COLLIDE

COLLIDE

Kimberley Dian

Cover Image © Inus12345 | Dreamstime.com

Published by **Mason Jar Jaunt**

Acknowledgements This novel would not be before you were it not for the help of the following people and more. Thanks, first and foremost, to Mom for countless reasons, including for reading to me before I could read for myself. Thanks also to those friends and family who also love to read and who were willing to share their feedback, Sloan May, Lisa Neff, Jennifer Hutchinson, Jessica Everett, Melanie Taylor, Vikki Paredes, Tammie Haug, Elly Hoeser, Melissa Keen, Sherry Holley, Kristin Paige and Kelly Santos. Friends who read the book at various stages and who also helped with the writing were Barbara Sylkatis, Valerie Johnson, and Leslie Thaxton Casas, who was tireless in her efforts. Heather Kobs deserves special mention because of her role in getting this work into print; her excitement upon learning I'd written a book was the wave that carried this book to shore after so many others had brought me within sight of land. And to my husband Chris and our children, Ryan, Abigail, and Jakob, thank you for inspiring me in so many ways and for giving me the time and freedom to write. The road this novel has taken has been less than straight but with it now complete I believe I am exactly where I should be and am surrounded by exactly those people whom I should be with.

ISBN-13: 978-0692366004

For Bonnie Lee Ray,
my grandmother.

All the goodness in me came
from all the goodness you are.

"You never really understand a person until you consider things from his point of view... until you climb inside of his skin and walk around in it."

Harper Lee, *To Kill a Mockingbird*

1

Carsen, 1992

I am not a quitter; more of a slow finisher. I thrive on conflict and confrontation. I am strong and smart. I own the mistakes I make. I am a realist, with a flair for the dramatic. I believe the girl should always get the boy. I believe in white picket fences and happily ever after. I believe in happy endings. I am eighteen and smarter than most adults I know. I am capable. I am careful, though at times can let the moment sweep me away. I trust easily. I do not forgive quickly.

I am pregnant. That was not in my plan. This is NOT who I am supposed to be. I want to become a journalist, a writer. I want to attend college and after graduation go on to do an internship in New York City and work for some big name magazine.

As I drive home from Planned Parenthood I can't help but think of a scene from *Terms of Endearment*, the one where Debra Winger's character calls to tell her mom, Mrs. Greenway, that she *thinks* she might be pregnant again and the camera pans out revealing that she is in fact well into her pregnancy. I think that this is how I feel. Like I *thought* I might be pregnant, but if I didn't know for sure, if I didn't have confirmation, then that somehow made it less real. This just wasn't supposed to happen to me.

I am driving down a road I have driven down countless times, but now it feels so different. In the matter of one hour everything I feared came true. *Knowledge is power*; that saying is so true. *Knowledge can also be devastating and painful*, but no one goes around saying that part too much. At the end of school last year we had to write an essay. We were asked to write 500 words describing who I was today and who I want to be tomorrow. None of *THIS* was in my essay.

I do not want children. Scratch that. I did not think I wanted children. If *the road to hell is paved with good intentions* then I have the purest intentions of anyone I know. I have lived in chaos and drama all of my life to the extent that I actually thrive in it.

I think I have suspected that I am pregnant for a while now. I've been so tired all the time. I've been nauseated almost all day long to where it's not simply *morning* sickness but more like *all day* sickness. However, having never been pregnant before, I really had nothing to compare it to. So, just not addressing it has been so much easier. Until, I just couldn't ignore it anymore. My period is now well past two months late.

As I listened to the nurse practitioner tell me I was definitely pregnant, I just zoned out. I saw her. I heard her. I just couldn't actually comprehend what she was saying. I looked around the room. It was covered in posters. There were warnings about STD's. There were warnings about unplanned pregnancy. There were warnings everywhere.

I heard *Girls Just Wanna Have Fun* playing in the background. The irony did not escape me. I didn't even crack a smile though. This was totally not funny. The nurse handed me a packet to take home with me. The packet was neatly divided so as to cover all my options. It went through the choices the clinic had decided I have.

Choice 1: Keep the Baby

Here there was literature about how great having a baby truly is: *Pregnancy is a miracle.* Really? Let's call a spade a spade, I thought, 99% of the time it's a mistake! As I thumbed through the packet, the middle aged, tired looking nurse told me how lucky I was to have already graduated from high school. Yes, that is great, and I was feeling so very lucky.

Choice 2: Adoption

Choosing adoption meant I would be pregnant for nine months, then hand the baby over to complete strangers. I wondered if that is how a momma dog feels when her puppies are taken from her. The pamphlets made it seem so simple. And not to mention the gift I would be giving to someone else. But right then, at that moment, I could only think of myself; what being pregnant and having a baby meant for ME! What about me? I was being very selfish, perhaps. It wasn't even a real baby yet. I mean, if I went into labor at that very moment, it wouldn't survive. It's an embryo. It's not even a fetus. It's not a baby!

Choice 3: Abortion.

Her voice changed when she said *the* word, like it was a dirty word. I looked up at her just then as she used words like "humane" and "terminate." Finally, I had something to say, I looked her right in the eyes. And after an hour of silence, I found my voice. It was low and guttural. It was scared and shaky. I barely recognized the voice.

"Why are you calling these options choices? Choice implies something positive. I can see nothing positive about any of these options. I do not have a choice to make. I have a decision to make."

The chubby nurse with her simple yellow gold wedding band on her left hand giggled.

"You may feel like that now, but you just found out, take some time. Talk to the father, your parents and your friends. Talk to people who know you and love you. That'll help you will make the right choice for you and your baby."

Then she patted my hand. That makes me feel so much better. Right!

Your baby? Oh. My baby. Joshua's baby. Our baby. I continue to drive back to Seabrook still in shock. I just keep saying the words out loud, to myself.

"I am pregnant. I am pregnant…"

No matter how many times I say it, I still can't believe it. He always wears a condom. He prides himself on being careful every single time.

Smart girls do not get pregnant. Girls who do get pregnant are in long term relationships and are having lots of sex. Girls who get pregnant probably think it will make the boy love them more. I don't believe that. I don't have a boyfriend. We are not in love. Well, let me rephrase that, he is not in love. I think I am in love with him, but he is only *deeply in lust* with me. We are having lots of sex, but that is all it is. I know how it is. I pretend like it is okay.

"I am pregnant."

Why? Why did this happen and why now? I don't ask "how?" I'm not that stupid! I know HOW, I just can't believe it. But why? Why now?

For about five seconds I consider telling my mom. For about

ten seconds I consider telling Joshua. For a whole minute I consider telling my friends. But I am not sure that I am capable of having any of those conversations right now. The reactions of shock and awe would just be more than I can handle. I am NOT the kind of girl that gets knocked up when she's eighteen. I have a good plan and I have goals. Boys and babies were NEVER in my grand plan. I don't know what I am going to do. I don't know what I want to do.

I get home and I go straight to my room. I close the bedroom door quietly. I turn on my jam box and *True Colors* comes on. I love this mix-tape. Joshua made it for me a few months ago. He thinks I'm obsessed with sad songs and being sad. He thinks he knows me. I curl up on my bed and pull the comforter up around me. I hear footsteps in the hall. I begin to make deals with God. If my mom walks in right now, then I am supposed to tell her. There is a knock on my door.

"Car, you okay?" she asks.

I sit up involuntarily, waiting for the knob to turn.

"I'm fine."

I hold my breath, if the door opens, I will have to spill. I close my eyes and brace myself for the disappointment and the anger that will certainly follow my confession.

"Okay, good. I'm heading over to Mike's. Call over there if you need me."

She doesn't come in. I don't have to tell her. This is definitely a sign. I lay on the bed, staring at the ceiling. My eyes won't stay closed.

I wish I could tell her. I wish I could get up, go into her room and tell her everything. I can't do that because I can't handle what will come out of her mouth. I can't handle the look that will be in her eyes. I can't handle the disappointment, the anger, the frustration, or even her pity. I know what she will say. She didn't want this to happen to me.

She was older and in college when she got pregnant with me. She didn't get a fairy-tale ending. My dad left after my brother was born, like, literally he left me at the hospital with my mom and said he was going to go run some errands and then come back later.

Sixteen years have passed and I'm still wondering what errand could take that long. I learned an important lesson from him. If you don't really love someone, when the going gets tough, the tough leave. They run away. Never to be heard from again.

My mom will see this as a colossal screw up on my part. She will remind me every single day going forward of what I have done to my life and how it is ruined. I hear these words from her all the time as it is. I mean she has never said "You ruined my life. I wish you were never born." But she does say things like, "Well, if I hadn't gotten pregnant and had to drop out of college who knows what I would have or could have done or been" I always feel like the look in her eyes, when she dares herself to go back there, is filled with daggers directed at me. If there had been no baby there would not have been so many closed doors and lost opportunities.

I stare at my small room. I can't see a crib or a changing table ever being in it. I can't see a rocking chair fitting in over there. I can't see me rocking a baby to sleep right here. It is too small even for me. This room is too small, this house is too small, and this town is too small. I want bigger and I planned better.

The double bed is on one wall, with the dresser beside it on the next. Big windows make up the third wall, and the closet on the fourth wall, nestled between the sink and mirror, rounds out the space. It is tiny and messy. *Mums* from past Homecomings cover a wall. One of those mums is from Joshua. We went to our Junior Homecoming together. There is also a bulletin board of pictures that represents my life up until now. Parties, dances and lots and lots of fun!

I stop and look at the 8x10 picture in the middle of my bulletin board. It's a picture of Joshua and me at some dance. We didn't go together, but he wanted to get a picture taken. We are looking at each other and both of us are smiling. I know we are both thinking totally different things, but we look happy. I sit up and grab a frame from my dresser. It is a picture of me and Josh on my 16th birthday. I keep it on my dresser, right next to my alarm clock. It is the first thing I see every morning and the last thing I see every night.

I stare into his eyes. I think he was in love with me back then. It feels like I have never looked closely at this picture before. He is wearing plaid Bermuda shorts and a white knit shirt. Naturally, it is not tucked in. He is much taller than me. He's at least 6'2". His light brown hair is cut short and looks as if it has been kissed by the sun. His blue eyes are brilliant against his summer tan. His smile captivates me, even still, even after everything that has happened.

I have on a pink halter top, which is tied behind my neck, and green shorts. It is September in Texas, but is still plenty warm enough to wear summer clothes. My chestnut hair is really long and I have it swept to one side, away from him. My head is resting against his chest and my hand is on his stomach. I couldn't have weighed more than 115 pounds in that picture. I am very well-tanned. I had spent most of that summer at the pool while baby-sitting. I am staring at the person taking the picture, probably Allie. Joshua is looking down at me. His arm is wrapped tightly around my waist. The smile on his face is genuine. I might have been a little drunk. I try to remember that night. I look so happy. I want to go back to that night. Things weren't as complicated then. We were really just friends.

My hands are drawn to my belly. I trace it over and over with my fingers. My baby. Joshua's baby. I am 9 weeks pregnant. I heard the heartbeat today. I saw the heartbeat on the sonogram. The baby is real, it is "viable" and it is growing.

Everything is normal. At least that is what that obnoxious nurse told me. REALLY? What have I done now? Will the baby look like me? Green eyes, apple cheeks and lots of brown hair? Or will it look like Joshua? Blonde hair, piercing blue eyes and a killer smile?

The phone rings and I jump just a little bit. I have to run out to the living room to pick it up. I make it on the fourth ring. I reluctantly answer it.

"Hello?"

"Hey," Joshua says.

"Oh, hey," I said.

I sound bothered, I am definitely bothered. We have an extra-long chord on the phone so I walk over and sit down on the couch. I am so tired.

"What's wrong with you?" he asks.

"Nothing. Why?"

Another deal with God, if he asks me what is wrong again, I'll tell him.

"You sound weird."

"No, I'm fine. Just tired, I guess."

I hold my breath, I cross my fingers, squint my eyes.

"You are always tired these days. Tired and bitchy."

There is a long pause. I don't say anything. I know it's true.

"Do you want to come over tonight?" he asks eventually.

He didn't ask again, so I don't have to tell him, at least not today.

"My mom is gone for the night. You can come here if you want."

There is no excitement in my voice. He of course ignores that.

"Cool. Do you want to get dinner or anything?"

"I'm not hungry, but you can bring something if you want."

"Later."

"See ya."

I close my eyes. Every new beginning signals the end of the previous new beginning. Was this the beginning or the end then? Was this the end of my relationship with Joshua? Is it the beginning of one for me and the baby? Is it the end of my adolescence? Is this the beginning of adulthood? Is it the beginning of a different sort of relationship for Joshua and me? I pull my pillow over my head and begin to cry.

2

Carsen, *2010*

As the alarm goes off at 5 am, I wish it was Saturday. I hit the snooze button. I figure I can go back to sleep for just ten more minutes.

I hit snooze a couple times more.

I get to the point where I realize I won't get it all done if I don't get up immediately. I pull myself out of bed. I feel old. Maybe it has something to do with me celebrating my 36th birthday last fall. I know time has passed, I've watched my child grow every day. But in this moment, and all of a sudden, I realize that half of my life is probably over. How depressing! On top of that, Tyler will be going off to college soon and I will be alone.

I think this has been becoming more and more of a reality lately because he is never home. I can remember times when I wished for silence and for just a little bit of time to myself and now that's really all I have. What was I going to do with myself when he left?

I have wrapped my life so tightly around his that I am not sure who I will be when he isn't here for me to mother every day. The thought of being alone scares me. It's the part of my *decision* that I'd never really given any thought to. "Decision" is still the word I use to describe what I did; I never came to like the word *choice*. In fact, I don't believe in choices.

I make the bed out of habit. I walk into my bathroom and stare at myself in the mirror. I try to look at myself objectively. I can see the small double chin I've been working on for years to get rid of. It has lessened lately and I am proud of that fact. It just isn't a big priority; I am not my priority. Tyler is my priority. He always has been and always will be. It seems like he is never here around dinner time and it's no fun to cook for one, so I just don't. Not a bad diet really.

My face is very round and I still have those apple cheeks that my grandmother loved to pinch. My eyes are probably my best feature, big and green. I do love that my lashes are thick and dark so I don't really need to wear much make up.

I can see the beginnings of tiny lines at their edges. I remind myself to pick up some more moisturizer. My hair is as wild as it has ever been. I have a mess of unmanageable brown curls that are usually piled into a ponytail. As I gather them up, I think I should probably get my hair cut and colored soon. Maybe I need a new look.

Perhaps today I will blow dry it out, and see if that helps me look a little bit younger than I am feeling.

I look down, I have small boobs and my hips are too wide for my legs. I was athletic at one point in my life, but after Tyler came along, I just didn't have time. I haven't let myself go entirely, I am still attractive, in a 'mom' kind of way. I do try and dress a little bit hip and young once in a while, but I know I am only fooling myself when I do.

I wash my face and brush my teeth. Routine is good for me. As I brush my teeth, I turn and stare out the window and look at my yard and at all the beautiful flowers. It is April and it's still a bit chilly. But it is definitely springtime. One thing I love about living in Connecticut is the transition from one season to another. In Texas we seemed to go straight from summer to winter and from winter to summer.

The sun is peeking out and it looks like it will be a beautiful day. That's good. The wedding is being held outside, and I have prayed for weeks that there will be no rain.

I turn back to the mirror and go on with the routine. I feel like I am on auto pilot most of the time these days. Life is happening all around me, and as much as I try, it feels like nothing is actually happening TO me.

If I pick up the pace, I can get to the shop a few hours before my staff does and that way I can get a lot done before they arrive. I hurry downstairs and fix Tyler's breakfast. He doesn't have to be at school for a few hours, so I leave his eggs and bacon in the oven on low.

He's a growing boy who plays a lot of hockey and if I don't give him protein, he'll grab Pop Tarts or something even less nutritious. I put a note on the oven. I grab my purse and lock the door behind me.

I get into my beautiful 2008 navy blue Land Rover and drive to work. The local station, that plays 80's music comes on, like clockwork every morning. It's funny; sometimes I think I am permanently stuck in my youth, while on other days I can't even remember who I was back then. But, all it ever takes is a song to remind me of him and of what I did.

My car is truly the only luxury I have "afforded" myself. I figured that since I would be in debt the rest of my natural life, I might as well make it worth my while on one front.

I didn't anticipate the shop doing so well so quickly. But, with my eye for color, attention to detail, and a little splash of determination, my floral shop quickly became not only the best in town, but the best for at least 100 miles. I didn't *choose* to become a florist, though; it was just something I fell into. I do love the smells and the colors, though.

Customers are always commenting on my choice of colors and blossoms. I try to do something different and non-traditional. I treat each arrangement like it's the first one I've ever done.

I adore that first look a client has when they see what I have created. I live for that moment of delight for them, and the acceptance for myself that comes with it. But I am also afraid they might find out that what I am really doing is trying to seek forgiveness for my sins. I am always looking for absolution. I believe that if I bring enough happiness to others, it will erase the damage I have done. I hope their happiness rubs off of me. Unfortunately, to this point it hasn't happened yet. So I bring happiness to other people, and I save the pain and the darkness for myself. I am selfish that way.

I park behind my shop, and walk towards the Caf Shack. This too is one of my daily rituals, and yes I know I could make my own tea, but then I would miss out on the town buzz.

I am not very social, for many reasons, so I feel that my daily tea habit is an indulgence I am entitled to. I walk up to the counter to order my non-fat chai tea latte from Fred, the owner. He begins our daily banter.

"Well there she is folks, its Ms. Carsen Wylder. How is the most beautiful lady in Beacon Falls?"

I smile at him, and begin looking around.

"The most beautiful? Hmm ... I don't see her," and I wink at him. "How is the most ineligible bachelor doing today?"

He blushes and says, "You are the sunshine of my day, young lady".

He is old enough to be my grandfather, and in many ways he is my surrogate one.

I never knew either of my grandfathers, and when I moved here, Fred was the first person my grandmother introduced me to. He has the sweetest spirit, and his body swims in a light pink aura. As my grandmother often says, "Fred is good people". He is also about 15 years younger than she is, but no one knows that fact, except for me.

The town of Beacon Falls, which I now consider my home town, has—according to its welcome sign—a population of 28,299. It is located in southwestern Connecticut and is bisected by the Naugatuck River which meanders through it. It is true that nothing much exciting happens here. I have always reveled in this. There's no drama, no tragedy. Life is just simple and easy.

I don't know what I would have done without my Grandma Lee. When I called her all those years ago I was almost hysterical. Barely able to talk, I mostly just cried. Finally, she said, "Pack your stuff and come here, honey. We can figure it out together."

Granny Lee is Dad's mom. She hadn't heard from my dad since he left us, so essentially he left us all. I am her only granddaughter. Our relationship is more special than any other relationship I've had in my life. She just loves me, mistakes and all. She even kept my secret from the family for years, waiting until I was ready to tell everyone. Coming to Beacon Falls allowed me to leave Joshua and my dreams behind. It allowed me to make all my own decisions when it came to Tyler. It also allowed me a lot of time to wonder if I did the right thing. That's the thing about the past, you can run but you can't hide from it.

I know that I am just an average woman with an average existence. Falls has some beauty queens, and we know who they are, but apart from that small group, folk here just aren't that pretentious. I know that after all these years, I blend in and I feel like I belong.

As I wait for my tea, my thoughts return to this morning. I consider how my life is right now. It's perhaps best described as stagnant, if I'm honest. Not to have a "significant other" was a decision I made for myself a long time ago. I did, however, seriously consider getting married at one point, to Michael who was so great. But, he wanted more kids. He deserved more kids.

He had been wonderful to both Tyler and me, but I didn't want to rob him of the future he desperately wanted. After we broke up, he married a sweet girl from a neighboring town, and they've since had four kids. He comes to the shop every now and then. I notice there is no regret in his eyes, he only sees me as his friend

11

now. It is comfortable and nice. Here, at least, I always knew I made the right decision, for both of us.

I am currently in a comfortable non-committed relationship with Alex, who doesn't ask any more of me than I can give. We go to dinner and we hang out. He accepts the times when I am distant and quiet. He knows that at those moments my mind and my heart are somewhere else. He believes that we are two lost souls and that this is what makes our relationship work. I enjoy being with Alex because there are no questions or expectations. It just is what it is.

He lost his wife to breast cancer about 7 years ago. He moved to Beacon Falls to get away from the pain and the memories. He came into my shop to send flowers back to his mom in Hartford. He had a nice smile, and a broken heart. There was an immediate connection, but it wasn't love, we were just comfortable together. Sometimes the best things for you are those things you don't plan on or wish for. I feel lucky to have a friend like Alex. I am grateful that he wandered into my life and that his expectations are zero.

I should learn to love what is good for me. But, in all honesty, I don't believe in love anymore, not for me. I know I had the great love of my life, and he didn't love me back. Tyler is what makes my life what it is. I am not bitter anymore. I am settled and resigned to my life here. I know that if I had to do it all over, I would do it all exactly the same way. I know that when I left Joshua I left the only chance, the only choice; I ever had to be in love.

3

Carsen, 1992

I am not going to tell Joshua about the baby. I am afraid that if I do, he won't go to college. I am afraid he will do something totally stupid, like marry me. I am even more terrified that he won't. I am afraid he might ask me to have an abortion. I am horrified at the thought of being rejected by him, again.

Maybe I should just leave. If I leave, do I tell him I am leaving?

No, he might ask me to stay not because he is in love with me but because he feels guilty. He might want me to stay out of pity or so he can do the "right" thing. I have made so many mistakes where Joshua is concerned, but this time it isn't about him. It isn't even about me.

Joshua and I are not dating, in fact I am not really sure what we are. Joshua isn't ready to call me his girlfriend, so there is no way he is ready to be a father. And if he's not ready for a relationship with me, he really isn't ready to be in a relationship with a pregnant me. I can't be with him the way I want because he doesn't want me like that. I can't stay!

For all of five seconds I consider telling him and I wonder how different my life might be: I'll be a wife and a mother at 19. Ridiculous. He will never marry me.

I am in love with him though. Is that important?

Anyway, I can't let how I feel about him matter now or how he doesn't feel about me. It totally sucks being in love with your best friend. Typically this would have been something I would've gone to him about, and we would've hashed out the pros and cons of it. Like when I was dating this bull rider and the guy hit me. I didn't know what to do. Do I tell my mom, or call the police? For over 12 hours we went back and forth about what the right thing to do was. We finally decided the jerk just needed an ass kicking. So after his next rodeo, Josh went with me and stood on the guy while I punched and kicked him. Not my finest moment, but I'll never let another man hit me and that guy never looked my way again.

Anything is possible, and if I know one thing to be absolutely and completely true, it's that Joshua is not in love with me. This fact and this fact alone will drive every other decision I make. It hurts to think it and it kills me to admit it, but it's what is true.

This baby could be my only chance at unconditional love. That thought makes me sound like a pathetic lovesick teenager. This thought makes me sick to my stomach. It sounds ridiculous and I will not let myself think it. More than anything, I fear that Joshua might do "the right thing," and that isn't what I want for myself. I want to be the one he chooses because he loves me, not because we made a mistake. No one should choose to be with someone else because they were forced into it due to an unfortunate accident.

I want too much from Joshua when it is only he and I involved. I always wanted more from our relationship than he did. I have just never had the courage to risk our friendship by telling him how much I love him. I think that if I put a baby into the equation, especially now, he will hate and resent me for the rest of his life. He will never believe it was an accident. He will never believe me again. So what else can I do?

He is on his way over now. My head hurts from all the thinking and the range of emotions I have been putting myself through. I need to figure this out and quickly.

I have already registered for my first semester at Southwest Texas State University this fall. I won't be following him to Austin. Instead, I've chosen to be 30 minutes away from him. He would have to make an effort to see me. I had made that decision months ago.

Now, though, college will just have to wait.

I will spend the rest of tonight with Joshua. I will try to make it seem like any other day. But, in reality I will watch his every move. I will watch for some sign that he really loves me; that we can get through this together.

4

Joshua, 1992

High school is over! I am now a Seabrook High graduate, class of 1992. Today was crazy. I had been waiting for years for today, but now that it was over it all seemed so anti-climactic. I drove myself out to Lance's instead of riding with the guys. I'd been hoping to find Carsen. I didn't mean to get out here so late either. But, we had been drinking and talking about all the crazy shit we'd done over the years.

I had been looking for Carsen since I'd gotten to the graduation party, but she was nowhere to be seen. And I didn't want to look like I was looking for her either, so I just kind of wandered in and out talking to whoever I ran into. The Outfield was blaring *I Don't Want to Lose Your Love Tonight* and I immediately thought about her again. Where the hell was she?

It felt oddly weird to know that high school was over. The real world was where we would be living soon enough. I couldn't wait for the fall. I had nothing but one trip planned for this summer and the rest would be spent doing a lot more of this, and hanging out with Carsen. She was being ridiculous about next year though. I have no idea where she is going, or if she is going anywhere actually.

I am kind of pissed at her. Part of me thinks that maybe she wants me to ask her to go to UT with me, but I'm not about to force my dreams on her. She can do whatever she wants, go where ever she wants.

"Hey, Allie?" I said loudly to a group of girls huddled on the front porch.

She sauntered over to me, almost seductively. She is Carsen's best friend and I immediately wonder how much she might know about me and Carsen.

"Hey, Josh! What's up?"

She bats her eyelashes at me and licks her lips. She must know NOTHING. She certainly wouldn't be flirting so shamelessly with me if she did. I smile to myself realizing Carsen loves the secret as much as me, which is good. That's what we agreed to a long time ago and it just works.

"Where is Carsen? Didn't she come here with you?"

Immediately she shifts her stance and her eyes drop to the floor. Disappointment is all over her face.

"She got a ride home with Clay. She didn't look like she was having any fun. She said she had a headache or something."

She looks me up and down now, a slow smile returns to her face.

"Do you want to have some fun?"

Yea, I do want to have some fun, but not with you, I thought. I had already been there and done that. Allie is beautiful. Dark hair, dark eyes and a killer tan. She is very thin and gorgeous, but she is also a head case. I know I shouldn't think of her like that. I did sleep with her before I slept with Carsen, but Allie is a shitty friend to Carsen. I guess that makes me a shitty friend too.

Carsen trusts Allie completely. If I were a better friend to Carsen, I would've admitted it to Carsen right after it happened. But, she knew before I ever told her. Carsen doesn't have high expectations for people and everyone had slept with Allie.

I never have understood the connection between Carsen and her, and when I have asked, Carsen's face gets very soft and she says she loves Allie as much as she could love a sister. They certainly fight like sisters, too. It's an obnoxious relationship. For Carsen, trusting and loving comes so easily, and I know I take advantage of that side of her. She loves and trusts me more than I deserve. However, if you cross her then that was that, too. She doesn't forgive easily and she has her friends back no matter what. Loyalty is by far her best quality. Of course, I knew she had other talents, too. I try not to think about sex every time I think about Carsen, but I can't help it. It's a big part of our friendship. Sometimes I think she regrets we ever started doing it, but she never says anything and I'm certainly not going to stop us.

I wonder again if Allie herself had ever told Carsen that we'd slept together. I haven't been with anyone besides Carsen in months now, but still, Carsen and I aren't public knowledge. I assume Allie knows though.

"Thanks, Allie. I appreciate the tempting offer, but I've got to get up early to leave for Cabo. What time are you girls leaving for Port A?"

Most everyone from Seabrook goes to Port Aransas, Texas, after graduation and also at Spring Break. This time though, I wasn't going. I was going to Cabo with a group of guys. I couldn't wait to get out of here and away from all the drama. I was hoping there would be lots of girls to meet too. I smiled to myself, thinking about looking for the next best thing.

Allie had already started turning away from me, irritated by my lack of interest.

"I'm picking Car up at 6.30 am," she said over her shoulder. I was being dismissed. But then she turned back around and looked at me with a strange grin.

"Please remind her of that, I mean, if you happen to see or talk to her tonight."

She flipped her hair in my direction as if she were flipping me off. I do not understand girls. They are so confusing to me. I am just glad there is nothing confusing about Carsen.

I decide that that's where I want to be anyway. I know she is expecting me. She is always expecting me, so I say my good-byes and get the hell out of there. These parties are pretty stupid anyway. It amazes me to see all the losers who have already graduated that are here. Dude, grow up! Move on! I know I will never come back to this town once I'm gone.

I park my car a few houses down from Carsen's like always and sit there for a minute. I don't know what I feel for her exactly. I feel a twinge of guilt for thinking about being with other girls, when I've clearly come here to have sex with Carsen. I know it's not just about the sex, but I don't know what else it's about either.

She's the first person I usually talk to every day either on the phone before school or at school. I always tell her everything. I don't even think about it. I just do it. We have a history and we have chemistry which means I'm sleeping with my best friend.

It isn't just a one-night-at-a-time thing either. It doesn't just happen each time. We both know we always end up together, no matter where we start our nights.

The first time we had sex it was a well-planned activity that we'd discussed for months before we actually did anything. I'm not sure why she was so weird about that first time. It had been months, and I was honestly getting tired of the "teasing" she had been doing, which is why I ended up sleeping with Allie.

There had been so much anticipation leading up to that morning.

I rest my head on the steering wheel. I think that morning is my favorite memory of me and Carsen. I tap my fingers on the dashboard and think back to then when our relationship was simpler.

Carsen had been at her grandmother's in Dallas for the first month of the summer before our senior year. Allie and I picked her up at the airport when she flew back on the night before what became *that morning*. Allie and I had spent most of that month together. She was wild and she was fun. We both missed Carsen. And we'd had fun, but that all changed at the airport.

Even Allie, I think, noticed the difference in me when Carsen got off the plane. She looked simply breathtaking when I first caught sight of her. It was like I hadn't really looked at her before, or as if I was seeing her for the first time or something. And then the look she gave me caused a feeling in me that I had never felt before. She hugged Allie first, but she was staring at me. Allie quickly let her go, and grabbed Carsen's bags, I wrapped my arms around her and could smell her shampoo and buried my face in her neck. I felt a longing and an urgency to be with her.

I dropped them both off at Allie's house and while I was bringing Carsen's stuff in and trying to decide what to do next, Allie got on the phone. She was talking to some dude who was apparently on his way over. I smiled to myself wondering if that was true, or if it was purely for my benefit. I decided it was too weird to be around them both, so as I left Carsen walked me out to my car.

Looking back, I now know that Carsen knew something was up. She always knew things before I told her. Carsen and I walked out to my car holding hands. We stood at the trunk looking up at the sky.

"Tomorrow," she whispered leaning into me playfully.

"Are you sure, Car?" I said.

"Joshua Ames Hattinson, we have been discussing this for what 6 months? If you don't want to, then I won't come over. It's okay if you've changed your mind. It's up to you."

She sounded hurt, scared and like she was trying to sound indifferent about it all. I stood in front of her and pulled her towards me.

"I want to. I want you. I have wanted you for months. You have kept ME waiting, remember?" I whispered in her ear.

"Tomorrow then." She said as she turned away from me. I instinctively grabbed her and pulled her back to me. I kissed her. At first she just stood there, motionless. I put my hands on both sides of her face and kissed her harder. She parted her lips and let my tongue reach hers. Then she was kissing me back, and next she wrapped her arms tightly around me and pressed herself into me. I wanted her right then.

I maneuvered her gently towards my car and her back arched

against the trunk. All of a sudden though, she stopped and pulled away, putting her hand on my chest.

"Tomorrow, Joshua."

She walked away then suddenly stopped in the middle of the yard. Her back was still to me as she said, "Don't think I don't know about you and Allie either. I don't want any details, and I don't want to discuss it. Do not insult me by denying it and do not admit it."

She turned around and faced me. She looked beautiful in the moonlight, but her eyes showed the hurt she felt. She was barefoot and in a plaid thin sundress. Her hands were on her hips, as usual, and her long curly hair was blowing in the wind. Her lips seemed full from our kissing.

She began walking back towards me. She was biting her lip as she usually did when she wanted to keep herself from saying something she might regret. I leaned up against the car with my hands in my pockets. My head hung a little bit in shame. I should have known she would pick up on it. She knows me so well. She put her hand under my chin and looked me right in the eyes.

"If we do this tomorrow, if we actually have sex, then you can't ever sleep with her again. EVER. So, if that is something you think you might want to do again, then give me a call in the morning and I will not come over. If I don't hear from you, I will see you around 9:15."

She grabbed the back of my head gently with her hands and kissed me hard. Again she pressed her body completely into mine.

That kiss seemed to reveal a little of what I would be in for tomorrow. I kissed her back. She knew I wouldn't be calling her in the morning to tell her not to come; and I knew that I would be lucky if I got any sleep that night.

5

Carsen, 2010

It was impossible not to relive my own teenage years as Tyler was going through his. I've tried so hard to repress the memories and the pain from that period, but I guess when some business is not completely finished, the heart and the mind still searches for closure. I have woven a web of lies for all these years, and I just don't think that I can ever do anything to right my wrongs. I just have to live with the choices, no, not choices, the decisions I have made.

Ever since Tyler's birthday last month, I have been replaying my own high school memories in my head. All the important ones were wound tightly around Josh. The pain was lying dormant, just under the surface and I struggle to keep it there. I've also found my yearbooks and old letters. I should've gotten rid of those a long time ago, instead I find myself searching through them.

In the Caf Shack, it's on with the routine. I walk over to where Fred keeps the newspapers. As I stroll over there something, someone, at one of the tables, catches my eye, and I get a strange feeling, and the hair on the back of my neck stands up. I'm staring. I stop myself, but then I slowly glance back over that way again. I have to do a double take.

He is older, definitely, but is it really him? I shake my head a couple of times, it can't be. I have just been thinking about him so much lately that now my eyes are playing tricks on me. That has to be it. I walk the other way, and try to clear my head. I turn around again. I focus on the man seated near the window.

I sit at the farthest table from him in the small shop. I close my eyes. I count to ten. I take another look, certainly I am just seeing the things I want or need to see. Anyway, I don't really know what he looks like as an adult. I have to think. Everything and everyone seems to be moving in slow motion. I continue to stare in wonderment. It could be him. It could be Joshua.

His back is to me now. I can't tell for sure. I grab my tea and walk out quickly. I hide on the other side of the window. Fred looks around, a bit confused. Then he smiles and helps the next customer. He finds my $5 on the counter, and he puts it in the drawer. He is still shaking his head a bit. It feels like an eternity passes as I stand there staring inside through the window.

I can't be sure it is him. I'm sure my mind is hoping, wishing that it is him. There this man sits, nonchalantly reading his newspaper. He is alone. He is drinking coffee and eating a bagel. I don't like the feeling that begins to boil inside me. Every feeling, every thought, and every word Joshua and I ever exchanged stream through my mind. Every touch, every look, every moment we shared reverberates through my body. The love, the hurt, the denial, all of it comes flooding back right through my heart. I remind myself to breathe and take a few deep breaths.

So many things are rushing through my mind. Why is he here? Is he looking for me? Had I been wrong all those years ago? Why now? Why here? Did she tell him I was here? Did Granny Lee betray me? I gather myself together, and close my eyes. Maybe it was just my mind playing tricks on me. How could Joshua be here? It couldn't be him. I have to fight back the tears.

I start walking towards my shop as fast as I can. I can't help but wonder what it would mean if he were here. He definitely isn't here for me, right? Somehow he just ended up here, but that isn't even feasible. She must have sent him here. Why after all this time? She must have told him, or at the very least pointed him in my direction. Why? Why now? Why after all this time would she do this to me?

My heart that had slowly been put back together with time and distance felt like it was being torn to pieces again. I could feel old wounds opening up and there was nothing I could do to stop them.

I just stand at the door of the shop while my head tries to process his presence, and I try to reconcile my past with this reality. Again, rationalizations of the situation start to play in my head. I had made the right decision. If I had told him, and stayed, then eventually he would have ended up hating me, and I just wasn't going to do that to my life.

While the decision I made was difficult for me in the beginning, it had never been difficult for Tyler. He doesn't know any different. He couldn't mourn for the life that he didn't have because nothing had been taken away from him. He knows he is loved and he has never wanted for anything. I always surround him with a blanket of love and understanding. He has the most pure love in his heart, and I pray that he will never know true heart break. I think somewhere in the back of my mind I thought that the sacrifices and decisions I had made would somehow protect him from that kind of pain, that kind of trauma.

I run back towards the Caf. I have to know if it's him or not. I peak in the window, but he is gone. I laugh at myself. Clearly, I am going a bit crazy. I shake my head and feel my heart stop racing.

Of course, I keep thinking of Joshua as I unlock the door to the shop. A smile forms on my lips, I used to believe it was fate that interceded and made Joshua and I into the couple I wanted so desperately for us to be. I thought our relationship was stronger than most marriages I knew. It had all the right pieces just not in the right places. There was friendship, and there was attraction and there was passion. And I had hoped my love for him would prove to be enough for him one day.

It was a relationship we fell into too easily. It was just the wrong kind of relationship. It never meant to him what it meant to me.

I don't want to think of him. I don't want to think of any of it. I had done so well over the years forcing myself to NOT dwell on it. I won't allow myself to think of him now then either. Out of sight and out of mind.

There is work to do, and I need to get busy. No time to spend wasting on what could have been. I was living what *was*, what had turned out, and that was how I had meant for it to be.

As I keep my hands busy making table vases, my mind inevitably wanders back to him again. Most likely he had moved on, and not given me a second thought over the years. I'm sure at first he wondered, but not enough to cause him any real concern. He knew how strong I was, and he knew that once I made my mind up, that was it. But, I had also thought he knew me. I thought he knew, or could feel how much I loved him. I had hoped that he would come after me, that he'd want to find me.

I had hoped and I had been wrong. Everyone knows first loves don't stand the test of time, or fate, or the unthinkable. I had put all those memories, my *Joshua Chronicles*, into a box and locked them away in my mind. The pain was just a part of who I was. But, I never let myself wallow in it; there wasn't usually time to do that. I had Tyler to keep me busy. I had a business to run.

Raising Tyler had been a full time job, especially since I'd been doing it on my own. And I had a life to figure out. If being a single mother wasn't bad enough, I'd been a teenage single mother. I glance at the clock and am grateful that it's close to ten o'clock. The girls will be here soon, and I will no longer be alone with my thoughts. Lately, I'd been fine unless I was alone.

I constantly worry about Tyler turning eighteen. I constantly worry about him going off to college. I also worry that the day will come when I'll have to answer for the decisions I've made, and that the world I had built for Tyler and I would crumble, and that I would lose him because I'd never allowed him to have a relationship with his father; a father who didn't even know that he had a child, a son.

Without any warning, a memory that I had buried very deep inside of me, made its way to the surface. And to the forefront of my mind. I could smell him, the soap, the cologne, the very essence of him. I couldn't believe the pain that it evoked. The images and the clarity it aroused. It was like watching a movie, only it was in my head, and it was so real. I sat down at the island in the middle of the shop and gave the memory the audience and attention it was craving. I let my mind go back to a time and a place that I had tried so hard not to visit.

6

Carsen, 1992

I had to get out of that party. Lately, I don't want to be anywhere that I can't be with Josh. And when I say "be with Josh" I mean be with him the way I want to. It's getting harder and harder to hide how I'm feeling. I'm beginning to not want to keep this secret anymore. We are almost adults! I want to hold his hand in public. I want everyone to know that we are together. I just don't have the balls to do anything about it!

He didn't even show up on time tonight. I am sure he was hanging out with the boys, but he told me he would be there. I am pretty sure that Allie knows something is up. I haven't confessed all, but I've let a few things slip. We've never addressed who though. As long as I don't say it out loud, I can still try and pretend I'm okay; that I'm okay with this arrangement and that I haven't fallen in love with my best friend. As long as she doesn't know the truth, she can't tell me how stupid I am. Lies – I just tell everyone lies all the time these days. It's become really exhausting!

It's getting late now...I'm sure he will come over, but there is always the nagging feeling in the back of my head that he won't. That tonight will be the night I lose him and there will be nothing I can do to stop it. How did I get myself into this mess, a mess I can't get myself out of? How and when did I become so stupid, one of those stupid girls that I try so hard to pretend that I'm not?

I go to my bedroom door and lock it very quietly. There is no noise, except for a small snoring sound coming from the living room, I think. I picture everyone sleeping soundly and somehow know that no one will be disturbed while he is here, if he shows up. I turn on my stereo very softly, so that if by chance someone does hear anything and they listen closer they will find it is just my music playing.

I open up the window, and then sit on my bed. It never ceases to amaze me how nervous and anxious I am in the moments before I am alone with him. I lean back against the wall, hugging my knees, wondering how tonight will go.

And then there he is. In a pale blue Izod shirt and plaid shorts, and he looks beautiful. His broad shoulders, muscular calves and, my favorite part, his strong arms, altogether cause me to gasp just a little bit. After he climbs in the window, he closes it slowly and locks it. I shut my eyes again for just a second, because when I am not looking at him, I can almost convince myself that I am okay with this arrangement, and that deep down he might someday really love me, and that all of this will have meant something and that all of this will have been worth it.

"Hey you!" he says in barely a whisper. His face inches from mine.

I open my eyes and smile.

"Hey yourself."

He kisses me on the forehead before plopping down next to me. There is an electric charge in the air between us. I look to see if he feels it, but he seems very calm. I can smell the beer, too. Great, this wasn't shaping up to be the night I'd hoped for.

"How much have you had to drink?" I ask, grateful for the darkness so he can't see the anger in my eyes.

"I just had a couple of beers with the guys."

His voice is light and I think he might even be smiling. He's teasing me, as always.

"You sure left early. Allie said you had a headache?"

More like a heartache.

"Oh, I just wasn't in to all that tonight. I guess I'm just feeling sad and a bit worried, too."

Both of our views stayed fixed, and forward looking, neither one of us watching the other.

His breathing became even with mine.

I enjoy the silence between us but eventually he moves closer to me. Our legs are now touching from the top of my thigh down to my ankle. That charge is setting my insides on fire.

I glance to him to see if he feels anything. He is sitting there very calmly; I don't know what he is thinking about. I could ask him, but instead I choose to stay quiet. He starts leaning in closer to me with his shoulder. I push back into him, just a little bit.

"Are you in a bad mood or something?"

"Like I said, I'm sad and worried."

"You are always worried, nothing new there. What exactly are you worried about at this exact moment?"

He was teasing me. He's always teasing me.

"Change. The unknown."

"You shouldn't worry about those things, not tonight. Not while I'm here."

And then I am underneath him. In one swift movement he has

moved me, and we are lying down, and I am looking up towards his gorgeous blue eyes. I think he grins as he shifts his weight.

"Wow, Car. You looked beautiful tonight."

"Thanks! I don't think you've ever said that to me before."

I was glad the room was so dark. I knew I was grinning from ear to ear; he thought I was beautiful.

"And you are going to look even more beautiful in about 5 minutes, when all your clothes are laying in a pile on the floor."

We both laughed.

I rolled onto my side, away from him. I didn't know exactly why I was feeling so sad. I tried to just feel his body against mine, and forget about what might happen over the next two weeks or two months. He was here now, and that was all I should be thinking about. His arms were wrapped around me, my back to his chest. His face buried in my hair.

"God, you smell good," he said, kissing my neck.

His hands are tracing circles on my stomach. It always starts this way. A little bit of a game we play. He knows I will surrender, but I think he secretly enjoys pretending he doesn't know how it will turn out. I smile, and try not to really respond to his touch. I lie, very still, and let his lips move slowly up and down my neck. His fingers continue to dance on my stomach, then onto my thighs, then back to my stomach again.

When he is like this, he makes me feel like I am the only one in his universe. He can't hide his feelings, everything is so exposed. So, I roll over and face him. We stare into each other's eyes for what feels like a lifetime. I am wishing I could actually read his thoughts. I keep staring into his eyes, and feel like I can see into his soul. My arms are around his neck and I am running my fingers through his short, thick hair.

Then he is kissing me, my throat, my lips, my shoulders. I can hear his sweet voice, but not the words he is saying. He isn't talking to me at all, he is talking to himself. I close my eyes and listen.

My body continues to react to his kisses and his touch, but I am more interested in what I am hearing. If this isn't real, then I know I don't want it to end. And if I am going crazy, then that is okay too. It is all so surreal.

He whispers, "I love being with you."

There is a pause, and then "I can't imagine not being with you. When I'm with you there is nowhere else I want to be."

He is starting to breathe heavier. "God, talk to me Carsen."

I know his words are more a reaction to what's going on in his body, than to any real desire to know my thoughts. I have learned not to respond and to just act as if I don't even hear what he is saying. It's all just part of our "routine." I have heard that love does crazy things to people, maybe now I am officially a nut job. It is so easy for me to forget everything else, especially my resolve when I am with him like this. I can sometimes let myself go and enjoy the moment. But, I will feel guilt and anger at myself tomorrow. But, here, now, I don't care about tomorrow. I only care about being with him.

I don't even notice that while he's been kissing me, he's down to his boxers. I help him pull his shirt over his head. He feels a slight shift in my body, and he misreads my reaction. I want him to slow down, but instead he speeds up.

He pulls me closer into him. Then I am further beneath him and he is kissing me hard and fast. As fast as his lips are moving, our hands are moving faster. He doesn't take his time removing my clothes like he usually does. He literally pulls my tank top over my head in one movement. In the next moment, he is pulling my shorts down, and throwing them on the floor. He slows down enough to move his eyes from my face, down my body. I can't breathe. I am afraid to. In the dim light he is tracing every inch of me with his fingertips. Then he puts his mouth on top of mine again.

My fingers are wrapped in his hair. My hands slip down his back, and then I have his boxers, and he is helping me take them off of him. He tugs slightly on my panties, and I shimmy out of them.

All I can think is how I have never wanted him more than I do right now. I try pulling him into me, catching up to where he is. But, he whispers, "Not so fast. Let's take it slow."

I think this is weird, he never shows much restraint once we get to this point. My head hears him, but my body is too aware of him on top of me, I groan very softly, so he'll know how much I want him, how much I need him. I let my hands brush his back gently.

He smiles down at me. Then he continues to kiss my neck, biting it here and there very gently. I wrap my legs around his waist. I push my hips into him. I can feel he is just as excited as I am. I begin to lose myself. I quit thinking about where I am, and instead I concentrate on his kisses and his touch.

"This is so easy. I want you so much. Every day I tell myself that I will end this, and every day, we are back here. I don't know what it is," he says very softly and slowly, kissing me in between each thought.

I open my mouth to tell him I do know what it is, that I am in love with him, but his mouth comes crushing down on mine and instantly he is inside me. Our bodies move together like a well-rehearsed dance. He knows where to kiss me, where to touch me. He knows when to speed up and when to slow down. My fingers are digging into his back, and he is still trying to run his fingers through my hair but eventually gives up. I can feel the blackness begin to fill my head which I welcome, it is familiar and I am no longer worrying about anything else other than being with Josh in this moment.

The feelings are too much for my brain to grasp. Our bodies are in tune, I let myself go. I feel my body react to his, and his to mine. I lose track of time, everything is going so fast, my head feels like it is spinning.

At almost the same moment, both of our bodies are rigid. The end is near for both of us. We are gasping, very slowly and very quietly. There are guests in the house, and none of them will be too pleased to find my best friend in my bed.

We are still and quiet. He has both his arms wrapped under my head, and his face is resting on my shoulder. I hear him say "cocoa butter," and then a small laugh escapes his throat.

"What?" I whisper.

"Cocoa butter is what I smell. And it reminds me of you".

I keep one of my legs wrapped around his thigh and the other draped over his other leg. I run my fingers through his hair and down his back, still kissing his ears, his face, his neck. I can't get enough of him, even as exhausted as I am. I am always left wanting more from him.

His breathing is slowing. He is still inside me and I don't want him to move. I just keep rubbing his back, gently while inside I am holding on to every second like it was the last one I will have with him. Then I force myself to close my eyes, and begin replaying the images in my mind, eventually I drift off to sleep underneath him.

When I wake up, I begin thinking about what had happened last night. I'm not sure what's real, and what isn't. Maybe I was just having a really vivid dream. I move to roll over and find his arms wrapped tightly around me. I smile, he is still here. He's sleeping so hard. His breathing is slow and even. He had turned me on my side and has both arms wrapped tightly around my chest.

His mouth is by my ear. I strain to look at the clock, to see how long I've been asleep. It is almost 5 am. I have a trip to get ready for, and so does he, just not to the same place. He's going to Carbo with the boys for two weeks, and I'm headed to the beach with everyone else from Seabrook.

I knew when we got back things wouldn't be so simple. College and real life were the next natural steps. He had made his decisions, but I hadn't told him mine yet. Thinking about this made me sad. I couldn't imagine not seeing or being with him like this every day. I had gotten my acceptance letter to UT even before he'd gotten his, I hadn't ever told him because I didn't want to lose him before I had to. I would eventually have to tell him I would be in San Marcos and not in Austin.

"Hey, it's almost time for you to go." I whispered to him, rubbing his arm to wake him up.

I hated this part more than anything; the time when he left me. I never knew for sure if he would come back, and if he did how things would be. I had no real hold on him. He wasn't my boyfriend. I don't think we knew what to call this, a mess at best, life altering chaos at worst. I gently shook him again and wriggled free of his grasp.

I watch his face as he begins to wake up and I hear his voice. His eyes were still closed.

"I don't want to leave. I don't want to leave this."

I watch him, figuring he's just talking in his sleep. I sit up in the bed. I'm so confused. I've hoped this might be more than something physical for him. It was love for me. I knew I was in love with him.

He on the other hand, wasn't there yet. And I didn't know if or when he ever would be.

He looked up at me, and moved over to me, putting his head in my lap and his arms around my waist. I played with his hair relishing this time with him. I wanted to say so many things, but instead, I pushed him from me. I did not look down at him; I couldn't look him in the eyes.

I got up quickly and headed for the bathroom. I locked the door, turned on the shower, and climbed inside. I started to cry. I knew that no matter what he had thought, or said or whatever, that this relationship was still going nowhere. And for this I was terribly sad.

After my shower, I put on my tank top and shorts, and went over to my bed. I gently shook him again, this time he rolled over.

"Why aren't you in here with me?" he asked.

I smiled down at him,

"Its 5:30, the girls will be here to get me soon, and you need to head out. If my mom catches you, I won't be going anywhere for a long time."

I was so grateful I had come home early last night and packed everything.

His hand was rubbing the outside of my thigh.

"I should have chosen to go to the beach with you. I'd much rather do what we did last night for the next two weeks."

He winked at me.

"Well, unless we went somewhere totally alone, we wouldn't be doing THAT anyway."

He grimaced, and it looked like I might have hurt his feelings. So I turned away, let out a nervous sigh, and said:

"Besides, you will find someone the day you land, and you'll forget my name all together."

I was only half teasing him. Teasing him made it easier to express what I believed to be true. For a guy like Josh, finding a willing participant wasn't very difficult.

He grabbed my hands, spun me around and with a very serious

face said, "Why is it so complicated with us?"

I looked down at him and shrugged my shoulders. I sat down next to his feet on the end of my bed, which looked so small with his beautiful body lying in it. I smiled to myself thinking that for now he was in my bed. But it's always so easy to get him in there. If only it was as easy to get into his heart.

"I think we set it up that way a long time ago. I'm just not sure how to change the rules now. Besides, two weeks away will do us some good, don't you think? You can figure out that I'm the love of your life, and I can become the woman you want me to be," I whispered, but I couldn't meet his eyes. I knew I would never be what he wanted me to be. I wasn't really even sure he knew what he wanted only that he knew it wasn't me.

I looked over at him, but he wasn't looking. His head was resting on his arms which were crossed, and his eyes were closed. There was a slight smile on his lips though. Before he could dissect what I'd said, or overanalyze it, I straddled and kissed him. There was definitely no denying how his body felt about me. I could feel the intensity in his lips, his arms, his thighs. It was a soft kiss. There was no fury behind it, like there had been last night. There was just him and I and nothing else mattered at the moment. I wished that I could make it stay like that forever.

I opened my eyes, and saw the light from my alarm clock. He caressed my back and I pulled him up with me, to where I was sitting in his lap.

"Gotta go," I said into his ear. I kissed his cheek. I kept my hand on his other cheek, just wishing time didn't move so fast.

I crawled off of him, and went and grabbed my bag and my flip flops. I pulled my hair into a ponytail. He grudgingly put on his clothes and we started to walk out of my bedroom. Just as I opened the door, he put his hand out and turned me to him quickly.

"Please be good down there, Car. Don't do anything stupid."

"Hmmm, what could I do that would be stupid?" I wondered out loud.

"Lots of things… just don't okay?" he begged. I thought I saw something different in his eyes, but he was probably just saying what he thought I wanted to hear.

31

We walked very quietly out of my house, and we waited in the front yard for my ride. Luckily I'd said my good-byes to everyone last night, and no one was any the wiser that he'd stayed over. He kissed me on the top of my head, and I instinctively pulled away from him. When he looked at me confused, I glanced down the road.

He knew what I meant. We didn't want anyone to see. I don't know how we had managed this relationship this long and generated no gossip, no rumors, and no one knowing. It made me feel ashamed sometimes, like he was ashamed of me. And then at other times, like this morning, I felt like I had the most delicious secret in the world, and I loved not having to explain it to anyone else. But, then again, I wasn't sure that I even trusted myself with my own thoughts on the subject.

Self-preservation is a very powerful instinct. Sometimes the subconscious knows more than we know about ourselves consciously. But, of all my fears, I knew my deepest darkest fear best. I was afraid that if we were no longer a secret, then we would be nothing at all. That would mean I would lose his friendship as well as everything else. So I made the decision, again and again, to continue on this course, because living without him was something that I just wasn't ready to do.

If someone who didn't know us had driven by, they would have seen a couple of teenagers holding on tightly to one another. They might even have blushed, and felt like they had intruded on a private moment. But, I knew all too well that things weren't always as they appeared. I was good at pretending this was okay, and that I was getting what I wanted from this relationship.

He kissed me again gently, and then he jogged off towards his car. As I watched him go, my heart began to ache. We had graduated from high school less than 24 hours ago. Everything would be changing in the months ahead. I was so in love with him even to where sometimes I couldn't think straight. Would I ever share these thoughts and words out loud with him?

7

Carsen, 2010

I was so focused on prioritizing my long 'to do' list that the ringing of the back door startled me. It was Jesse and Laura, my student helpers who were supplementing their studies by doing floral work with me.

They were both bright and so very funny. One of the things I loved most about my job was the kids that worked for me. Jesse was engaged, but she and her fiancé were taking a break for the summer. The way she explained it, they wanted to see if their love could sustain them being separated for a time. Joe, her boyfriend, had gone to Europe with two buddies, and they had agreed the only form of communication was to be through the written word; they were going to write letters to one another. Jesse was an old soul. She was a tiny thing with dark hair and darker eyes. She always looked like she had a tan, though she swore up and down she'd never "fake 'n baked."

I was grateful they had gotten in a little bit early today. I wiped away the tears that had formed in my eyes and hoped they wouldn't notice my crying and reminiscing. I knew that Jesse would notice though. She had a kind of sixth sense about these things. It gave her an incredible ability to convey emotion through her floral arrangements.

Laura was a different story. Laura was the beautiful "girl next door" type. She had shoulder length blonde hair that she wore board-straight. She had a perfect pug nose, perfectly arched eye brows, high cheek bones and piercing blue eyes. She dressed a little more conservatively than most girls her age, but always looked very pretty.

Laura had grown up in Beacon Falls and therefore knew everything about everyone there, and then some. She kept me on my toes for sure. She and Jesse had been roommates their first year of college and had been inseparable ever since. Laura was casually dating a few boys, but her path was all mapped out, and she wasn't going to let a stupid boy, with his own agenda, ruin her plans. I envied her strength and determination. I was drawn to them both because of their ability to put themselves first.

It cracked me up to no end when they wanted my opinion on something. I wondered what the topic of discussion would be today.

"Good morning ladies," I said as they walked in through the back door.

"Hey Momma Car," Laura sang.

Jesse waved; she was sipping her coffee. When she'd set down her coffee tumbler she stared at me.

"So where were you right now?"

"Huh? What do you mean?" I asked as I looked away from here and down at my vase.

"You were a million miles away, Momma C. Talk to us."

They both came over to the work-island and huddled up close to me.

"I'll talk a little while we work. Laura, please go get all the baby's-breath in the walk in, and Jesse can you get the gerbera daisies, please."

I considered telling them about what I thought I'd seen this morning, in part to see if they would surmise that I was going crazy. I loved their perspective on my odd behavior. They didn't know much about my past. They knew, of course, that I'd had Tyler when I was young, which they both thought was so "brave and liberating." They also knew that the father wasn't involved. And again, they thought that was totally cool.

So I walked them through what had happened earlier in the Caf. I told them that I thought a guy I knew in high school might have been there. Jesse was deep in contemplation, while Laura said the first thing that came to her mind.

"It could be him. He could be here. What did you say he did for a living?"

"He's a lawyer. I'm not sure what he practices though."

"Why didn't you just go ask him?" Jesse wondered out loud. I knew she'd put two and two together faster than Laura.

My eyes told her not to go down that road right now.

"I just didn't want to embarrass myself. I mean what are the odds?" I laughed it off.

Jesse wasn't letting it go, I saw the wheels spinning.

"Oh, well. No harm, no foul. I'm sure it's just my wild imagination," I quickly added. Then I turned to Laura.

"So, how many daisies are going in that vase?"

We got everything done faster than I expected. My part-time high-school girls arrived after lunch; Violet and Emma. They were part of a program that allowed them to leave school early to gain work experience. They both knew Tyler and I think they both had crushes on him. They made me laugh whenever he was around. It wasn't hard to remember being awkward and embarrassed around cute boys. It just struck me as funny that it was over my son, who was totally oblivious to girls in general.

I put them all to work on different tasks, and we started getting through the do list. I tried to stay busy and focused, but my thoughts kept going back to the man in the cafe. I wasn't 100% convinced that it wasn't him, but the rational side of my brain thought it knew better. No matter what I tried to do, every thought and every feeling made its way back to Joshua. Jesse could tell that I was pre-occupied. She came up behind me and asked if I wanted to go along with her to get the afternoon caffeine jolt. I smiled and was grateful for the distraction.

Jesse took everyone's orders. They all tried to give money, even my two drivers, Alan and Lucas, but I told them this time it was on me. It was payment enough to see the reaction on their faces. They all worked hard for me; I appreciated them and they knew that.

Jesse and I walked towards the square where we knew we would find the old fashioned ice cream parlor, Triple Dips. They had the best cola-freezes and we all enjoyed those. There were so many more offices filling up the space around the square. It was looking more like a business park than our town square. I guess that was the price we paid for growth.

As we walked past the Caf I couldn't help but look in. I knew he wouldn't be there, but it was like I just had to check.

This proved enough to provoke Jesse.

"I can't stand it anymore, Carsen. Please talk to me."

"There really isn't a lot to say, Jesse."

"Sure there is. This isn't just some random guy from high school, is it?"

I smiled to myself. I knew she would have put it all together given a little quiet time.

"Perhaps not. If it is him he really is a guy from my high school, I pinky promise." I smirked at her.

"Fine, but he means more than that. You didn't see the flush on your face when you were talking about him. You didn't notice how your hands were shaking. Whoever he is he means more than you're saying and letting on."

"Oh, Jesse! I think YOU should be a lawyer! You read people like we are books. But, I don't think I'm ready to talk about all this. Not out loud anyway. Besides, I don't know that it was him. It was probably just my mind playing tricks on me."

"Maybe it was," she paused, "or maybe, just maybe, he is here by some bizarre twist of fate, and you guys are destined to be together."

She looked off into the distance. I imagined she was picturing a scene from *The Notebook*. She was an engineer major by day and a hopeless romantic by night. This was one of the reasons she worked for me, flowers are just so romantic.

We got to Triple Dips and ordered all the drinks, it was going to take a while, so we walked out to the middle of the square and sat down to enjoy the fresh air. I perused the names of some of the new businesses that were opening. There was a tax accountant and a kid's re-sale shop. Their real signs weren't up yet, just vinyl banners hanging in the windows. There was one that caught my eye though. Jesse saw it, too.

Martin & Callum Law Firm

"What did you say he did?" Jesse whispered.

"I said he was going to be a lawyer. Is that a new law firm, or was it always here? Why are we whispering? Anyone could be moving into that space."

"Well, Laura will know. I'll write the name down, and see what she knows. Do you want to walk over there?"

"Of course not! I'm sure it's just a coincidence, Jesse. We better go get the freezes before they wonder where we are."

I got up and turned towards the store.

My heart skipped a beat at the thought he could be with that law firm. My mind pushed that idea far away, protecting my heart, as it often did.

We got back to the shop. There were still a few of the larger arrangements that needed to be completed. I went into the smaller room where the bouquets were patiently waiting for me. I could hear the kids out there laughing and working. I wished that I could find that carefree spirit I used to have again.

I was alone again with my thoughts.

Damn it!

8

Tyler, 2010

I heard her leave this morning. She tries to be so quiet but the house is too small and the doors are too old and everything creaks. I actually enjoy being alone in the house. I like the silence. My mom is always trying to flood the silence with mindless chatter. Sometimes I feel like she is trying to fill up all the space so there'll simply be none left. No questions to ask, no time to wonder.

I reach over and pick up my iPod, and put in my ear buds. Band of Horses, *Ghost in my House* is on, and I get lost in the song. It's funny that this song came on; maybe I had been listening to it before I went to sleep. I don't remember, but that's probably because I was thinking about her. When I woke it wasn't but a few seconds of consciousness before my thoughts turned to Lilly. I smile, thinking about our conversation yesterday.

One of the things that sucked about living in a small town is that you know everyone and they know you. I grew up with these kids, and sometimes it's all just a little boring. I am always wanting more, feeling like I should be somewhere else or doing something different. But, every morning, to my disappointment I wake up in my bed in my house in Beacon Falls. But, now that she is here, everything feels different.

Lilly. Her name is Lilly. She has been here for almost a month now, and everyone has been all over her. I didn't want to do that. I can only imagine how hard it is for her. Being the new girl in a town this size has to be the worst. So I waited. Since she was a sophomore and I was a junior, we didn't have any classes together. I had to wait for just the right time to approach her.

I was a little thrown by the attraction I felt towards her. I didn't even know her. There was no denying she was beautiful, but, not in the ton-of-make-up, too-tight-clothes, hey-look-at-me kind of way. She has long, light brown, wavy hair that most of the time is just kind of flowing behind her. She seems to be most comfortable in T-shirts and jeans, and a hoodie. I think she likes the color green, it seems like she wears it every day. Not the same clothes, just the same color of green.

This in itself makes me crazy. Why do I even notice what she is wearing? I know that means nothing about the person I have come to believe she is. She seems smart, but not nerdy. She appears to know her way around a computer, but she is not geeky. She seems fairly typical, for all intents and purposes, but I have this nagging feeling that she is far from typical.

Of course, I am not your typical teenage boy either. My mother would have died before letting me be just typical. Ever since I can remember she has surrounded me with music, literature, art and what she calls "enrichment." I sometimes wonder if she forgets where we live, and that some of this crap just isn't important to me.

She often says it doesn't matter if I don't like it or use it, but that knowing about it is the key. I don't quite know how to break it to her, but here in this town, most people don't even know what literature is. My mom is smart. She is incredibly witty and definitely has a way with people. Everyone in town likes her, but they love her floral arrangements more.

I think she over does stuff because she doesn't want people to judge her and our "situation." She isn't married and she has a kid. And maybe a million years ago that mattered, but now, it's not a big deal. Although, I've sensed something when I've caught her on a day where she wasn't chatty and her gaze was lost and far away. Then, I know it matters a great deal to her. Not because it bothers her for herself but because it bothers her for me.

But, you can't miss what you don't know. I have plenty of friends whose parents are divorced and who get shuffled from one place to the next. I also know kids who are being raised solely by their fathers. I don't think the nuclear family is what it once was. I have never felt slighted because I don't have a father, it's just the way my life is and I accepted that a long time ago. I think she beats herself up over it more than she needs to.

She has never shared very much information with me, so I don't have a whole lot to base my assumptions on. When I was younger, she just said my father wasn't with us. I never really wondered too much. But, then there was the first t-ball team I was on. I was then painfully aware that it seemed I was the only kid who didn't have a dad on the bench.

But, as luck would have it, I was a natural at sports, so every dad wished I was their kid. So, even though I didn't have my own father, I had a lot of substitutes, and lots of people cheering. Many of these guys, who were married, would even hit on mom sometimes. It was crazy. She would just smile, like she totally didn't get it.

Then one day, I think I was twelve or thirteen, I saw a picture in her room. She had accidentally left it out, and she had gone into her bathroom. When she came out, I was holding it.

I looked at her and said, "Who are these people?"

She smiled at me, and took the picture.

"That is me the day I graduated from high school."

"You were beautiful, Mom."

"Hmmmm. Thanks. That was a lifetime ago."

"Who is the guy?"

She hesitated looking directly into my eyes, smiled a little bit, her voice cracking,

"That is your father."

She took the picture from me and stared at it for some time. I waited for more information, but none came. I wasn't a little kid, I knew where babies came from, and it all kind of clicked for me.

"So were you married then?"

"Oh no, of course not," she said emphatically, "We were too

young to get married."

"But, you weren't too young to have a baby? That makes a lot of sense, Mom," I said sarcastically.

She got up quickly and looked down at me, she spoke firmly but softly,

"Clearly you are not mature enough to have this conversation right now. One day we will, but not today. You will someday realize that things are not always as they appear, and the world is NOT black and white, it's a hazy gray."

She walked out of her room. She stopped at the door and turned back to me, her arm was stretched out like it was saying "come on," so I got up and walked out.

I was confused, but I also knew I didn't want to push her. I felt a bit scared too, like what she was going to tell me was going to hurt me or something, so I just pushed past her and went to my room and closed the door. I was mad at her, but I hated fighting with her, so I just turned on my stereo and let Pearl Jam drown out what I was feeling. *Don't Call Me Daughter* started playing which made me laugh.

After a little bit, she knocked on the door.

"May I come in, please?" she asked, yelling over the music.

"Sure," I said with no enthusiasm whatsoever.

She came in and sat down on my bed. She listened to the music for a moment as I turned it down.

"I bought that CD with your Dad."

"He liked Pearl Jam?" I asked excitedly.

"He did." She smiled at me. "I know you have questions, Tyler. And, I know you're getting older. So, maybe, it is time to have this discussion. What do you think?"

Finally! Finally I would get to know something, anything about my father. I didn't think of him like a real dad but I did think of him.

"Where is he? Why isn't he with us?" I asked.

"Wow! You want to start with the hardest ones first, huh?" she looked down at her hands which were folded neatly in her lap. She reached over and took my hand. I sat up in front of her. We were about the same height then. I think I may even have been taller than her.

"He lives in Texas, I believe. At least that is where he was when I left fourteen years ago. I am sure I could find out for sure, if you want to know." She paused, looking at me.

I raised my eyebrows,

"Uhm. I don't know."

"Well, you let me know if you do. The part why he isn't with us is a bit messy. It's really all my fault, to be honest. I never told him I was pregnant with you." Her eyes filled with tears then.

"Why? Why wouldn't you tell him you were having a baby?"

She shifted on my bed. She cleared her throat and looked me in the eyes.

"I was scared. I was terrified, really. We didn't have the most conventional of relationships. We weren't really dating, Tyler. We were best friends. I knew I wanted you, but I wasn't so sure that he wanted me. So, I decided not telling him was the best thing to do."

She looked up at me, waiting for my reaction. I couldn't read her face. I think she was still scared and this was obviously painful for her to talk about, but I didn't really have a reaction there and then, it was all still sinking in. The mystery was solved, sort of. I wanted to see if I got it right.

"So, you guys were having sex, right?"

"Yes."

"You got pregnant?"

"Yes."

"You didn't tell him?"

"Right."

I considered what she had said. Interesting.

"So, it's not like he didn't want me, because he never even knew there even was a 'me' right?"

"Exactly. It's not like he didn't want you or that he ran out on us; I ran out on him." Her voice faded at the end. It was almost like by saying it out loud she was just now realizing the severity of what she had done.

"Mom? Why didn't you tell him?"

She thought for a long time about that. Her eyes were red and she was wiping the tears from her cheeks with the palms of her hands.

"Back then, I thought I knew it all. I thought I was doing what was best for him. I was afraid if he knew he might change his mind about his future and about me. But, now I know how selfish I really was. I guess I just didn't know any better at 18. You kind of think you know everything about everything at that age. And, no one can tell you any different. But, coming here and having you *was* the best decision I have ever made. You are my whole life, Tyler."

"I know that Mom, but what if he wanted to be a part of our lives? That would have been awesome." I wasn't mad, just a little disappointed.

"I have just one more question, Mom. Why didn't he ever come looking for you?"

She closed her eyes. I could see the pain when she opened them again.

"I don't have an answer for that. But, that's how I knew that I'd made the right decision, Tyler. He never did come looking for me."

I decided then and there that I wouldn't ask any more questions about him. If he didn't love my mom, then I couldn't love him. A lot can change over the course of a few years though, I realize that now. Things can change in just a few days or minutes. Like, I know my whole life has changed now that I've met Lilly.

Mom always tries so hard to be both my mother and father, to the extent that most of the times I never even miss having a "man around the house." And Mom is so careful to make sure I have everything I need, almost to excess. We aren't rich, but we are definitely comfortable. I got a used Jeep Wrangler on my 16th birthday. It was 5 years old, but it was a jeep. I worked summers at her floral shop because I had to pay the first years insurance, up front. I know how important hard work is so the work didn't really bother me.

But, all I can really think about these days are two things, Lilly and getting out of Beacon Falls. I don't really want to get out of this town because I hate it or anything. I just want to see more of the world. I am ready to get on with the rest of my life. I have this great little plan. I will head down to Austin, Texas and go to the University of Texas. I haven't decided exactly what I want to do just yet, but I know Austin is where I belong. It is such a neat place. It isn't a huge city, but also not a podunk town like Beacon Falls. Mom has friends there that we have visited religiously all my life. And, when we are there I feel like I have come home. So for the past three years, I have been counting down the days.

Now, though, there is Lilly. I've had girlfriends before and I've had my share of fun and flirtation. But now there is this new girl. A girl I haven't known my whole life. A girl who I don't know anything about, but who was really all I can think of.

She is always reading. Most days at lunch, she sits in the school courtyard and reads. I have been watching her for weeks and find it fascinating. My keen observations reveal she reads a lot about England and also books about kings. I've seen a few other classics in her hands too, including *The Scarlet Letter*, which I thought was funny. We didn't have to read that until senior English and here she was getting two years ahead. People who read for leisure usually strike me as odd. To my mind if a book is any good it will eventually be made into a movie, so why bother wasting the time to read it? And if we had to read it for school, well there are Cliff Notes or the internet to get the gist of the story. Lilly, on the other hand, is in her own world, and I could tell she likes it there.

A few times she has looked up and met my stare. Neither of us turns away, and yet neither of us moved either. I usually end up looking away first, a little embarrassed. But, she just slowly puts her head back down and picks up where she left off, but perhaps with the trace of a slight smile on her lips. That leads me to believe that she likes that I am watching her.

So yesterday I decided I needed to just get it over with. I needed to introduce myself to her. But, she wasn't at her normal spot at lunch, so I spent most of the break looking for her. As I came around from the courtyard, I looked into the library and there she was. She gave me a huge smile when she saw me. It looked like she was almost laughing, like she knew the joke, and I didn't. Then she waved. She pointed to the doors, and we started walking towards them.

She opened the library door, and whispered, "Hello stalker boy."

I looked down. I could feel the blood rising into my cheeks, and I knew the embarrassment I felt would soon show on my face. Then she reached out and touched my arm.

"I'm only teasing. I enjoy being stalked by you".

I raised my head and my eyes to meet hers. She winked at me, and I immediately felt relieved. This wasn't going to be as hard as I'd thought it would be.

"I wasn't stalking you, really. I was just letting you get to know the entire student body before I introduced myself. I didn't want you to forget my name, so I thought I'd wait to say 'hi.' "

"Oh okay. Well I totally appreciate you thinking of me in that way. But, to be honest, it's been driving me crazy that you haven't spoken to me yet, until now. So, let me introduce myself to you. Hi! I'm Lilly. Oh, but I bet you knew that though, didn't you?"

By the look in her eyes I could tell she was still teasing me.

I lowered my voice, and stuck my chest out just a little bit.

"I did know that. The whole town knows that. But, do you know who I am?"

"I've done my homework: You are Tyler. You are the Captain of the Varsity Hockey Team. You also swim and play basketball to boot. You do not currently have a girlfriend, but I couldn't find a girl in school who hasn't wanted to date you or who hasn't already dated you."

Again, she was still teasing.

"Well, you're good. Everything is true except the girl thing, and we both know that!"

I winked at her.

"So, do you ever study Tyler? Because I am really having a hard time in Geometry and could definitely use some help".

She had to have known that I was a math mentor at the elementary school. And, if pressed, I would readily have admitted that elementary math and Geometry were not similar, that Geometry was much harder. But, really, numbers had always made sense to me, so I'd probably be able to help.

"I've been known to help out my friends, every now and then," I said casually. I motioned elegantly towards the table she had been sitting at when I'd seen her through the window.

"Friends?" she asked. "That's okay, for now," she said over her shoulder as she led me to the table.

I followed her and saw that she already had all her books spread out. I already knew that there was no way I would be able to get any studying done. All I could think of was how beautiful she was, and how now she was talking to me. And, to top it all off, how she wanted to be talking to me.

After we sat down, she leaned over and whispered in my ear:

"I don't really need any help with geometry. I just wanted to get to talk to you some more."

We both smiled. Lunch was going to be over soon, and I knew I didn't have much more time before we would both have to go to class.

"Hmm.., no tutoring necessary?"

I leaned back in the chair, putting my arms behind my head, and looking right at her said:

"Then I guess we will just have to hang out after school and find something we have in common to do. What *do* you like to do, Lilly?"

I wanted to put the ball in her court to see just what her level of interest in me was, maybe she was just having fun and being polite.

"I'm interested in seeing all the ins and outs of Beacon Falls. Do you think you could manage that?"

"Well, I *have* lived here my whole life, so I doubt you could find anyone who would know it better than me."

"Great! You're hired! You are my very own personal tour guide now!"

She grinned like a Cheshire cat, her plan was obviously working.

I had a feeling she was going to have me being whatever she wanted or needed. When I looked into those piercing blue eyes, I couldn't ever imagine myself telling her no. The bell rang, and we both stood up. I helped her gather up her stuff, and asked,

"Would you like a guided tour to your next class?"

She looked up at me, beaming.

"Absolutely."

45

9

Joshua, 2010

I can't believe I'm in another small town. I swore once I left Seabrook and moved to Austin that I would never live in a small town again. Of course that was before my life took an unexpected detour to where I now find myself a single father at 36 raising a 15 year old daughter. I am grateful to have Lilly but still so worried about doing this on my own. Daughters need their mothers. I need her mother. I still can't believe that Lauren is gone.

Sitting in this unfamiliar coffee shop, in this unfamiliar town, I can only hope that I made the best choice for us. My sister Sarah had almost insisted that this was where Lilly and I belonged. I argued with her for what seemed like weeks. I didn't quite understand how leaving everything and everyone we knew and loved behind could be the best thing for us. But I did agree that it would be nice not to be reminded of Lauren everywhere I looked. I knew I would have to sell the house regardless. Lilly and I had agreed on that just a few days after the funeral. But how was moving to Connecticut actually the answer? I had never lived outside of Texas.

I remembered though how earlier in the month, as we'd driven into Beacon Falls, I'd felt a deep sense of relief. But it was relief tinged with guilt. I was grateful for my sister, Sarah. She had found us a cute rental house and enrolled Lilly in the high school. She'd made the move almost seamless for me. But while I'd had Lilly's company as we drove up here together, we both seemed very much alone.

It had been a terribly long drive. There was so much pain and anger between us. It was just so apparent in each of the conversations that we'd had. I did not blame Lilly for the accident; it was an accident, after all. It was a terrible tragic accident. I did not blame Lilly. Lilly is just a child.

No, in fact, I blame myself. I should have been the one that went searching for Lilly. It never should have been Lauren. When I recall that fateful night I see how many bad decisions I made and how if I had just made one different one, at any point along the way, my wife would not be dead, and I would not be living in Connecticut.

Staring out of the shop window, absentmindedly, I allow the guilt to wash over me like a torrential down pour. Within a few seconds, I feel like I am standing in our old kitchen, arguing with Lauren about Lilly, one more time. It is in these moments that I feel like I truly have no control over my life whatsoever. It feels like there is someone else pulling the strings, someone else making the decisions, someone else dragging me down into the abyss.

We'd learned early on that Lauren was unable to conceive children. She had gone for a routine checkup just a few months after we'd been married and had come home devastated by the news. I wasn't as upset or devastated as most might be. My older sister, Sarah, was adopted, and I was a big supporter of adoption. Even before we knew we couldn't have our own children we'd decided we should adopt. It just seemed like such a normal thing to do. My family, after all, was complete only with Sarah. She made our family what it was.

What Lauren and I hadn't planned on, though, was a baby basically falling into our laps. Sarah at the time worked very closely with a placement agency. She'd gotten us placed high up on their waiting list. The agency felt that people already close to the adoption process made the best candidates. We were told the process from there could be as soon as six months or as long as five years. We applied, were accepted and then we waited.

When you're waiting for something like this to happen, time still passes. You don't necessarily count the days; you just know that one day it might happen. You go to work, you have dinner with friends, you take vacations that you might not want to take with children; you go about your life. But, looming back in a deep part of your mind, each and every time the phone rings, you wonder if you'll be told you've been picked.

Even then though, things began to change. Laura's focus shifted from just us to preparing for a life with a baby. I felt like I was more realistic than she was; I really believed it might take a very long time. So, I didn't see any sense in making drastic changes to the house or to our lives. Lauren quickly began working on the third bedroom to turn it into a nursery, although she would never call it that. I continued to work, and to travel, and I became increasingly happier on Sunday evenings when I knew I would be gone until the following Friday. It wasn't that I didn't still love Lauren, it was just hard dealing with the fall out of another week when things didn't happen the way she had so carefully envisioned. I saw the depression it was leading to, and I just wasn't so excited about going through that again.

I had never really been exposed to anyone who was severely depressed until Lauren's grandmother passed away suddenly and unexpectedly. This was just a few months after we'd met, and she spiraled into a place that really scared me. It's hard to watch someone you care about go through something like this. What I did learn was that I never wanted Lauren to go through something like this again. I felt I needed to protect her from being exposed to anything like that. And here I think I confused how much I cared about not hurting her with just being in love with her. Now these seem like two very different things, but at 20 I didn't know the difference.

I was by no means ready to get married. When we began to date it was very comfortable, which I think was what drew me in. There was no drama. There were no arguments. It seemed like she just wanted to make me happy. And this was so far removed from my only other serious relationship that I felt myself gravitating to her.

In the beginning, it was nice to be adored. It was nice to have her take care of me. She did everything too, even things I didn't ask her to do were done. After all of six weeks we were living together. She believed the sun rose and set with me, and that felt really good. My ego definitely loved Lauren. My heart, I suspected, would forever be lost to someone else; to someone who'd never even known I loved her.

I realized that not loving Lauren like I'd loved Carsen was actually fine with me. The relationships were so totally different. It made it easier to compartmentalize my emotions and feelings. I had Lauren who loved and adored me, but it was Carsen who had disappeared with my heart and soul in tow.

I proposed to Lauren on our two month anniversary. She was so ecstatic you would have thought I had done something phenomenal. She wanted to get married quickly. Looking back now, she probably was afraid I would change my mind. So, later that year, in October, we did.

It was in December that we learned of Lauren's infertility.

It was in February that we got the most startling news of all. It was a typical Sunday; I was getting ready to leave to go out of town for the week. Lauren was getting my clothes washed and packed and the phone rang.

"Hello?" I answered.

"Josh? Hey it's me Sarah. I've got the most unbelievable news." She was almost out of breath and was talking so fast.

"Hey sis, slow down, please, and tell me what's going on."

"Your baby was just born".

"WHAT? What did you say?" I screamed into the phone.

"I know it's so fast! But isn't this the best news ever?" she said, almost cautiously.

"Uh, yeah." I paused to think. "Uh huh, yes of course it is."

She sighed heavily.

"Oh good! I knew you would want her. You will need to get to the hospital as soon as you can. We are at Austin County Hospital. Just come straight to Labor & Delivery. See you soon."

And, with that, the phone went dead.

I couldn't move, I stood, paralyzed by the news. A baby? Now? I didn't know what to say, or think. After a few deep breaths and a glass of water, I went upstairs to tell Lauren, and before all the words were out Lauren was grabbing me and her purse and pulling me out the door.

Sarah had been working with a young girl during her pregnancy. Sarah just knew the girl would want to give us her baby once she delivered. Sarah had shared photo albums and stories about Lauren and me. She had shared our heartache, short lived as it was. I mean, I knew people who had had to wait years for a baby. Suddenly though, here we were with a beautiful strawberry blonde, blue eyed beauty.

Her first dozen years went by so quickly. I continued to work really hard at the firm I had joined right after law school. I was determined to make partner by the time I was 35. I still travelled quite a bit, but that never seemed to bother the girls. They just loved doing everything together, and Lauren was just the best mother to Lilly. We stayed on the list to adopt, but sadly we were never chosen again. And after a few years, that didn't seem to matter. This was our life. This was our family. And I knew I was a blessed man.

Then Lilly turned thirteen. At first we thought it was just normal teenage rebellion. She wasn't always where she was supposed to be, she wouldn't answer her cell phone or it would be misplaced or even stolen. Whatever happened, there was always an excuse.

Now, looking back, I wonder whether it was just easier to believe the lies? Confrontation only leads to empty threats from us and angry hateful words from Lilly. Dealing with teenagers can be like being blind-folded while running an obstacle course. No matter where you go, you run into something, and it was usually very painful.

Once she got into high school, it was almost unbearable. Things got to the point where I couldn't travel during the school year, which really made things quite difficult for us financially. Telling the firm "no" had previously been unheard of for me, but I couldn't abandon Lauren to parent Lilly alone.

Lauren would cry that her needing me to stay home was only temporary, and that she just couldn't do this alone at that moment. Lauren was such a fragile soul. I had always been aware of this, but now it seemed like she was being dominated by her own child. Lauren backed down when Lilly's voice rose. I was frustrated by the lack of respect Lilly showed her mother.

Yet, when I was home and Lilly behaved like this, if I spoke to her sternly her attitude would change. She even seemed remorseful, and she would go to Lauren and apologize. However, the longer this went on, the more I believed I was witnessing my daughter develop into a great method actress. I no longer trusted what she said and questioned her motives when she did things she knew we disapproved of.

Lilly had been sneaking out, and it took us a while to actually catch her at it. This was partly because it was easier just to turn off the lights, close your eyes and say a little prayer that she would stay put. I had even quit getting up and checking on her in the middle of the night, because like Lauren, I was simply worn down.

That last night at dinner, though, something was definitely different... Although actually, if I'm really honest, I'm not sure if it really was, or if that's just the way things seemed in hindsight. Lilly was telling us about her plans for the evening. She was babbling on about this new boy she liked, who was a junior, and who was picking her up at 8 pm, so that way we could meet him.

Then they were going to his house for a small gathering. His parents would be home, and we could call them if we didn't believe her. I was staring into her eyes trying to see if there was any truth in what was being said. I immediately felt guilty for doing this. I think we always want to believe the very best in the people we love most in the world. And sometimes that love clouds our instincts.

I remember Lauren asking questions, and Lilly becoming agitated by them. She got so angry; she threw her plate at her mom. I jumped up and slapped Lilly right across the face, yelling,

"You will not EVER treat your mother with such disrespect. You are not going anywhere but right up to your room. And don't even think about sneaking out. You think I don't know about that young lady?"

Lilly looked horrified. Lauren wrung her hands in her lap, her head hung low, and I knew she was crying. I grabbed Lilly by the arm and took her to her room. It felt like this was something I'd done when she was three and misbehaved; when I would have taken her to the "naughty chair". I was never, as a rule physical with Lilly, but tonight, it had just been too much, the entire situation was just too volatile. I shoved her into her room.

I walked in behind her and picked up her cell phone, her laptop and her iPod.

She screamed at me,

"I HATE YOU! I HATE YOU SO MUCH! I am going to leave

and never come back. You can't DO THIS TO ME!!"

And with that she flailed onto her bed.

I turned to her, a little calmer now,

"Unfortunately you will have to wait to leave until you are no longer grounded. And all of these things I am taking with me will have to be earned back, at some point. You are NOT to leave this room young lady. I will speak to you tomorrow."

And with that I swiftly exited and locked the door from the outside.

I walked slowly down the stairs to my wife. I noticed as I came up to her, how small and frail she appeared. She was 34, but she had the frame of a teenager. I put my arms around her, but she only stiffened under my embrace. She looked up at me, and I instantly realized that I was the one in trouble here, not Lilly.

In a voice I was sure I had never heard before she said,

"How could you? YOU ARE A MONSTER! YOU struck HER! You HURT her!"

I stepped back and just looked at Lauren. I waited a few moments before I spoke.

"Lilly was and has been out of control for a while now, something needed to be done. Maybe she'll think over her actions and realize that she needs to be making better choices. But, I will not apologize to you, or to her, for slapping her. Can you imagine what would have happened if that plate had hit you in the face?"

She sat back down in the dining room chair and I knelt next to her, rubbing her back.

"I promise it will be okay, Lauren. I promise she is fine. Her ego is hurt more than her cheek. Please," I begged, "look at me."

Instead, she stood and started cleaning up the mess that our daughter had made. I wanted to help her, but I just couldn't, I was too angry.

We had tried reasoning with Lilly, we had tried grounding her, taking away privileges, made plenty of idle threats, and nothing had worked. Something had to give. And, I knew I was the adult here, but sometimes her behavior and attitude just sent me reeling. I was only human.

I decided to go sit outside in the yard. I grabbed a couple of Miller Lites from the outside fridge and got comfortable on the couch on the patio. It sure was peaceful out there. After my second beer in this oasis, I started to calm down again. So I got up and went to grab a few more, and in the process decided just to grab the rest of the six-pack. There was a slight breeze and the night sky had turned such a brilliant hue. I could see pink, orange, yellow and white smeared across the sky as the day began to turn to night.

Some time passed before I got up and walked to the other side of the back yard and peered up at Lilly's window. There was a lamp on, but there didn't appear to be any movement. It had been about an hour since the incident, and my hope was that she'd picked up a book, or just fallen asleep.

Maybe the worst was behind us, at least for tonight. As I made my way back to my chair, I peaked in the kitchen. Of course, it was spotless. Lauren was sitting alone in the living room, in her favorite chair. On normal nights she could be seen reading a book or magazine. But, tonight she sat there in the dark. I thought I saw a glass of wine on the table next to her. "Good for you," I thought. All we needed was some time apart; some space in which to calm down and gain some perspective.

I turned on the outside music, keeping it real low, and smiled as I heard Jack Johnson playing. I lent my head back, closed my eyes, and just allowed my mind to wander back in time. I knew the beer had a lot do with this. It usually did when I let myself revisit my past. I didn't entertain those memories often because some were painful. Tonight though, I guess I was willing to trade the pain of the present, for the pain of past.

I popped open another beer, and drank it down in one huge swallow. They were only memories, but even to bring them out, even for just a little while, required a little liquid courage. Now with the 6th beer in my hand, resting on my thigh, I closed my eyes and there she was, there was Carsen, as if she'd never left me.

Carsen Wylder was my very best friend and the girl that totally and completely broke my heart. I knew that things might not work out the way I'd wanted them to, but I'd never seen it ending quite the way it did.

We had the most amazing connection. And we guarded our friendship above and beyond anything else. For a couple of years, we down played the attraction. It was easy to do, I dated other girls, and she dated other guys. But, we always hung out, and did stuff that I might have done with my guy friends, like go hunting or fishing, as well as things she might have done with her girlfriends, like shopping and gossiping.

And for a long time, we kept saying that being best friends meant more to us than anything else could. But, as we got older, and the lines started to get fuzzy, we decided we needed rules and boundaries. It was those rules and boundaries that eventually made her run away, to never be seen or heard from again.

I was so lost in the memory of her that I could smell her lotion, her perfume. It was a combination of cocoa butter and Anais Anais. It felt so real, like she was right here with me. I imagined holding her, and playing with her mess of hair. I remembered graduation night. And all those nights that had preceded it.

I don't even know what you'd call what we had. I liked to think it was so special that there wasn't a word to describe it, and that no one else had ever had what we had.

Then my mind started remembering touching her, making love to her, and I was overwhelmed by the raw emotion I felt. It had been years.

At least 17, I thought. As I concentrated harder on the timeline, I fell into a beer induced sleep where I knew I would find Carsen.

I was woken up, what felt like days later, by Lauren. She was shaking me viciously.

"WAKE UP DAMN IT! WAKE UP JOSH!" she yelled over and over.

I rolled over and opened my eyes and saw that it was pitch black outside. I no longer heard the music playing either, and Lauren was frantic. She had on her coat and she had her purse.

"I'm up now. What the hell is going on?" I asked.

"Like you have to ask, really? It's Lilly. She's gone."

And with that my wife began to sob. She fell against my chest and let me hold her for a second. As I began to speak, she quickly pulled away. Her eyes were red and angry; I wasn't forgiven.

"We'll find her Lauren. Don't worry. She doesn't have her cell, so her options were probably limited. Just please calm down."

The irritation and frustration were like sour milk on my

tongue. My head was pounding, and I just needed some silence to think straight.

"My daughter, MY ONLY daughter has run away. She took all her clothes, two suitcases and all her stuff from her bathroom. Do NOT tell me to calm down."

I noticed then that her eyes were bloodshot, and not from crying. I glanced over my shoulder into the living room, and next to the glass of wine I had noticed earlier, were two bottles of wine. The light from the moon was beaming in through the side window and I could tell both bottles were open and empty.

"And she is gone because YOU HIT HER! YOU HIT HER JOSH! YOU BASTARD!!" and she began to hit and slap at me. I grabbed her by both her wrists, begging her to calm down.

"I'm going to find her. You stay here in case she calls or comes home", Lauren said.

I was paralyzed. I knew she wouldn't let me go because I'd had three glasses of wine at dinner and then a six-pack of beer. I knew I was in no condition to drive, but I had quickly sobered up, and knew I needed to go look for Lilly.

Lauren looked at me again.

"Did you HEAR me? I AM GOING! NOT YOU! If you found her, she wouldn't come with you anyway."

She was right about that. I sat back down on my chair, and put my head in my hands. What have I done? Where is Lilly? What have I done?

I heard the garage door going up and before I could get there, Lauren was pulling out of the driveway and heading down the street. She was gone into the Austin night, alone, and not knowing where she was going to look for Lilly. A wave of fear washed over me. Now both my girls were alone on the streets, one hiding, one searching, and I was here, drunk, doing absolutely nothing to bring either of them home.

I went inside and made some coffee. I see that the microwave clock says 2:40 am. I walk into my office, and find Lilly's laptop. If I am lucky, maybe there will be some e-mails, or something on Facebook that might lead me to where she is.

After I log on, I immediately access her email account. Fortunately, it isn't password protected. I open it up. There are no new messages. So I scan through to see when the last one opened had been received. That was at 6:12 pm tonight, before dinner. Good. Maybe this will tell me where she went.

It was from some John Krause, someone I of course had never heard of. He was giving her directions to a party down under the Park City Bridge. He told her to bring cash if she was ready to party like they did last weekend. My stomach churned. She is 14! Then I notice there is an attachment.

Oh. My. God.

There is a picture of my beautiful Lilly, barely dressed and barely coherent. There is one boy kissing her mouth, another one kissing her bare stomach, and another kissing the inside of her left thigh. Lilly is just lying there like she doesn't even realize what is happening to her. There is nothing behind her eyes, they are black and empty. I am enraged.

I grab my phone and dial Lauren. She answers on the 2nd ring.

"Is she home, Josh? Is she there? Did she call?" Lauren asks, begging me for answers.

"Uh, no, sorry. But, I think I know where she might be. Try the Park City Bridge, the closest part to the lake. But, Lauren, I'm going to call the cops. I think there is a lot more going on down there than some kids hanging out and getting drunk," I hesitated and then asked, "Lauren?"

"Ok I'm headed there now. I'm about 15 minutes away. Please call the cops, they can meet me there." I know she didn't hear everything I was saying.

"Lauren?" I asked, slowly and more quietly than the first time.

"What Josh? What now?" she said and her words were full of agitation.

"I'm really sorry about tonight, honey. I know I screwed up. It's my fault entirely. I promise to make it up to you, and to Lilly. I swear."

I am sure she could hear the defeat in my voice. I expected her to yell at me again.

"We both handled things badly tonight it's not just you Joshua. We are both her parents. We are just going to have to make some serious changes once we get her home tonight," she said, and I thought I heard a smile in her voice.

I knew we would be okay. I knew this would just be another storm we'd weather together. And while the issues with Lilly might not be so simplistic, our relationship was. All could be forgiven, if I just admitted I was wrong.

I smiled and said, "Please be careful. I'm calling the police now. And I'll see you soon."

She whispered, "I love you Josh so much. And I love Lilly, too. Maybe I love you both a little too much. I'll call you when I talk to the police or I find Lilly."

Relief washed over me, the pounding in my head seems to have subsided, and so has the nausea. I said, "Love you."

And we both hung up.

10

Lilly, 2010

I would never admit it to my Dad, but coming here was the best thing EVER! I got to start over. I got to leave the old Lilly behind. When Aunt Sarah first mentioned Beacon Falls, and showed it to me on the map, I totally freaked out. I remember screaming at her, "CONNECTICUT? What the HELL is in Connecticut? Doesn't it like snow there or something?"

She had just smiled at me and said, "I really do know what is best for you Lilly. But, more importantly this will be good for your Dad. Sometimes growing up means you have to be less self-ish, and more self-less."

I remembered thinking that I only knew how to be selfish. My mother had been selfless, but also pathetic. She was nothing more than a door mat. And I'd read enough books to know that what she and my Dad had, was NOT love. I mean, they had said it to each other all the time, and they even kissed occasionally. But, it wasn't love.

There is just no way my Dad was in love with her. I think he loved her like I loved our dog. But, there was no spark, no chemistry and no fun. EVER. She was boring, predictable and so irritating. It's one of the reasons I think he drank so much. Just to escape from being her husband.

But no matter what I did, she couldn't bring herself to punish or discipline me. And as I did worse and worse things, I expected that she would eventually blow up, and act human! It never happened.

Thinking like that makes my stomach turn. Even now, after her death, and the part I'd played in it, I still didn't feel the kind of remorse I should have. I don't know what it is. The counselor tried to tell my Dad that I had never really bonded with Lauren. That being adopted was something that was so openly discussed and brought up, that I became kind of immune to it. And by doing that, I pulled away more from Lauren. I shouldn't talk about her like that. But, the truth is, I'm not sad that she is gone. I'm not sad that we have moved. I am not sad at all anymore.

I love my Dad so much. It's like he IS my biological father. We are so similar and we get along so well. I know he would never admit it, but sometimes I think he's glad things happened like they did.

I, for one, do NOT believe in coincidences. I believe that every little thing happens to us for a reason. I believe I was conceived and delivered by a terrified teenage girl. I believe that my Aunt just happened to help that girl out so much, that she felt indebted to my Aunt.

And I believe I was supposed to be Joshua Ames Hattinson's daughter. I just never believed I was supposed to be Lauren's daughter. I never meant for anything bad to happen to Lauren though. That was a tragic accident. I would never have expected her to go out late at night searching for me.

There had been some serious drama at dinner that night, and I was slapped by my Dad. I deserved it for throwing a plate at my mom. I was out of line and definitely out of control. I can see that now, but when you are in the middle of all that hate and anger, it's pretty hard to see anything but red.

I remember that night like it was yesterday. I watched my Dad out on the back patio for a while, noticing how many beers he was putting away. I knew that eventually he would pass out, and then I wouldn't be heard leaving.

I had also snuck out to the landing at the top of the stairs and seen Lauren drinking wine. I thought if I gave her enough time, she might be out, too. But, that sixth sense she was always talking about must have kicked in. Her gut must have told her to go check on me.

I had seen her face as I jumped out the bedroom window. She came rushing to the open window. She yelled for me to stop, but I just looked up at her, picked up my bags and smiled at her. I was on the other side of the fence in a split second.

Stephanie was waiting there for me. By the time Lauren made it back downstairs, we were almost out of the neighborhood. I guess she sat there, drinking, and waiting for me to come back. But, I had no intention of doing that. I wanted to prove a point to both of them that they couldn't cross me. And I could do whatever I wanted, whenever I wanted because they were both totally clueless when it came to what I did in the hours between 11 pm and 6 am most days of the week.

When I first started sneaking out, I guess a year ago. I would only go for like 15 minutes. I had to make sure I could get out, and not be heard, and then I had to make sure I could get back in without getting caught. Jumping out my window from the 2nd floor only hurt the first few times. Coming back in was tricky though. I always ran the chance of one of them being downstairs, going to the bathroom or just roaming the house. After the first few months, I got the patterns down, and realized as long as I left after midnight, all was quiet on the home front.

Tonight was different because I had been provoked. I didn't leave to sneak back in, I left to stay gone. I wasn't sure for how long, but long enough for them to really feel horrible. They had adopted ME. They had wanted ME. Nothing said I had to want them. So, I would make them worry and miss me. And then I would come back on my own terms.

I had been able to sneak my phone back from my Dad, but not my laptop. That totally pissed me off. But, whatever, I was out of there, for now. I didn't need the email to tell me where we were going anyway. Stephanie was dating this older guy, he was 17, I think. And it was him that organized the Park City Bridge parties.

I was always surprised that the cops never came. Relieved actually, because I feared what might happen if the cops did show up? There were kids drinking, doing drugs, having sex and on occasion a fight. And that was on a slow night!

As we drove there, I was slightly amused that Lauren would be totally freaking out now. I was sure if she told my Dad that she saw me leave, he would blame her for not stopping me, or at least waking him up. He might have been able to stop me.

But, the truth was, I hated hurting him. I just didn't hate it as much as I loved torturing her. I laughed to myself about that. She was such a pathetic woman. I have always wondered how she got so lucky to have married my Dad. And now that I was grown up, I knew there could only be one way. My Dad must have been running from one hell of a broken heart, one that must have caused him to not be able to see what he was running into. Lauren was nothing but a train wreck, no matter what anyone else thought.

We got to City Park Bridge, and the party was in full swing. It was almost 1 am. We had been taking shots of Vodka on the ride down here. So when I stood up to get out of the car, I was totally buzzed. I looked around to see who was here, and more importantly who wasn't. I didn't see Jared. That figures. He couldn't really "hang" down here. Which I thought was quite bizarre, since this is where I met him.

But, once I'd "matured" and started partying MORE than he did, he went all parental on me. He became so over protective, I couldn't even TALK to someone else, much less kiss or fool around with anyone. I kept telling him that I was way too young to have him acting like I was his property. He kept telling me how much he loved me. But, I knew how to end that, quick and dirty.

A couple of weeks ago, I actually let Jared take me to dinner before we came down here. He's only 16, but compared to me, he was way more mature. I wore a cute outfit, even put on nice make up. He was a nice guy. But, after dinner, I took too long in the bathroom of the restaurant, and told him to go get the car. When he pulled around to pick me up, I was dressed like a Catholic school girl. A tight white button down shirt, unbuttoned too low, and wrapped too tight around my waist. I had on a plaid skirt that was two sizes too small, and when I bent over, you could see my g-string. I had on the tube socks and the saddle shoes too. He smiled when I approached the car. It was just as I had hoped he thought this little get up was for him. PERFECT!

I got in the car, and he immediately slid over to kiss me. And I let him. This was all part of my plan. I kissed him back and let him touch me. Then I shyly pulled away and asked if he had any X on him, Ecstasy, that is. It makes you forget all your inhibitions and is so fun to trip on. Of course he had it on him, he dealt it to almost everyone that hung out under the bridge, which was the only reason I showed interest in him to begin with, free drugs. I popped a couple yellow baby domes, and kissed him again.

Then we were off, and headed down to the bridge. I had already talked to Jason and Norman they were cool with what I wanted them to do. Friendships were more or less a liability down here. Someone was always getting hurt, somehow. I just hated to do this to Jared, but it was really the only way.

I jumped out of the car as soon as he put it in park, the X was kicking in, and I was suddenly very aware of my body. I loved how this drug made me feel. I was pretty much too scared to shoot anything and I didn't smoke and couldn't snort, so this was pretty much my only illegal vice. And it made me feel invincible. Jas and Norm saw me coming. Their smiles told me that while I had asked them to do me a favor they both felt more like they had just won a prize. I smiled to myself, stupid boys!

Jas walked up to me and kissed me hard. In the next second, Norm was behind me caressing my body. I so wasn't into either of these guys, but if it made Jared leave me the hell alone, and for that I was willing to do pretty much anything. I let Jas kiss my neck and my chest. And I whispered to them, "Hey! Watch it! I'm not having sex with either of you. This is all for show. Remember?" I looked at Jas and realized he was so messed up, I seriously doubted that he even heard me.

Whatever! I shouldn't let this go on too much longer. I tried to turn myself, so I could see Jared, but couldn't free myself enough to. I thought to myself this is NOT what I had in mind. Suddenly Jared was there, and punching Jason and Norman. These were two of his best friends. Crap! This was NOT the way it was supposed to go.

I turned to Jared, and screamed, "What are YOU doing? I want to be with them. I'm not YOUR property or your problem. LEAVE. ME. ALONE." I saw the hurt and pain in his eyes, and he backed away. He just kept watching me as he walked backwards towards his car. He peeled out, and I hadn't seen him down here since.

Unfortunately, I had to deal with Jas and Norm though. Jared had busted up Jas's face pretty bad, and kneed Norm in the groin. My buzz was totally killed, so I decided to just get someone to take me home. The only good that came out of all that was that now I had a reputation. If I wanted to kiss someone, I did. If I wanted to do more, then I did. It was all on my terms and no one really gave me too hard a time about Jared. Thank God. I hated clingy boys more than anything.

So I was happy to pull up and not see him there, again. I kept thinking he might show back up, but he didn't. And since we didn't go to the same High School, I figured I really never had to see him again. I was so buzzed though. I really needed something a little harder. I could still see Lauren's face, the sadness and the disappointment, and it wasn't settling well in my stomach. I just needed to forget all about her, and tonight.

I walked over to where the fire pit was, and sat down. It didn't take long for a couple of guys to wander to over. I didn't say much, I was still drinking my vodka, straight. I could still see Lauren's face, and that was quite a problem. One of the guys sat down next to me. I looked over at him.

He was kind of cute, I think. I couldn't totally focus on his face, so I started giggling. He was talking to me, too, but I wasn't quite sure what he was saying. It was so loud down here, and I really didn't care what he was saying. I lifted up the bottle from between my legs, and shook it at him. He quieted then, and nodded. He moved closer to me, and stuck his hand out, so I gave him the bottle. I was rocking back and forth, listening to the sound of the lake, the music and just trying to relax.

He put his arm around me. It felt nice. I leaned into him. We sat like that for quite a while. Then his friend reappeared from somewhere and sat on the other side of me. He was even cuter than the other guy. I giggled to myself, "Thing 1 and Thing 2." I looked at Thing 2 and smiled. He was rummaging in his pocket for something, and then he looked up at me and smiled. He held his hand out, and I saw there were three small white pills. "X?" I screamed. He laughed, glanced at Thing 2 and said, "Yes ma'am. You interested little girl?"

If I hadn't been so drunk, I might have been offended that he called me little girl, instead I giggled again. Instead of answering him, I just took the three little pills, and popped them in my mouth. As they went down, I couldn't wait for them to take effect. This would be the perfect ending to this dreadful night. I leaned into Thing 1, only to find myself flat on my back. Now they were both standing above me, and they didn't look very happy. I couldn't focus, but I did hear Stephanie's voice. All I heard her say was, "RUN! RUN Lilly, RUN!" I was up in a flash, and running towards her car. I guess I wasn't supposed to take all three pills! Oops!

I got there just in time, and she locked the doors. The guys were right behind me, beating on the car. I rolled the window down and dropped $30 out the window. Such losers! I looked at the dashboard and saw that it was almost 3 am. I wasn't sure what we were going to do now. But we peeled out and we were gone. Stephanie turned up the music, and I rolled down my window. We were both singing so loud, it must have sounded like screaming to anyone who could hear us.

I knew we were going fast. I could feel it. Stephanie was drunker than I was, and the X had finally hit me. It wasn't as strong as I had hoped it would be, even taking three, cheap crap. I thought I saw something up ahead on the road. It looked like someone was walking across the street. I looked over at Stephanie, and she didn't even seem to notice it. She looked over at me, took her hands off the wheel and we both started dancing in our seats. I could feel the car accelerating. The silhouette in the distance was still coming towards us.

We slammed into something, head on. And then Stephanie swerved the entire car, it went on to the sidewalk and came to a stop, I closed my eyes. I heard a terrible sound. It sounded like a wounded animal screaming. Stephanie backed up, to see what we hit, and then the car rolled over it. And then all I could hear was the music inside the car, and there was silence on the street. We looked at each other briefly, and then Steph started driving again. Neither one of us looked back or said a word.

Some rap song came on just then, and the mood in the car shifted as Stephanie was singing at the top of her lungs, and we continued to drive. There were no cars around and no people. I figured we hit an animal of some sort. It couldn't have been too big because it made very little impact to the car. I looked behind us, but it was too dark. The road wasn't very well lit, and all I could see was a lump in the road. I felt a little nauseated. That was really cruel to do. As soon as I had that thought, I shoved it out of my mind. Stupid animal shouldn't be running around in the middle of the night. The X was hitting me hard now, and I just turned up the music and swayed a long.

"Where are we going?" Stephanie asked me a while later.

"Your house, I guess."

"We can't go there. I told my parents I was staying with you", I thought I heard annoyance in her tone. But, she was probably just ready to pass out.

"I guess we could call Michael. I'm sure he wouldn't care if we crashed there," I said giving it little thought. Michael was 19 and believed that we were 18. I'd had a thing with him, but in the interest of keeping him out of jail, and me being sent to some boarding school in the North East, I had decided to make it a once in a while kind of occurrence.

I grabbed my cell phone out of my purse. I called him. He sounded happy to hear from me. But, what guy wouldn't when a girl was calling him in the middle of the night. Stephanie turned around and we headed back towards Michael's apartment. I was ready for this night to end.

I was too wound up when we got to Michael's to sleep. Unfortunately for me, Steph passed right out. Michael kept trying to coax me into his bed, but I didn't want to sit still. I just wanted to be anywhere but here. I wanted to be dancing, moving, something. I was really regretting taking all three of those pills. My mind was racing and I was feeling very out of control.

I walked out of Michael's apartment and sat on the stairs. Out here it was cool. I began to try and talk myself down, but my heart was pounding out of my chest. I started to think about what happened at dinner with Lauren. I felt a twinge of guilt.

It really wasn't fair of me to be so mean to her all the time. She loved me, I knew that. And when I was mean to her, it was almost like abusing a small animal. Lauren appeared to be helpless, defenseless. She didn't have it in her to fight back. Sometimes I thought it was because I was adopted, and she always wondered how long I would be "hers." If I was hers biologically, then maybe I wouldn't feel so disconnected from her. I don't know. Why was I even thinking about her at all?

I smiled to myself wondering how much trouble I was going to be in, once they found me. Or once I decided to go home. I still hadn't decided what I was going to do. Michael said I could stay here, but really, that was a joke. I didn't mind the guy, honestly, but I didn't want to be with him either.

Guys were all the same. They listened only because they thought that was what we wanted, all the while they were scheming on how to get you out of your clothes. I seriously didn't understand what all the hype was over sex. It was just a physical thing. It wasn't like they showed in the movies or for that fact even what they showed on TV. These were just illusions to make you feel worse when you couldn't achieve what seemed to come so naturally in movies. It was pretty sickening.

And then I thought about my Dad. UGH! I couldn't deal with his worry and how bad he must feel. He shouldn't though. I deserved that slap. I was out of control. I knew it. I started to feel really, really guilty. I wanted to go home. I needed to see my Dad. I'm sure he was beating himself up so much right now. I didn't want that. No matter what I felt, or didn't feel for Lauren, I really loved my Dad.

I checked out the clock in Michael's room, and saw it was 6:30 am. I still showed no signs of coming down off this X yet, but I went and lay down next to him anyway. I let him wrap his arms around me, skin on skin always felt nice, no matter who it was, and I was so thankful that he was too asleep to do anything else.

I started thinking about my Mom, too. All of a sudden I felt something I hadn't felt in a long time, I was sad. I was sad for the animal. I was sad for my mother. I was sad for me. Who was

I turning into? Where was I going? I began to sob then. It was more than evident that the drinking and the drugs made me a little bit nuts. Eventually I guess I fell asleep.

11

Carsen, 2010

Everything was loaded into the vans. It was just in time to get everything delivered for the weddings and receptions. There were two tonight, and so I needed 4 drivers. Tyler was supposed to be here right after school to help drive one of the vans. He still wasn't here. He knew we had to leave no later than 4.30 pm and it was almost 4.15 pm. He was never late. But the last few weeks, he had been totally pre-occupied. He listened, he talked to me, and he did his chores and worked at the shop. But, something was definitely going on.

I picked up my cell to call Tyler; we needed to leave in less than 2 minutes. The phone rang twice and then went straight to his voice mail. Great! He's avoiding me. But, just as I was about to dial again, in he walked.

He looked different. He had this smile on his face that I was sure I had never witnessed before. He was almost in a daze. "Hey Mom, sorry I'm late, "he casually said. "Which van am I driving?"

I raised my eyebrows at him, and smiled, "The last one on the left. I'm riding with you."

"Cool."

We both took off out the back door of the Shop, I pushed in the code to lock everything up, and we fell in behind the other vans.

I reached over and ruffled his hair. "How was school today? Anything exciting happen?" I asked. I wasn't really trying to pry, but I figured something must have happened for this temporary vacation from sulking and grunting at having to work.

"School was good, Mom," he smiled.

"What was so good about it?" I teased him.

Tyler took a deep breath. I knew he was contemplating telling me what had happened and what he was thinking. He reached over and turned up the music. "Can we talk about it after the delivery, please?"

"Of course," I said. I was just grateful that we would be discussing it all. I stared at my son as he drove. He was humming along with the music and totally oblivious that I was even sitting next to him, staring at him. He was so handsome. His blonde curls had long been replaced with darker, shorter hair. His blue eyes were still as piercing as they had been when he was a baby. His eyelashes so long and dark, it looked as though they weren't even real. I had to search to find any of me in his physical appearance, and usually I came up empty. He looked so much like Joshua to me that sometimes I had to turn away. Those memories had long been buried, and tucked down deep in my heart. But, Tyler could surface them with a smile, a nod, or even his laugh.

It amazed me how much he was also like Joshua. His mannerisms, which of course he couldn't of learned from him. I looked away from Tyler, and was immediately taken back to Seabrook, and a day that I had spent with him that last summer. Occasionally, I had to let myself relive that. It makes everything else I had done to this point seem rational and deliberate.

It was the summer of 1992. It was supposed to be a carefree summer, one where Joshua and I spent a lot of time together. He would be leaving in the fall, and I hadn't decided yet what I was going to do. The days passed at a very rapid pace. We had a good summer. We partied with all of our friends; we had lots of camping trips, spent many nights holed up at my house, discussing whatever politics we didn't agree on. The physical part of our relationship had gotten much more intense. It didn't feel like we were just having sex anymore. There was so much more emotion involved, from both of us.

One night, sitting on the back porch of his parent's house, we had a very frank discussion. He was sitting on the top of the porch stairs and I was cradled between his legs on the next step down. He had his chin on the top of my head, and my arms were wrapped around his legs. You could hear the lake beneath us, and boats passing by. It was so relaxing and peaceful. I leaned further back into him, just relishing in this alone time with him.

I could tell he wanted to say something, but as always I was afraid of what I might hear. I wasn't going to make it easy for him this time. Instead I started humming to myself.

"What song is that?" he whispered in my ear.

"Uhm...it's not a song really. It's just some tune to something my Dad used to sing to me," I answered flatly.

"What are you thinking about, Car?" he inquired.

I thought for a second, and then realized, he wasn't going to be brave enough to bring whatever it was up, so I might as well just give him what he wants. I always do. "I'm thinking that you have something to say or ask or tell me, and I'm thinking that you should just get it over with and say it. Quit over analyzing it, and just say it".

He took a deep breath then, and I felt him slightly pull away from me. I held on tighter to his legs, and pushed myself into him again. He might have something to say, but I wasn't going to make it any easier for him. For once, it felt like self-preservation was kicking in. Like maybe for once, I was thinking about my heart and my feelings, instead of always thinking of his first. I groaned to myself. But he heard me.

"Are you mad or something?" he asked.

"Not yet. But, I'm guessing by the way you are behaving, I'm not going to be happy about whatever you want to say am I?" I turned around to face him. I was surprised to see the intensity in his eyes. His mouth in a straight line, and a crease between his eyes, he was thinking really hard about this. I quickly turned back around away from him.

In my gut, I thought he was about to end everything. I was waiting for him to tell me that this had gone on long enough, that he wasn't ever going to be in love with me, and that while this had been great fun, it was just simply over. Girls like me never get the boy. And Joshua was so much more than just that. He was my best friend. He was the first boy I had ever really kissed. He was the first boy who had ever touched me. He was my first.

He pulled me closer to him, and I felt his lips near my ear. He kissed it very gently, and then sighed. "I always think you know me too well, but then occasionally you get me all wrong. You are totally wrong tonight, Carsen. You are wrong."

In a swift movement, he had me by the waist and pulled me up onto his lap. I was facing him now, and his hands were moving slowly up and down my back. I kissed his forehead, and then wrapped my arms around his neck. I got this unfamiliar feeling in my stomach, and my breathing started to race a little bit. My legs tightened around his waist, and I was scared that he was going to leave me. I felt like I was drowning and if I let go, I would lose him. He brushed through my hair with his hands, and whispered, "Its okay. Calm down, Car. It's going to be okay."

I started trembling and the tears were burning my eyes and the back of my throat. I wanted him to tell me what he needed to say, but physically I couldn't control my reaction. I half expected him to just pull me away, and bring me out of this mess. But, instead, he pulled us both up and he was now standing, but I was still wrapped around him. I had my face buried in his chest, my arms tightly around his neck, and my legs still around his waist. Through my tears, I begged him, "Please don't do it tonight. Please not right now. Please." I barely heard the words I was saying, and wasn't sure if he could even understand me.

He hugged me tighter. His body didn't recoil or try to move away from me instead he turned around and carried me just as I was into the house. His parents were out of town for the week. I had stayed here with him many times before, but this time everything felt new and different. It was like this was the first time we were going to make love.

He continued to carry me through his house, and I wasn't about to let go. I was holding on for dear life. I feared most what would come tomorrow morning when he got a better hold on his thoughts, and less on his physical needs. The physical part had never been a problem for us it was only the emotional that caused so much uncertainty. I was lost in my thoughts and my own desires. But his voice broke my own silence.

"I want this to happen. I want to be with you. I need you, Carsen. I will always want you".

His lips were busy kissing my throat, my neck, my cheeks. I immediately reacted to the words I had heard. The tears began to flow more, but out of happiness not sadness. I realized I had been reading him all wrong. He was always telling me how pessimistic I was. I smiled to myself and began to relax.

He felt the calmness in my body. He kissed me again as he sat me down on his bed. He walked out of his room to the front door and locked it, and I just watched him go, and it was easy to do because I knew he was coming right back to me. I was marveling at his body, his smile, the look in his eyes that was just for me. He was so beautiful and for now he belonged to me. With that clarification, I was able to give him everything that I had – my heart, my soul, my life. I lay back on his bed and waited for him to come to me.

The next morning, well it was more like noon or so, when I woke up. I lay very still, reveling in what had happened last night. It was so tender, so amazing. I don't think he left one piece of me untouched or un-kissed. It really felt like we had never done this before. I kept my eyes open the whole time, I was afraid if I closed them, it might all disappear. Certainly I wasn't allowed to feel all of this now. We were so young, who meets their soul mate in high school?

I was playing it all back in my mind still laying on my side with my back to him. I wasn't sure what I would look like in the sun light, I knew I was a mess. The tears had certainly smeared make up all over my face, and my hair must look like a rat's nest. I wrapped my arms around myself, and tried to drift back off to sleep. Maybe I could make this dream continue.

I could hear Joshua's breathing change. He rolled over and yawned. I kept very still. I was waiting for him to do something. I knew that last night was incredible. It was like nothing I had ever experienced before, but I was so afraid that it wasn't the same for him. And I was even more afraid, that in the sun light, he wouldn't want me the same way. I feared that last night was more like a goodbye than a turning point in our relationship. I know what I heard him say last night, but I wasn't sure I could trust those words in the daylight.

I could feel his eyes on me now. I had gotten up earlier and put on one of his shirts and a pair of boxers so that I wouldn't be any more naked than I already was. I bore all to him, both emotionally and physically, last night. It was more difficult than I could have imagined worrying about what he was thinking and feeling now. He was my very best friend. He was the love of my life. I just wasn't sure where I fit into his life anymore. We had crossed so many lines, broken so many of our own rules. I was terrified that he would blame me. But, I was more terrified that he wouldn't love me back.

He started to move and I froze. If he got up and left then I would know what that meant. That would have mistake written all over it. He wouldn't want to face me. He wouldn't want to talk to me. He didn't want me.

I was so lost in my own thoughts, I barely felt him snuggle up next to me. His arm wrapping tightly around my waist and his leg swung over the tops of mine. He moved my hair out of the way, and he was kissing my neck. My stomach started fluttering and I was sure he would hear the sound of my heart racing. I put my hand on top of his on my waist and pushed back closer into him.

"Good Morning Sunshine," he whispered into my neck. His kisses were so light, so delicate, and so sensual. I kept my eyes closed because if this was my vivid imagination in action, then I was going with it.

I felt his grip tighter on me as he got as close as he could to me, and he began speaking, so softly. "I had such a speech planned last night for you. I had so many things to say." He paused and my body instinctively tensed up, waiting for him to say, "But".

"And now, I can barely remember any of it. I never could have imagined last night in my wildest dreams," and he let out a nervous laugh. "Where have you been hiding? I feel like you really let me in last night, you were so open, so vulnerable."

I began to panic. I knew it was different, I knew I had let my guard down, but it was because I thought he loved me. I thought he was going to tell me that he was in love with me, so I had done everything I could to make it a night worth not only remembering, but a night worth fighting for, too. But, what was he saying now. I was so confused, I couldn't say anything.

"Hey! Are you really awake?" he asked, moving his face around to mine. I opened my eyes to his.

"Sort of, I guess. I am convinced this is all a dream, a really incredible dream. And if I stay still, with my eyes closed, then it won't end." I'm sure he heard the anxiousness in my tone.

"You are such a silly girl, Car. It's not a dream and it's not going to end." He rolled me toward him, and kissed me on the lips. His hands found their way to my neck and he traced my collarbone with his finger. I felt like dead weight beneath him. I was too afraid to move or react, afraid one little mistake would change things. I felt like I was about to get everything I had ever wanted and some things that I hadn't even known to ask for. I felt all the emotions meshing together. I was no longer going to have to keep my love and our friendship separated. We could have a real relationship. We could be together. I knew why this feeling was so unnatural for me I certainly wasn't used to being euphorically happy.

He propped himself up on his side, facing me. He was looking at me like he was seeing me for the first time. I just stared back, unsure of what to say. I was sure nothing I could come up with would accurately describe how I felt, what I wanted. And I was sure that it would make no sense at all. I just smiled at him, all the while hoping he would see everything I was feeling in my eyes.

I leave in a few weeks for school, Carsen. And maybe before I wasn't sure what I wanted, but I know now. I want to be with you. I want you to come with me," he sighed heavily, but continued on. "I just want out of here. I want to leave and never come back. I think that is why I have fought so hard to not let this happen between you and me. I didn't want any ties to this place. My parents are going to move in December, and I don't want anything to make me come back here. If you come with me, there will be no reason. It's not that I hate it here, I just never felt like I really belonged here. But, once we became friends, and then more, I finally felt more myself than I ever had here."

I was listening to him intently. I didn't want to interrupt him. I was afraid he might realize the implications of what he was saying, of what he was asking me.

He went on, "I don't know if I'm in love with you yet, but I know if you come with me, I might fall in love with you. I know that we're awfully young for this to be it, so I don't want you to think I'm asking you to marry me. I don't want to get married, now or maybe ever. I don't know what I think about having kids either." He looked down, he almost looked ashamed. I was afraid he thought he had gone too far.

I sat up next to him, and took his face into my hands. "Hold on, Josh. I am still reeling from last night, and you are talking about moving away together. That you might fall in love with me one day, but then again you might not. How did this conversation become about marriage and kids?" I looked at him in total amazement. Maybe he was going crazy, just a little.

His eyes had been closed since I touched his face, so I let my hands drop, and waited for him to say something. After what felt like a few torturous minutes, he spoke again. "I know that I have no right to ask you to come with me. I have no right to ask you to do anything, especially since I am basically asking for you to do it with no guarantees, no promises. I am probably the most selfish person in the world right now." His words slowed down, but he continued. "I just know that something changed last night. And I don't think it would be wise for either of us, to just let it go".

I did not want to be having this conversation right now. It wasn't going the way I had expected, but this certainly wasn't the way I'd hoped it would go either. Basically what I heard him saying was, someday, I could love you, maybe, but this feels so good right now, I don't want to lose you. Again, I am at his mercy. I had been in love with him for so long now, and been so good at repressing my feelings from him, and even from myself. I really thought that last night we had both gotten to the same place. I was painfully aware that once again, I was wrong when it came to him and his feelings.

And then all the memories of the past year and half came flooding through my mind. It had always been about him. He made all the decisions. I had let him. I was so afraid of losing whatever part I had of him, I had given up myself in the process. I knew that I couldn't continue to do that anymore. I couldn't allow him to affect every part of my life. I realized that if you truly love someone, then you have to let them go. If they love you back, then you will find a way to be together one way or another. I realized just in this moment, that I would have to let him go.

"Josh, we have three more weeks before you leave. We don't have to decide today if I am going or not. I think the best thing for us to do, is to enjoy this. Enjoy that you and I have a few more weeks together before adulthood slaps us in the face. We can just be together the rest of the summer, and see where we are then," I spoke slow and calm. I didn't want him to hear the hurt and the disappointment in my voice.

I knew I could do this, I would do this. I knew that he would never love me like I loved him, but I could either spend the next few weeks without him, or spend it with him, knowing how it would all end. At least the wondering, the hoping, the exhaustion of not knowing was over. For the first time in months, I felt like I had a little more control of the situation. I knew I would never go with him because he didn't really want me to go. He was giving me just enough so I wouldn't, couldn't walk away from him. I knew it would end, and that when it did he would never come looking for me again.

He was smiling now. The relief was evident in his eyes. He had gotten just what he wanted. The best of both worlds and he knew it. He would still have me for the next few weeks, and then he would be able to walk away because he knew I wouldn't follow him. He would be able to say it had been my choice, my decision. But, we would both know it was all really his doing. He would never owe me anymore than this. He had laid it all out there, and given me the option of going or staying. And I knew, in my heart, that he would not mention these things to me again.

He started kissing me then. At first it was slowly on my cheek, moving down my neck and then finally stopping on my lips. His hands were cupping my face, and he was totally relaxed. I felt a tear roll down my cheek, and I was sure he had felt it, too. He rubbed my cheeks with his hands, and the tears came faster. He didn't quit kissing me. Eventually I forgot what he had said, and how bad it had made me feel. Instead I kissed him back and was grateful we had three more weeks together.

"Mom? Hey! Mom? Hello???" I was suddenly jerked back into reality. And my son was calling for me. I snapped my head around and looked at him. All I could see was Josh.

"Yes, honey. What is it?" I asked.

"Geez, where have you been? You like completely zoned out."

"Sorry about that. I just got lost for a moment, sorry. Oh! We are here", I said and jumped out of the van. Tyler and I had both been in our own little worlds for a few minutes, I suddenly realized he didn't tell me what was going on with him. I would have to ask him on our way back home.

After we unloaded all the arrangements, the bouquets, and set up everything for the reception, it was time to head out. We were all tired. I sent most of my staff home from here, they had driven in their own cars, and there was really no sense in them coming back to the shop with us anyway. There wasn't much to unload, and Tyler and I could do it together. I hoped that maybe he would tell me what was going on with him. Although, he is a teenager, and keeping me in the dark, is part of the whole act.

I decided that I would drive back to the shop. Maybe if he wasn't concentrating on driving, then he would open up to me. I couldn't decide if I should pry, or stay quiet. A few minutes passed, and he reached over and turned off the radio. I took a deep breath, and waited for him to speak.

12

Tyler, 2010

After 7th period today, Lilly was waiting for me outside of the gym. I ditched hockey practice because she'd asked me to go somewhere with her. Of course I would have to drive, she'd told me with a wink, since she was only fifteen. And she may have been only fifteen, but something in the way she'd spoken told me she was not your average fifteen year old girl.

I am sure that I didn't act nearly as cool as I had hoped I did in my head. I saw people staring at us as we made our way across the parking lot to my jeep. I wasn't sure if I should open her door for her. I didn't want to look like a geek. I double clicked my key chain, and her door was unlocked. I took her backpack and put in the back of the jeep. She hopped onto the front seat.

I stayed back just staring at her beauty. I tried to get it together because I didn't want her to know how nervous I was. I mean, I had been with girls, had girlfriends. It's not like this was the first girl I'd ever had in my car, but it felt so much different. I wanted to be near her and to know everything there was to know about her. I was actually a little frightened by what I felt.

I climbed in next to her, and when I put the key in the ignition, immediately *Use Somebody* by Kings of Leon, came blaring out. I fumbled to turn it down, but she grabbed my hand and said, "No, leave it up. I love this song."

She didn't show any sign of letting go, so I opened up my hand, and she laced her fingers with mine. She leaned over towards me, and started singing along to the music. I could smell her now, more intensely than before. It was a combination of fruit, flowers and spice. She smelled incredible. She looked up at me, "So, where are you taking me?"

"Hey now, you asked me if I wanted to go somewhere with you. I thought you had a plan." I teased her.

"I've been in this town all of five minutes, I have no idea where the cool hangouts are. Besides, I thought you were going to be my personal tour guide. Or have you already forgotten?" She winked at me again.

Of course I hadn't forgotten I just needed little more time to plan. I was racking my brain trying to think of where we could go to be alone but not too alone. I was afraid I would not be able to control myself around her. All I could think about was kissing her and touching her, but since she was younger than me, she might not be ready for all that. I wasn't even sure I was ready for all that either.

"So, where are you taking me?" she asked again. I turned to look at her, and found her beautiful face staring straight at me. I had to remind myself to breathe. It just shouldn't be right for someone to be as extraordinary as she was. Her thick long curly hair the shade of mahogany that flowed down her back like rippling water was blowing gently as the wind caught it. I was sure she could see directly to my soul with her brilliant blue eyes. I looked forward again just in time to slam on the brakes, or I would have run the stop sign.

Lilly giggled. "You really should keep your eyes on the road. I don't think my father would approve of me being in the car with someone who can't pay attention."

"Uh, yeah," I stumbled over my words, "I'm sure." This seemed ridiculous. I knew how to act; I knew how to be cool. She's just another girl, I thought.

Finally I composed myself, "So how about we go to River Road? It's off of the Naugatuck. It dead ends at the dam where lots of people fish, so it's usually quiet. I imagine there won't be too many people out today anyway."

"Why do you think that?" Lilly asked as she leaned closer to me and touched my shoulder.

"It looks like a storm is coming. See all those dark clouds to the north-east," as I pointed out the front window.

"Oh, yeah, I guess I have been so distracted today, I hadn't even noticed." I smiled at the sarcasm in her voice.

We drove along for another fifteen minutes. She started asking me questions about various people in school and about me. I think she asked just about everything.

"So why hockey?" she asked.

"Why not?" I replied. I was totally teasing her. "I don't really know. My mom enrolled me in any and every sport that I mentioned wanting to try. I played football, basketball, and even spent some time swimming in the summers. But, it was hockey that I enjoyed the most. I was fast, and it was like second nature to me. So what brought you to Beacon Falls?" I inquired.

She sat up straight and pushed her back against the seat, staring out the passenger window. After a minute, she answered softly, still looking away from me, "Look Tyler, I am having a really great time with you. Would it be okay if we talked about all that another day? It's a long, sad story" and she locked her green eyes on mine, "And I just want to be here, with you, right now. I don't want to think about Texas today."

I nodded just enough to let her know I wasn't going to push her. I could appreciate her request, remembering when I first went to school, kids would ask about my Dad. I hadn't known that I had been missing anything until other kids started pointing it out to me. Then I had become painfully aware of what I didn't have. What little I knew about Lilly was probably more than she would have wanted me to know.

My best friend's girlfriend, Jessica, worked in the office at school. It wasn't often that we got a new kid, so when Lilly's records came in Jessica took the liberty of reading them. She found out her grades were okay but she definitely had a rough beginning to her freshman year. I guessed she was here with just her father, because her mother had recently passed away.

I knew we would have a lot more time to cover the big stuff, so I turned up the music and we both sang along to another Kings of Leon song. She broke our silence, "Are we almost there yet?"

I turned to look at her, "Just about 5 more minutes... Are you sick of me already?" and I instinctively smiled.

"We're just getting started," she said. She closed her eyes and laid her head against the back of the seat. I watched her slipping away into her thoughts, and I was okay with that. In that respect, I was opposite of my mom. I enjoyed the silence, welcomed it with no need to fill all the space up. All I needed was to know we would be spending a lot of time together. If I hadn't been so sure of that, I might have mistrusted her silence.

We got to the dam, and it was just as I had thought, desolate and abandoned. We got out of the jeep and walked towards the grassy place near where the water ran off the dam. I usually sat here and watched the water spill down below. A huge man made waterfall. The sound of the water crashing against each other was enough to drown out the questions and thoughts I usually came here to untangle. Today was different. I had never brought someone here with me.

There were rocks forming a questionable path to the other side. The depth of the water was clouded by the bubbles and rushing water. I imagined it was shallow though. I couldn't tell if she wanted to cross it. The other side was shaded and inviting, the dark grass looked like silk from where we stood and along the bank were bunches of wild flowers dipping into the river bank. It was breath taking.

Before I could decide what to do, Lilly grabbed my hand and lead me onto the rocks. I was staring at our hands. She had just reached out, so quickly and so easily, like it was nothing to hold hands with me. That made me aware of how natural being with her felt. It had never been 'easy' for me with girls. I was always anxious and stammering. This felt different, like we had been holding hands forever. I was still mystified that she wanted to be there with me anyway.

Lilly easily stepped from rock to rock, and took little jumps across the large gaps until we reached the other side. Once there, she turned to me quickly and wrapped her arms around my neck. "Now all the hard stuff is over. We have nothing to worry about now."

I had absolutely no idea what she meant by that. All I did know was that she was in my arms. She fit into my embrace like she was molded for me. I reminded myself to breath as we just stood there holding each other and watching the water break across the dam. She eventually backed away, but only to pull me down to the ground right next to her. I wanted to kiss her right then, but I was afraid it would be too soon or too awkward. So, I put my arms behind me and leaned back. Lilly did the same thing.

Again, we were silent. We could hear the water crashing against the rocks and I thought I heard a few rumbles, too. I would have worried about getting someone else out of the rain, should it fall, but not Lilly. I had a feeling she might like it, maybe even love it. She crossed her leg over mine, and looked over at me. She smiled, batting her eyelashes a little, and said, "Can I ask you a question?"

"Of course, anything, "I replied quickly.

"And do you promise to tell me the truth, no matter what?"

"I can't imagine what you could ask me that I couldn't tell you the truth about it," I said, hoping she would hear the confusion in my voice.

"Oh!" She looked away from me then. "I was just wondering if this is your place."

"My place?" I asked. "It's public property. It kind of belongs to everyone, I think".

She threw her head back and laughed. It was such a sweet in-fectious laugh. I began to chuckle a bit, nervously and a little frustrated. And then we were both laughing so hard. I still wasn't in on the joke, but that didn't matter much to me.

She calmed down, and said, "What I meant was, do you bring all the girls here? Like if I were to tell someone I came here with you, would they say, 'Oh yeah…that's typical for Tyler".

I thought for a moment. I hadn't ever brought anyone here before. I began to grin at her before answering. I was trying to decide if I was offended that she thought this was 'what I did' or flattered that she thought there had been so many other girls. I usually came here alone, to think, read or fish. On occasion, my best friend Scott might come, but lately he was too busy. Lilly was patiently waiting, but sort of pleading too.

When I looked into her eyes, I could see she was desperate for me to be honest with her. She really had no idea what kind of a person I was, and no other way to find out. We'd only been talking for the last hour or so. But, then I wondered if maybe other guys hadn't treated her the way she deserved to be treated.

I sat up and she mirrored my movement. I took her hand from her lap, and placed it in mine. I put my other hand over the top of hers and began tracing her delicate skin with my finger. I brought her hand to my lips, and as I kissed it so very gently. I could smell her sweetness again, like no one else. Then I stared intently into her dazzling blue eyes. "I know you don't know me very well yet, but you can trust me. I won't hurt you, and I won't ever lie to you. I have never brought anyone here except for Scott, and it wasn't quite the same as being here with you." I had expected a laugh, but she was quiet.

I saw her shoulders move slowly up and then back down. She tried to hide it, but she even let out a small sigh. She scooted closer to me and leaned up against my arm. She rested her head on my shoulder. We sat there for a while, just being together. A million dishonorable things ran through my mind, after all, I am a seventeen year old boy. But just being with her was good, for now, I thought.

We sat quietly discussing the weather and the River. I was filling her in on all the history of our little town. I happened to glance down at my watch and realized what time it was. "Crap! I gotta go!" She looked over at me.

"I'm so sorry Lilly. But I work for my mom and we have two huge weddings tonight, and I am one of the drivers. Please don't be mad. I totally forgot the time." I looked at her, begging for forgiveness.

"Well, I can't stand in the way of a man who earns money. How else are you going to pay for our first date?" she smirked and winked at me. "Tomorrow night? Will you make it up to me, tomorrow night?"

"Absolutely." I stood and pulled her up with me. We ran back across the rocks, and she splashed some water at on me. I wanted to spend the rest of the evening with Lilly, but I feared what my mom would do to me. Besides, we would have all the time in the world, another 3 months of school and then the whole summer. All of a sudden, I saw my life revolving around Lilly. I paused for just a second, and then I realized that just such a whirlwind of an existence was exactly what I wanted.

13

Carsen, 2010

Both weddings went better than I had expected. I was so glad that the day was almost over. I loved to sit back and marvel in my creations once everything was in place. I didn't have any experience with flowers until I moved here, and started learning everything from my grandma. She showed me colors, textures, smells and taught me to make sure that the flowers and plants arranged complement one another. She would often compare floral arrangements to adult human relationships.

I could not relate to those analogies though. I had never experienced a real adult relationship. I was too wounded and my heart was too bruised by my adolescent relationship and choices. Sometimes I did miss having someone I could share everything with, and my grandma had been really good at not prying.

I was lonely more often than I would ever admit, but I wasn't lonely like people probably imagined I would be. I think most people figured I made my choices and I should be happy with them. And I was happy with having Tyler and moving here. I was happy in the choices I'd made since I got to Beacon Falls. But, I still wasn't 100% sure that I did the right thing in never telling Josh about Tyler. In the dead of night, I would wake up in a cold sweat and the thoughts were always the same. Did I make the right decision? And then I would feel the emptiness in my bed. That is when the loneliness took over.

I missed the friendship. I missed the emotional benefits. I knew a physical connection was important, too, but I figured that need would fade with age anyway. I was very cautious about the decisions I made regarding men, mostly avoiding them.

When I decided to have Tyler and raise him by myself, I knew that I was trading my own happiness for his. Every day proved that it was the right decision. He was a good kid. He made mostly good choices. I wanted him to be and feel as loved as possible. I never wanted him to feel like he was missing something or someone.

In the beginning, when I left Joshua, I had believed that I would get over him and all that would never be. I convinced myself that by moving on, I could let him go and find love again.

But the only other man I could love was our son. I became so consumed with that bond, I abandoned the thought of any consequences. Tyler would grow up and have his own life. It began a bit earlier than I had hoped for, when he started high school. As an accomplished athlete, he naturally had the girls all over him, but I was not worried about him making the same mistakes I did. He was different.

He was confident. He was smart. He was beautiful. He had a heart so grand and pure, there was no room for cruelty or spite. I had taught him to accept things at face value, however if that didn't make sense, ask. I had encouraged him to ask about people's thoughts and feelings. I had begged him to be honest with himself and others about what he wanted. I could tell at the time he was a bit confused, probably wondering what would prevent someone from telling the truth or speaking up.

I knew all too well the damage not being open and honest would bring. I lived that every day. I would never want Tyler to go through this kind of regret.

I saw him question others about their motives and feelings often. Mostly he did it to me. I was the one that hadn't learned to be honest, not even now. He could see right through me. It happened on his last birthday when I was really feeling melancholy, realizing he was getting older and would be leaving me soon. My head knew that it was right and what should always happen.

The house was full of teenagers and music. They were dancing in the living room and on the front porch. He had wandered out the back door and found me sitting on the steps, gazing at the full moon. He plopped down by me and put his arm around my shoulder. "What are you thinking about Mom?"

I peered into those eyes, and I didn't see the young man I had raised. I saw the baby that was put into my fearful arms seventeen years ago. I knew better than to lie to him.

"I was just thinking about your life."

"What about it?"

"Your future, actually."

"What exactly?" He smiled at me, crinkling his eyes almost squinting, as if we had this conversation a million times before and he already knew my answer. He gave my shoulder a reassuring squeeze.

"I was thinking that no matter what, you will be okay. You will find your place in this world, and though it most likely will take you away from me, I will always be right here, whenever you need me. I just hope that I have done enough for you, and been the right kind of mother."

I could feel my throat starting to constrict and knew the tears were about to come.

"Mom, I know it's not always been easy for you. But, you are the best mom. Besides, I don't know how far I will go. But, I will always come home."

He hugged me tightly until I smiled and instructed him, "Go back to your party before someone realizes you are gone, especially Jen. She might think you are doing something you shouldn't be doing!"

He laughed and got up. Then he walked back in the house, leaving me alone with the knowledge that he had read MY mind. He had known I was sad and where to find me.

The same bewilderment was looming among the flowers, and my mind needed to clock out for the day. Joshua's presence was conjuring up memories of Tyler's childhood. I wasn't surprised that my mind could flow so easily between the two most important men in my life. One had been gone for so long, yet just thinking of him could cause butterflies like I used to feel every time I saw him.

The other one, well he held my heart. Tyler was already out with friends. I left the shop alone. On the drive my thoughts returned to Joshua. It didn't sadden me to think that I had given him the best part of me. In return I got the very best part of him. I had long ago accepted this was my fate.

Joshua being in town didn't really change much for me. He didn't know I lived here. It wasn't like he came looking for me because he loved me. I knew that things would change but only because of Tyler.

I had lied. I hadn't technically committed perjury, just what some call guilt by omission. I was still agonizing over the ramifications of that decision. I could only hope that Tyler would forgive me. I didn't really care if Joshua did. All of a sudden I was in the shadow of my empty home, sitting in my driveway, exhausted and drained. I went inside and straight up the dark staircase to my room.

I went directly to my sanctuary, my huge bath tub. I planned to decompress and regroup as I poured the bubble bath, watching it swell into a cloud of refuge around the streaming hot water. I slipped off my clothes, grabbed my book, and stepped into someone else's life, a life that was nothing like mine and had absolutely nothing to do with my reality. I found comfort in knowing that at the end of most books there was a happy ending.

Unfortunately, I knew in my timeworn heart that my own story was no fairy tale. There would be no star crossed lovers reunited because the depth of the pain of separation was too great. There would be no Prince Charming to kiss me awake and carry me into my happily ever after.

14

Tyler, 2010

I knew that Lilly was going to the movies with Jen and Meredith. They should be out soon though. I hoped I wouldn't look like a stalker when I showed up at the theatre. I was also worrying that Jen would say something to Lilly about 'us' even though it hadn't been that big of a deal. We had been over for months. I dated her because it was convenient. Scott had dated Meredith and the girls were always together. Since Scott and I were also hanging out a lot, it just sort of happened with Jen, without much effort from me.

While we dated there was a lot of drinking, hanging out, and fooling around, but no sex. I could have done it with her easily because she was totally into it, and me. But, for some reason I had a conscience when it came to girls. I was painfully aware of the rumors though. The rumors I never tried to set straight. I never admitted or confirmed them, but I guess I was still lying. It's just that in a small town, the gossip is far better than the actual truth. Anyway I didn't feel like I owed anyone anything. But, Lilly being out with Jen and Meredith was making me nuts.

I sent her a few texts, and she responded. I didn't see anything to make me think they had said something that would shame or embarrass me. I mean, I am seventeen and obviously I've been with other girls. I'm sure she's at least dated other guys, too. I could only picture Lilly having sex with me though. How stupid was that? I didn't want her to know about me, yet I was idealizing her.

I tried not to think about it at all. I didn't know what, if anything was going to happen with Lilly. That isn't exactly true; I'd been around enough girls to know that what happened at the dam definitely meant something. It was like nothing I had ever felt before. I could have just sat with her all day long, not even speaking. I wondered, can you meet your soul mate while you're still a kid? I just might have to talk to mom about that.

I didn't know much about my father, but I did know that Mom said he was 'the one' for her but she had chosen to leave because she got pregnant. She felt they both deserved more than settling. I don't think she believed she was 'the one' for him. And that if she'd stayed, things would have gotten worse and not better.

She'd always been honest with me about love, relationships and sex. She was good at making me see things her way without preaching to me. I was convinced she didn't want me to make

85

the same mistakes that she did. I guess that was the reason I had never had sex before. I knew that it could alter the course of my life, and I wasn't prepared to do that yet. That was until I was alone with Lilly.

I had changed clothes at home and hoped I didn't look like I was trying too hard. I wore khaki shorts and my button down polo un-tucked. I also had on a hoodie and my Sperry's. I couldn't worry about my outfit. She would either like me or not, and what I wore shouldn't change that. I was sure I'd put on too much cologne, but better to smell too good than to smell bad, right?

There I was, standing outside of the movie theater, just waiting for her to get out. She expected me to meet them at Jen's. I hated even thinking about what Jen might have told her. I just hoped since Jen had started dating John she wouldn't feel the need to say much more than we dated; it didn't work out, end of story. I doubted it was ever that simple when it came to girls though. I knew if Lilly showed interest in me it might spark some jealousy in Jen because everyone had thought we were perfect together. Only we had known the truth. And in a town this small, the secrets and gossip were the threads that held it all together.

I got another text from Lilly. "Movie is almost over. CU n 15".

I smiled, she had no idea! I would see her the moment she walked out of the theater. I was still surprised at my nerves and anxiety. In reality, she was just another girl. I just couldn't convince my racing heart to believe that. It's not like she could turn me to stone or ice with one look. I laughed out loud at how ridiculous I could be.

My phone vibrated, and I saw a text from Scott. He was pissed I'd skipped practice, not that it mattered to me. Screw him, I thought. He blew stuff off all the time. I guess the team depended on me just a little bit too much sometimes. I always ended up doing the right thing, even when we were all doing something we shouldn't.

If we were out drinking and I noticed everyone else getting hammered, I would stop drinking and make sure everyone got home. I was the only one without a curfew, so I could drop everyone off. But, every once in a while, I wished my friends didn't depend on me so much. I seriously considered being a little more dangerous, a little more carefree. I'd be eighteen in a few months, and I didn't want to think that I'd always done what was expected of me.

Of course, truth be told, I was a little fearful of my mom, too. She was so used to me doing everything like I should, she might freak if I did something crazy. Maybe, but maybe not. She surprised the hell out of me on a regular basis. Sometimes I wished she was like other parents in that she didn't care so much about me and that she wasn't so damn honest with me. I knew though that's how she developed the trust between us.

She had never lied to me, not even about my father. She said that he didn't know about me, and that she thought at the time she made the best decision. She also swore to me that when the time came, and I was ready to meet him, she would do her best to find him. She made no empty promises and she never apologized for what she had done. Maybe that is why I didn't feel the need to find him.

I always wondered why he never came looking for her though. She told me about their relationship, and she said there was another side of the story, his side. But, that really didn't interest me much. I just knew that if I was ever lucky enough to find someone that loved me like my mom loved him, I wouldn't be so stupid. I would know it. I wouldn't be arrogant and hide. I would face whatever happened with her, not let her deal with it alone. She would just smile at me and say, "Remember Tyler, you only have my side, not his. You can't ever really know someone else's heart. Try to be fair".

There was a rush of people exiting the movie and I saw the girls coming out of the theater, and I had to catch my breath. Lilly was stunning in just her Miss Me jeans and a UT Austin sweatshirt. Her long hair was pulled up into a bun and she had on just a touch of makeup. She was smiling and talking with the girls and seemed oblivious that anyone was watching her.

She sure didn't look fifteen. She walked with confidence and her head held up. Not like Jen, who moved like she wanted to be swallowed up by the ground. Meredith was shaking her butt a little too much and bobbing her head side to side in an effort to appear way more casual than it came across. Meredith was as confident as Lilly, but the difference between them was easy to see. Lilly didn't know she was beautiful and she just seemed to be content with who she was. Meredith on the other hand knew how beautiful she was with her dark curly hair, crystal blue eyes and a body that looked like something right out of the Sports Illustrated swimsuit edition. Meredith was someone that most guys within a 300 mile radius wanted to be with, sleep with, date or just have her notice them. But, I was not one of those guys. I knew that bothered her. A few drunken nights together and she had let me have it. She got over it eventually and we became good friends.

Lilly still hadn't seen me, so I just continued to watch her, continuously tapping my foot to remind me this was real. Her coming to Beacon Falls felt like a dream. I just didn't know what I had done to be so fortunate. I tried to relax, but thinking of being alone with her again in a few minutes made my hands sweat and my pulse race.

I cleared my throat, and yelled "Hey!"

All three girls turned in my direction and smiled, but I focused all my attention on Lilly. She smiled and waved at me, and began to walk across the parking lot. Meredith and Jen followed her.

Before long Lilly was standing right in front of me, wide-eyed. "I thought you were meeting us at Jen's?"

"Guess I couldn't wait that long. Hey Meredith! Hey Jen!"

Jen popped off, "So is it true? You skipped hockey practice today?" The tone in her voice was as sarcastic as her one arched eyebrow.

"I did." My tone was sweet as pie and I tilted my head a little to the left.

"Ugh. Whatever! Are you going to go get Scott and John or what?" she rolled her eyes at me.

"I didn't know about that. What are the plans anyway?"

Meredith chimed in. "Well, we were going to go over to Jen's. Her parents are out of town, and we thought the six of us could hang out. Maybe play quarters or something? Unless of course you are still anti-fun?" She punched me in the shoulder a little harder than I expected, and her demeanor suggested she was just teasing but not very much.

"He's not anti-fun. We had a lot of fun together earlier today," Lilly said, not quite as innocently as she tried to make it sound.

Both Jen and Meredith appeared to be surprised by this fact. I was glad to know that she hadn't told them earlier. I wasn't trying to keep it a secret, but I didn't want people speculating about actions we hadn't even decided to take yet.

Lilly took my hand, and having her beside me was so natural, like we had always held hands. I hoped that my hands weren't too sweaty. I looked down at her and smiled. She smiled back, and leaned into my arm. I liked the way it felt with her that close to me. I could smell her hair which was the same scent only stronger from earlier. I didn't know that girls could smell and be as sweet as Lilly was. I leaned in and I noticed Jen staring. I flashed a crooked smile at her, kind of trying to say "Don't be mad at me," without saying a word. Her half-smiling response made me think she seemed to understand. I hoped this would be the end of whatever she was toying with doing or saying.

"So text Scott. Let's get going!" Jen said.

"I'm going to ride with Tyler," Lilly said. Jen and Meredith smiled at each other, and then at us. I watched Lilly turn towards me, her back to the girls, and I saw the girls give each other this 'look'. I'm not sure if that look meant they were okay with this or what. But, I didn't really care what they thought.

We walked to the car hand in hand. I opened the passenger door for Lilly who got in and immediately grabbed my iPod. She began flipping through songs, and I worried that some of it might offend her. The music I listened to before a hockey game, or any sport really, upset my mom due to its vulgarity and lewd lyrics. But it helped me get my mind into the game and let everything else go.

She settled on Kings of Leon's *Use Somebody*. I am pretty sure we had heard that together earlier. Interesting choice, I thought. She kept playing it over and over until we got to Jen's. She never once let my hand go. I introduced her to John and Scott who for some reason, laughed like idiots. I guess it was because I called her 'my new friend' since she smirked too. I didn't really know what else to call her. 'The Love of My Life' sounded a bit ridiculous.

I knew I was falling in love with her. I had never been with a girl before and wished that we were alone. Usually I didn't plan anything. I just ended up where ever everyone was and with whoever was there. I saw girls more as a nice to have rather than a have to have. Until today. Until Lilly. I wished we were going somewhere alone and not to Jen's. I convinced myself that we had plenty of time ahead, and there was no reason to rush into it all in one night. Besides, I didn't trust myself alone with her so soon.

15

Lilly, 2010

Dad had dropped me off at Jen's. He had gotten to know her parents well enough that he didn't feel the need to come up to the door anymore. And that was good! Because her parents were not home, in fact they were out of town. Jen had assured them she would stay with Meredith. I claimed to be staying with Jen, and Meredith said she was spending the night at my house. But, really we were all staying at Jen's. I felt a bit guilty about lying to my dad; I hadn't lied to him once in the last six weeks. I only did it tonight now because I didn't want the girls to think I was some 'goody-goody' two shoes. I wasn't back to the bad girl I once was, but the amount of guilt I was feeling did disturb me.

I decided while we were at the movies that I was going to have Tyler take me home instead of going to Jen's. I resolved to do the right thing. I smiled to myself thinking how odd this new behavior was for me. I felt proud that I was going to do the right thing. I was beginning to believe I really was changing. That Beacon Falls was changing who I was.

Maybe when you have done the wrong things for so long, and then you try to do things right, it was true, you really could change. Maybe my Dad was right and that a new place could really make all the difference. The best part was I wasn't really struggling to do the 'right' thing. It seemed to almost come naturally. I was putting my past behind me. I did feel a lot different here.

I felt almost normal although I'm not exactly sure what normal really is. I just don't feel so out of place or so angry anymore. I feel like what I imagined most teenage girls felt, and after being with these girls, I believed I was just as good as they were! The only thing making me different was that my mom was dead.

In this small town, everyone's history was so interwoven that it seemed just shy of incest. It was bizarre to think that Jen's Mom and Meredith's Dad had dated for two years in high school. I wondered if when they saw each other if they ever thought back to how they felt back then. I wondered how uncomfortable that might be.

As we walked out of the movies, I heard a loud "Hey!" above the noise from the crowd of kids pouring out of the theater. Jen must have seen who it was first because she grabbed my left arm and pulled me in that direction. All three of us turned at the same time.

I saw him then, across the street. He was leaning on his jeep, looking like the hottest guy in an Abercrombie & Fitch advertisement. We made our way across the parking lot to his car. Instantly I forgot about going home. All I could think about was being alone with him.

Jen and Meredith started discussing what we were doing next but I wasn't really listening. I took his hand and leaned on to his shoulder. Jen and Meredith's conversation slowed and their watchful eyes seemed intense. I wasn't sure if they were happy or jealous about Tyler and I. We had talked about it earlier at Jen's house while we were getting ready for the movie and they both seemed to think that Tyler most definitely was into me. I mean they had known him forever. But, Jen did say something that I didn't quite understand.

She said, "Lilly, just know one thing about Tyler. What you see or even hear about him, isn't really who he is. Tyler is a really, really decent guy."

I already knew this though. He hadn't even tried to kiss me all day. Any other guy would have been all over me at the river. It made all of this so much more exciting.

I wasn't sure he was playing hard to get at all. I thought he might actually care about me, and want to take this slow and do this right which would be so out of the norm for me. Then again just about everything in my life was unusual. I didn't want to do anything to ruin what might happen with Tyler. This just felt so different than anything else.

I never believed in love at first sight, but now that I had met Tyler. I believed that anything was possible, that everything that was wrong with me and my life was really behind me, and a whole new future lay in front of me. I just held on to his hand while he drove to pick up the guys. I found 'our song' on his iPod, and let it blast. I was thinking now, I can't go home, even if I want to. To spend the night with Tyler was all I could imagine.

It was kind of funny when he introduced me to Scott and John though. He sounded nervous. They laughed out loud because of course they knew me already. Scott and I were in the same Algebra II class. He and John were pretty much dumb jocks, but not Tyler. I couldn't really figure out how they were alike, except for the whole athlete thing. I guess that is how guys bonded.

When we got to Jen's, the guys both hopped out on Tyler's side before he even killed the engine. Tyler tugged on my hand. I looked straight ahead but I knew I was grinning from ear to ear. He wanted to be alone with me. I almost dropped his hand because mine began to sweat a little bit.

He rolled down his window and said to the boys, "Hey! We will be in later."

They looked at each other, and gave Tyler a juvenile wink and thumbs up.

He rolled the window back up and turned to me with an embarrassed frown and said, "Sorry about that. They are about 10 years old when it comes to girls."

"Oh that doesn't bother me at all. Boys will be boys, right?" I said hoping he would hear the flirting in my voice. I probably didn't have to try so hard, I realized. But, I wanted him to know how interested I was in him.

"Look," he said quietly, "I know we just hung out earlier today, and I know that it is virtually impossible to think that you could possibly feel like I do, but I want to make sure that we are moving in the same direction."

"What direction is that exactly?" I was toying with him, and it was kind of fun. I began tracing his fingers in my hand with tiny little circles while glancing up every few seconds to look at him.

"I don't know exactly, yet. But, I do know that I don't want you to move in the same direction or even in the same vicinity with anyone else," he said, while looking down at his shoes.

"I mean, like I said, I know it's crazy and totally unrealistic. But, I have honestly never felt like this before, and I want us to have a real chance, to find out what this is, together."

He was so beautiful. His green eyes were sparkling in the reflection of the garage flood lights. He had this wrinkle between his eyebrows; he was choosing his words very carefully. He was tapping his fingers of his free hand on the steering wheel nervously.

He had no idea my heart was beating so fast that I thought he might actually hear it.

I had to rescue him from his misery, and I knew there was nothing that I could actually say that would put him at ease. After all, words are just words. We all use them and we don't always tell the truth.

But, actions speak so much louder than words, so I undid my seat belt. He dropped my hand and took off his seat belt as well. We were now facing each other. "Tyler", was all I said.

I leaned over and touched his cheek with my hand. I traced his jaw line with my finger until I was at his lips. He kissed my finger so gently, if I hadn't been watching I might not have known. He closed his eyes, and took a deep breath. When he opened his eyes, I was right in front of him, I could see him pleading for a kiss. I leaned into him and gently obliged.

He kissed me back so tenderly I could barely feel his lips. I slowly wrapped my arms around his neck, and then ran my fingers gently through his hair. He put his hands on both of my cheeks, and continued to lavish me with many slow, delicate kisses.

I dropped my hands to my lap, and just surrendered to his embrace.

I couldn't help moaning a little bit, or smiling when he said "Thank you," in between kisses. Unable to move away from each other, we stayed there kissing. I could tell he was holding back, and as much as I wanted more, I knew that didn't need to happen tonight.

I wouldn't make the same decisions I'd made before. I wasn't inhibited by drugs or alcohol, it was just me and Tyler and kissing him felt like the first time I'd ever been really kissed before. Even though this felt so right, and I was sure that Tyler wouldn't hurt me. But for the first time, I was thinking more about Tyler and his feelings than my own. I didn't want to hurt him. I didn't want this to be just about sex. I wanted more from Tyler.

Then I heard laughter and saw the flood lights flashing in Jen's driveway. We pulled away from each other hesitantly and both laughed a little nervously. He grabbed my shoulder and quickly kissed me on the cheek. "At least now we don't have to wait until the end of the night."

Tyler squeezed my hand and then opened up his door. I did the same. We got out of the car and he instinctively waited for me at the front of his jeep. He reached for my hand and we headed into the house and with the luck I was feeling, a future together.

16

Carsen, 2010

The more I tried not to think about him, the more I did. I was almost obsessed with figuring out how he got here and I began to suspect how it'd happened. There were only 3 people who knew that I had moved to Beacon Falls, and two of them would never have led Joshua here. My mom and brother knew this was the right decision for me, and they had never second guessed it. We all had our own lives and they would never interfere with mine. It could only be Sarah.

Sarah is Joshua's older sister and the first person I told that I was pregnant. But, she had agreed with me. Joshua had a full ride to the University of Texas and that package did not include family housing, me or a baby. She wanted what I wanted, for Joshua to be happy. Although, she thought that Joshua did love me, and that he would have welcomed the baby. But, she knew as well as I did, that he wouldn't go to UT, and that his life and choices would be very limited.

I loved Joshua enough to let him go and have the life he deserved. I never made him happy. And I knew that I was getting the best part of him, without a doubt, by having and keeping Tyler. I didn't have it all figured out back then, and I still didn't really.

But, she sent him here for a reason. I just didn't know what that was! I hadn't heard from her in at least five years. I would have to try the last phone number I had for her, to figure out why she betrayed me. I KNEW that Joshua didn't just happen to land in Beacon Falls.

My thoughts led me to the last night I had spent with Joshua. It was the worst night of my life. I knew I was leaving the next day. If he had walked me out that night, he might have noticed that everything was packed and the car was ready to go. Things might have ended differently.

I have always believed that everything happens for a reason, and when no clear signs occurred that I was making the wrong decision, I assumed I was making the right one. I drove to Joshua's house. His parents were gone, I don't remember *why*. But, he had been playing golf that day with his buddies and had come across a hornets' nest. I don't remember how it happened, exactly, but I think that one of them knocked it out of the tree, and then somehow Joshua ended up falling, his knee landing right on it. There must have been 50 stings on his knee.

The guys dropped him off at home, and he had called me to come "take care of him". I picked him up dinner and went to the store and got bandages plus what the pharmacist recommended. When I arrived, I let myself in. The house was dark and quiet. Josh was asleep on the couch.

I put his dinner in the oven and sat down in the chair across from the couch. I watched him sleep. For a brief minute, I tried to picture us together with a baby, *but* I just couldn't see it. This boy jacking around with a hornets' nest wasn't ready to be a father.

Not that I was ready to be a mother, I was just too selfish to know what I was really doing. I was trying to hold on to the only part of Joshua that would be mine. Watching him sleep, I thought about how much I loved him, and how I wished I could tell him.

I wasn't expecting for him to love me back, I knew that wasn't possible, but I felt like such a coward not telling him. If he was nothing else, he was my best friend.

I hated that I would be giving up so much, but I knew in my heart, I was giving him what I thought he would want, and exactly what I thought he needed. He woke up, and caught me staring at him. He gave me a mischievous smile. The smile that I couldn't resist no matter how much will power I exerted.

I smirked at him, "Hey sleepy head".

"How long have you been here?" I could tell he was drowsy.

"A while".

"Why didn't you wake me up?"

"I figured you needed to sleep. Your knee looks awful. Is it hurting much?"

"Not too bad right now. My mom had some pain killers, and I took like 3".

He put his head back down on the pillow, then looked over at me and patted the couch.

"What?" I grinned at him.

"Come here."

"How about I heat up your dinner?" I got up and walked into the kitchen.

His mom collected all kinds of knick knack things, and they were displayed in neat little boxes on the walls of the kitchen. I noticed many were little mice and I hate mice! I had never really paid much attention before, but they were a bit creepy. It was very 'country', and I thought that maybe someday I might have a kitchen like this, with a husband and a son but no mice.

"You want something to drink, too?" I yelled from the kitchen.

"Yeah," he said. "There are some cokes out in the garage. "

I walked out there and grabbed one for him and a diet coke for me. I came back in and filled two glasses with ice. I came up on the other side of the couch and reached over to hand it to him. When I looked down, I couldn't help but take in a quick breath. He had rolled over exposing his shirtless chest and the waistband of his plaid boxers. He had one arm bent behind his head. He took my breath away again. How was I going to walk away from him? He must have seen the look on my face.

96

"What is wrong? Are you okay?"

"I'm fine," I said as I turned abruptly around and went back into the kitchen.

I took his dinner out of the container and felt that it was still warm. I positioned my hands level on the counter and tried to get that image of him out of my head. It was so hard to know that I loved him, that I wanted him, and that he didn't feel the same way about me. Ever since the pregnancy was confirmed, my feelings for him were growing more intense. They terrified me.

I instinctively rubbed my tummy, my consolation prize. I wouldn't get the boy, but I would have his child. I put his food on a plate, got the silverware, wiped the corners of my eyes, and walked into the living room. I placed the food on the coffee table in front of him.

"Can you sit up to eat?"

"Uh yeah, I can."

He sat up, not even concerned that he was sitting there in his underwear right in front of me. How many 18 year old boys could feel that secure with themselves? Or that secure with the person they were with? Then it clicked, he would hang out like this in front of any of his guy friends. I literally felt like I had been kicked in the stomach. I got up abruptly and headed to his parents bathroom which was closer than Joshua's.

I locked the door and sat on the floor in front of the shower. I pulled my knees up to my chest and rocked back and forth. The tears were streaming now, through my anger. I am so stupid! How could I have been so clueless? It wasn't that he was hiding being in love with me, he truly wasn't. He didn't regard me as anything more than a friend. I was just a friend that he also happened to have sex with whenever he wanted. He never made love to me, he never wanted me, I was just convenient and I was his friend.

I allowed myself to fall in love with my best friend. I felt like I betrayed him. I had promised to be his friend and that the sex was just an extension of our friendship. But, I had broken that promise and he didn't even know it. I glanced over at the shower.

I recalled the first time we had slept together, and how we had ended up in the shower afterwards. We had sex again in there as well. I had never let myself be so vulnerable with a boy. I remembered how he caressed my breasts, my hips, kissing me everywhere. I remembered how gentle he was with me.

I realized that the first time we had been together I had fallen in love with him. I was barely 16 years old then. And now, it all was coming to an abrupt halt. He would never know our child, and he would never know that I loved him *enough to leave him* so that he could have the life he deserved. There were so many things he would never know.

I heard a soft knock on the door. I didn't say anything. I didn't want him to see me crying. I had kept all of this from him for so long certainly I could pull it together for a few more hours.

He knocked again. I turned on the water, hoping it would stifle the sadness in my voice.

"Yes?" I half way yelled.

"What is going on with you?"

"You shouldn't be up, Josh. I'll be out in a minute".

"Please let me in, Car."

I looked at myself in the mirror. My eyes were red, and my face was streaked. I splashed cold water on my face several times and blotted it dry with a hand towel. I dried my hands and then opened the door.

"Nothing is wrong, Josh. See, I'm fine."

He knew I wasn't fine. He wrapped his arms around me at once.

"Talk to me. What is it?"

This is why I fell in love with him. He did love me. But, he loved me like he loved any one of his guy friends. He had a good heart. I cried hard into his shoulder. He lightly guided me back into the bathroom, and spun me around. He was leaning against the counter now, no weight on his knee, and I was leaning into him.

It wasn't long before I felt the heat between us. He was rubbing my back and whispering "Shhhh, shhhh," into my ear. I kept my hands near my face and just kept crying. I was crying for everything we had been through over the last two years. I was crying for everything we could have had, and everything we never would. I remembered hearing that whenever a boy and a girl were friends, inevitably one of them would fall for the other. I just never believed it would be us. I thought I would be able to let him go, that I was being smarter than other girls. I guess I forgot to protect my heart.

I was stupid to think that sex didn't matter. I was naive to think that I could have this kind of relationship and not fall in love with him. Just another growing pain, I supposed. It was a hard lesson to learn. I was continually learning things the hard way, the wrong way.

He began to kiss me. I pushed him away. I was shaking my head. He kept rubbing my back, and kissing my ears, my neck, whispering into my hair. I didn't even know what he was saying, I just heard his voice. I tried pushing him away again. But, eventually, like always, I gave up and relinquished myself to him.

I wasn't strong enough to make him stop, and I didn't really want him to. As with every other time we had been together, my heart hoped that this was the time that he would fall in love with me, and he would realize we belonged together. We made our way to the floor of the bathroom. He was beneath me, and I straddled him. I didn't want to hurt his knee. He reached up and slipped my tank top over my head. He was looking at me above him. He was staring into my eyes.

I thought I saw a flicker in his eyes, something I hadn't seen there before. It was almost as though he was seeing me for the first time. He didn't rush through the motions. He was slow and careful. With each movement, he watched me, and then would bring his eyes back to mine. I was aware there were still tears. He reached up and put his hands on my face, cupping my cheeks in his hands. He wiped the tears with his thumbs.

"Why all the crying tonight?" he murmured.

I looked at his stunning smile and his incredible physique. I considered saying everything I felt. I debated telling him everything that was going on inside of me and the words were on the tip of my tongue. His hands found their way to my stomach. He was drawing circles there, and looking at my tummy. I thought for a second that he noticed there was a slight bulge. Instead his hands found their way to my hips, and he was pressing against them softly. I glanced at his face and saw the boyish grin that I had never been able to deny. I beamed at him.

"Summer is almost over. Just a few more days and you leave

for Austin."

He unbuttoned my shorts, and I moved to one side to help him slide them down. Then he tossed them behind me. His hands lingered on my thigh, just lingering there. I was so careful not to touch his knee.

"Yeah, so? That's been the plan all along. Have you decided not to go?"

I sat down on him then and I was in just my bra and panties. He was in just his boxers. We were both very exposed and vulnerable. Typically we didn't stop to talk, but I guess my tears caused him to wonder what might be going on. I was so good at hiding my feelings from him, it was almost second nature. To let him see me cry made me feel weak and more susceptible than I wanted to be.

I shifted a little on him, feeling very nervous. Thinking about the question he was asking. I decided I had nothing to lose. Maybe it was time we had this conversation. Maybe it was time I let some things go, and let him figure out what to do or maybe we could figure this out together.

"When you say 'Come with you', what do you mean exactly?" I studied his eyes, his mouth, even his hands. I was expecting to see some emotion that would let me know what he was thinking. He was lying beneath me, looking more like a child than a man.

He looked so content, so happy. I thought for a second that maybe that I was responsible for his happiness. Maybe I was enough for him. "Well," he moved his hands from my thighs, to my waist. He was gripping me, holding me in place.

"I thought you were considering moving to Austin. Have you made up your mind?"

"I have, actually," I said. I lay my body down on his. My face just inches from his. I was looking for a sign, a sign that he wanted me to go with him, a sign that said he loved me, even if he couldn't say the words.

Immediately, his hands made their way to my back, and he was pulling me closer to him. I strained to keep my face just above his, and tried to quit thinking about kissing him.

"When you say you have decided, what do you mean exactly?" he was teasing me.

He was careful with his words. I didn't want to have to say it I wanted him to read my mind, read my thoughts, read my body. I wanted him to know me well enough to know that I needed and wanted so much more from him.

"Well, if you want me to go with you, as you keep saying, what would I be going with you as?"

I wasn't even sure I had said it out loud, so I knew he could have barely heard me. I examined his face for an answer. He closed his eyes and was quiet. His hands went from my waist to moving along my back. I rested my head on his shoulder, and kissed his neck. We remained like that for a little while. My words were occupying the tiny space between us.

I told myself I wouldn't be the first one to speak, and I wasn't going to acquiesce and have sex with him either. I needed to stand my ground, make him give me an answer. Make him make a decision.

I wanted him to tell me what I meant to him, so that I would know without question, that the decisions I had made were the right ones. I didn't want the baby to be the reason he chose me. I wanted him to pick me because he loved me, and couldn't imagine his life without me. No matter how strong I tried to be, and how comfortable I had pretended to be in this friendship/romance/mess, I was still a teenage girl with romantic notions. A girl who dreamed of falling in love and having the boy love her back. I believed in the fairly-tale ending and happily ever after.

I didn't want it to be the 'We were good friends who also had sex. It worked for us.' That wasn't the ending I day dreamed about when I was away from him. I just wasn't sure how to get what I wanted. My heart must have been trying to protect my mind because my mind continued to be delusional.

I was holding out, against all hope, that he would declare his undying love for me. That everything I had done for him, with him and because of him, would finally all be worth it. That he would finally find me worthy and tell me that he loved me. The tension began to rise in me as his silence seemed never ending. Finally he spoke, in a hushed tone, "I guess that depends on what you want to go as."

I sat up quickly. He brushed the hair out of my eyes and tucked it behind my ear and tugged on it gently, he thought this was a game, me just teasing and playing with him. I found my shirt and shorts. I stood before him, embarrassed and humiliated. He lay there totally confused. He propped up on one elbow, and grabbed my leg. "Hey. Sit down."

I remained standing defiantly, with my arms hugging my chest and pouting like a five year old. If I didn't control my foot, I just might stomp it, too. Why did I always have to give in? Why couldn't he just once know me well enough to know what I was thinking, and say what I was so desperate to hear?

"I'll stand. What do I want to go as? What kind of question is that?" I put my hand on my hip and glared at him.

"One that I would like the answer to, please?" he asked, smirking at me a little. I was so confused.

Did he want me to say it, so that he could just outright reject me? Could he be so cruel? I wish now I had just stayed where I was, kissed him, and kept his mouth and mind occupied with other things.

This was not going to end the way I wanted, and I knew it.

Would it be so wrong to have my last memories of him be me wrapped in his arms, with him loving me the only way he knew how? I kneeled down slowly, taking my place back straddling him again. He batted his eyes at me and sheepishly grinned. I tilted my head a little to the right and pursed my lips at him. I was really trying to find the right words. I was struggling, and he could tell that I was. He was watching and waiting.

His hands wandered to the top of my panties, and his fingers lingered there for a while as I struggled to figure out what to say. I grabbed his fingers, and brought them to my lips. I kissed all of them. The whole time my eyes were fixated on his, trying to interpret what he was feeling. Was this purely physical for him? Was there more than friendship here?

"I am not going to go to Austin with you. I don't think we are really ready for that just yet. I think you need some time to figure out what you want."

His eyes looked sad now. "You aren't coming?"

"No. Josh, I have been, we have been doing this for over a year now, haven't we?" I muttered.

"I guess so, yeah."

There was a severity to his response like I had wounded him. I immediately felt awful. I loved this boy, but he was a boy, and he was not ready to be the man that I needed. That wasn't his fault, I didn't blame him. I wasn't even angry at him. I loved him so very much, but I knew the best thing to do was to let him go.

"And, we have had a lot of fun, right?"

I leaned over him and kissed him on the forehead.

His hands found their way to my hips, just as they had many times before. I believed that he was my soul mate, and that no one else would ever fit to my body quite like his did. But, I also wasn't selfish enough to trap him into a life that he wasn't ready for, and certainly didn't want.

"And I love you, you know that. You are the best friend I will ever have. And I'm guessing you feel the same way about me?"

I was aware that his body was moving slightly. His hips were pushing ever so slightly into mine. I tried to ignore the yearning inside me, because I wanted to say these things, because I knew I would never have this chance again.

"I do feel the same way about you, Carsen. I do love you. I can't imagine not having you in my life. I can't imagine not talking to you every day. Who am I going to call when I'm too drunk to drive? Where am I going to go when I don't want to go home? What am I going to do without you there?"

And in those words, he answered my questions. He was not in love with me. He just didn't want to lose me. And that was not enough for me or for the baby that I was carrying.

I realized I wasn't being totally honest with him, that I wasn't telling him I was IN love with him. A part of me thought that might have changed the rest of the conversation, but I just wasn't willing to risk it. I took his face into my hands and kissed him. I opened my lips and let my tongue find its way into his willing and open mouth.

It was a kiss that was so familiar, I couldn't remember a time of not knowing how it felt. Instead of answering his questions, I gave into our desires and made love to Joshua. If he felt the urgency and the difference in how I was responding, he certainly didn't say anything. He let me be completely in control. A couple of times I thought I felt him pause or stare at me a little too long. He might have felt the difference in me, the urgency and the desperation that was in every kiss. But, he never said a word.

We didn't move fast, every time that he tried to speed up, I slowed him down. I knew that I would need these moments to last me a lifetime. I would need to recall them to draw the strength that would be required to raise his child alone. And I hoped that one day he would look back, and realize how much I had loved him. I finally quit thinking, and let my body love Joshua in the same way my heart did, without boundaries or reservations.

We eventually made it out of the bathroom, and he was starving. His knee looked worse, and needed some doctoring. I got him settled in his bed, and brought him the cold dinner. He was being playful and swatted me on the butt, and instead of teasing back, I left his room. My mind was made up. I was resolved in my decision, and there was no changing it. It wouldn't matter what happened the rest of the night. I loved Joshua so much, that I was willing to live without him, to ensure his happiness. I wasn't sad anymore, although I was terrified of what lie ahead of me, but I was sure I was making the best decision for him.

I came back into his room, and climbed into bed next to him. There was no way I could feel any more pain than I already did. I wanted him to think of me and these moments with some sort of happiness.

He wrapped his arms around me, kissed me on the top of my head.

"You didn't answer my question earlier, Car. I mean, I'm not complaining about the delay tactic, but that doesn't mean I forgot about the conversation."

I nuzzled closer to his ear, and let my hands wander up and down his chest. "I'm not going because I don't think I belong there. And I don't think you really want me there either."

I paused.

"I know you will miss this, but you will find someone else, you always do. We both know I'm not really what you want. I'm just who is here."

There was no anger in my voice, maybe a hint of sadness. But, I knew that if I made him believe that I didn't have any expectations, then he wouldn't feel the need to make something up to make me feel better. I expected some kind of reaction, but he didn't say anything. I did feel him take a few deep breaths. He put his other hand to his head. I wondered if he was feeling relief. His voice was low and I thought I felt him shaking a little bit.

"Carsen, you are not always right, you know that? You think you know so much more than me, about everything, including me. Maybe I got it all wrong. Maybe you don't know me at all. If this is all, if this has all just been about sex, do you think it would really would have lasted this long?"

I closed my eyes. He still wasn't saying what I wanted and needed to hear.

"It's gone on this long because you got comfortable. I mean, it made everything so much less dramatic didn't it? You didn't have to worry if Julie or Ann or whoever else you were dating was going to put out, did you? It never even crossed your mind. You knew you would get laid because all you had to do was look at me, grin at me, talk to me!"

I was yelling now and had sat up next to him on the bed.

"So, you are just a slut then aren't you? I wasn't the only one you were sleeping with was I? I heard rumors in the locker room and from some of my friends, but it was true wasn't it?"

"Of course NOT! I have not slept with anyone else BUT you! You are the only one I have wanted. You are the only one I can even imagine kissing! I'm not the one dating other people that would be YOU!"

I didn't want it to go like this.

But, now he was sitting up too, and he was fuming. I closed my eyes and shook my head. No, no, no.

I will not let it end this way. I don't want him to hate me, regardless of anything else; I don't want him to be angry.

"Look, wait." I said, "Let's not do this, okay? We don't have to do this to each other. We both have made mistakes, and this 'arrangement' just doesn't really work anymore. We are not just stupid high school kids anymore. We are adults now. And as adults, I think we need to respect each other enough to let each other go."

I felt the tears coming again, but I didn't look away from him. I moved close to him, caressing his arm. I ran my hand through his hair, reached up, and kissed his ear. He moved into me, too. He was shaking his head. He put his head on my chest, and hugged me close to him.

"I will always be your friend, Josh. It's okay that we never became more." I bit my lip; I hated the bitterness of letting him go.

"You will go meet some brilliant woman and make beautiful babies. You will be a phenomenal lawyer, and I can say 'I knew you when.'"

The tears trickled slowly when I stopped trying to resist them, and I brushed them away so he wouldn't feel them. I kissed the top of his head and began massaging his back. I wanted him again. I wanted to be with him one more time. And then I knew I could let him go. He raised his head and studied me. There were tears on his face as well. I brushed his cheek with my finger and felt the wetness on my hand. I wanted to tell him it was okay. We would be okay. But neither of us said anything, instead Joshua and I made love for the last time.

I rolled over in my bed. I felt the tears, and for a second I thought I had been dreaming. I was flooded with a range of emotions, just as I had been that night, and I knew I had just been reminiscing. I had left him a short note on his pillow. It just said:

Joshua,

Timing is everything. And this is YOUR time. I wouldn't rob you of this, no matter what. We will always have our memories and you will always be my very best friend. You are so much more than that. I wish you nothing but love and happiness.

Always yours,

Carsen

I gasped at the sting in my heart, and it subsided to a dull ache. Something I had always felt when I remembered those days. My mom had called that afternoon to tell me that he didn't take it well. But, I comforted myself by believing that one day he would be grateful.

17

Joshua, 2010

Lilly was gone for the night. I had dined at a local restaurant with one of the law clerks in the new office. He was young and eager and I remembered those days. That fire. I once had that burning desire to leave my mark on this world.

It is unfortunate that fierce energy gets wasted on the young. It's only after you have lived, loved and lost that you can truly appreciate the irony in the world. That you can be the best employee, the best lawyer, but that won't necessarily make you the best person. If you don't work hard at the relationships with the people you really love, then no matter what you do in your life, you will one day be alone and empty.

Experience is easy to gain. You do things enough times, you will master it. And with experience comes better jobs, better perks. But, when you don't put forth the same efforts with your wife and your child, then you end up like me. Alone and drinking more than I have any business doing.

The law clerk, I believe his name is James, insisted on driving me home. He talked incessantly the entire ride about some of my more famous cases. I nodded politely, as he conveyed to me how brilliant he thought I was. I almost told him he was an idiot, because I was no one to idolize. But I needed this job and I needed no one to know what a tortured soul I really was. I had to keep appearances up, much as I had done my entire life.

Regret.

There is nothing quite like the after-taste of regret, it is hard to stomach and more bitter than curdled milk. I took little comfort in knowing that I had always been so arrogant, so right, that I had not realized what a charmed life I had before it was too late. Most people spend an exuberant amount of their life looking for someone to complete them. We compare ourselves to romantic movies and books to convince us what we are missing or what we should be seeking. We develop unrealistic definitions of what that is.

I had married Lauren assuming that she was the right kind of wife for an aspiring young lawyer. She was petite, soft spoken and most importantly she placed me on a pedestal. She couldn't have been more wrong for me, but back then no one could tell me anything, because I knew everything.

I walked in to our rental in Beacon Falls. I was still not sure why I had let Sarah convince me to move here. But, I had to admit, I liked the small town pace. It reminded me a bit of where I grew up in Seabrook, Texas. I already saw Lilly thriving here, and knew that alone was reason enough for this transition. She had been so adrift in Austin and now she was the daughter that Lauren and I had imagined she would be. She hadn't given me any trouble so far. It was a nice change. Unfortunately, for me, with her being so agreeable and 'good', I found myself with a lot of alone time.

And when I was alone with my memories and my 'what if's', I drank until the past got hazy and I became unconscious. Often, I found myself waking up fully dressed and slumped over the chair, not even making it to my bed. Often feeling like I had spent the night with a stranger, waking with more guilt than I had the night before, it was a vicious cycle I had fallen into.

I usually over indulged after Lilly excused herself to her room to do homework, or so she said. I was certain she spent more of that time Skyping and texting that boy, and I honestly didn't care that much. I didn't want her to think I was a drunk. But truth be told, I was wrestling my own demons by drowning them in a bottle of Jack. Unfortunately the answers I was seeking were not going to be found in the bottom of a bottle.

Her memory came so much easier when I was inebriated. It was like she was lying dormant, just waiting for me to find her. She came to me and consumed me. I might conjure up a fight we had, or some function that we attended. But, it was always unchanged Carsen haunted my drunken stupors and taunted me in my dreams. I wondered if it was because I was intent on finding her someday if for no other reason, than to tell her how wrong I had been and how sorry I was.

Tonight I was embroiled in the day I found out she was gone. My ego took a significant blow because selfishly I had always assumed that she would just be there. I had never taken the time to define our relationship because once we'd gotten started, she was always just there. When you get so comfortable with someone and having them there for you, you don't have anything to analyze. You give it little thought, and absolutely no attention. You accept it as fact that this is the way it's going to be. That is until, it isn't.

Carsen and I had spent the whole night together. It wasn't really any different than a hundred other nights. It was almost time for Freshman Orientation at UT, and I knew she was floundering, but I wasn't sure why. She was definitely the brightest, most driven girl I knew and she was my best friend. And in all fairness to her, she was even more than that. But, I was 18, and I was focused completely on myself, and was hopeful that my future wouldn't involve anyone from Seabrook. I had expectations for my life. I had no romantic ideals about soul mates or being in love. It was all fun for me, but in retrospect, I think I feared never knowing another girl like I knew Carsen and always wondering if there was someone else better suited for me. I did assume that there would be time to figure it all out. I didn't know I had run out of options and time.

I woke up expecting to find her curled up on her side of my bed. Instead the bed was empty. For about five seconds, I thought she might be making breakfast. My stomach rumbled as I realize I hadn't finished eating last night. I put my hands behind my head and closed my eyes and replayed last night. I smirked as I remembered I wasn't really worried about food, being with Carsen typically caused me to forget everything else at the moment. That is why I needed her so much. There was no thinking when we were together, it was easy, it was comfortable, and it was always so good. I hadn't been with a lot of other girls, but I assumed that no other guy was getting it as regularly as I did, but I was very careful not to brag or ever discuss my sexual relationship with Carsen.

At the time, I convinced myself that I didn't want anyone else to know. I mean she wasn't the hottest chick in school. She was definitely not like any of the girls I dated. She was quite the opposite. But, at the same time, she was also so much more. She was always there for me. No matter what I did, where I was, or what ridiculous antics I got myself into, I called her, and she was there. I expected it from her without giving any consideration to her feelings.

On graduation night, I sensed things were changing. I could feel it in the way we kissed. I could feel it in the way we touched. It was more intense, more dangerous, too. We were taking risks and not being as careful about not being seen together. We never spoke about it though, and I guess my 'teenage boy self' adopted a 'don't ask, don't tell' policy. She didn't express that anything was wrong or different, so I allowed myself to believe it was okay. That is until that last night and of course, I only realized it in hind sight.

I wish now I could remember her exact words. It was something about her not being what I wanted. I remember thinking to myself how juvenile she sounded. How could she think I didn't want her? My entire body reacted to her touch, her lips, even the sound of her voice. How could she not know that?

When I found that she was nowhere in my house, I went back into my room. I picked up the phone on the nightstand, and found her note. It made no sense. It was like a terrible 'Dear John' letter, leaving me with more questions than answers.

I got dressed and drove to her house. I knew we needed to have a face to face conversation. It was going to be difficult. But, I felt abandoned. I was more alone than I had been in years and I knew it had to do with Carsen. I had to tell her how I felt, even if at this moment I wasn't sure what it was, I knew it was something. I easily identified that being without her was more devastating than the fear I had of being with her.

Her mom let me in. She looked as if she had been crying but offered me no explanation. I asked if Carsen was there. Instead of answering me, she motioned to the hall. I walked past her and made my way to Carsen's room.

I expected to find her there sulking and brooding. Instead, her room was empty. All her stuff was gone from the walls. The walls were bare where her pictures that had been framed and hung had been for years. Her bed was neatly made I chuckled and thought how bizarre that was. I don't think I had ever seen her bed made. Carsen was messy and her room was always a disaster. I walked towards the bathroom, and saw the same. It was clean and nothing was there. I was so confused. I turned around and her mom was standing there in the doorway, staring at me.

"Look, I don't know what happened between you exactly. Carsen told me very little. I knew a few weeks ago that she was planning on leaving. At first, I thought she was packing for college. She got her acceptance to UT months ago." She paused. I rolled my eyes and slowly shook my head in disbelief.

"Yeah, I was sure she hadn't told you, although I wasn't sure why." I was watching her mom, and I struggled to see Carsen in her. But, then she tilted her head just a little bit to the right and started twisting her blonde hair, and I could then see the resemblance. I used to tease Carsen about this because she seemed to do it without noticing. It was a nervous habit.

"She is gone, Josh. She wouldn't tell me where she went because she didn't want me to have to lie to you. She said that it was for the best, and that one day, she hoped we could forgive her. She told me to tell you a few other things, as well."

She crossed the room and sat down on Carsen's bed, I did the same. I remembered the last time we had been together here and I felt the guilt punch me in the stomach. It had been weeks ago, she had been distant. Something had been on her mind, but instead of asking, I just started kissing her, and soon I forgot that she had been upset.

I wondered now, how many times I had unintentionally silenced her. I realized that while I always called her my best friend, I probably had not been a best friend to her. I was always more interested in having sex with her.

Back in the present, I shuddered at the thought. I know, I was an 18 year old boy, stupid, selfish and believed I was invincible. Why is it so hard for boys to see girls as they should be seen? And just like that day, the guilt and shame engulfed me. I cringed at the thought of some boy treating Lilly this way, I would kill him. I recognized the irony of me having a daughter and surmised it as my punishment for being so awful to Carsen.

Without much effort, I was back on Carsen's bed, my head in my hands. Her mom put her arm around me. After a few minutes, she finally spoke. "Again, Josh, I don't have many details. I do know that she felt this was the best thing for you. She wants you to go to Austin, be a lawyer. She wants you to be happy. She felt that if she stayed, then neither of you would live the lives that you were meant to lead. Do you know what she's talking about?"

I didn't know then, or at least I couldn't verbalize the words to her mother. I ascertained she didn't know the depth of our relationship, and I wasn't about to have that conversation. I just kept looking down at my wrinkled shorts and shrugged my shoulders.

"Would you like to hear my theory? Because that is all it is," she asked me.

"Yes, please. I am completely in the dark here."

That wasn't entirely true, but it was true enough for Liz. I am sure she saw right through me, it wouldn't really matter what I said anyway. It wasn't going to change the facts as they were now at all.

"I figured it out a few months ago, and I asked her if you and she were more than friends. She looked away from me for a few minutes, and she adamantly denied it. She said that you were her very best friend, and she would never do anything to jeopardize that. She said that she needed you more than she needed anyone else in her life." Liz had tears in her eyes. I knew she was sad that her youngest daughter, her little girl, had left. I knew she felt helpless because she didn't know how or why or where she had gone. I still wasn't following what she was saying.

"Wow! You really are clueless aren't you?" She laughed uneasily.

"Joshua Hattinson, Carsen was in love with you. She was so in love with you, that she believed it was better to leave you, than to stay and just be your best friend. She would never have asked for more than she thought you could give to her. I guess she thought the only way to get over you, was to let you go."

"She was in love with me?" I asked. I wasn't really talking to Liz, I was talking to myself. I said it again, "Carsen was in love with me?"

She patted my knee. "Like I said, she never said a word. It was just a feeling I got."

She got up and left me alone in Car's room. I could still smell her perfume. Her absence didn't feel real yet, it was as if I was just waiting for her to get home like I had done a million times. The only difference knowing now, she wasn't coming back. There was a hole in my chest. I was struggling to catch my breath. She left me? She left?

I tried to play our conversations back in my head searching for a clue, but I still couldn't see what had been said or done that would have caused this kind of reaction. I had always known she had a flare for the dramatic, but even for Carsen this was too much.

I honestly don't remember how long I sat there. It was dark when I began to grasp the fact she wasn't coming back and I had to get out of her house. I don't remember the drive home either. I don't recall much about the next three days. I guess I was in shock and looking back, I was heartbroken. But when you are surrounded with more questions than answers and the one person that you depended on is gone, it's really impossible to do anything but sit and question everything you thought you knew.

What made it even harder was that the one person I would have gone to for comfort, conversation and just to be held was Carsen. I started to piece the last few years together. It was grueling for me, I had been so focused on myself, I had ignored what was happening for months. I could remember little things, like the balloon bouquet and homemade cookies before a big football game. I remembered the night my grandfather died, and how she held me all night long while I cried. She never said a word, she rocked me, she rubbed my back, and she loved me. I had been such a stupid, stupid guy! Carsen had no idea how much I lost the day she left.

The third bottle of wine was empty. I didn't think I had any more on hand. I might have to hit the hard stuff now. No matter how much I drank, I was never going to be able to correct the mistakes of my past. I couldn't apologize to Lauren for not being the husband I should have been to her. I couldn't tell her that she deserved so much better than me.

I could never wrap Carsen in my arms and whisper to her that I was such a self-centered clueless boy. I could never erase all the hurt and pain that I'm sure Carsen had been through. I had thought about looking for her over the years. I was sure I would come across her somehow with the Internet and Facebook. But, I never have. Maybe that wasn't such a bad thing. There were no words to express how deeply sorry I was. How does a man apologize for the mistakes he made as a boy? How does a woman forgive the man that didn't know any better as a boy?

I got comfortable in my leather Lazy Boy recliner, my eyes heavy from the alcohol and anticipated finding Carsen in my dreams. The recollections were too painful, but in my dreams the outcomes were different. In my dreams, she didn't leave. In my dreams, we were together. In my dreams, there was no pain, there was only happiness. Happiness is what dreams are made of, right?

18

Tyler, 2010

I honestly can't remember my life before Lilly. I don't know what filled my mind, my time or even my hands. I still played hockey, I still hung out with the guys, but now everything had more purpose. I got up early for school, eager to pick her up. I knew that as soon as she got into my Jeep, she would kiss me. I was only able to get through Physics in the afternoon because it was my last class of the day, and I was that much closer to being alone with Lilly. After school and before I had to have her home, we would drive out to the river. It was almost a daily ritual now. We didn't spend a lot of time there each day, but it was just enough.

Things got a bit out of control the other night at Jen's, and things could have gone too far. It would have been so easy to make love to her. It was obvious we both wanted to, but I refrained. We messed around a little bit, but then we talked the rest of the night. I am certain that was the night I fell in love with Lilly.

The party got wild. I think everyone who was anyone at Beacon Falls High attended. It was around 1 am when the cops showed up. They cleared everyone out except for the six of us. Sometimes it was convenient to be best friends with the sheriff's son in our small town. John's Dad sat us all down, gave us a lecture, and then told us to just go sleep it off. I hadn't really drank that much, we did a few shots when we all got there, but then I realized that I didn't want to be drunk when I was with Lilly.

It was a little harder to convince Lilly to slow down on the drinking. She had been drinking more than me. She eventually passed out, and I cleaned up the mess. Again, being the responsible one. I did let my mind wander and imagined making love to Lilly. I believed when it did happen, it would ruin every other girl for me. My heart and my body had never been in total agreement about any girl. I realized I was falling hard and fast, yet I didn't find myself running from it. Instead, I was running straight to her.

It was kind of hard to believe it had been almost five months that we had been officially dating. School had been out for almost two months, and we had fallen into a routine over the summer. Everything was so easy with us. My mom seemed to really like her, too. They cooked together on most Sundays. I learned a lot more about Lilly from those meals than in any of the conversations we'd had alone. I guess when we were alone, we were too absorbed in ourselves to talk about or think about anything else.

When she talked to my Mom, she really opened up to her. It was hard to grasp that her mom had died only last winter. When she talked about her, which wasn't very often, it seemed like she had been dead for years. She didn't tell us everything, but from what I had understood, they had a fight, and Lilly took off mad and her mom had gone looking for Lilly.

I tried to imagine the Lilly she had described to my mom. The Lilly she had been before she came here, but it was virtually impossible. The girl I knew was sweet, kind and amazing. She did let it slip once that she and her mom hadn't been close. Her eyes looked distant and detached when she spoke about her mom. I also wondered about her relationship with her father. He seemed to not pay much attention to us when we were at their house, which really wasn't very often. He worked a lot and Lilly preferred being at our house.

One Saturday night, we decided to not go to any of the many bon fire parties and to just hang out at my house. We rented some DVD's and Mom had gotten everything to make her famous honey fried chicken, mashed potatoes and green bean casserole. She knew it was my "comfort food". She used to make this meal for me whenever I was sad, happy, frustrated. It was just one of our many 'things'.

I guess most people might think I am pretty spoiled. I knew that being an only child had its perks, but being Carsen Wylder's only child also had its downside. I didn't try to think of it often, but lately, it had been on my mind a lot. Maybe it's because Lilly's Dad is not so involved in her life. He was a nice guy. I had hung out there a few times, but we usually came here. Mainly because Lilly thought her dad relished the silence, while she thought my mom loved having us around here. I don't think he even knows my last name. It's a little irritating how he calls me 'Ty' all the time. Lilly has corrected him and said, "Dad, his name is Tyler. Tyler Wylder. He doesn't even go by Ty." But he just smiles and nods. I don't think he hears anything she says.

Dinner was over, and we were all cleaning up in the kitchen. My mom was talking about her dad and how she missed him, and how hard it was even now as an adult. She was reaching out to Lilly, wanting her to open up. Lilly began to tell us about the night she lost her mom. It was a freak accident. There was no way it was Lilly's fault. She was just a kid, doing some stupid kid stuff. I didn't know everything that she had done, but that was because I didn't want to know. She had tried to tell me, more than once but I always kissed her and told her that I was only grateful that she was brought into my life. I know that made me awful, I mean I wasn't glad her mom died or anything. I was just glad to have her here with me.

My mom hugged her after Lilly broke down in tears. The words she said were barely audible to me. Lilly kept saying it was her fault. If she hadn't been out looking for Lilly, than she wouldn't have been walking in the street in the middle of the night and she wouldn't have been hit by a car. My mom just rubbed her back and let her talk it out. She thought that her dad had moved here because he just couldn't stand to be in the house that he shared with Lauren.

Lilly was afraid that deep down he blamed her, and she was sure that was something that he could never get over. She also mentioned that her father drank a lot. And that she hated to be at home with him because it seemed he just waited for her to go to bed or leave. Then she began to cry harder. She said, "I feel so guilty being happy living here. And I know that if one single thing had happened differently, then I wouldn't be standing in your kitchen and I wouldn't be in love with the most wonderful boy." She glanced over at me, smiling through her tears.

They kept talking, and I felt like an outsider. On the one hand, I felt very proud that Lilly felt she could share such intimate details of her life with my mom. But, on the other hand, I didn't even know some of these things. I knew that what was best for her was talking. I knew that she needed a woman to talk to. How could she have 'girl' talk with her dad?

I left them in the kitchen and went to my room and turned on my iPod, I laid down on my bed. I was bothered by the fact that her dad was a drunk. I guess I hadn't noticed but in all fairness we don't spend a lot of time at her house. It's not like I would know what to look for anyway. My mom had an occasional glass of red wine, and I'd seen her drunk maybe once or twice ever. She always got very emotional when she drank. She hadn't done much of that lately though. Not since she had been seeing Alex. I knew she really liked him, and I even tried to talk to her about him once.

"So, you and Alex?" I grimaced at her.

"What about me and Alex?" she replied. She gave me that look where she raised her eyebrows, while squinting her eyes at the same time. She had a slight smile on as well.

"You like him, don't you?" I asked.

"Yeah, I like him, Tyler. Do you like him?" She was teasing me now.

"Mom! I am being serious. What we can only talk about MY sex life and NOT yours?" I tried not to sound too serious, but I wanted to know.

"Well, yes, we do talk about your sex life, or the lack there of, I hope. You are the child and I am the parent. However, since you are asking, I guess you deserve an adult answer."

I waited. This was going to be good. How could she tell me what she was doing ok, sleeping with Alex, while I was supposed to wait and NOT sound hypocritical.

"It's simple, Tyler. It's easy."

I waited again. I was expecting more.

She looked at me like she wasn't going to say any more. "That's it? That's all I get, it's simple?"

"That is the truth, Tyler. I'm not in love with Alex. It's comfortable, it's easy. We aren't going to get married. We aren't going to ever be any more than we are right now. Like I said, it's easy. It's simple."

I felt so bad for her. She didn't want to be in love? Now that I knew what that felt like, I couldn't believe that anyone wouldn't want this. I could have just let the conversation end there. But, I couldn't understand why she didn't want or more importantly, need more.

"Mom, that is sad. Don't you ever want to fall in love?"

She smiled at me. It was such a serious and sincere smile. She was thinking again, looking for just the right words to explain to me why she didn't view love like I did. She moved closer to me on the couch, and she took my hand. It looked so big compared to hers. I towered over her at 5'10 and there was no sign I was done growing yet. She traced the back of my hand with her fingers. She was being cautious and careful, knowing the weight of the words she would say to me.

"I have been in love Tyler. I was in love with your father. I thought that we would eventually spend our lives together. But, I made a fatal mistake. I never told him exactly how I felt. "

Her eyes looked frightened, but she was still smiling at me. "And then I got pregnant with you, I left and then I had a broken heart. My heart was broken into a million tiny pieces. I always knew that I got the best part of him, when I had you. I just never wanted to feel that kind of pain again. I just can't open myself up like that."

I was blown away. I couldn't believe that she could talk to me so honestly. I looked away, feeling almost ashamed for bringing it up. A few moments passed, and she began to speak again.

"But, Tyler, that is my story, it is NOT yours. Your story is still being written, and the ending is nowhere near. I made my choices, and I have to be resolved in those decisions. I may have some regret, but I can't go back. I can't change the things I've done. I can only look forward."

I thought about how strong she was. How strong she had to be to raise me alone. I knew that she was a good mom, and I was glad Lilly was opening up to her. But, I couldn't help but mourn for the father that I never knew. That was such a tragedy to me. Not just for me, but also for her. Although, she had done so much to make sure things are okay. But some holes were never meant to be filled and some wounds would never heal. Ever since I'd met Lilly things I never thought about filled all the empty space in my head. And sometimes I felt almost crazy, but I guess it's just part of growing up. I hoped they had done all their talking and I headed back downstairs.

They were still in the kitchen, only they were hugging. I felt like I was intruding, but mom heard me and motioned for me to come take her place. I walked over to her, and my mom let her go and turned to face the sink. I thought I saw Mom drying her eyes a bit as she turned back to face us. I'm sure the story had moved my mom, too. I was sure she felt bad for Lilly, just like I did. Lilly turned and folded into my arms. I looked over her head at my mom, and motioned towards the living room. She nodded. Lilly let me lead her to the couch. We snuggled together there as she pulled her legs up, and lay her head on my chest. I wrapped both of my arms around her, resting my chin on her head.

I waited for the tears to stop. But, they just kept coming. Occasionally she would mumble: "It was my fault." "I wanted it to happen." "I should never be forgiven." I just held her. There were no words that could be said that would make her feel better, and I wasn't about to say things that might make it worse.

Eventually the sobs came less frequently. I didn't feel as many tears falling on my shirt, and her body stopped trembling uncontrollably. Mom had long since left us alone, and gone up to her room. I must have dozed off a little bit, too. I woke up and

Lilly's head was in my lap. She was crashed. I moved her head off my lap, and pulled the blanket down on her. I leaned down and gently kissed her beautiful pink lips. A part of me was sad that she was asleep. I wanted to kiss her and tell her it would be okay.

Instead, I turned off all the lights, and headed up to my mom's room. The hall upstairs was dark, but the light from mom's bedroom lamp was just bright enough that I didn't have to turn on the hallway light. Things always seemed worse in the dark of night. A chill ran through my body. I was so worried about Lilly.

I took a deep breath and was surprised at the smell. I could smell mom's floral, fruity kind of perfume that she wore. She had actually worn it forever. I knew she had lots of other scents on her counter, but she always wore this one. I meant to go see what it was. I decided I should know these things about her. Now that I had Lilly, I had noticed a lot of different things about my Mom lately. I was concerned that she was lonely. I knew she was worried about me and that she thought of my future much more than she thought of her own.

I put my hands in the pockets of my shorts, my head was hanging low. She would expect that I would be upset. The whole conversation kind of had my head spinning. I was hoping that maybe Mom could make some sense of it for me. She was always able to explain things so that I understood them. Even though she had a wicked temper, she also had a loving and patient side to her. That of course was my favorite part about her.

Her book was already lying on her chest, her glasses pushed on top of her head. She was completely ready for bed, and she had been waiting for me to come in and say good night.

"I didn't hear your Jeep. Did Lilly's Dad come get her?" she asked.

"No, not exactly. She is asleep on the couch." I didn't make eye contact with her. I wasn't sure if this would make her mad, or if she wouldn't mind.

"Hmmm," she said. She sat up and closed her book. I tried to see what she was reading, but she closed it upside down, and placed it on her night stand.

"So, what is your plan then, exactly?" There was no anger in her voice.

"Can she sleep here tonight, Mom? Please?" I was pleading with her. I didn't want to wake up Lilly and have to take her home right now. I thought she might need me when she woke up in the morning.

"Did you call her father? Does he know she is here and asleep?" she asked quietly.

"Not yet, I wanted to check with you first. Does that mean it is okay?" I gritted my teeth to make a full grin.

"Well, it is late, and I know she was really upset. The right thing to do would be for me to call him, and let him make his own decision. If it were me, I'd be fine with it. But, we have a different relationship. And if the things she said were true, he might not trust her like I trust you, Tyler."

I nodded, of course she was right. But, I wanted to call him. I wanted to be the responsible one. "Can I call him? I want him to know that I am taking care of her. I want to show him that I care that much about her. "

She smiled at me. "Of course that is what you would want to do, but what do you think Lilly's father might interpret that to mean?"

I thought for a second. Why would he think anything other than what I was saying? I mean, it's not like we were sleeping together. He might not know that though. He might just assume that we were.

"Oh, I see your point. I will go grab her cell phone." I turned to walk out of her room. Then I came back, and kissed my mom on the forehead.

"And that was for what exactly? Letting you have a sleep-over with your girlfriend?" She winked at me.

"No, not at all. It was for just being you."

"Will you sit down for a second, honey?" she asked. Her face was serious now.

I immediately sat down across from her. I waited for her to speak.

"I need to say something to you okay, Tyler? But more importantly, I need you to listen to me." She paused. I nodded slowly at her.

"I remember being in love at your age. I know that it is hard for you to imagine, and probably even uncomfortable to think about. But, I was in love. It was love, Tyler. I didn't even appreciate that until recently. As I have watched you fall in love with Lilly." Her eyes were misty, and I wanted to reach out to her, but I was almost frozen, listening to her.

"I am guessing that maybe you are wondering if this is the real deal. I know you both are young, but please, don't discount it because of your age. And if you do really love Lilly, like I think you do then make sure you tell her, every day. It doesn't mean that she will be the only girl you will ever love. It doesn't mean that your whole future is her. It's just that the worst thing you can ever do, in my opinion, is love someone so much, yet never have the courage to tell them."

She continued. "A broken heart will heal with time. I know that from experience. I also know that if you are not strong enough to tell people you love them, you are not worthy of having them love you back. It's hard to tell someone you love them, especially if you think they might not return that love. I don't think that is the case for you and Lilly, at least not right now. It's all new and exciting. Just remember that love, in its truest most raw form, is love worth fighting for. It really is better to love out in the open with your whole heart instead of suffering with love in silence."

She had little tears forming in the corners of her eyes. I wondered what brought this on, but I knew she was speaking about my father. I hated to see her sad. Then it occurred to me, what if I had it wrong? Maybe she wasn't sad at all. It's true that we don't ever truly know our parents. They were different people before we were born. I wondered what she had given up to have me. I hoped I had been worth it. I wasn't bold enough to ask her though.

"Go get her phone, call her Dad. Sleep tight, sweetie." She leaned towards me, ruffled my hair and kissed me on the cheek.

I ran down the stairs to get Lilly's phone. When I came around the corner, I saw that she was awake, and she was already on her phone. I stopped not wanting to intrude on her conversation. But, I wasn't able to stop myself from listening.

"I know it's late. I'm sorry I didn't call sooner. I fell asleep, Dad."

"I don't know, I guess he went upstairs, it's dark, I'm sure they are both asleep."

"I really am sorry, Dad. Are you mad at me?"

"No, I didn't do it on purpose. We were talking about Austin and Mom. I got really upset I guess I just cried myself to sleep."

"No, I'm not slipping back into my old ways." Lilly's voice had an edge to it, she wasn't angry, not yet, but she was certainly getting there.

I didn't know if I should go in and let her know I was awake or if I should just let them think I was asleep. I wasn't sure I wanted him to know I was awake, he might get more upset and possibly come get her. I didn't want her to go home. So, I sat down on the bottom stair, and continue to eavesdrop.

"Are you? Well, I'm sure you can't come pick me up anyway, can you?"

"Look, I promise it's not how it looks. In fact, you can call Tyler's mom tomorrow or if you want, you can come pick me up and meet her. Then you will see that it is just as I have explained it. I'm just really tired, and would like to go back to sleep."

"That's fine then. Again, I'm sorry, Daddy. I really want you to trust me again, and I know this doesn't help that. But, I am being good. I promise. Besides, you trust Tyler, don't you?"

OH I wish I could hear what he was saying. Did he trust me with his daughter? He might not if he knew how in love with her I was. I'm sure dads get more worked up about the whole sex thing, but that wasn't what was happening with Lilly and me.

No one believed me. None of my friends and none of her friends believed that we hadn't slept together yet. Everyone thought that we were definitely "hooking up". But, nothing made my stomach turn more. That kind of thing insinuated that what we had wasn't special. That it was just some juvenile high school romance. Lilly and I both knew we were young, and probably too young to feel like this, but regardless of our ages, we both did. We were careful not to say "I love you" in front of other people. The more people knew, the more I thought it cheapened it.

I would have kept our entire relationship a secret, if the way we felt wasn't so obvious to everyone. I knew in my heart, that I would never love another girl the way I love Lilly. I didn't know if we would be lucky enough to survive high school and college. I wasn't so naïve to think that we would go our whole lives without ever loving anyone else, but I knew what was in my heart today, at this moment. And I knew without any doubt that Lilly felt the same way.

"He is a good guy, Dad. He's better than I deserve."

"I love you, too, Dad. I will call you when everyone gets up tomorrow. Good night."

She hung up her phone. I was still sitting on the bottom of the stairs. I was caught up in my thoughts of her. I often found myself just thinking of Lilly when I wasn't sitting right beside her. I knew it was crazy. I was seventeen years old and had only one more year of high school. Lilly had 2 more years after I got through. I hated to think of anything past my graduation. A lot could happen in those years.

She lay back down on the couch and wrapped the blanket back around her. I wanted to go to her. I wanted to have her in my arms. But, I knew my mom was waiting for me to come back up and tell her what Lilly's Dad had said. I quickly moved up the stairs.

Mom put her book down again, but this time only looked up from her glasses.

"I didn't have to call him. She was on the phone with him when I went down there. I don't think he was happy about it. But, apparently he wasn't in any condition to come pick her up either. So, I'm going to head on to bed." I couldn't look at her because I think we both knew I wasn't going to go to my room.

She watched me for a minute. Then she closed her book, took off her glasses and turned off her light. "Okay. Night again, Tyler. Will you please shut my door?"

I was surprised. I knew she trusted me, but even though she trusted me, she also knew I was a seventeen year old boy. Didn't she remember what those were like? I smiled at her.

"Sure thing, Mom. Love you."

I closed her door. I walked to my room and stood there for a few seconds. I felt the pull from downstairs. I wanted to go to Lilly. I told myself not to over think it. I changed into gym shorts and headed downstairs. I was sure I'd pay for it, but I knew it would be worth it.

I stopped half way down the stairs. If I had learned anything from my mom, it had been to always be safe. I went back up into my room and rifled through my night stand drawer. I remembered the conversation we had a few years ago.

Mom knocked on my door one night, right before the summer between my freshman and sophomore year of high school. I remember how serious she looked, and I was afraid that I was in trouble, but I couldn't figure out what for exactly.

"Can we talk, Tyler?" she asked me.

She was in her pj's and her hair was pulled up in a ponytail. I didn't think she looked old enough to have a son my age. She was cute and with her glasses and ponytail, she looked about 20. That made me smile. I loved how my friends were always talking about how young and pretty she was. She tried to make everyone feel comfortable when they were here. She always said it was important for us to have a place to hang out. She was cool about a lot of things, but I could tell by her tone, this wasn't going to be a casual conversation.

"Sure, Mom."

I sat up and put my book down. I was working on my summer reading list, lame as that sounds now. But, I had definitely gotten my love of reading from her, among other things. Shakespeare was my mom's favorite of all the classical writers and I was totally getting into *Macbeth*. She promised to help me through any of the parts that I didn't understand.

"We are about to have a very serious conversation, Tyler. It is not a time for jokes or sarcasm, on either of our part. Is that understood?" There was nothing but seriousness in her tone.

I sat up straighter in my bed. I was curious as well as concerned now. The first thing that ran through my mind was that this conversation was going to be about my father. I couldn't think of any subject that she would hold with such reverence. I wasn't sure I was ready to hear what she had to say.

I must have looked petrified because she giggled.

"It's not life or death, Tyler. I apologize for my tone. But, I wanted to make sure that you were listening, and are going to take me very seriously." I smiled back at her, and felt a little bit of relief.

"So, I wanted to discuss sex with you, Tyler. And before you try to persuade me or convince me that it's not necessary, know that we ARE having this conversation."

She cleared her throat and continued.

"You just turned fifteen and I know that what you think about more than anything right now are girls. I'm not going to embarrass you by asking what you have or have not done yet. Let's just agree that we both know the mechanics of sex, right? I am sure the basics have been covered in Health classes since you were in what the fourth grade?"

I nodded.

"Do you have any particular questions, before I go on, about the mechanics, that is?" She waited a few minutes.

I shook my head slowly. Of course I knew how it was done. They showed us all the 'basics' and then some. I wanted to laugh, remembering how the coach had told us about masturbating, and how natural it was and we shouldn't feel guilty for doing it. I certainly never felt guilty about it. I was a guy after all it was just something that we did. I was however looking forward to when I didn't have to do it on my own.

Mom was staring at me. "May I continue or do you want to share your thoughts with me?"

I knew that was a rhetorical question, so I just half smiled at her. She went on.

"Sex is just that. Sex is a biological need that all of us have. Boys. Girls. It's a physical reaction to touching, kissing and it always feels good. You don't have to be in love with someone to have sex with them." I guess my eyes kind of bulged at that statement. "What?"

"Well, I didn't think that girls, I mean, moms thought like that," I said, looking down as I spoke.

"Do you really think, physically, it's much different for girls? It's not Tyler. Girls are just told by their parents, by society, by everyone that only 'bad' girls enjoy sex. I am here to tell you, that mechanically, the actual act can be very pleasurable for females. Girls, good and bad and women just the same, enjoy having sex. But, there is a difference." She paused.

"Here is where the difference is between boys and girls, men and women. Most girls have feelings when they are having sex. Sure, there are some girls out there that just might not care, but the vast majority would agree, no matter what they say do have feelings deeply attached to the boys or men that they choose to have sex with. That is not to say that a woman is in love with every man she has sex with. Women are just as capable of one night stands as men are. Women can detach themselves physically and emotionally, but it's less common for women in my own personal experience."

Mom twisted away from me and gazed out my window. She looked like she had left my room, this house and was somewhere far away. I didn't say anything. I knew she had ghosts and skeletons that haunted her. I heard her nightmares sometimes. They aren't nearly as often now, but I can remember when I was younger, she had startled me awake several times with her screaming. She had dismissed them as 'night terrors', but I always thought it was something more than that.

She looked back at me and suddenly she was refocused on the conversation we were having. Although it wasn't really a conversation, she was talking and I was listening. I was really listening to her. I knew that this had to be hard for her, sitting here discussing sex with her son.

"I want you to remember that. I know that it will be hard to remember this when you are physically in the moment. But, if you don't let yourself go there until you are ready, really ready, and she is really ready, then you will make the experience enjoyable for the both of you. I know it will be hard for you, Tyler. You are a guy. And sometimes, it's all guys think about. Just don't be THAT guy, Tyler." She reached into her pocket and pulled out condoms. My mouth fell open.

"Mom, really? I'm not even seeing anyone, really."

"That doesn't mean that much, Tyler. I hope that you do believe you need to be in a relationship and in love before you have sex, but just in case that doesn't happen. Just in case your hormones get the best of you, I want you to always be safe."

I seriously couldn't believe she was giving me condoms. I wasn't sure if I should take them from her or not. Luckily, she put them on the night stand.

"I will buy these for you whenever you need them. If you are too embarrassed or whatever, and I will never judge you or your choices. I just want to make sure that you are informed and you are making these decisions for the right reasons."

She had tears in her eyes now. I wasn't sure why exactly, but I knew better than to ask.

"There is nothing wrong with being prepared, Tyler. There is nothing wrong with planning. And there is absolutely nothing wrong in waiting. And if you wait, it will not be just sex you are having, but you will be able to make love to the person you love. And no matter what anyone else says, there is a difference. Sex is mechanical. Making love can be magical and riveting. I would always choose the magic over just satisfying a physical need. But, please hear me when I say this. It only takes one time. It is much better to make the decision ahead of time than have to make harder decisions when you no longer have a choice."

She leaned over and hugged me tightly. She kissed me on the cheek and stood up.

"Tyler, I am always here for you, no matter what. I trust you. I trust your judgment. Just promise me that you will plan and be prepared, that's really all I ask."

She had kept her word all these years. She had never had to replace this box though. We never had another conversation about it again. But, tonight I was so grateful for her words. I had waited. I had planned, sort of. And tonight I was not going to have sex with Lilly, I was going to go downstairs and make love to Lilly. I knew I loved her and that I would love her for the rest of my life.

I grabbed a condom, and went back down stairs to Lilly.

Lilly, 2010

It felt weird to wake up in Tyler's house, mainly because he was not here with me. It took me a few minutes to acclimate myself, where I was, why I was here, and why I was alone. Then it came back to me. I had a mental breakdown tonight. His mom had been so great! She just held me while I cried, and then she let me go to Tyler. I wonder how long I cried. But, it felt good. I felt good. Like I had let all the guilt and anger and sadness get cried out of me. My heart was healing. I could actually feel it healing. Tyler was the reason.

I grabbed my cell from the table, and freaked. It was almost 1 am. Definitely a few hours past my curfew, although I wasn't sure that Dad even knew when I was late. He was drunk all the time it seemed. He drank at night, after he thought I was asleep. I also knew on the weekends he really over indulged, especially when I wasn't going to be home for hours or was spending the night at a friend's house. I figured he was working through his own guilt, just with the help of the bottle. Jack Daniels was his best friend. It was sad really. We came here for a fresh start, but we both had ended up with some addictions. At least mine is good for me. I was completely and totally addicted to Tyler.

We were moving very slow, too slow in my opinion. But, I didn't want to freak him out. He knew I had a 'history', but we had agreed it was in the past, and had little relevance on our relationship. Tyler was a 'live in the moment', and don't look back kind of guy. Again, I felt so totally lucky and addicted!

I called my dad. I could tell he was very drunk. He didn't like that I was going to spend the night here, I mean, it wasn't Tyler he didn't trust it was me. I was immediately remembering the pictures he had found of me. I was sure he had been scarred for life, and never looked at me quite the same way. But, I was so different now. I was so 'small town', it wasn't even funny. I seriously couldn't believe I had adapted so well.

I knew that it was only because of Tyler. Tyler was TOO good. He was always doing the right thing, for everyone. Finally my dad just caved and told me I could spend the night. I got my way by reminding him that he probably couldn't come get me anyway. And we both knew it was totally true. It was kind of pathetic really. But, I had won this round. I knew he wouldn't show up here tomorrow either.

He would be too embarrassed that he couldn't come get me. It struck me odd how our roles had reversed. I hung up and lay back down on the couch. I really wish Tyler would come back down here. I guess I could sneak up to his room, but I cared about how his mom felt about me. I knew she liked me, and that was important to me. It was important to me because it was important to Tyler. I laughed at myself. I couldn't believe I had turned into one of 'those girls'.

It was really ironic. I tossed and turned a bit, trying to get comfortable. I closed my eyes and started to think about Tyler. I loved how he smelled. It wasn't just his cologne, it was just him. His green eyes melted my heart when he stared at me, which seemed to be a lot lately. I thought about how he kissed me, how he touched me. A while back he made this speech about how we were going to keep our relationship innocent. He promised he would never force me to do anything that I wasn't ready for.

He didn't know that I dreamed about being with him all the time.

I knew he would be so tender and gentle with me. I also knew that I would have to play it down a bit, being it would be his first time, and not mine. That made me a little bit sad. I wish my first time could have been with Tyler. I wish that so many things I had done with Tyler first.

I thought I heard talking upstairs, but I couldn't make out the words. I was happy to hear them talking, I was hoping he would come to check on me, find me awake. Then it was quiet.

UGH! He was going to do the right thing. He was going to go to his room. And all I could hope for, was that I could fall asleep quickly because knowing that Tyler was upstairs half naked, was making me feel restless. I wanted Tyler. I knew that once we had sex, that he would totally be mine. I pretended not to mind waiting, but it was seriously becoming harder and harder.

Everyone at school assumed we were sleeping together anyway. Not that I cared too much what any of them thought. They were mostly jealous. That made me a little bit happy. I liked people being jealous of me, instead of looking at me like a freak or feeling sorry for me because my mom had died. Jealousy felt like a normal thing for someone to feel, and I so just wanted to be normal.

I turned over to face into the couch. I thought if I was away from the windows and the moon light, then I could fall asleep. I was thinking of Tyler though. I was wishing he was kissing me and running his fingers through my hair. I started to get a little flushed. I took a deep breath, and willed myself to fall asleep. After a few minutes, I actually began to feel Tyler touching me and I knew I had started dreaming.

I clenched my eyes closed tighter and it was like Tyler was there. I could feel his hot chest against my tank top. His arms were around me. He was kissing the back of my neck and my ears. His hands were everywhere. I leaned back into him, hoping that nothing would interrupt this amazing dream. I had dreamed of Tyler before, but it had never felt this real. I heard him whispering my name over and over. I rolled over and opened my eyes just a little bit.

He was there. He was really there. This wasn't a dream. He must have felt a shift in my body. He stopped. He looked down at me. He looked almost a little embarrassed. I must have looked startled to see him. I did think it was a dream at first.

I smiled at him. He seemed to relax for just a second.

"Is this okay, Lilly?" he whispered. He was breathing harder than usual.

I stared into his eyes. "Yes."

He lips came crushing down on mine, like he had never kissed me before. His mouth was open on mine, and his tongue was darting in and out of my mouth. I put both of my hands on his face, and kind of pushed him back a little bit. I wanted him to slow down. He stopped kissing me and pulled away.

"No, Tyler. Please don't stop." My breathing was staggered. "Please don't stop." I said again, "Just don't go so fast."

He smiled at me then. It was the most beautiful smile. His eyes were smiling as well as his lips. I moved myself underneath him, and he quickly was on top of me. I was very aware of every muscle, every tremble in his body. He ran his hands through my hair. He kissed my forehead. He kissed my eyelids, my cheeks, my nose, my chin. I kept my hands moving up and down his back, gently using my nails. As I got closer to the top of his shorts, lingering there, he let out a small groan.

He kept one of his hands pressing against the couch, trying not to put all his weight on me. The other hand was moving down my neck, to my breasts, to my stomach. He hesitated at the bottom of my tank top. I could tell he wasn't sure if he should start to remove it or not. So, I reached down, underneath him, and pulled it up over my head. When our skin touched, we both had a hard time catching our breath. He pulled away from me, staring down at me.

His hand was back on my face, and I just let my hands grasp the waist band of his shorts. He looked at me, his face flushed. I closed my eyes for just a second, hoping that he wasn't going to stop. I wanted to make sure he knew I didn't want him to stop. I lifted my head up to his, and kissed him hard.

He pulled back again, watching me. I tilted my head to the left and grinned at him. I was trying to flirt with him without saying anything, but I wasn't sure he was reading me.

Finally, he spoke. "Lilly, I love you. Are you sure you are ready?" he whispered to me, while staring deep into my eyes. "We don't have to we can just kiss or whatever."

His eyes moved away from mine, and I thought he looked a little bit embarrassed. He really had no idea how much I wanted him, how much I wanted this to happen. How badly I needed him!

"Yes, please, Tyler. I love you so much. I've never wanted anything more."

He was kissing me so gently and slowly. I was giving myself to Tyler for the first time. And I didn't care about what I had done in the past. All that mattered was Tyler and right now, this minute.

He was prepared and whispered to me, "We have to be smart about this too, and I want to keep you safe." I melted into him.

Afterwards, we lay there side by side on his mother's couch. We were wrapped around each other. He was such a wonderful person. He loved me. He really loved me. These weren't just words he had shown me how much he loved me. And I had loved him right back. It felt like it was my first time.

I felt adored and protected. We both eventually fell asleep, face to face on the oversized couch. I woke up first, and began kissing his neck and his shoulders. He began to moan every so often, so I knew he was waking up. I knew I should have felt tired, but I didn't.

"Hey sleepy head…Do you want to go up to your room now?" I asked him.

"And leave you? I just couldn't".

I could tell the thought of doing so upset him.

"I don't want you to go, Tyler. But, your mom will be up soon."

The mention of her name brought him back to reality. He grabbed my phone and saw that is was 8.30 am.

"Oh GREAT. I didn't even think about that."

He quickly got up and pulled his shirt over his head. He came back to me quickly, kissed my forehead and said, "Go to my bathroom, and get dressed. I'm going to start breakfast."

I smiled at him. I could so get used to this. Tyler made me feel like a princess. It had been the most amazing night of my life. I couldn't imagine anything ever being as perfect as last night was. I could never imagine being with anyone but Tyler. I wasn't paying attention but I thought I heard footsteps. I didn't even double check to see, I was too caught up in thinking about last night.

I got to the top of the stairs and took a left to Tyler's room. I tip toed into his room, shut the door. I then walked into his bathroom, and shut that door, too. I turned on the water and began washing my face. I smiled to myself, so this is what true love is supposed to be about?

I didn't hear Tyler's mom open his bedroom door. I had no idea that she saw his bed was still made.

I finished up in the bathroom, got dressed and ran back down to Tyler. I found him and his mom laughing and making breakfast. I felt like I belonged. I watched them from just beyond the kitchen.

They weren't like other kids and their parents. They seemed to just get each other. I started to feel this emotion brewing from down inside, at first I thought it was jealousy, but then it hit me.

It was guilt. And I knew that feeling all too well.

I had never had this kind of a relationship with my parents. I had never wanted to. Actually, I didn't think it was really possible. I thought about my dad then. I'm sure he was hung over and trying to piece together last night. He probably didn't even realize I wasn't home yet. Then it occurred to me how odd it is that he and Tyler have barely said ten words to each other.

It was one night a few weeks ago, and Dad had just gotten home from work. I could tell the way he slurred hello to us that he must have gone to happy hour before he headed home. He was probably grateful that I had Tyler and that he didn't have to deal with me that much. After all, I was being good.

My grades were good. I was home by curfew, as far as he knew.

I had introduced them, but Dad didn't even make eye contact with Tyler. Tyler had been very understanding that night, and I didn't have to tell him what was wrong. He saw my embarrassment. He just kissed my cheek and said, "We are not responsible for our parents, Lilly."

And now, standing in his home, watching him with his mother, I wondered where that kind of empathy had come from. I couldn't imagine Carsen doing anything that would bother Tyler. Tyler saw me then, and came right over to me. He wrapped his arms around waist and kissed my forehead.

"Good Morning," he whispered.

Pretending we hadn't already seen each other. I tucked my head into his shoulder, not quite ready to make eye contact with Carsen. I looked over at her then, and she was smiling at me.

"Hey there! I hope you slept okay on that lumpy old thing!"

"Oh, it was perfect," I said, squeezing Tyler.

"Well, I must say having Tyler up first and making us breakfast, we just might have to have you over more often." She winked at me then.

I wasn't sure how sincere she was being, but I wanted to believe that she didn't know. I wanted to believe that she didn't hate me. I wanted to believe that I still belonged here with Tyler and with her.

"Well, I doubt there will be any more sleepovers. My dad wasn't very happy with me last night. So, Tyler after breakfast, do you think you could take me home?"

But before he could answer, Carsen stepped towards me, and said, "Oh let me! I would really like to meet your father, and maybe it will smooth things out for you."

She rubbed my shoulder, and turned and walked away. I felt so much better.

"Really? You would do that, Ms. Wylder?"

"I think you can call me Carsen from now on, sweetie. And yes, I would love to meet your dad. Now that you and Tyler have been together for how long?" she asked.

At the same time we both said, "Almost five months." We both laughed.

"Well, I think it's time we met then."

19

Joshua, 2010

I suck as a dad. I shouldn't really be too surprised though. I sucked as a husband, too. I just can't seem to pull it together. And when my job isn't affected, well, who else is going to tell me to slow down? Take it easy? Quit drinking? No one.

I answer to no one. I use to try to keep it together in front of Lilly, but she's got her own life and a boyfriend. She's just not around that much anymore. I guess a better father would care where she was, care that she doesn't want to be here. I do care. I just care about drowning myself more. She called in a panic around 1 am.

Lilly knew I'd been drinking, so she knew I wouldn't come get her; that I couldn't come get her. I hung up and took a huge gulp of Jack Daniels right out of the bottle. No need for the glass, I'm alone. I drink alone. I drink every night. I drink first thing in the morning. I am a functioning drunk. My work has not suffered at all. I keep it together most of the day, most of my work is done over the phone and I have one hell of a paralegal to do all the other menial tasks.

I knew I was starting to screw that up though. I didn't mean to sleep with her. Well, I did. I just didn't mean for her to get all over emotional about it. We are both relatively young and not married. Of course, she is divorced and I am a widower. I guess I didn't realize the difference that makes on one's view of 'dating'. She was still looking for the fertile ending. I was just counting the days as they passed. Another day since I killed my wife. It was another day that I was alive and Lauren wasn't. It was another day where my beautiful daughter was growing up without her mother and with an alcoholic for a father.

I came home last night after leaving Emma's house. She begged me to stay, but I just couldn't bring myself to spend the night. I liked her enough and the sex was okay. I mean it was sex and it felt good. It even felt nice to be with someone. But, the truth was when she talked, I didn't hear a word she said. I nodded in all the right places, and I pretended to pay attention. But, I was just counting down to when we could just get to the sex. I was only there for that. I figured she knew that, deep down.

We had never really talked about it. I didn't want to mislead her either, but the fact was I needed her for work and for sex. I am the man I swore I would never be. I wonder if I get points for at least being aware of that fact. I don't think I care.

The house was empty when I got there. No surprise. Lilly didn't want to be there. I felt it. I knew she was dating that boy. But his name escapes me right now. I'm sure it was getting hot and heavy. I envied them. I envied their ability to believe in love. The ability to believe in a future that they most certainly believed they would share together. I'm just assuming they are like all young people in love, in such an idealistic way.

I didn't believe in either anymore. I didn't believe that I would ever find love again. I know I'm slowly killing myself, and I just don't care. Lilly is going to be 16 soon. I'd already bought her a new car, a red 2010 Ford Escape. I was great at giving her things. She took good care of herself, too.

I hated it here though. And if she wasn't doing so well, we would have headed back to Austin. I couldn't believe that I had let Sarah talk me into moving here. She had promised that it would be good for both of us. I could only see how much it was helping Lilly. I knew as a dad, I should be grateful for that. I knew that my child should be the most important thing to me, but the truth was, I wasn't wired that way.

I did love this house though. I loved hanging out in this back-yard. I had done a lot of work out here, too. I laughed to myself. I had paid to have a lot of work done out here. I could buy just about anything I wanted, but I had no one to share it with. Twenty years ago I thought all that mattered was being successful. I knew what I wanted and I went after it. I went to UT and got my undergrad in Business and then went on to Law School at SMU.

I practiced Business Law. I made a lot of money in Acquisitions and Mergers. The first few years with the practice had been the hardest, but now, it was all something I could do in my sleep, which I did many days lately, well not asleep but hung over.

I stripped off my work clothes. I noticed my white polo had pink lipstick on it. I thought back to earlier, with Emma. She is so eager to please me. I honestly don't know what she sees in me really. I mean, I have money and that is about my only redeeming quality these days. Maybe she is just that desperate for attention that she would take it from me.

I passed out on the patio as I do most nights that Lilly is gone. I just hate being alone. At least out in the backyard, there are sounds and there is usually a breeze. I can just drink until it all goes black. Unfortunately, I usually was startled awake by a terrible dream. Who am I kidding? I don't have dreams I have recurring nightmares.

I have had the same one for months. I am running down the street, its pitch dark. I hear Lauren screaming for me. She says my name over and over. I keep running towards her. When I think I've found her, she is lying on the ground, on the turn by the bridge. She is white and bloody, just like the last time I saw her barely breathing. I kneel down to touch her, to wipe the hair from her eyes. Her eyes pop open and she screams, 'NO!' at me every single time. I wake up in a cold sweat. Shaking.

It was always the same. I was consumed by guilt then quickly it turned to relief. Some nights, like last night, I sat up and began to cry. I cried for the life that I had lost when Lauren died. I cried because a big part of me wasn't even sad that she was gone. I cried because I didn't miss her. What kind of a man doesn't miss his dead wife?

I missed what having her in my life had represented. But, I didn't miss her. I got up and went inside, and opened up a new bottle of Jack. He was really my only friend. He listened, he sympathized and he never judged me. He was a good friend.

I eventually found my way to my bed. I was still thinking about the nightmare. I was sure I was going to pass out again when my memory drifted to Carsen's face. Her beautiful smile whenever she saw me. The way she lighted up in my presence. I remembered that once Jake had commented on how nice it must be to have someone so in love with you.

I think I slugged him. "What are you talking about? She's my best friend."

Jake looked at me, "Man, you are so stupid. If she's just your friend, than I definitely need to get one of those."

"Look asshole. We are just friends." I was starting to get defensive. She wasn't in love with me, no way.

"Yeah, dude, keep telling yourself that." Jake shrugged.

Carsen had never been in love with me. In fact, I was certain that it was quite the opposite. She abandoned me, leaving some stupid ass letter. Not even telling me herself, like I didn't deserve a face to face explanation.

I think I had hoped she was in love with me. It would have been so easy with her. Even those last few weeks, I thought we were really getting closer, if that was possible. Then she was gone.

I suppose I could have tried to find her, made an effort to figure out what had happened. I'm sure her mom and brother knew where she went, eventually. Instead, I'd been a stubborn ass and decided if that's what she wants, then that is what she gets. Lauren had come along soon after, and she adored me. She was what I thought I wanted and needed.

Regret is the worst tasting emotion. I should know. I get a heavy dose of it every single day. It's hard to live with regret because some things just can't be corrected. You just can't get a do over. I passed out with Carsen's face on my mind, and I knew that face would take me back to a kinder and gentler, less complicated time in my life.

The phone rang again, pulling me out of my stupor. Not another phone call? I hope it isn't Lilly. I was in worse condition than before. I wouldn't be able to keep from slurring. It would be pointless. I looked at the clock, it was actually 9 am. Wow!

I had slept for quite a few hours. I looked around for my phone. I had to actually get out of bed. I saw it on the floor. I cleared my throat, hoping it wouldn't sound so bad.

"Hello Sarah. It's been a long time."

"Hey Joshua! It certainly has been," she said.

There was something off in her voice, even though we hadn't

talked recently, I still could tell something was wrong.

"What's wrong? Is it Mom?" I sat back down on the bed trying to ground myself. The room was spinning a little bit.

"Uh, no, Joshua. We are fine. How are you? How is Lilly?"

"Lilly is great! She's doing really well in school. She's a totally different kid here. You would be so proud of her, Sarah."

"Really? Well, that is great news. And you? How are you, Joshua?"

"You know me. Working a lot and trying to stay out of trouble. So did you just call to check on us? Or are you finally going to come for a visit?" I asked, hoping she would say yes.

"Well, there is something wrong, Joshua. It has to do with Lauren. And with Lilly."

"What are you talking about?" I stood up quickly almost involuntarily. I began to sweat a little bit, and I could feel the shakes coming on. I began to feel very anxious.

"Well, the investigation was re-opened, regarding Lauren's, uhm, accident."

"Why? Do they know who hit her?"

I was all of the sudden optimistic. Maybe if we could punish who killed Lauren, then maybe I could quit punishing myself. Yeah, right, that was unlikely.

"That's just it. They have identified the car and driver. It was discovered during another hit and run accident in the same area."

"This is GREAT news, Sarah."

"Yes, it is. Do you remember Andrea, Lilly's best friend? Do you know if they have spoken lately?"

"No, I really don't. I think she's pretty much done with all that. She's got a few good girlfriends here, and even a boyfriend. I sure hope she isn't still talking to that girl, anyway. Why do you want to know?"

"It was her car. She is who hit Lauren."

"Are you serious? Are you sure?"

"Yes, Josh. They are sure. She has confessed. But there is more."

She paused. I had to sit back down. I had a splitting headache, I wasn't sure if it was from the news or from my hangover.

"What else could there be, Sarah? What else matters?"

"Joshua, Andrea says that Lilly was with her that night. That

139

Lilly was in the car."

"What does that mean?" My head was spinning faster now I thought the room was actually moving. I felt like the bottom had fallen out, and all I could pray was that I would be sucked into it.

I could hear the strain in Sarah's voice. "The girls had been drinking and had taken Ecstasy. Do you know what that is?" She paused.

"Yes I do know what that is."

"Apparently they thought they just hit an animal. Andrea says that they realized they hit something, but when they looked in the rear view mirror they didn't see anything. She panicked and put the car in reverse, believing they hit her a second time. Then they drove off. Of course not realizing it was a person that they hit." She sniffled and I could tell she was crying.

There was no way this was possible. Lilly was troubled and she had been a royal pain in the ass for a good three years, but she would never want to physically hurt a living creature. It was impossible.

"I don't believe it, Sarah. I just don't believe it."

"Well, they haven't officially charged either one of them with anything. But, you and Lilly might have to come back to Austin, Josh. I have spoken with a criminal attorney and put him on retainer. His name is Chase Albrighton. I will give you his information. He said he should be able to get everything he needs from you guys over the phone. But, Joshua, this doesn't look good."

This wasn't happening. This couldn't be happening. Lilly was doing so well. She was thriving here. I didn't care about myself I only cared about protecting her. She was all I had left. No matter what happened, nothing could bring Lauren back. There was no way that Lilly could have known that it was her mother that she hit. Could she have?

Of course not. My thoughts were racing, so was my heart.

"Sarah?"

"Yes, I'm still here."

"Is there any way to keep Lilly out of this? Any way at all?"

"You can't protect her from this. Chase says that if the girls' stories match up, then they can be charged with involuntary vehicular manslaughter. If everything you have said about her is true, if she has really turned herself around, then maybe it won't be as bad. It is worse for Andrea, of course, she was driving."

Lilly had been through so much and I didn't know what this was going to do to her. I didn't know much about criminal law. But I knew that if Lilly had been in the car at a minimum she was an accessory. And I'm fairly certain that carries jail time. SHIT.

"Okay, Sarah, please e-mail me all the necessary information for the attorney. I will have to call him tomorrow morning. I will talk to Lilly today, when she gets home."

"I'm sorry this is why I'm calling now, "Sarah said. "Is everything else okay there? Besides this, are you okay? Are you seeing anyone?"

"I don't have time to date, Sarah. I'm working all the time and raising Lilly," I said dryly.

"And the drinking, Josh? Better or worse?"

"Whatever, it's not a problem, and it never has been. It's just what I do. Please don't start worrying about me now. I've been doing just fine on my own."

I didn't think for one second that she believed me, but more importantly I didn't even care. I guess that is what happens when drinking literally becomes THE most important thing in your life. I hated being reminded of it. I didn't want to discuss it. I knew that if I wanted to, I could stop drinking. And it looks like I would have to now. I would have to find the strength to make sure that Lilly got through this okay.

"I can tell by your voice that you aren't fine. What sent you down this road again? Did something in particular happen?"

It sounded like she was fishing for something, like she already knew the answer. Of course she knew the answer was Lauren's death.

"Oh I don't know, Sarah? Maybe my wife dying? How about that?" I said sarcastically.

"I didn't mean it like that, I'm sorry. I know it's hard on you, Josh. I just thought that the change of pace and scenery might do you some good. Haven't met anyone interesting?"

"Again? I'm not dating. Good God."

"I'm just worried about you. And if you are holding on by a thread, like your voice indicates, then I am terrified of what this is going to do to you. Why don't I fly out there?"

I paused for a second. It might be nice to have her here. Help me through this, help with Lilly. She was very nurturing and always a pillar of strength when I couldn't hold myself up.

"Okay. That would be nice. I could use some help." I didn't realize until I was saying those words that I had started to cry.

"Just let me get a few things settled today, and I will take a flight out tomorrow, okay? Then we can work through everything together. All you ever had to do was just ask."

"Thanks, Sarah. It's hard to admit what a mess I've made."

When I hung up with Sarah, I wasn't even sure what I was feeling. I still couldn't quite grasp what she had told me. It didn't seem plausible. I mean, how could the girls have hit something, and not pulled over to see what they had hit? Could they have been trying to hit something? They were wild, yes, but cruel? I just couldn't wrap my brain around that. What I needed was a stiff drink. But, with Sarah coming tomorrow, I should probably start trying to slow down a little bit.

I lay back in the bed. I just wanted to erase the last year of my life. Go back to before things had gotten so difficult. I would try to love Lauren the right way. I should have tried harder. I hadn't been fair to her, and now I was paying for that. I deserved whatever I got for being dishonest and judgmental and mean to her. I just didn't want my legacy of failure to project on to Lilly. I had to get one thing right in this life, and it would have to be her.

Maybe if you don't love the person you are supposed to love like you are supposed to love them, maybe you get punished. Maybe this was fate's way of telling me what a colossal screw up I was. I have always thought that I had all the answers. I was driven, I knew what I wanted. I knew what it took to get the life I deserved.

Yet here I sit widowed, a drunk and the father of a wild child who might be in serious trouble. I swore to myself that I would live my life with no regrets, yet I deal with too much of it every single day. I wonder where exactly it all had gone wrong? At what moment in my life had I made the worst decision that could have possibly led me down this path and to this day? I have no clue!

I looked over at the clock. I wondered when Lilly would be

home. I didn't think I would say anything to her today. I would wait until Sarah got here. I have never been good with the emotional stuff. I have them, I have all kinds of emotions but expressing them with words was not my forte. I mean, I'm a man. We DO things, we don't really discuss the feelings around those things, not too much anyway.

I got up and walked through the house. It seemed so empty. It was definitely too big for just Lilly and me, but I loved it here. I loved the space. I loved not having to face her too much. I again was smoldering in guilt. I was going to have to make some changes. I walked into the kitchen and opened the refrigerator. Wow! There was nothing in here except a 12 pack of Miller Lite, Cokes and Diet Dr. Pepper. I would have to go to the store today, and maybe Lilly would want to go with me.

I reached in and grabbed a Coke. I opened the can and took a huge swig. Nothing worked better on my hang over than an ice cold Coke. The fizz alone had healing powers. I leaned against the kitchen counter, and my eyes wandered to the window.

There was a navy Range Rover in my drive way. I didn't know who it belonged to. That boy, whose name I couldn't remember, drives a jeep. I kind of leaned further back, not wanting whoever was in there to see me. It was a woman. Someone I'd never seen before.

I heard the front door open and then Lilly's voice, "Dad? Daddy? Where are you?"

"I'm in the kitchen, Lills." She came prancing in. She looked a little upset and was staring me up and down.

"Hey," I said.

"Hey! Uhm, Tyler's Mom is out in the car."

We both looked outside. The woman in the car saw us and began to wave. We both waved back at her.

"She would like to meet you, Dad."

I looked down, I didn't have on a shirt, and my shorts weren't even buttoned or zipped up all the way. My hair was a mop of oil on my head. Lilly stared at me.

"But, I guess this isn't the best time. Your eyes are bloodshot and you stink. You smell like whiskey. Forget it. I'll make something up."

Lilly stormed out. I hated to see her so angry, but it was my own fault. I watched as she ran up to the driver's side window. The woman, Tyler's mother oh right, that was his name, Tyler. The woman was running her hand down Lilly's hair and patted her shoulder. I couldn't imagine what Lilly was telling her, but I certainly hoped it wasn't the truth. I didn't need gossip in this small town getting around.

I should just go out there and have a few words with the mom though. She allowed my daughter to sleep over there last night, presumably because everyone had fallen asleep. A good father would not have allowed that. Maybe I should just go tell her what I thought about all that. I could do that. But, of course, I wouldn't. Lilly was right.

I looked like I hadn't had a good night's sleep in days and I smelled. I wasn't exactly the poster child for the model parent.

I looked back out the window, and the woman was waving goodbye to Lilly. Lilly was standing there, like she didn't want her to go. I guess that was normal, Lilly would be looking for someone to be a 'mother' to her, since I was not capable of being a father or a mother to her. But, tomorrow that would change. Sarah would be here. We would figure all this out together. I would tell Lilly that we would have Tyler and his mom over for dinner in a few weeks. I just needed some time to figure out this whole ordeal back in Austin.

Carsen, 2010

As I pulled out of Lilly's driveway, I began to have a panic attack. I related too well to Lilly. She was so excited to introduce me to her father. She jumped out of my car and skipped into the house and had asked for me to wait a few minutes before coming in. Once she disappeared behind the front door, my eyes were drawn to a silhouette in the window just to the right of the garage.

Based on other homes in this sub-division, I imagined I was looking into the kitchen and saw him standing in there. I couldn't make out his face, but he didn't have a shirt on. He didn't look ready for company. I suspected that many fathers were never ready to meet the mother of his daughter's boyfriend. Not to mention the fact that this mother was considering ambushing him with the great possibility that our children had sex.

But, then I saw Lilly and he arguing and I immediately was rethinking this plan. This wasn't the time and probably not the place. I should probably talk to Tyler first, and possibly Tyler and Lilly together. I respect Tyler enough to do that.

Lilly came rushing out of the house, and she was fighting back tears. She leaned up against my car and whispered sheepishly, "Carsen, he is really, really hung over. He smells like whiskey and BO. There is no way you can meet him today. I am so sorry."

"Oh, sweetie," I stroked her hair and patted her shoulder.

"I know how hard that can be, trust me. We can meet another time. It's really, really okay." I thought for half of a second that I shouldn't leave her. But, this was her home, and this was her father. I smiled and winked at her. "Call us if you need us."

I backed cautiously out of their driveway while her father was still staring out the window. I waved as I left. I couldn't begin to know what he was going through or why he thought he could find comfort in this manner. But, I know what it's like to grow up with an alcoholic. I know what you give up and the feelings you learn to hide. You learn early on how to lie and lie well just so no one finds out the truth. No one ever tells you that it's a secret or that you shouldn't tell anyone. You just know, instinctively.

You are able to create two worlds for yourself. The world where things were 'normal' and that really means the days that he didn't drink. Then there was the world when he was drunk, when anything that could go wrong, would go wrong.

I remember many dinners getting cold on the table while we waited for my father to come home from work. Our growing hunger would fuel Mom's anger, but she would wait in a spine-chilling silence. At least once, when Daddy stumbled in late and drunk, Mom couldn't hold back. I can't remember their words, but I can't forget their actions. Mom shattered a casserole dish against the wall, and Daddy shoved her past the refrigerator into the pantry. I fled to my room, hungry and scared, as the screaming ensued. There were many long nights of screaming and broken dishes before she'd had enough.

I never understood why it hurt me so badly when he finally left us. But, it did. Even though things were bad, at least to the outside world we appeared normal. Once they were divorced, we weren't normal anymore. Maybe that is why I let Joshua take advantage of me. Maybe because I didn't feel important to my father, I didn't expect to ever be important to any man.

Great, an epiphany – I had Daddy issues! But, I also loved my father very much. That is what really screwed with my head. I hated what he did and I loved him. And no matter what Joshua did, I loved him too. Wow!

I couldn't believe how much sense this actually made to me. I'd have to give Lilly a big hug the next time she was over, although she wouldn't exactly know why I pulled up to our house and it looked like a cottage compared to the house that Lilly and her father shared. Nevertheless I was willing to bet that our house was more a home than theirs was. I felt ashamed even thinking that, considering all they had lost over the last year.

Lilly was wounded. I could see it in her eyes. I could see the same look in her eyes that I saw every day in the mirror. I think that drew me to her. The need to help out total strangers was one character trait I knew I inherited from my father. Lilly was not totally broken though. She had found Tyler, and he treated her like she needed to be treated.

I desperately wanted to take credit for this, however maybe he was just that kind of man. I must have played a part. It is much easier to want to help people you don't know so well, because it is can be too daunting to apologize to the ones you love and have hurt. It's so much easier to be the hero for a stranger. They don't have all the facts; they don't know the real you that struggles to get through every day. If you are busy attending to outsiders with their issues, then you don't have to look in on your own demons.

I had worked hard for eighteen years to 'get over' what I had done. I guess it is true that no matter how far you run and how often you tell yourself you have moved on, your past catches up with you.

I just didn't want to ruin who Tyler was, or who he was becoming. He was a gentle compassionate boy and he was growing into a responsible, respectable man. I knew I had done my very best with him. I had raised him right.

But, the years were slipping by so much faster than I had anticipated. I could see the difference in him this morning. I was positive that he had consummated their relationship last night. I could tell by the way she came running up the stairs without a care in the world. She was flushed and glowing. I know they believed they were in love. And I believed it, too. But I wondered how Tyler had learned that.

He had never seen love like that up close. I was grateful that he could tell her and show her how he felt. I probably should have been more concerned about the fact that my teenaged son had sex on my couch. But in reality, I was a bit jealous which made me absolutely crazy! I actually envied their passion.

I was bitter that I would never feel those things again. I resented myself because I had not been strong enough to fight for Joshua, I should have at least tried. I was not a quitter, but when I abandoned him, I surrendered whatever we could have been.

In the same heartbeat, I realized that I had managed to raise a good son, one that had fallen in love so effortlessly. Telling him now would be selfish. He was so happy and in such a good place. I also knew there would never be a good time. I had lied to him for so long; that didn't mean that it didn't hurt me. It didn't mean that I wasn't aware of the pain that my decision was bound to cause him one day. It just wasn't going to be today.

He must have seen me sitting in the driveway. He walked out on to the porch. He was always such a beautiful child. His hair was darker now, but his intense blue eyes were as vibrant as they always had been. He was evidently no longer a child.

But, when I looked at him, I could see him missing his front teeth and that silly grin he used to flash no matter what the circumstances. Physically, he reminded me so much of the Josh I first met. Even without having ever met Joshua, he possessed many of Joshua's traits. I never stopped dreading the day that I would have to tell Tyler.

I expected that he would feel that I had betrayed him. I could only hope that he would remember how much I loved him and that I had always thought I did the right thing. My mother used to say that I did what I wanted and begged for forgiveness later. I could only hope begging for forgiveness would work with Tyler. Although, the severity of this choice, paled in comparison with some of my more trivial decisions and the consequences weighed heavy on my soul.

He sauntered over to my car. "What are you doing just sitting here, Mom?"

He looked around my car, the disappointment in his voice. "Oh, so Lilly is at home now?"

"Yes sir," I said and smirked at him.

"I went to take her home, remember?"

"Yeah, I know. I guess I thought she might be able to come back over."

He looked down and I could see he was frustrated that he wasn't with her. I try so hard to remember what that feels like. I can remember the anxiousness and the anticipation. But, in truth my relationship with Joshua was nothing like Tyler and Lilly's relationship.

There was an innocent honesty between them. They hugged and touched each other out in the open. They were kind and considerate of each other all the time. They could sit and just be together with very little conversation between them and you could tell they were so comfortable with each other. Their relationship was easy. Easy? It is all so easy until it just isn't anymore.

Easy becomes more difficult as you grow up. Responsibilities and day to day life takes place of lulling away the afternoon day-dreaming of your future. I knew a few people who survived their first love and were actually lucky enough to marry one another. And I supposed there are people who have never kissed another person or had sex with anyone other than 'the one'. I both envied and pitied those people. I envied the stability. I envied the comfort they had found. I felt sorry for them because you cannot truly appreciate love until you have had your heart broken. I just don't believe it can happen!

Looking at Tyler I didn't want him to experience that kind of hurt, but I also wanted him to appreciate what he had with Lilly. I wanted him to savor it. I wanted him to be gracious and thoughtful. There I was again sounding like a broken record. Maybe everything had really been about what I wanted and what I thought, and I gave no consideration to the other lives my decisions affected. That's the thing about regret; you just can't outrun it, no matter how far you go. Yet, appreciation can only be achieved when there is pain to offset the happiness. Whoever first said "It's better to have loved and lost, than never to have loved at all," was so right!

"So, did you meet her Mr. Hattinson, Lilly's Dad?" Tyler asked.

I froze. I stared at him. I couldn't have heard him correctly. Did he say Hattinson? Couldn't have? Didn't I know Lilly's last name? I thought it was 'Hattie'. He was always calling her 'Lilly Hattie'.

"Who?" I asked trying not to appear caught off guard.

"Uhm, Lilly's Dad, Mr. Hattinson," he said sarcastically.

"I thought her last name was 'Hattie'. Don't you always call her 'Lilly Hattie'?" I inquired.

"Yeah, I do. But that's just a nickname. Mom, we were going out for like a month or two before you met her. I just always have called her that. But, really her last name is Hattinson. H-a-t-t-i-n-s-o-n. So, did you meet him or not? I think he's weird. He is always so quiet and so uninterested in anything we do or say. Was he different when you met him?"

My head was spinning. My stomach was in knots. I knew I was going to throw up. I coughed and swallowed hard. I had to get out of my car. I had to get into the house, be alone.

"No, I didn't meet him. He wasn't feeling well, Tyler."

I got out of the car and darted through the front door. I left Tyler standing there in my jet stream, staring at my absence. I wish I would have looked back at his face for just a second. I hustled up my stairs, taking two at a time. I locked my bedroom door behind me and pulled out my old address book and searched for Sarah's number. I couldn't recall her married name, so I feverishly flipped to the H's, and there I found it. I grabbed my cell and dialed the number.

It was disconnected. My mind screamed, this could not be happening! It had to be some bizarre coincidence. I also had an e-mail address for her, but it had been more than 5 years since we had last communicated.

I booted up my laptop and went to my e-mail. I searched for old correspondence from Sarah, but there weren't any. I had the same e-mail still – cWylder2229@yahoo.com. She could have looked for me, and I would have been easy to find. I e-mailed her and it bounced back almost immediately. I decided to Google her and discovered she was an adoption attorney in Austin. Or at least she had been. Lilly had told me she was adopted. My mind was still not so quick to believe that was a convenient coincidence. She must have placed the baby with Joshua and his wife. I couldn't remember now if it had been a boy or a girl. I only remembered crying myself to sleep for several nights after she had e-mailed me about it. I never heard from her again, and I'd just assumed it was her way of letting me know he was happy, he had a family and his life was full. I tried to picture the man I saw earlier in Lilly's kitchen. I wasn't looking for Joshua then, had no reason to believe that he was anything more than Lilly's father.

Oh.

My.

God.

I knew I was going to be sick. I ran to my bathroom and threw up. I vomited at least four times before there was nothing left in me but disbelief. As I progressed to dry heaving, the vilest truth emerged. If Joshua was here and Lilly was his daughter, then his son was dating his daughter! The fact that she wasn't his biologically would be of little comfort to Tyler. This would kill Tyler. This would destroy Lilly.

Every time I allowed myself to imagine the worst case scenarios from my choice, I never could have anticipated something like this! A decision I made when I was eighteen years old was going to tear apart our lives, gauging all the seams of comfort and love that I had spent years creating. It would not unravel neatly. It would be ripped and shredded until there was nothing left. And the only person that I could blame was me.

I lay down on the tile floor in my bathroom, pulled my knees tight to my chest and cried. I continued to cry. I couldn't stop crying. There were no words running through my mind or coming out of my mouth. There was nothing lucid to be said. There was nothing worthy of thought or consideration. My mistake would have colossal repercussions. And there was absolutely nothing I could do to prevent it from happening. Instead, I had to stand by and wonder and wait.

No, that would be the worst thing I could do. I at least had one strand of control left. I could tell Tyler before he happened to find out. Before the kids had to be told, I could go to Joshua. I would try to repair as much of the damage ahead of time as possible. I rose to my knees and tried to throw up again, but there was nothing left within me. I lay my head on the side of the toilet.

20

Tyler, 2010

For some unknown reason my mom had totally lost it. Over what? That I wasn't sure of. She freaked out over Lilly's last name. How bizarre was that? I probably should have gone after her, but I just didn't. I couldn't contain my happiness. I couldn't stop smiling. I went back in the house and cleaned up the dirty dishes. All I could think about was Lilly.

Lilly and me.

Lilly and me last night.

I did feel a little bit guilty that we had done it here in our house, on the couch. I had really thought our first time would have been somewhere more romantic. I had hoped to plan a get-away for a weekend this fall. I never imagined it would happen here because I never imagined she would spend the night here.

I don't know if I did things right or wrong. It wasn't even like I had to think about it. It all just happened. It was so natural. I didn't have time to be nervous or worried. I just wrapped my arms and mind around her and made love to her.

I missed her already. I went to my phone and sent her a text.

LAH – I'm thinking about you love you
Just the sight of her initials made me grin.
Lilly Angela Hattinson.

Again, I wondered why that mattered to my mom all of a sudden. I decided to go check on her, just to make sure she was okay. I walked up the stairs and noticed that the whole house seemed different to me. I felt different. I couldn't exactly say what was different about me, but I knew that last night had changed everything between Lilly and me.

I'd heard from my friends that sex really changes things for girls. I just figured that none of my friends had felt the same way I felt. I loved Lilly. I knew that. I wasn't like the guys who thought of nothing else. I had never regarded any woman like that. I guess that is what happens when you are raised by a mother and a great grandmother. All I've ever known are the sacrifices and the struggles.

Mom has always said I was the only thing she did right in her life, and when she said it, I believed her. She took raising me more seriously than anything else. I didn't realize it until recently, but I had always been her first and sometimes only priority. I had friends whose parents were divorced and all they seemed to care about was dating. A few of my friends had lost a parent, and the other parent usually fell, like into a brief coma. Eventually of course... they were out on the prowl, too.

Not my mom.

She had dated a few guys, and she really cared about Alex. But, even I could see she kept him at arm's length. He had even come to me one time, asking what was wrong with her. His exact words were, 'Who hurt her?'

"I guess it would be my father. She left him, and he never came to find her. I just don't think she has ever gotten over that."

"You know, not even death causes this kind of gut wrenching hurt. I can't get to her heart. I don't think anyone does, but you."

That was sad. I felt sadness for her now because I knew what it feels like to love someone so much that it is all you can think about. I also knew how it felt to have someone love you like that back. I was an expert on love. I laughed at myself. That was such a joke!

If any one of my friends heard me talking like this, I'd get the crap punched out of me. I mean I didn't get into it with the guys too much. I listened to them talk but just never had much to contribute. I thought how most of them were just like their dads, real assholes. I guess that is what made me different.

I stood outside Mom's door and lightly knocked before turning the knob, but it was locked. That was a first. I couldn't remember a time she had locked her door; very rarely did she even shut it. That took me back to last night. She had asked me to shut her door. Had she been giving me permission to have sex with Lilly? Did she know now? Is that why she was so upset?

I banged harder and kept turning her knob, like if I turned it enough, it would all of a sudden open. I yelled, "MOM! ARE YOU OKAY? WHY IS YOUR DOOR LOCKED?"

I put my ear to the door and listened hard for her to say something or make a sound. I heard the toilet flushing.

"Mom? Hey?" What was she doing in there?

"Calm down, Tyler. I'm fine." She said behind her closed door.

"Well, can I come in?" I asked, almost pleading with her. I didn't like the weird feeling of being locked away from her.

"Can I have a few minutes Tyler? Please?" she murmured. I could tell she was inches from me, standing behind her locked door.

"Mom? Just let me in, please?" I was begging now.

It was really quiet now. I couldn't hear her at all. She must just be standing there.

"Please, Mom. Please let me in." I slid down the door and sat with my back leaning against the door.

I put my head on my knees. I had never seen her act like this and she was totally freaking me out. I really couldn't remember a time when she'd just fallen apart. There may have been days like this, probably more than a few that I just hadn't known about it. She had always been so strong, stoic really. She was only a year older than I was now, when she got pregnant with me. It was kind of hard for me to visualize her like that. I knew she had struggled a lot.

But, I had a good life. I always considered myself so lucky. I didn't really think I had missed that much, until lately. I wished she had a husband. I wished I had a dad or at least some man I could talk to about last night. I had questions. I'm just not sure they were questions I wanted to ask my mom.

I felt my phone vibrate in my pocket. I had a text from Lilly.
TMW – love you back! Come get me, please!! Xoxoxo
I couldn't help but smile. Lilly made me that happy. I wanted to go to her, but what about my mom? She wasn't letting me in, and clearly she didn't want to talk to me. After a few more minutes, I walked to my room and decided to take a quick shower. I got dressed in a t-shirt and shorts. I laughed to myself; it was kind of my uniform. If I wasn't working or playing hockey, I was in shorts and a t-shirt. This was difficult in our terrible winters!

I walked back over to Mom's door; this time I knocked softly. I put my ear to the door again and heard her moving around in there. That was a good sign, even though the door was still locked. I took a deep breath and tried not to feel so agitated. I didn't know how to deal with her when she was like this! I'd never seen her like this!

"Mom? I'm going to go pick up Lilly. We are going to go get something to eat. Is that okay with you?" I noticed I didn't really ask. I was more or less telling her what I was going to do.

"That's fine, Tyler. Just remember you have practice early in the morning, so don't stay out too late." Her voice was flat.

Interesting! I was leaving at like 2 pm on a Sunday afternoon with my girlfriend, and was basically told I could stay out all day. Something was definitely wrong here, but I so didn't care. I ran down the stairs. I went into the trunk in the living room and got an old comforter. I went out to the garage and found a small ice chest, too. I grabbed some bottled waters and a few sodas. I noticed an unopened bag of chips on the counter and took them, too. I knew I would take Lilly to the river, and we could spend the afternoon there.

All I wanted to do was hold Lilly. I knew we would discuss what had happened last night and I'm sure she would want to talk it all out. She was a girl after all and girls loved to talk. I would listen and make sure that she knew how much I loved her and how important it had been for me.

I really didn't think we had a whole lot to discuss. Nothing changed, really. Except that I was more in love with her and I wanted her in a way that I couldn't really explain.

I got in my old jeep Wrangler and looked back at our house.

Suddenly it was no longer just my house, I could envision Lilly and I living in a house similar to this one. I visualized my whole future wrapped around her. It was easy to see. Suddenly, I felt like I got the wind knocked out of me. I had my future mapped out before. It hadn't included Lilly.

She was younger than me. She had two more years of high school, where I only had one. I was dead set on going to the University of Texas. It is all I ever imagined I would do. I suddenly was painfully aware of how far away that was. I would be a thousand miles away from Beacon Falls.

Then something struck me as totally ironic. Lilly was from Austin. I'm sure she had family there. My mom is here. During the semester there would be breaks and I could come home a couple of times. It would be fine. We would be fine. I just needed to calm down and not stress about things that were out of my control. That I totally got from my mom. She was always playing devil's advocate, wondering and worrying about things that may or may not happen.

I wasn't about to waste the next year and a half doing that. My senior year was going to be great. I was captain of the ice hockey team. I'd be starting strong safety on the football team. I had Lilly. Nothing could get any better than this! I looked down at the gas gauge and realized it was almost on empty. I pulled into a 7-Eleven and saw John walking out.

"Hey, Tyler!" John came jogging over.

We did our 'guy handshake' which is actually a hand swipe, grip and shake followed by a shoulder bump.

"Hey Buddy! What's going on?" I asked as I lifted the gas nozzle and placed it into my tank.

He stood next to me. "Not a lot. Haven't seen you much this summer? What have you been doing? Or should I say who have you been doing?" He knocked his elbow into my ribs and then punched my upper arm.

I almost blurted out what Lilly and I had done last night, but realized that I didn't want him or anyone to know. Not because it was a secret, but because it was that special.

"I'm not doing anybody, John. You know I'm dating Lilly. And it isn't like that! She isn't even 16 yet!" I tried not to sound too

155

pissed off at his insinuation.

"Geez, dude, chill out! I was just messing around." He looked annoyed.

"I know its chill." I said, not really meaning it, but not wanting him to think I was a douche either.

"We need to hang out, man. There is a party tonight at Danielle's house. I've been seeing her this summer. Her family's out of town, so it will be cool."

"Danielle, huh? How did that happen?"

We had gone to school with Danielle since like kindergarten. She was one of our best friends, too. Then when we all got to junior high, we divided into 'boys' and 'girls'. On occasion, if our moms got together, we would hang out and pretend that we hated each other. We were jerks for a couple of years, acting like we were too good to be friends with girls.

But, in reality, Danielle was cool. Whenever we would run into each other at school, she just nodded at me with a 'hey what's up' gesture. I just couldn't believe she was going out with John. He's got a reputation for treating girls more like objects than people. She was too good for him.

"It was kind of cool actually. Our parents got a beach house together this summer down in Destin. We were there for two weeks. At first, we were hanging out just because we were the only ones remotely the same age. Then one night, we went to watch some fireworks and while we were there, she reached over and held my hand." He paused. I could see that he had actually grown up *some since* the end of school. It was kind of nice to see.

"Then, I moved closer to her and we sat there for a long time, just holding hands. It was really cool. I didn't even kiss her that night."

"Wow! You? Really?" I teased him.

"I know, right? She was even kind of shocked. In fact, I didn't kiss her until the last night of our trip. I didn't want to screw up what was happening." He seemed like a little boy when he said that. I wondered if he was in love with her. It was weird to think that we might actually be growing up.

"Well, maybe we should double date then." I said.

I hadn't hung out with anyone but Lilly all summer, and I realized I kind of missed just chillin' with the guys, doing nothing.

"Yeah, let's do that. But, tonight, you guys will come right? It's not going to be a big blow out or anything. There will probably be beer and stuff. Just hanging out."

"Sounds good, bro." I slapped him on the back.

"See ya."

"Later."

I was really looking forward to senior year, and apparently I wouldn't be the only one with a girlfriend. That would make it even better. I wondered if Danielle knew anything about Lilly. It's not like our high school was that big.

I got in my car and heard U2's '*With or Without You*' playing on the radio. I love that song, even though it might be old. But long ago, Mom made me realize U2 is awesome. I cranked it up, and headed over to Lilly's. When I turned onto her street, I saw her sitting at the end of her driveway. She had a bag with her. As I got closer, I could see it wasn't her purse, but a pink polka dotted duffle bag.

I definitely didn't want her to think she could spend the night again. Mom would not be cool with that. I grew anxious and worried. I was not very good at telling Lilly no.

I pulled up and before I could even get to the driveway, she was running towards the passenger door. I reached over and opened it for her just as she got there and jumped in. She had evidently been crying. A lot. Great! She must have regretted last night and probably hated me. I prepared myself for the 'I love you, Tyler, but last night was a mistake' conversation. Damn it! I had screwed this up.

I looked up towards the kitchen window and saw her Dad glaring at me. Well, no actually, he was glaring at her. He looked furious. When our eyes met, he moved quickly away from the window.

"Go! GO Tyler! Go before he gets out here!"

For a second I froze until I noticed that their front door was opening. I quickly backed up and peeled out with Lilly's dad running after my jeep.

Lilly was bawling. "Keep driving Tyler, don't look back! Keep driving!"

21

Lilly, 2010

It is amazing how the best day of my life can become the worst in a matter of seconds. I was so exhilarated leaving Tyler's house this morning. Tyler was mine. I had hoped he was before, now I knew it for sure. I never imagined that I could love someone the way I love Tyler.

Driving home with Ms. Wylder, I mean, Carsen was so comfortable. We talked about next year and she knew I was so excited to be on the cheerleading squad. I was whining a little bit because on the junior varsity squad, I wouldn't be actually cheering for Tyler.

She said, "I have season tickets, so if you want to sit with me at the games, I would love it. Of course, it might be more fun if you ran around with your friends." She smiled at me. She looked like how I envisioned a very proud mother to appear. She graciously was letting me into their world and I was bursting with happiness. I couldn't remember ever feeling this good ever.

"Oh wow. That would be so much fun. Do you go to the away games, too?" I asked.

Right after I said it, I knew it was a stupid question. She didn't say anything, she just nodded. I didn't know how I had gotten so incredibly lucky. It was as if Austin and my mom didn't even exist. Like none of that had ever even happened. I had this great boyfriend who had a great mom and life was just going along as it should. Until we turned on to my street and I was slapped in the face with the reality of my life. My real life.

The life that I tried to run from every chance I got. I couldn't stand being at home. My father, my "Daddy" was now a total drunk. He was even drinking before he went to work in the morning. His 'coke' always had a funny smell to it. I don't think he realized that I knew. I knew a lot more than he thought I did.

I suspected he was sleeping with his paralegal. I'd heard her slither out one morning when they assumed I was still asleep.

I knew he was no longer working out or taking care of himself. As much as I wanted to hate him, I couldn't. He had brought me here and saved my life. So for that simple fact, I tried to cut him some slack. And look the other way as often as I could. It wasn't doing either of us any good, but I was too caught up in Tyler to honestly care too terribly much.

I wanted him to meet Carsen. I wanted him to see how a single mom did it, so he could try parenting with some dignity. I wanted him to get over the guilt, anger, sadness and whatever else was eating at him. I wanted him to be my Daddy again. I wanted him to be sober.

I thought if we got there early enough in the morning that he might not be visibly drunk, that I could introduce them. They could talk for a little bit, and then I might not be grounded for spending the night at their house. Although part of me thought I deserved to be grounded.

I did feel guilty for having sex in Carsen's house with her upstairs asleep. Even if she didn't know, I still felt like she would be disappointed in us. I had this sick feeling as we pulled into my driveway.

"Do you mind if I go in and make sure he's decent?" I asked beaming at Carsen.

"Of course, go right ahead," she replied.

She was really pretty. She didn't look like everyone else. She also didn't seem to be as self-absorbed as some of my friend's moms. I liked how she didn't feel like she had to wear make up everywhere. She had her curly hair pulled up in to a ponytail, but it was all tucked into the rubber band. She had beautiful eyes. They were big, green and she had the longest eyelashes. I knew where Tyler got his good looks.

I smirked at her. "I'll let you know when the coast is clear."

I hopped out of her car and jogged up to the front door. I expected the door to be locked, and instead when I went to turn the knob it pushed open.

"Dad?" I yelled.

"In the kitchen, Lilly," I could hear the agitation in his voice. I took a deep breath as I walked through the living room and crossed over to the kitchen. I could see that the back door was wide open and on the table by his favorite chair near the pool, I could see an empty bottle of Jack on its side. No wonder he couldn't come get me last night. I stopped just short of the kitchen. I took another deep breath, and made myself put on a smile. Kill him with kindness, I told myself.

"Hey you!" I said.

"Hey yourself! I can't believe you spent the night at your boyfriend's house!" He glared at me, staring me up and down, cutting into me with his disapproving stare.

"You look like you got rode hard and hung out to dry. You are turning into quite the little whore, aren't you?"

I felt like he had just slapped me in the face. I didn't know what to say. No matter what I said it would be a lie. But, I didn't think he should be talking to me like that! So even though I had no room to talk I decided to speak to him in the same way.

"Then I guess this would be a bad time to meet my boyfriend's mom, huh? You smell like whiskey. And it's more than apparent you are drunk! How about I go get her, huh, Dad?" I knew how important his reputation was to him.

He took a step back and peered out the window. "I'm sure she has already noticed you standing in here, without a shirt on. Lucky for you she can't see your eyes or smell you."

I was furious! How dare he be angry with me! If he had been able to pick me up last night, I wouldn't have HAD to spend the night.

"Besides, I should go tell her what a drunk you are! And that was why I couldn't come home last night! What would she think of you then?" I screamed at him.

"Look Lilly, I have a massive headache. I don't want to fight with you. But, the bottom line is spending the night at your boyfriend's house when you are fifteen is slutty. I shouldn't have called you a whore. That was wrong." He wouldn't look at me, but he still sounded very angry.

I tried to seem calm, "I'm sorry. We all really did fall asleep. In fact, that is why she is here. She wanted to explain to you how sorry she was, and to assure you that I slept on the couch, and Tyler slept in his room. There is nothing to tell, but she thought it would be better coming from her. I guess she was right. I'll go get her." I turned around to walk away from him.

"No you will NOT go get her! You will go out there and tell her what-ever the hell you want. But, she will not come into MY house. Do you hear me young lady?"

I hollered back over my shoulder, tears welling in my eyes and the sarcasm dripping off my words, "Yes sir."

He would die if he knew I told Carsen the truth, even though she so understood not getting to meet him. I figured the chances of them meeting were slim to none at this point. He was spiraling further and further out of control, and I seriously doubted they would ever run into each other, because Carsen didn't hobnob around town like my dad.

She didn't kiss anyone's ass. She was her own person with her own rules. That could be why I was so drawn to her. I wanted to be that kind of woman one day. But, I also secretly hoped to be married to Tyler one day, too. I thought I could have it all. I know that the odds of a high school romance being long term are a shot in hell, but it was done. I couldn't imagine ever not being with Tyler. He was the one!

When I came back in from talking to Carsen, Dad was waiting for me.

"Look, we need to talk," he said.

I walked right past him and went out to the pool. I picked up the bottle of Jack Daniels, and said, "Will you and I be speaking? Or will I be talking to Jack?" There was a sharper edge to my voice that he definitely picked up on.

"It doesn't matter what I do, Lilly. I'm the adult here. You are the child. So I'm the one who's going to give the lecture here, and you are going to sit down and listen."

I wondered how we got here. I guess while I was busy being a teenager and falling in love with Tyler, he was left to his own devices. In those months he had turned into a belligerent drunk.

I began to feel less hostility, only because I felt sorry for him. I sat down willing to admit at the very least, this should be inter-esting. I wondered if I would get the 'sex' talk now. Certainly he knew that I was long past needing that. He had seen the pictures. He knew I wasn't a 'good' girl. I just don't think he knew or real-ized how much I had changed. I'm sure that was hard to see from the bottom of a bottle.

"I got a call from your Aunt Sarah last night. She is coming in tomorrow."

He sat down right in front of me on the coffee table. He was staring at me and for just a second, I was a little bit scared.

"Did something happen to Grandma? Is Seth okay?" I questioned.

"No, they are all fine," and his face tightened, "Have you talked to your friend Andrea lately?" His eyes turned almost black. He looked so angry.

Hearing that name, I immediately tensed up. It was odd that he was mentioning her. Since the first few weeks after moving here I hadn't heard from her. But, she had recently texted and called me more times than I cared to count. I hadn't returned any of them. I didn't want to do anything that would remind me of those last few days in Austin.

He was studying my reaction. I tried really hard to not shift or move. "No, I have not spoken with Andrea in months." That was the truth, that wasn't a lie.

"Interesting," was all he said.

"Is that all then, Dad?" I got up to leave.

"Sit down young lady. NOW."

I sat down quickly. "What is your problem? If you are mad because I stayed at Tyler's last night, then…"

He interrupted me, "It's not really my problem, Lilly. It's more your problem." He cocked his head sideways, keeping his eyes on me. "Could you maybe tell me what the problem might be, Lilly? Do you have any idea?" He was beyond angry. I didn't even recognize this tone.

I stiffened. Something had transpired. It must have something to do with that night. The night I never let myself think about. I never let myself consider the possibilities. I knew what it could mean, but if it wasn't, I didn't want to bring it up. Maybe it was something totally different. But, he had asked about Andrea. And the last time I was with Andrea was the night my mother died, the same night that we hit something down by Park Bridge.

I began to shake my head. I was not going to think about it. I was not going to consider it. I was not going to say a word. I would let him tell me what he knew.

"I don't know what you are talking about," I tried to keep my voice steady and even. I couldn't look at him in the eyes though. It had been so long since I had lied to him, it was as if I didn't know how to anymore. I didn't mean to, but I could feel the tears starting to build. I bit my lip and fought against them very hard.

"Well, how about this then, Lilly? Your Aunt Sarah will be here tomorrow with all the details. Just make sure you have a good story to tell her since you obviously aren't going to tell me anything." He got up and walked to the wet bar, he took out a new bottle of Jack, and opened it up. He poured himself a drink and gulped it as our eyes were locked.

"Enjoy the rest of your day, Lilly. It all ends tomorrow." He glared at me and slammed the back door to the pool.

I grabbed the phone out of my back pocket and there was a text from Tyler. I told him to come get me. I ran back into my room, and I stuffed a few t-shirts, shorts, panties and a bra into a duffle bag. Then I went into the bathroom and grabbed my make-up bag and my toothbrush. I was not going to think about tomorrow, or last year or my mom the rest of today. If my world was going to come crashing down tomorrow then I was going to spend the rest of the day with Tyler.

I ran out the front door, half expecting my Dad to come running after me. I waited for a few minutes, expecting the front door to open. It never did. I began to cry. Everything was going to fall apart tomorrow. There was nothing I could do to change that. No matter how far we had gone, I was not going to be able to outrun my past. I was going to have to face it head on.

I just prayed that Tyler would be able to forgive me. I wasn't quite sure if I would tell him today or not. I would have to wait and see how the day went. I continued crying, thinking about not having Tyler love me anymore. It was more than I could stand.

When he pulled up, I jumped up and ran to his jeep. When I looked back at the house, I saw my dad come outside yelling at me, and I just begged Tyler to drive and get me out of there. Tyler loved me enough to drive away as fast as he could.

I still wasn't sure what I was going to tell Tyler. A big part of me wanted to tell him the truth, tell him everything. But, a small part of me was hoping he would never have to know about anything that happened in Austin. I was a totally different person since moving to Beacon Falls, and a lot of it had to do with meeting Tyler. But I had also made a conscious effort to change. I had decided to become a better person and live my life in a less self-deprecating way.

Last night was proof that it had worked. Tyler had made love to me, Tyler loves me. I wondered how strong that love was though. It was new. I wasn't sure it could withstand my past. I just didn't think I could tell him now. My day had already been awful. All I wanted to do was get wrapped up in Tyler and forget about what was happening tomorrow.

Tyler reached over and took my hand. He took my hand to his lips and kissed it gently, while keeping his eyes on the road. He didn't say anything. He respected my silence.

I leaned my head back and closed my eyes. I tried to push my father's words out of my head. I just wanted to be with Tyler, one more time just in case something happened tomorrow, and my choices were no longer my own.

I looked over at him. I wished I knew what he was thinking. I had an idea though. I assumed he was worried about me. I loved that he worried about me.

"Hey, Tyler?" I finally said.

"Hey Lilly Hattie!" He said in a sing song way trying to lighten the mood.

I smiled at him. "Where are we going?"

"Where do you want to go?" He glanced over at me, and I could see confusion in his eyes.

I glanced in the backseat and saw the cooler and huge comforter. He knew exactly where I wanted to go.

"You are too good to me, Tyler Mathews." I turned a little in my seat to face him. I just wanted to watch him. I still couldn't believe that we were together. That we were dating or that we had fallen in love. I didn't even used to believe in love.

I thought of my dad and our fight. I wondered if he had ever loved anyone like this. I seriously doubt it. That made me feel almost happy inside. He had turned into such an awful person lately. I couldn't stand to be near him. I was dreading school starting, because that meant my time with Tyler would be limited and my time at home would be more than I could take.

We pulled up at the dam. Tyler parked his jeep, but didn't get out immediately. Instead he took off his seat belt and turned to me. He put his hands on both sides of my face. It was like he was holding my head above water, so that I didn't drown. I closed my eyes trying to stop the tears from coming. The next thing I felt was Tyler's lips on mine. They were short, sweet kisses.

"Lilly? Did you tell your dad about last night? Is that what is wrong?" Tyler questioned.

I shook my head.

"Good. What happened then? If you want to tell me, then I am here for you. If you don't want to tell me, I am still here for you. You just let me know what I need to do to help you through this," he whispered in my ear.

He got out of the car and came around to my side. He opened the door for me. I just couldn't seem to move. He reached in and undid my seat belt for me, and took both my hands. He pulled on me just a bit, and I began getting out of the jeep. I wanted to speak, but I couldn't find my words.

"Come on, we just have a little ways to walk, Lill."

We walked over to our spot. He put the comforter down and pulled a couple of bottled waters out of the cooler. He sat down and opened his arms to me. I fell into his lap. I rested my head on his chest and curled up between his legs. He began playing with my hair at the nape of my neck, he knew it relaxed me. He kissed me gently on the back of my head and then rested his chin there.

I had never felt more loved or protected. I closed my eyes and relied on his strength.

22

Carsen, 2010

I couldn't face Tyler. I was relieved when he said he was leaving. I had so much to think through.

I had so many things to consider. Yet every time I tried to digest the fact that Joshua was here, living in Beacon Falls, I had to run to the bathroom. There was nothing in my stomach, but that didn't stop the urge.

I had known this day would come, but I always thought that I would be in more control of it. I always thought I could plan for it. Obviously Joshua didn't know about Tyler. Tyler had spent time over there, not much time, but I know he had met him.

I could only believe that Sarah could have done this. But, I didn't understand why. Why would she send him here and not warn me? Did she think we would just run into each other and think it was a coincidence? Did she think that either of us even wanted to see the other?

I had tucked away my feelings for Joshua. I had them locked in a vault in the recesses of my heart. I didn't let myself access those feelings. I didn't let myself go there very often, because after all these years the pain was still as devastating as it was the day I left Seabrook. We had unfinished business; we had unanswered questions, and those things allowed me to hold on to the tiniest thread of hope.

I hoped that one day I could reconcile my choices, my decisions, and my fears and protect my son in the process. But now, it was all going to come crashing down and there was nothing I could do. I forced myself from my bed and unlocked the door. Tyler had been gone for over an hour, and I assumed they weren't coming back here.

As I walked slowly down the hall, things looked different to me now, I feel like everything is tainted now. I descended the stairway in a haze of trepidation. I got a glass of old-fashioned tap water and stared out my kitchen window. I had worked so hard to build this life for Tyler and myself. I felt a powerful need to protect him.

Joshua couldn't hurt me anymore, but he could hurt Tyler. I couldn't even let myself think about Tyler and Lilly. I recognized they weren't related, but found little comfort in that. This was a mess that I had made. And I had to figure out the right way to clean it up.

I leaned against the counter and thought about Joshua. I discerned he wasn't doing well. I would assume losing your wife, the love of your life, could lead you to drink. I knew what it had done to my father and our family. I didn't want that for him or for Lilly. She was a great girl.

He had done a good job raising her until the last few months, according to Lilly. I couldn't believe that I had been staring at him just this morning. Joshua had been less than 20 feet from me and I had no idea.

I walked out the back door and sat on the steps. I could feel a slight breeze sweep over my skin. I wanted to just go back in time. Back to yesterday when everything seemed less important, less urgent. I wanted to go back so that I didn't have to deal with what was paralyzing me now. A night that we spent together that last summer came back to me. Memories are so shrewd. They are like an uninvited, unannounced house-guest appearing from nowhere.

A bunch of us girls went to the movies in the late afternoon. I can't remember what we saw, maybe Pretty in Pink? I don't know why I thought it was that movie, but I think it was. He just showed up there. I remember thinking, 'Oh great, he must be into one of my friends now. '

I wasn't sure I could handle that. So far, anyone that had seized his attention had been younger than us, and I just pretended that I could care less who he dated. I recalled Gabby asking me why he was there. He had overheard her question, and when I looked his way, he nodded at me and grinned. It was still our secret. I had blankly stared back at him.

At some point during the movie, I got up and went to the bathroom. My stomach was upset, and I thought I was going to get sick. I bought a Sprite and went back to my seat. He was sitting in it however when I got back. I remember thinking 'what a dork.' I sat in the seat next to him and stared at him totally irritated at how careless he was behaving.

I leaned over and whispered, "What are you doing?"

"I didn't like sitting way over there. Is that a problem?"

"Not a problem, but don't you think somebody will think it's weird?"

"You are so paranoid. Who cares? These are your friends anyway. Won't they ask you if they think something is up?"

That bothered me. He usually is the one trying to make sure no one knows anything. I tossed my hair back I so just didn't care right now. He is just too hard for me to figure out. I lifted my legs up and rested my ankles on the chair in front of me. I felt a tickle under my right thigh. His hand was resting on my seat. I was completely enamored with him. It was part of the fun of our secret, possibly getting found out. He was getting brave or stupid, I'm not sure which. He scooted closer to my seat, like he was going to lean over to whisper something to me, but instead he put his hand inside my shorts. I brought my left leg down and shifted as I crossed my legs over his hand. He leaned back in his chair, a sly devious smirk on his face. It was that grin that got me every single time.

My heart recalled that smile, that grin. It skipped a beat.

When the movie was over, we all walked out together. When it was time to get into cars, he yelled out "Hey, Carsen? Ride with me?"

I quickly looked at my girlfriends but no one seemed to suspect a thing about it. Gabby looked at me and said, "Ok cool, go with him, then I can take these guys home. They are on my way. You are not!"

I hadn't thought of Gabby, Stacy or Vivian much over the years. We had been really close our senior year of high school. But, once I started sleeping with Joshua, I distanced myself because I hated lying to them. That was the last night I saw them. None of us had any idea that it would be the last time we would spend together. I wouldn't come home for reunions, weddings or visits. I felt very sad about that. I felt like a terrible friend.

I was only now, as an adult, fully grasping everything else that I had given up. But, all I had to do was think about Tyler and I remembered why I did what I did. I had hoped one day I would be able to explain it to them. I had thought that if they were truly my friends, then they would understand.

I said good night and then walked with Joshua to his Dodge truck. I couldn't remember which number vehicle this was. I knew he had wrecked at least one other car, maybe two. "I can't believe your parents got you a new truck. You are so spoiled."

"Yeah, I am. I am used to getting what I want."

"I know. I'm used to giving you what you want," my voice sounded sadly submissive. I wondered if he would even notice.

"You say that like it's a bad thing, Car."

He was watching me intently now waiting to start the car until I said something. But, I didn't know what to say. Do I start a fight with him? Would that make things easier? I took a deep breath, but no words came to me. I twisted in my seat away from him. I just stared out the window, waiting for him to just start the car.

"Do you have to go home, Carsen?" he inquired.

I hesitated before answering. I still hadn't decided what I was going to do or say. I wasn't able to fight the attraction, it was too great. And if he made any attempt to kiss me or touch me, I would be putty in his hands. If we fought, he'd just drop me off and that would be that.

"Why?" I wondered out loud.

"Did I do something? Are you mad at me?"

I spun around and looked at him, but instantly my willpower melted away. The way he looked at me said he was genuinely concerned that I was angry with him. "No, I'm not mad at you. I'm just in a bad mood," I lied. I really wasn't angry, I was incredibly sad.

"Well, I know just what to do about that." He moved closer to me and kissed me. He kissed me gently at first, but then they came faster and soon we were both breathing heavier. I pushed him back gently, trying to get him off of me. He looked rejected.

I batted my eyelashes at him and playfully said, "Now now, you big baby! I'm not saying no, I'm saying not here. Do you not notice we are under a light sitting here in this parking lot?"

"Woman, you know when you do that with those big green eyes, I can't think straight," he looked away slowly.

"Where do you want to go?" There was a little bit of teasing in my tone.

"Why don't we go swimming?"

"Well I don't have a swim suit. I don't think I can go swimming." I reached over and took his hand. He started the car, and drove out of the parking lot.

"Well, that makes two of us, then." He looked over at me and grinned, lifting his eyebrows. He is the devil and he knows just what to do and say.

He turned on the radio and The Outfield came on. "I Don't Want to Lose Your Love Tonight" was playing. I took my hand out of his, and punched him lightly on the arm.

"Are you kidding me? Did you like plan that? Just in case I said I wanted to go home?" The playful smile on my face and the flicker in my eyes gave me away. Sometimes he was just too much. I leaned back in the seat and closed my eyes. He rolled the windows down, and I got lost in the song. I would think about everything else tomorrow.

I hadn't made my mind up yet about what to do about the baby and telling him. Tonight would be just like any other night I had spent with Joshua. I deserved to enjoy it. And maybe one day, he would recollect and smile when he remembered me.

We were going to the same place we had been frequenting all summer. It was a new subdivision developing along the river, a few miles from the state highway. During the day, it was buzzing with construction workers and traffic, but at night it was desolate. None of the houses were complete; our haven was a slab and frame near the water. Joshua had found our secret retreat early in the summer, so from then on we'd come here when we wanted to be alone.

There was a constant rhythm to the moonlight dancing on the lake and to the sounds of the croaking frogs and chirping crickets fighting to be heard. Some nights Josh and I just lay under the stars and talked. One breezy night we had fallen asleep and woke up when we heard a truck pulling in. The construction guys whistled and made crude gestures. Joshua signaled them a 'thumbs up' while I threw a towel over my head. We'd been hiding out for so long that I didn't even want strangers to know we were together.

I was still so terrified that he would lose interest once we were no longer a secret. I should have been able to tell him my fears since he knew everything else about me. I just couldn't bring myself to trust him wholly with my heart. I feared he would unintentionally break it.

When we got to our special hideout, I noticed the moon wasn't shining very brightly. We got out of the truck and he pulled my old comforter out of the trunk.

"How did you get that?" I inquired.

"I stole it from your house," he said playfully.

"Obviously. But, why? You don't have any blankets at your house?" I stood with my hands on my hips, baiting him.

"My mom catalogs every sheet set and blanket. I would be dead if I took one from our house."

"Ahhh. I see your point. My mom won't notice though?"

"No, I told her I was taking it." He held the comforter up to hide his face.

"WHAT?" I raised my voice at him.

"Well, she kind of caught me taking it. She snuck up behind me! So, I turned and told her that my vinyl seats were really hot in the summer and I wanted to lay it down on the back seat. She said that was fine."

"Well, what else would she say? Oh my God, Joshua. She's not THAT stupid!"

Of course, I knew that she already suspected that we were more than friends. I just had tried to play it off, but now, I'm sure she knew. It didn't really matter though.

Nothing really mattered that much to me at this point. Nothing but him. It had always been him. It would always be him.

"Whatever, Josh. I swear you are so stupid sometimes."

"Yeah, but you know you want me!"

I whipped around, facing him. "Yeah, I do want you. It's that obvious, huh?"

He was in front of me by now. I was so short I barely came up to his shoulders. He bear-hugged me and took me down to the ground in one quick movement. He was fast when he knew what he wanted.

I rolled myself on top of him and sat up, straddling him. His hands were on my thighs, rubbing up and down gently. There was that smile again. I flipped my hair over to one side and leaned down over his face, my hands on either side of his body. Our eyes were locked. I stayed there, gently rocking back and forth. He bent his knees and I rested against his thighs. I sat up again. I was nervous!

I leaned back over him and kissed him. Normally, he would

pull me down on him, and then it would all just happen so fast my head would spin. Instead he just kissed me back, gently. He pulled my hair back away from my face and smoothed it down my back. He cupped my face with his hands.

"What is going on with you?" he whispered.

He didn't let go of my face, he was staring hard into my eyes, searching for something.

I looked past his face, off into the distance. "I told you, I am in a bad mood."

"No you aren't, at least not anymore. There is something different, something is wrong." So he must have decided now to be perceptive. Now was the time he chose to give some sincere attention to me and my behavior? Seriously?

"Summer's ending soon. Maybe I'm just a little sad."

He was studying me as if he had never seen me before. "Maybe, but I think there is something you aren't telling me. Something you are hiding from me."

He dropped his hands from my face, and I rolled off of him. I had my back to him now, and he wrapped himself around me. I'm sure he was worried that now he wasn't going to get laid. I always assumed that was in the forefront of his mind every time we were together.

"Well aren't you Mr. Know It All tonight," I scoffed. "Does it really matter if there is something wrong with me? It's not like it matters to you one way or another."

He removed his arms from my body and jostled himself away from me, turning on his side. "Great! So you do want to fight. So, what are we fighting about tonight? Let's get it over with." His shitty sarcasm was dripping off every word he said.

"Yeah, let's get it over with so you can get off, right Josh? I mean that is all I am to you." I had to fight back the tears.

That wasn't fair; I knew that wasn't all I meant to him. He didn't have to get it from me; there were lots of other girls who would love to be with him.

"I hate it when you do this. You get mad at me, and I don't even know why. You know very well it's not just about the sex, Carsen. We are friends... we are best friends." He stopped for a minute. "Are you not okay with this anymore? All you have to do is say the word and it's done."

It was just as I had always suspected. "I'm not doing anything, Joshua. I am just wondering why we ever let it go this far? Why we have been doing this for so long? I mean, it seems like we ARE dating. Doesn't it?"

We were still lying back to back, not touching. I was breaking all the rules and I was grateful that I didn't have to look at him. But, I had nothing to lose. I heard him take a deep breath. He seemed a bit more relaxed and less tense than he was a few minutes prior. This wasn't our first fight on this topic.

"Carsen, we never said we wouldn't start dating. I thought you didn't want to ruin our friendship. It's what we agreed to." His voice was calm and the tone was even. "Are you saying you want more now? Do you want to be my girlfriend, Carsen?"

I couldn't ask that of him when I knew what I might be doing to him soon, leaving him and taking his child with me. I remained still and kept my back to him. Did I want to be his girlfriend? That is precisely all I had ever wanted. I had just never let myself even dream about it.

"Maybe," I whispered through my soft sobs.

He was quiet again. I had no idea what he was thinking. I had no idea what he was feeling. I was too embarrassed to turn and face him. I knew if I rolled over and started kissing him, we could just pretend this conversation never happened. But, I was still looking for some sign to tell me what the right decision was, so instead I lay still and waited for him to say something.

If felt like forever, but he finally snuggled up next to me again and wrapped his arm around my waist.

His lips were at my ear, and I could feel his slow and steady breath. I covered his hand with mine and entwined my fingers into his. I leaned into him, but still said nothing.

He spoke first, "How long have you felt differently?"

I sighed. "I don't know. It just kind of happened," I tried to repress the embarrassment in my voice.

"I wish you would have told me when you realized it."

"Why does it matter when I started feeling more than friendship for you? It's not like it changes anything, Joshua," I whispered to him.

173

"Of course it changes things, Carsen. I just don't know how."

"It doesn't have to change anything, I'm sure I'll get over it. Just forget I said anything. Please, Josh?" I begged him.

I rolled over to face him now, and I moved quickly to begin kissing him. His hands were on my hips and I pushed gently into him. He kissed me back hard. I melted into him. I wanted him to remember these sultry nights and still mornings long after the heat and I were gone. I didn't want him to tell me anything right now, I didn't want to hear that he didn't feel the same way about me.

He pondered his response for too long; the answer was revealed in what he didn't say, not in what he might have said. He was nothing if not predictable. To him, the conversation was removed as easily as my shorts. I didn't want to want him or need him as much as I did.

I hated myself for falling in love with him. I hated myself even more for not telling him how I felt.

Even if it didn't change anything, I should have told him the truth. We kept kissing for longer than usual; it felt like he was almost hesitant to go any further. I straddled him as I tossed aside my shirt. I just couldn't make eye contact with him. I was afraid that I would crumble and spill every detail of my feelings.

I was relying solely on the physical attraction I had for him, and trying to bury the emotions behind it.

I got up quickly. I flung off my bra and panties and ran for the water. He was up in a flash and a few steps behind me. Moments later, Joshua and I made love in the water. Then we made love again on the comforter. We fell asleep for a while, but I woke him up a few hours later and we made love one more time. That last time was very passionate.

Nothing had been resolved; the conversation had been forgotten, and he knew I wouldn't bring it up again. He had to know that by not saying anything, he had said it all. I kissed him with no regret and no hesitation. I wanted this to last. I wanted tonight to be the best night he ever spent with me. Who was I kidding? I needed these memories and I wanted to hold on to them for as long as I possibly could.

I needed them to get me through all the coming months and

years. I would only want to remember him as tender and loving. I wanted to pretend that he loved me back a little bit, just enough to hold on to. Every time he said my name, my heart fractured a little bit. There was so much familiarity between us, we knew what each other liked and we made love with persistence and ease.

I was voracious for him. Physically, I wasn't holding anything back. The benefit of knowing that you have already lost everything is that you have nothing left to lose and no reason to be reserved. Afterwards, I lay in his arms, as always with my back to him. We were both very quiet.

He finally broke the silence, "That was amazing, Carsen. I didn't even know it could be like that."

I wondered if he was thinking about our earlier conversation, but I didn't want to ruin the moment. I let my breathing become much slower. I wanted him to think I was asleep.

Eventually, I must have drifted off. In my dreams I heard him say, "I love you, Carsen."

Then he was kissing me awake. Mornings had always been his favorite time of the day. We made love one more time, it was quick. He kissed me the entire time. I just quit thinking about anything else but kissing him and him touching me. I savored the moment. The sun would be up soon, and we needed to go. He fell asleep again, so I got up and got dressed. I went to the water's edge and just sat for a few minutes.

I said goodbye to Joshua, the only way I knew how. I had given in to him last night, over and over.

I hoped that one day he would realize how much I must have loved him, to be able to do that, to be able to love him enough to let him go.

I walked back over to our spot and knelt down beside him. Ever since the first time I saw him sleep, I loved watching him. I glanced at my watch and it was 5:45 am. I kissed his cheek. "Joshua, we have to go. It's almost sunrise."

He looked at me like he was seeing me for the first time. His eyes were glassy and half open. I don't think he at first recalled where he was. He rubbed his eyes again. He was exhausted, I could see that too.

His eyes began to focus and he smiled at me, "Wow," was all he said.

While he got dressed, I folded up the comforter and ran my hand across it, trying to memorize how soft it was, how it had felt against our bodies last night. I wanted to make sure that I never forgot a single minute of last night. He popped the trunk open, and I let the comforter fall in, knowing it was going to have to carry me through a lifetime.

We drove in silence, except for some music playing softly in the background. I felt him look over at me more than once, but I never permitted myself to look back at him. I knew his face could change my mind. When we got to my house, he turned the car off. Before he could say anything, I was out of my seatbelt, and I was hugging him. He held me tight.

I brushed his neck with my lips, then his cheek before reaching his lips. We kissed for just a few seconds. I closed my eyes and sighed. How was I going to be able to say goodbye to my best friend?

His hands were on my waist and mine were in his hair. Finally, I pulled away. He had to know we weren't doing this again today.

I glanced down for a few minutes and then gazed up into his beautiful blue eyes. He was about to speak and as much as I wanted to hear what he had to say, I just couldn't let him say anything. I put my finger to his lips.

"Please, Josh, please don't say anything. Last night was incredible. It was more than I ever thought it could be. But, let's not ruin its perfection by talking about it. I just want to remember it for the perfect night it was. Can we do that?" I batted my eyelashes at him.

His eyes were telling me no, he almost seemed a bit hurt, but he nodded. He kissed my fingers.

I got out of his car and walked into my house. I turned back around to look at him one last time. He saw me, and he smiled at me. I saw him mouth the words "I will call you later". I waved at him, smiling.

I knew he would call me later. I knew I would see him again tonight. I also knew that he would never love me the way I wanted him to. In that moment, I decided that I would leave at the end of summer.

I had hoped for a change in our relationship, and I believed that one had occurred last night. Unfortunately, it wasn't the change I had hoped for. I would spend the next month untangling him from my heartstrings, carefully.

As I sat there outside my Connecticut kitchen, I remembered that summer day like it was yesterday. I was so afraid that I had made the wrong decision then. I couldn't afford to make the wrong decision again now. I conceded I had to go to Joshua.

I had to tell him I was here. I had to find out what he knew and tell him the truth about everything.

He needed to know, and I could no longer run.

For once I didn't over think it, I didn't over analyze it. I grabbed my car keys and left before I could rationalize anything else. I had to get to Joshua. I wasn't sure what was leading me to him, my guilt-ridden conscience or my forlorn heart. I realized it didn't matter.

By the time I reached his neighborhood, it was dark. I had lost most of the day. But, all I cared about was seeing him. As I pulled into his driveway, I felt sick again. I warned myself that he might not be happy to see me.

I had no idea how he felt about me, if he had even thought about me once. He might not care at all that I was here. I prepared myself as much as I could for the rejection I might face.

I walked up to his front door and paused before I knocked. Everything I had ever thought I wanted and everything that I had run from was on the other side of the door. The past I'd fled from and my future were about to collide.

I braced my body and soul. My heart needed protecting; it really hadn't strengthened much over the last eighteen years. My draw to Joshua had not waned. My thirty-seven year old heart wanted this. I knocked on his door and felt my heart start to rupture, again.

23

Joshua, 2010

I didn't want to really stop Lilly from leaving. I just had to make it look good. I needed her out of here. I had to think and I had to do it with as clear a mind as I could manage. I hadn't had anything to drink since that glass this morning. I knew the alcohol was still in my system, but I wasn't going to drink at all today.

Tomorrow I would have the police report, the facts and the information from the lawyer that Sarah had hired. Sarah would be here. I wouldn't be alone. We would handle this together. She would help both Lilly and I get through this.

I had changes to make. I couldn't keep living with all this guilt. I couldn't be angry with Lilly either.

She is just a kid. And she's had a rough time. I watched as she drove off with Tyler. He was a good kid.

He was always there for her. He was going to make one hell of a man someday. I felt a pang of jealousy.

I thought back to who I was going to be. The kind of man I envisioned myself growing into.

I sat down on the steps on my front porch. I'm sure the neighbors would be so grateful to see me sitting out here with no shirt on. I should probably get up and go inside. I should go out to the pool. The sunshine would do me some good.

I looked up and saw Mrs. McGrath staring at me through her window. I waved and got up. I shook my head I didn't even want to think what she or any of my other neighbors must think of my behavior over the last couple of months.

I walked through the house and went to my room and grabbed a polo shirt and put it on. Then I walked back through the house and opened up all the blinds. If I was going to face all that was coming, I would need to do it with my eyes open and all the lights on metaphorically speaking.

I started to feel a little bit better. I felt shaky and I knew that was due to the alcohol but I knew I could beat that. I went to the kitchen and cleaned it up. It was no wonder why Lilly couldn't stand to be here, it was depressing and dirty. Unfortunately it was Sunday afternoon, and there was no way I could get a cleaning service in here before Sarah got here. I would have to do it.

But, before I did that, I decided to take a couple bottles of water and head out to the pool. Why did I let it get this bad? Everyone deserves a chance at redemption, don't they? I had a lot of making up to do for Lilly. I owed that much to Lauren. I let myself grieve my wife. I missed Lauren.

I didn't miss her like most husbands might miss their wives. I hadn't loved Lauren like that. I had loved her more like a best friend. I had tried to give her a good life because I thought that made up for everything else that was lacking in our marriage. I guess she was happy. But I know nothing made her happier than being a mother. It was all she had ever wanted.

She was probably turning over in her grave seeing what I had done lately. I had done the right thing leaving Austin though. Lilly was in trouble. She was making terrible choices and throwing her life away.

Sarah had been so right to have us come here. It was the best thing for her. I should probably get into some counseling.

I would need some help getting through all that had happened and all that was about to happen. If Lilly had been in the car that hit Lauren, then things were going to crumble. Part of me wanted to crawl back into the bottle. It would make it all seem less real, less painful.

However, that was just a cop out. I never thought I would become that man. I had become the man that just gives up on everyone and everything in his life. In reality, it did make things easier, for a while.

And then when the booze wears off, everything is there again. The pain, the hurt, the anger and the despair and each time, it gets worse. The tears came easy then. I just let myself cry. I cried for Lauren.

I cried for Lilly. I cried for the life we lost. I cried for all the mistakes I had made since that terrible night.

I must have fallen asleep at some point. The next thing I knew I was waking up to pounding on my front door. It was dark outside now. I looked at my watch and saw it was after 9p. Maybe it was Lilly. When she ran out of here, she must have forgotten her keys. I turned on the front porch light and opened the front door. The woman standing there looked almost lost.

"Hello. Can I help you?" I asked.

She was staring at me. She didn't speak. She just stared at me. She turned a bit pale she looked like a deer caught in the headlights. She tilted her head to the right very slowly. Then she moved her hands to her hair, and ran them through her curls.

I leaned against the door, and asked again, "Uhm. I'm sorry, can I help you?"

She was a very pretty woman. She had huge green eyes and dark lashes. Her eyebrows were perfectly arched. She had a lot of curly hair. It was beautiful. She was wearing Capri jeans and an oversized white shirt. She had on little make-up. She had a full face with the cutest cheeks. I looked her up and down, trying to figure out if I knew her. She started to back away from me.

Instinctively I moved towards her. 'Are you okay?" I asked.

"I'm so sorry. I shouldn't have come. This was a mistake." When I heard her voice, my heart skipped a beat.

She turned and ran towards her car. I followed her. It was the same Range Rover that had brought Lilly home this morning. "Hey! Wait! You are Tyler's mom, right?"

She was trying to get her door opened. She stopped. She stood very still for a few minutes. I couldn't figure out what was going on. I walked closer, slowly. "Hey, did you want to come in?"

She still wouldn't turn around. This was quite awkward. I tried to think about her voice though. It had struck me when she spoke. It sounded familiar. It was comforting. But, I knew I had never met her before.

I decided she wasn't going to face me, so I started to walk away slowly, just in case she changed her mind. I looked back to see if she was looking at me, but she wasn't. I shook my head and continued up the walk.

"Joshua," I heard her whisper.

Her voice stopped me. I turned around and she was facing me

now. I walked slowly towards her.

I was staring at her. She had tears in her eyes. Her eyes were begging me, but I didn't know for what exactly.

"Joshua. It's me," she said timidly.

I reached her and cocked my head to the left. I could see that she knew me. She reached her hand out to mine and gently touched me. "It's me, Carsen."

My head shook involuntarily. I yanked my hand from hers like she had burned me.

"What did you say?" I almost didn't recognize the words that came out of my mouth; they were filled with anger and bitterness. "Who did you say you were?"

I didn't need her to answer for me. It was Carsen Wylder. Now I could see that it was her. She was older, but she didn't look her age. Her hair was a different color lighter or darker I really couldn't remember.

The years had been good to her. Her eyes hadn't changed a bit. My heart was beating too fast.

I never thought I would ever see her again. Emotions and feelings I wasn't comfortable with began to surface.

"I should go. I shouldn't have come. I just had to see if it was you. I'm sorry," she was crying now. The tears were streaming down her face.

"What? You don't get to come here and then just leave? What the hell are you doing here?" I yelled at her.

I couldn't piece this all together. She was Tyler's mother? She lived here in Beacon Falls?

"I will stay, I owe you that much. But, please, don't scream at me, not out here. Can we go inside, please?"

She didn't even try to hide her tears. It wasn't the first time I had seen her cry. She looked nervous and scared. It was amazing to see someone, standing in front of you, that you hadn't seen in what 19 or 20 years? Someone I really never thought I would ever see again. Carsen, the girl that I had thought of more than I should have over the years, was standing in front of me. I couldn't believe she was here, standing in front of me, crying.

"Uh, yeah, I guess."

I stepped aside to let her go in front of me. She walked past me like a timid animal that was going to be punished for chewing up a favorite shoe or something. I guess I had scared her with my yelling. But, I couldn't let her leave without talking to her. It was so surreal. We walked into my house. She moved over and stood in the entry way as I shut the door.

She had her arms wrapped around her chest, like she was protecting herself. The tears were still falling down her face. I wanted to reach over and wipe them away. I didn't ever like to see her cry, not now and not then.

"Let's sit down in the Living Room."

I couldn't bring myself to say her name out loud. I was afraid if I did, she might disappear and I would find out this was all a cruel joke. She sat down and immediately put her face in her hands. She was sobbing now. I didn't know what to do.

I wanted to go wrap my arms around her, but that didn't seem appropriate. I sat in the chair opposite of the couch, and waited for her to speak. It felt like an eternity passed before her sobs slowed down. I got up and went into the kitchen to get her some Kleenex. I brought them and a glass of water back to her.

I didn't say anything though I didn't know what I should say or what I could say.

"Joshua, I'm so sorry I am falling apart here. I thought I could come here and just talk to you. But, obviously, I can't," she let out a nervous giggle. She was still beautiful. She had put on weight, but I barely even noticed. It was hard to see her as an adult though, we had been kids the last time we saw one another.

"So, you are Tyler's mother?" I asked.

"Yes. Yes, I am." She said that with such clarity with so much conviction. I was a little taken aback.

"What are the odds my daughter and your son would be dating?" I tried to make a little joke of it, but she didn't even smile. Her face was free from any reaction.

"Why did you move here, Joshua?" she looked at me accusingly. I wasn't quite sure why.

"Well, when my wife died, Lilly and I needed a fresh start," I started to explain.

"I know that. But why HERE? Why Beacon Falls?" Her stare was intense.

"Actually, when I first started discussing moving, Sarah, you remember Sarah right? My older sister?" I waited for her to answer instead she just closed her eyes in agreement.

"She did some research and it was at her suggestion. How long have you lived here, Carsen?" I was starting to think this wasn't such a coincidence. She looked upset like she had been betrayed.

She took a deep breath. "I have lived here for almost 18 years, Joshua."

"Wow! You came here when you left Texas then?" I wondered out loud.

"Yes. My Grandmother lives here."

"Weird. Did my sister Sarah ever know that you came here?" again I was speculating more to myself than to her, but she answered my question.

"Yes, Sarah knew."

So Sarah sent me here to what? To find Carsen? Why? I was grieving my dead wife. I struggled to think of the words that Sarah had used. I began shaking my head. Why would she do this to me?

"Sarah said this move would be good for both Lilly and I. She knew you were here. Apparently she didn't know that you were married with a family of your own. How ridiculous!" I exclaimed.

I was ecstatic that she would be here tomorrow to explain all this in person. I felt like she had purposely done this to me, I just couldn't figure out why. Carsen and I had been best friends a million years ago.

Or did Sarah know more than I thought!

"I'm not married, Joshua," she softly said. She wouldn't look at me, not directly anyway. She looked above my head or to the left or right of me, but never in the eyes.

"Hmmm. That's interesting. I don't remember Lilly ever mentioning that you were single. Of course, I probably wasn't paying much attention," I said.

I was then horror struck! What had Lilly told her? How much did Carsen know about me? About Lauren? About my drinking? I closed my eyes and wished that something would swallow me whole. I didn't want her knowing all my dirty little secrets.

I couldn't believe I was sitting here with her. If I had been angry with her, I wasn't anymore. I was confused and nervous, but I was no longer angry with her. I did have a million questions though.

"I know that you have had a rough time, Josh. I didn't know until earlier today that you were Lilly's father. I am so sorry about your wife. I'm so sorry about so many things," she looked at me then. When our eyes met, hers filled up with tears again.

"Yeah, thanks. I'm dealing okay. Well, no I'm not. I guess you know that already though," I said sheepishly.

"Lilly is wonderful, Joshua. She is smart, funny and beautiful. She is a lot like I remember you being when you were younger. She's got a stubborn side, too," she smiled at me then.

"You know she's adopted, right?" I said.

"Yes, she told me that. I guess you are doing something right, she really has no desire to meet her biological parents."

"Really? I thought maybe with Lauren gone, that she would want to find them?" It was weird to think of Lilly discussing all of this with Carsen.

I guess I should have been more weirded out by the turn of events, but I wasn't. For the first time in a very long time, I was feeling oddly comfortable.

"She loves you so much, Josh. I love it when she calls you 'Daddy' just in passing. I thought that was so sweet. Now, knowing it's you she was speaking of, well, that makes it even sweeter."

She was finally calming down and seemed like she was relaxing a bit.

"Well, Tyler is a great boy. I mean, I haven't spent a lot of time with him really, but he's been good for Lilly."

Honestly, I could barely remember what the kid looked like which made me feel like the biggest asshole in the world. My daughter was dating this boy, Carsen's son, and I didn't know a damn thing about him. Well, that would all be changing immediately.

She nodded. She could see right through me. She knew I had been drinking a lot and that I'd barely been participating in my daughter's life.

"I guess I should thank you for all you've done with Lilly this summer."

"No need. She is great." She paused. "Look Joshua, I can't believe you are here."

Looking at her, she seemed like she was 18 again. I could remember that summer before she left.

I could remember it perfectly clear. The way she smelled the way she looked, the way she tasted when I kissed her.

"I can't believe it either. Well, at least we can ask Sarah about it tomorrow. She'll be here in the afternoon, I think."

She looked nervous again. "Oh Sarah is coming here? Why?"

I wasn't about to tell her about something that I didn't even know the whole truth about. "Uhm, she's coming for a visit."

"Oh. That will be nice for you and Lilly."

We were staring at each other now. I wanted to go sit by her, but she looked so jumpy I was afraid I might spook her or something. But, I was having such a hard time wrapping my head around her being here. How bizarre that we now lived in the same town again, thousands of miles away from where we grew up.

Without even thinking I said, "You left. You left ME, Carsen."

The hurt was back in her eyes. As soon as I spoke the words, I wished I could take them back. But instead, I went on. "I always wondered why you left like you did. I thought about trying to find you for a while."

She looked up at me and I knew she was going to cry again. I had wanted answers for years. But, I had obviously not cared enough to go looking for her.

"You did?" She seemed very surprised.

"I did at first. But, then I got angry. I figured if you had wanted me to know where you were, you wouldn't have left in the first place. So, I let it go. I went on with my life."

"I am sorry I left like that. I have struggled with that decision almost every day. I was a scared girl when I left Seabrook."

"Scared of what? Scared of me?"

She took a deep breath. She looked thoughtful as she watched me and I could tell she was choosing her words very carefully. I was hanging on every one of them.

"Joshua, I was scared of us. Well, I was scared that you were never going to feel the same way about me that I felt about you."

She looked down again and closed her eyes. She kept them closed as she continued speaking.

185

"I was terrified that you were never going to love me the way I loved you. I was in love with you, Joshua. I was so in love with you. I just couldn't tell you. I was too afraid that you would never love me the same way. I was scared that if I told you, you would leave me and I wouldn't have any kind of relationship with you. I couldn't stay in Seabrook or anywhere near you, I knew I wasn't strong enough to just get over you. So, I left."

She opened her eyes and looked at me, she appeared ashamed.

"So, I took the easy way out. I ran away. For a while, I told myself that if you loved me at all, you would come after me. But, of course, you never did. Which told me exactly what I already knew that you weren't in love with me and that solidified my reasons for leaving. I did you a favor, Joshua. I really believed that. I still do."

I wanted to interrupt her, but she had bottled this up for a long time, and I saw no reason to not let her go on. I had failed her all those years ago. I had not been the best friend she needed. We had always been able to talk to each other, about everything, so I had thought. I had been a pretty stupid boy, of course hindsight is 20/20. I smiled at her, hoping she would know that I wanted her to continue.

"I kept up with you for a while through Sarah. Please don't be angry with her. I begged her to keep my secret. She agreed only because I convinced her that it was what was best for you. As careful as you and I thought we were, she knew that were sleeping together. I told her I was afraid that I would hold you back or something and that the best way to end this was just for me to leave. I haven't spoken to Sarah in over 5 years though. But, she knew I lived here. She sent you to me. I guess she thought you could use a friend."

She got up from the couch and walked towards me. She knelt before me. I wanted to reach out and touch her, but I couldn't be that selfish.

"I hope that one day you will forgive me for the decisions and mistakes I have made, Josh. Just know that I always did what I thought was best for you. I knew I couldn't just keep being your friend. I didn't want to just be your friend. I wanted so much more from you. I knew it wasn't fair to change the rules on you like that."

She sat back on her knees. She smiled up at me.

"That all sounds so stupid now. I guess that was a rationalization of an 18 year old love sick girl. I was stupid back then. But, you already knew that didn't you?"

I wasn't sure what to say. I think on some level, I had known that she was in love with me. I used it to my advantage over and over. I wasn't thinking about her feelings back then. But, I had thought of her often since. She was why I couldn't give my heart to Lauren. She was why my marriage didn't really work. I looked for Lauren to be like Carsen.

"Carsen, I am so sorry. I know that I never gave you any reason to believe that I had real feelings for you. But, I did. It just took you leaving for me to figure them out. I am so sorry that I wasn't stronger then," I felt my heart swelling, it was filled with regret.

I wasn't sure how much to say to her now. I didn't know if she wanted anything at all from me.

I sat back in the chair and closed my eyes. I ran my hands through my hair. I realized how awful I must look to her. Blood-shot eyes, dirty hair, scruffy face. When I had let myself dream about seeing her again, I never thought it would like this.

"I have only one thing I really need to tell you, Joshua. The one thing I have regretted every single day. I love you. I have loved you since I was sixteen years old. You were my very best friend. The physical part of our relationship seemed like such a normal progression for us. I had hoped we would start dating, you would fall in love with me and we would get our happily ever after."

She was quiet for a second I'm sure trying to hold back the tears that were brewing again, her voice cracked a little bit.

"But, I realized a long time ago that what was my happy ending wasn't meant to be yours."

I heard her get up off the floor. I opened my eyes, she was turning to leave. I didn't know what to say, but I knew I didn't want her walking out that door, not again. I reached out and grabbed her hand.

"Wait. Please don't go." I whispered.

She turned to face me, my hand was still on her arm and I let it slide down until I was holding her hand.

She wrapped her fingers around mine. It felt so familiar, so normal. She looked down at our hands and then looked back up at me.

"I'm here, Joshua."

"I don't know what to say, Carsen. I still can't quite believe after all this time that you are standing here in my living room. All I am sure of right now is I don't want you to leave."

I reached for her other hand, and pulled her to me. I wrapped my arms around her tightly. My head still rested on the top of her head, just like it had a lifetime ago. She still fit into my arms just as if she had always belonged there. I could feel her soft sobs against my chest. She had her hands tucked up under her chin. I wished that she would wrap her arms around me.

But, it didn't seem she was ready to do that. I just held her. I wanted her to say something, anything.

The silence was deafening. I remembered how she was never able to stay quiet, how she hated those terrible lulls in conversation. I guess she didn't have anything else to say to me.

I knew I wanted and was asking far too much from her. She wasn't the same girl I knew; she was a woman, a mother and at one point someone's wife.

"I don't want you to say anything. There really isn't anything for you to say. I left. I disappeared. But, I want you to know that I was trying to grow up and be a better person. I was angry, so angry with you for not feeling the same way about me. Yet, I didn't have the courage to even tell you how I felt. I made the mistakes, Joshua, not you."

Her arms were finally making their way around my body. She was leaning into me more. My instincts were starting to kick in and I began to rub her back. I could smell her shampoo, her perfume. Feelings that I had long ago buried started brimming inside me. I wanted her. I had always wanted her. For a second, my life took on a different path.

I thought back to what might have happened if I hadn't been such an idiot. If I had done the noble thing and made Carsen not only my girlfriend, but more importantly my wife, I could see how my life would have been. I felt her hands moving up my back. She reached the nape of my neck, and then ran her hands through my hair. I jumped. She pulled away, misunderstanding my reaction.

"I wouldn't touch that if I were you. I am in serious need of a shower. Why don't I get you something to drink and you can sit on the patio while I go clean up. Is that okay?"

I suddenly felt very nervous and unsure about all of this. I didn't want to move too fast, but I also didn't want her to misinterpret how much I wanted her here.

"That would be nice. Do you have any red wine?" she moved a little bit away from me and started walking towards the back door.

"Is it out here?"

"Yeah, just go sit down and I'll bring it out to you."

I opened up a bottle of red, I hoped it was good. Someone had given it to me for something. I was just glad I had it, I didn't drink wine usually, but maybe I would start. I poured her a glass and stopped at the window of the back door. She looked like she belonged there. She was mesmerizing in the moonlight. She had sat down on the edge and had her feet in the water.

It felt like the last 18 years had never happened and this was just where we were. My head knew it wasn't going to be that simple, but my heart was holding out hope that it might be. I knew that I didn't deserve Carsen, not then and not now. However, that didn't stop me from wanting her. She looked over and saw me staring at her. She started to fidget with her hands.

She was so nervous, even still. It was so endearing. I opened the door and walked over to her. I handed her the wine. She smiled at me as she took the glass, I was right, she was nervous; her hand was shaking the glass just a bit.

"You will be here when I come back out?" I hesitantly asked.

"If you want me to be, then I will be."

"I want you," I paused. "I want you to be."

She smiled at me again and nodded.

I walked back into the house. My heart was pounding, my head was spinning. I was trying to figure out how I had gone from the drunk, lonely, pathetic bastard I was this morning to acting like a teenager full of hope. I thought if she could do that to me, even now, in the midst of all that was going on, she had to be my fate.

24

Carsen, 2010

It was him. He was here. Everything I had ever wanted was taking a shower just on the other side of the wall. I couldn't believe he had wanted me to stay. I had been surprised at first, at the anger, but more surprised how quickly it had disappeared.

He had been through a lot in the last year. I wasn't naïve enough to believe this was anything more than what it appeared to be. He was lonely. He was in a small town trying to raise his daughter alone. I'm sure he saw this as an opportunity to have a friend.

I was proud of myself though. I had stayed. I had also told him I loved him. There was no confusion there, for either one of us. I always wanted to just say those words to him. It didn't matter that he hadn't said them back, I never expected him to.

Sitting out here beside his pool, I drank my wine and did some soul searching. He didn't seem to have a clue about Tyler. He had said something about me being married, so he probably assumed that was who Tyler's father was. I didn't think that I could tell him now. I didn't know if I would ever even have to tell him. Tyler would leave for college in a year. Even if he and Lilly continued dating, I didn't see how it would ever come up.

Assumptions had already been made. I could see the similarities between Tyler and Joshua because I knew that he was Joshua's. If neither of them knew, then maybe they never would know. Was that fair? There was too much to lose by telling the truth.

I had to be here when Sarah got here. I had to find out what her 'grand plan' had been when she sent him to me. She couldn't know that Lilly and Tyler would fall in love. No one could have predicted that.

I felt the irony. Tyler had done fine without his father. He never even asked about him anymore.

I wondered if I could pull this off. And if I could, would I get everything that I ever wanted? All I had dreamed about.

I was lost in that fantasy. I was dreaming of my fairy tale happy ending when my phone rang. It brought me back to reality quickly. It was Tyler. I felt a pang of shame, I let the phone ring a few more times before answering it.

"Hey honey! Where are you?"

"Hey Mom! You sound better. Are you feeling okay now?

"Much better. Thanks."

"Good, I was really worried." I could hear him relax now, he believed me.

"Sorry about that. It was just one of those girl moments. Where did you say you were, Tyler?" I asked.

"Well, that is why I'm calling you. Lilly and I are on our way to our house. Is that okay? Or do you not want company?"

I didn't want to lie to him, but I also didn't want them coming over here.

"Uhm. I'm not home, Tyler. I should be there later though. So, why don't you guys go to our house. Just be good, okay? Smart choices, please." He was a good kid there was really no need for me to remind him.

I heard Lilly say, "Hi Carsen" in the background.

"Tell her I said Hi back, you guys just hang out there, okay? I will call you when I'm on my way home."

"Ok, thanks Mom."

"Love you, Tyler."

"Love you more."

"Love you most."

I realized then that I was not alone. Joshua was standing on this side of the back door, watching me.

"Oh, hey!" I started to get up.

"Don't get up, please. Are you ready for some more wine?"

I knew I should say no, but I needed some liquid courage. I was too aware of how much was at stake here.

"I'd love some more, but I can go get it."

"No no, I'll be right back."

He looked amazing. He had shaved and put on a clean shirt and shorts. I could see that boy I loved inside this man. His eyes had a sparkle that they hadn't had when I first saw him open his front door.

I wanted to believe it had something to do with me.

Instead, I was plagued by the same insecurities I had when I was with him a lifetime ago. I looked at our time apart as just part of our journey. I was hopeful that it allowed us both to gain better knowledge of ourselves. I wanted us to be able to break free from the chains of the past so that we could look ahead to our future.

I knew it would be extremely painful, but after all the pain we both had endured, was it really too much to ask for a little happiness as well. I knew if we could do that, together, then everything we had done to each other from then to now would have tremendous meaning to who we could be for each other now.

I should know better than to get ahead of myself. I had no idea what he was really thinking or feeling.

But, I knew this time there would be no mixed signals, there would be nothing left to chance. I would be open and honest about my feelings. But could I do that while lying to him about Tyler? I knew that if I could, I would hate myself a little bit.

I had once sacrificed myself and my happiness because I thought that was what was best for all of us.

I wasn't sure that I could be that selfless again. I wanted my happy ending. I believed my prince had come to take me out of my own personal hell, and carry me into our future.

Could it really be that simple? Could it really be that easy? I fought against myself, I knew better.

I was a grown woman. These kinds of things don't happen, and if they do they don't end well.

I heard the door shut, and I looked to him. He had been the hardest part of my past. I had been in undeniable pain over him. Yet as he walked towards me, all I could think was that my future had found me. I took my wine from him, and took a big sip. I noticed he had a bottle of water. For a second, I was disappointed. No liquid courage for him.

That couldn't be a good sign then. He noticed I was looking at his bottled water. He smiled at me as he sat down.

"I've been living in the bottom of a bottle of Jack for about 3 months now. I don't want anything clouding my mind now."

He kept his distance though. He didn't sit too close, he was about an arm's length away. I didn't know what to say. There were so many things I had thought I would want to say, need to say to him, if I ever saw him again. Yet, sitting here, quietly with him felt like too much.

He got up and I looked at him. I'm sure my face looked fearful. Had he come to his senses?

"I'm going to go turn on some music. It's just a little bit too quiet for me," he grinned at me.

I felt flutters in my stomach. Flutters that I thought I would never feel again. Little butterflies were dancing in my body. I just looked up and smiled at him, then looked back down to the water.

When the music began to play, it was a commercial for something in Hartford. It was just a random radio station. It was nothing sentimental which of course is something I would have done.

I blushed. I was totally crazy. I knew that I had been right about his feelings for me all along. He must have missed our friendship and the no strings attached sex. I wondered if he was thinking that would happen again now.

A chill rippled through my body, and he must have seen the little goose bumps on my arms. "Are you cold? Do you want a sweatshirt or something?"

"No thanks. I'm not cold. It was just a little chill in the air," I was embarrassed that he had seen that.

He sat down next to me, this time our thighs were touching. He leaned back a little bit on his arms, and I felt his stare on me. I didn't know what to do. I only knew what I was feeling and I knew it was too much, I could feel the emotions brewing just waiting for a reason to explode. I wanted to break the silence with something poetic and meaningful. Unfortunately I was coming up empty.

"Okay Carsen, I really can't stand the silence. Do you want to start with the twenty questions or should I?"

I needed to control the conversation because I didn't want it to veer too close to why I left. I didn't know how I was going to go about telling him about Tyler, so I was trying to think of things to ask leading away from that subject.

"May I start?" I asked hesitantly.

"Shoot. I would like to reserve the right to plead the fifth if anything I might say could be used against me at a later time," he was laughing just a little bit.

I leaned back the way he was, and looked over at him.

"Where did you meet your wife?"

"The University of Texas, freshman year. Oops! As a lawyer I know that I said more than what you were asking."

I gave him a half smile and said, "I see you are still a smart ass."

"And it seems you still can't take a joke?"

"Of course I can. I have relaxed over the years. I'm really nothing like I used to be."

"Really? You seem uptight and insecure. I don't see how much has changed."

"Interesting for you to notice those things about me now. And here I had thought for all these years that you weren't perceptive at all, that you were just totally clueless about me. I guess I was wrong." I am sure he detected the sarcasm in my voice and quite possibly the irritation, too.

"You can't seriously still be mad at me after twenty years? Are you?"

"I don't know. Mad isn't the right word. Disappointed. Bitter. Confused. Disenchanted. I think those are better more descriptive words for how I feel."

I looked over at him again. My eyes were hard and I could feel all those feelings, boiling, festering waiting for a reason to let it all go and just tell him everything. This was my problem, and I knew what he was about to say next. He was going to call me over emotional and erratic. He used to say those were my worst characteristics.

"Carsen, we aren't kids anymore. We have both grown up, lived a while now and we don't have to be those kids now. However, you haven't seemed to have changed too much you are still over emotional and erratic."

I laughed out loud.

"What? You are laughing at me now?" His voice was so sweet.

"I'm laughing at me. I'm laughing because not two seconds ago I thought you were going to say that to me."

"Some things don't change, huh?"

"I guess not."

"So my turn now to ask a question, is that okay?"

I nodded.

"Are you happy?"

I thought for a second, considering how I should answer that question. I inhaled and exhaled a very deep breath. I was just going to continue to be as honest as I possibly could be.

"Right now? This minute? Yes. Yes I am happy. I am so happy to be sitting next you, talking to you."

"That isn't what I meant. Let me rephrase my question. Have you been happy?"

"Ahh. Uhm. I love my son. I love the life that we have. He brings me a joy that I didn't even know was possible. I have a business that I own now. I work hard. I'm so busy being a mom and a boss that I honestly don't give my own happiness much thought. Happiness is fleeting anyway. It can change in a split second."

I knew I hadn't answered the question. I thought again before speaking.

"I have been content. It is not the same as being happy, but we don't always get what we want, now do we?"

He was staring up into the sky. I knew he was chewing on the words I had carefully spoken. I sat silent again. I leaned up and splashed some water on my legs. I had almost finished that second glass of wine and true to how my body reacted to alcohol I was beginning to sweat a little bit.

"Your turn. Question number 2."

"Was your wife your soul mate?"

He grabbed my arm, I gasped because he grabbed it hard. I hadn't thought before asking that question. It was the wine, the moon, his being this close yet still so far away.

"We can dance around the elephant in the room as long as you want Carsen. But we need to talk about the past. Not MY past, not YOUR past, but OUR past. We both deserve to know what drove the other to do what they did. And since you aren't going to start this conversation, I will."

He was a lawyer all right. I knew he was destined to be one. He was direct, to the point just as he always had been. I was the coward here, not him. Maybe I had always had it wrong.

I think as we get older we start to remember things not as they really were, but as we wished they might have been. Then it all gets muddied. We can't tell what the real truth is because our memories fail us.

"I know that what I did to you was wrong. I know that the way I treated you was wrong. Every time we were together, just hanging out, and nothing else happened, I would tell myself that we WERE just friends and that I wasn't attracted to you, that I didn't want to JUST be with you. But, it's not for the reasons that you must think." He looked down.

I took my feet out of the water and turned towards him. I pulled my feet in, until I was sitting Indian style across from him. He didn't move. I waited for him to continue. I knew the reasons that I believed were the truth, but I was anxious to hear his.

"And then, you would do something so sweet, so considerate and it would run through my thoughts that maybe you were falling for me. That maybe it meant more to you, too. We would fall into a pattern. Do you remember?"

I closed my eyes and nodded. Of course I remembered. I would think we were making progress, that we were going somewhere.

"But, then something would happen. We would have a fight. You would start talking to some random guy or even dating him and then I would do the same. We'd fight about that! God, I remember all those nights fighting with you on the phone until 3am. You can't fight with someone like that and think that you don't love them, unless you are a teenager."

I opened my eyes. He was shaking his head.

"How stupid WERE we?"

I pulled my knees up now to rest my chin on them. I was starting to feel the need to protect myself. I could feel some blame coming my way, and I wanted to be prepared to defend myself.

"But, that last summer, Carsen. It was clicking for me. I could feel something so real. I didn't know what it was then because I had never felt it before. I had felt lust and attraction, but not what I was feeling for you. I was so sure you were feeling it too."

I was just watching him. I could see the struggle in his eyes. I could also see the pain. I wanted to reach out to him, to touch him and to comfort him. But, I just couldn't make my body move. I was trying to protect myself still.

"But, you wouldn't make a decision about school. You wouldn't tell me what you were going to do. In the beginning, I thought you would go where I went. I expected it. It only made sense. I of course wasn't thinking about what you wanted, I just knew what I needed. All summer felt like a tug of war with you. One day you were in, the next day you were out."

I had never thought about how my actions had affected him. I had never considered that he was struggling as much as I was. I let out a nervous laugh, and he stared hard, his eyes squinting at me.

"I'm sorry. I am laughing at the irony. Best friends. That is what we told each other over and over that we were. We weren't. We didn't discuss the most important thing between us, Josh. You never asked me directly and I never asked you directly. Don't you see? We both were too stubborn or too stupid to ask the right questions. Good God!" I began to feel myself tearing up.

I had blamed him for everything. I blamed him for not loving me, I blamed him for not wanting me and I blamed him for the decisions I made.

"I know why I didn't tell you how I felt. I didn't tell you because I didn't believe that you could possibly feel the same way about me. I knew the girls you dated. They were beautiful, smart and most of them blonde. I was none of those things." I looked down ashamed.

It was so hard to admit all of these things to him, even now. He lay down with his hands behind his head. His eyes were closed. I still couldn't believe it was Joshua lying there in front of me.

"They weren't you, Carsen. Did you ever consider that? They were nothing like you and that was the point. Those relationships were going nowhere because I didn't want them to go anywhere."

I rested my head on my knees, hiding my face from him. I didn't want him to know I was crying. I was feeling nothing but self- loathing. I had betrayed him. I had hurt him. I had been so incredibly dense. I was still being stupid.

"I didn't want to be with you Carsen because I didn't trust my feelings. I mean who marries someone they knew in high school?

Very few people and if they do, the odds are they won't last. I could see my whole future, my whole life with you. But, I just didn't want it then. You were so strong. You were so smart and so intimidating. You were opinionated and convicted in your beliefs. It was like you were a 30 year old woman trapped in an 18 year old's body."

I knew he was talking to me, but it felt like he had said all this before, maybe to himself.

"I thought we had time. I thought I had time. I thought we would go off to college and we would do some growing up, make sure we still wanted each other. I didn't want to trap you into staying in Seabrook. You had big dreams. I didn't see either one of us living in Seabrook. I just needed time."

My body moved closer to him now. I didn't mean to, it just did. He opened his eyes and saw that I was leaning over him. I was so close to his face I could feel his breath.

"Why didn't you just give me some time?"

The tears were coming now, my big tears falling on to his chest. I sat back down quick. I straightened up.

"Why didn't you ask?" I whispered.

He sat up fast and forced me to sit back quickly.

"Why didn't I ask? I didn't ask because I trusted that you were going to be there. I trusted that you wouldn't leave. But you did. You left. You left me a note, Carsen. After two and a half years, you left me a note!!"

25

Tyler, 2010

Lilly and I were driving from the river and going back to my house. We had not been alone at our spot on the river. That was probably a good thing though. It gave us time to talk about last night. I was recalling part of our conversation and was fixated on something she had said earlier. When we got to our spot, I sat down on the blanket and Lilly came and sat in my lap.

"Too bad there are so many fishermen out today, "she whispered in my ear.

"Oh I don't know about that. I'm just happy sitting here with you."

She titled her head as she looked at me. "You really mean that, don't you?"

"Of course I do! When are you going to realize how in love with you I am?"

"I don't know. I've never been in love before, I'm not really sure how these things work."

"Well that makes two of us then. But, I do know that just because of last night, nothing changes. It only gets better."

"So are you saying you won't want to do that every single minute of every single day?"

"That's exactly what I'm saying. It was amazing, Lilly. YOU are amazing. And I can't wait until the opportunity arises for us to do it again. But, that is not all we are going to become about."

She had her head on my shoulder and one of her hands was on the back of my neck. She was running her fingers through my hair absentmindedly staring off absorbed in her thoughts.

"You really aren't like other guys are you?" There was a hint of surprise in her voice that almost offended me.

"If you thought that because we were together last night that either I was going to break up with you or expect to do it all the time, then no, I guess I am not like other guys." I wrapped my arms tighter around her waist and hugged her closer to me.

"I can see how it could become about sex. It feels really good and makes me feel so much closer to you, but in all honesty, this feels almost as good."

She pulled away from me so she could look me in the eyes. I saw a trace of speculation in her eyes. She didn't really believe me.

"Look, I'm sure I've said this before, Lilly, but I love you. I really love you. Every decision I make from now on isn't just about me. I consider you and your feelings as much as my own. You have to believe me, Lilly. You have to trust me."

She put her head back where it was before and she began kissing my ear. I wasn't sure if she was just kissing me to kiss me, or if she was testing me. She had to feel the shift in my body as she continued to lightly nibble on my ear. As hard as it was, I kept my mind on her and just held her tight.

"I do trust you, Tyler. You treat me like a Queen. I trust you with my life. I'm just not sure I deserve it. I'm not sure that I deserve you."

It wasn't hard for me to figure out part of what was going on. I knew there was a whole life she had before I met her. I knew she had been miserable and that she blamed herself for her mother's death. It was so difficult to think of her being any other way than she was right now. I didn't care what she had ever done none of it would ever change how I felt about her. But something was different about her today. I kept feeling like she was slipping away from me during our conversations. She was a lot more quiet and reserved.

As we pulled into my driveway, I noticed my Mom's car was gone. So I called her. She sounded weird. She was trying too hard on the phone. Her voice had an edge to it. I had no idea where she was or what she was doing. For once, it was kind of nice. I worried about her more than I should. She was the adult and it should be the other way around.

Lilly and I walked hand in hand into the house.

"Hungry?" I asked her.

"I could eat."

We were in the kitchen now, and I was rummaging through the refrigerator. She came up behind me.

"Move over, let me figure it out."

I kissed her on the forehead and sat down at the kitchen island.

"Something you said earlier is bothering me, Lil."

"What's that?" Her back was to me.

"Earlier you said something about how you don't think you deserve me. What did you mean?"

She acted like she was engrossed in the shuffling she was doing in the refrigerator. I just let the silence fill the space between us. If she needed time I would give it to her. I was willing to give her just about anything she wanted or needed from me.

"Grilled cheese? Is that okay?"

"I don't care. I'm not really hungry."

She got everything out and continued to make sandwiches for

a late dinner. I watched her closely. Sometimes it was hard to believe that we were still in high school. We had long given up going out very much. Most of our friends said we acted like an old married couple. I was perfectly fine with that. Of course, I had very little knowledge of what that entailed. I think that is why we were like we were.

I knew her parents didn't have the best marriage and I had never seen one up close and personal. We were winging this whole relationship. I worried that she would get bored with me. I knew that might come later, when I left for college.

"Hey," I said softly.

"Yeah?" she continued to busy herself.

"What did you mean earlier?"

She looked up from the pan and looked at me seriously. There was something unsettling in her eyes and I wasn't sure what it was exactly. I didn't think I had seen it before. She hesitated again.

I took a deep breath and sighed. "Fine, don't tell me. I'm going to go upstairs and shower." I stomped off and ran up the stairs two at a time. I went into my room and then the bathroom. I locked the door behind me.

It wasn't that I was really angry with her, just confused. If I had learned nothing else, I had learned to be open and honest with the people you love. It didn't matter to me if I didn't like what you had to say, but you had to say it. Something had been off all day with her. I could feel it, but I didn't say anything until now. I was hoping some time alone might give her some breathing room and time to think.

Women, I thought as I showered. I had my mother who was an open book. She told me and everyone around her exactly how it was. She was hard on me, but she only expected from me what she expected from herself.

Then there was Lilly. I felt like she was like my mom in some ways, but totally different in others. I couldn't figure that part out though. I guess that was because I didn't totally understand how their minds worked really. Times like these it would be nice to have a guy to talk it out with.

I tried talking to some of the guys about it the other day after hockey, but they all had one track minds. They weren't interested in long term anything, it was all about the hook up and the one after that. A couple of them thought I was an idiot and told me so on a daily basis. I just shrugged it off. I had never been one to care about what other's thought about me.

I got out of the shower and got dressed. I looked at the clock and saw that I had been gone longer than I had meant to be. I came into the kitchen and she wasn't there. She had eaten already because I saw the plate in the sink. There was another plate she had fixed for me. For a second, I panicked. Did she leave?

I went to the front door and found her sitting on the porch. She was staring into the night. She didn't even look at me as I walked towards her. I sat next to her and put my hand on her thigh, palm side up.

She didn't move at first. I could feel she was tense and I felt really bad for being mean earlier, I was just about to apologize when she took my hand and wrapped her fingers in mine. Her breathing was slow and steady, but her hand was trembling in mine. I just sat and waited for her to talk.

"Tyler, I am sorry I wouldn't answer you earlier," she closed her eyes as she spoke.

"There are just things about me that you don't know. Things I'm not sure I want you to know." Her voice was now low and shaking.

"You don't have to tell me anything, Lilly. I'm not asking you to. I just wanted you to explain to me what you meant earlier. That is all."

"My aunt is coming into town tomorrow. There has been new information in my mom's accident."

"Really? That's good news, right?" I tried not to sound too excited.

"Yes and no."

I was watching her, looking for a trace of enthusiasm, but I couldn't see any. I would have thought this would have been well received information. Instead it seemed to cause her a lot of pain.

"It turns out that one of my friend's cars was the one that hit her." She looked right at me, judging my reaction. I was stunned.

"Oh, Lilly. I am so sorry." I freed my hand from hers to wrap my arms around her. I knew that she had been out that night and her mother had been looking for her. I didn't know exactly what she had been doing, but it wasn't hard to guess. I'm sure they were things she didn't want to think about now. I knew she wasn't proud of who she was before she moved to Beacon Falls.

I held her while she cried. Soon her tears became uncontrollable sobs. I started to get worried that she wouldn't stop, but eventually they slowed down. I said nothing. I just rocked her and held her. I knew there was nothing I could say or do that was going to make any difference, so I did all that I knew how to do.

26

Joshua, 2010

I didn't mean to yell at her. I just couldn't stand how she was acting. I knew we weren't the same people that we used to be. But, she was being so cavalier. She was acting like what she did was justified because of how she felt. I honestly didn't realize where all the anger was coming from. But there was nothing I could do to control myself.

"You took off. You never called. You never wrote. I didn't know if you were alive or dead. I just don't know what could have possessed you to run like that?" I heard the sob come out of my mouth. I was starting to really lose it with her. "Can you possibly imagine how I felt when I woke up and you were just gone?"

She wouldn't meet my eyes. "No, I guess I can't."

"No you can't because you weren't the one that was left behind. You weren't the one wondering what you possibly could have done that would cause your best friend to leave without any warning or explanation." I had to take a deep breath.

I could really use a swig of Jack right about now. My voice was loud, but she sat there, not looking at me, just listening.

"And for the record, we were more than friends. I was a stupid boy, but I didn't deserve that. You didn't even give me a chance." My last words were no more than a whisper.

I felt broken. I had never gotten this emotional over her ever. I knew now why though. That boy that I was didn't realize what I was losing exactly, but this man, he knew now how rare what we had was, and I was grieving what might have been if she hadn't run away. I looked over at her and she was crying. Her back was heaving and she was wrapped tightly around her legs.

I wanted to reach out to her, but it seemed like the wrong thing to do. It was quiet for a while. I was thinking about Lauren, too. She had always known she wasn't my first choice, though we never discussed it. She always knew there was someone else out there.

I thought for a second that maybe everything had to happen for a reason, but quickly realized that Lauren's death was not meant to be. She had been killed and that was not part of anyone's master plan.

I went inside and brought out the bottle of wine to her and filled up the glass. I was on some natural high because Carsen was sitting here with me, thousands of miles from where we had met as kids.

She hadn't moved at all. Her head was still down and she was still crying, though softer now. I searched for the right things to say to her.

"Carsen?"

She didn't look up, but I did hear a timid, "Yes" from her.

"Carsen? Look at me, talk to me."

She looked up and took a huge sip of wine. She still wouldn't look directly at me though. She kept the wine glass close to her lips, and before I knew it, the glass was empty again. I sat down behind her. I put my legs on either side of her and I pulled her into my body. She was rigid, she didn't want to move.

I rubbed the sides of her arms until she finally let go a little bit and leaned back. But, now she was trembling.

I wanted to believe it was my touch, but something told me it was more than that, much more than that. I didn't say anything else I just wrapped my arms around her loosely, and laid my head back. I was lost in how right this felt, how normal. Like time had not passed, and we were still teenagers hanging out. Nothing had ever felt as right as being with Carsen. Finally, she spoke.

"I have to tell you why I left." I thought I felt her lean into me just a little bit, almost shifting her weight.

I really didn't think anything she said would make much of a difference to me.

This felt too nice and too perfect. I wanted to kiss her, but tried to push those thoughts away. She put her hands over mine. I could feel them shaking, even as I wrapped my fingers around hers.

I didn't remember her ever being nervous or scared.

Then I realized, she could have been both those things a million times and I probably wasn't paying close enough attention to have ever noticed. A flood of guilt came over me. I wish I'd been different with her.

"It was actually nice to hear you get angry with me, Joshua. I deserve that and a lot more. I am so sorry that I made decisions without thinking about you. I realize, only now, this minute, how selfish my decisions actually were. But, you have to know, you have to try and consider that I did those things because I was in love with you. I thought I was doing the right thing, for all of us."

She moved away from me and turned so that she was facing me. She was sitting Indian style again and she began wringing her hands together. She looked up at me, finally. Her eyes were pleading with me.

I couldn't stand to see her in so much turmoil. I wanted to reach out to her again and she must have seen me start to move towards her because she put her hand out between us, to block me.

"Joshua, I have to get through this. And after I tell you everything, I don't think you are going to want to do that. Again, please remember that I was in love with you and all I wanted to do was make you happy. I love you still. That has never changed nor even diminished over the years. It is a constant in my life, in my heart." She paused.

The tears were forming again. She was on the verge of crying. I hated to see her like this when all I wanted to do was comfort her.

"I left like that because I thought I knew what was best for you. You had this whole future mapped out, a future I wanted for you. A future I believed I was not supposed to be a part of. I realize now that was the wrong thing to do. I shouldn't have made all the decisions on my own. I owed you the chance to choose for yourself. I don't know that you will ever forgive me. I know I cannot forgive myself."

Her words had taken on a different meaning. I wasn't completely sure of what that was yet, but I was all of a sudden a bit fearful and totally confused. I was almost afraid to hear the rest of what she had to say. A part of me, a big part, didn't really care anymore. I was very aware of this second chance that we had been given. I thought that finding her was some kind of divine intervention. She looked down at her lap and her words were barely a whisper, but I heard them as though she were yelling them. "I was pregnant."

Everything started spinning. I felt like the wind had been knocked out of me or that the world was falling in on me. I struggled to look at her, to make sense of what she had just said.

"You were WHAT?"

"Pregnant."

I got up and walked into the house. I walked through the house, I had no idea where I was going, I just had to try and get away from her. I sat down in the chair in my room. I was thinking just one word – pregnant, over and over. Everything clicked. I now knew why she left, and it wasn't that she was trying to hurt me, it was quite the opposite. She left because she loved me? Isn't that what she had just said? You don't love someone so much that you leave them. That is the most ridiculous thing she had said yet.

She was pregnant and she thought the best thing to do was to leave? And what? Have an abortion?

I heard the door close and I heard soft footsteps in the hall. I got up quickly to shut the bedroom door, but she was standing right there. "Talk to me, Joshua. I don't care how terrible the things are that you want to say, just say them. Say them ALL!"

I couldn't speak. I couldn't look at her. I didn't even know what or how to feel. I had never imagined this. In all the years between us and all the reasons I had thought of, this had never been one of them.

Again, I thought to myself how completely stupid and clueless I had been. Or maybe I had wanted to be. If I had not been so self-centered then maybe I would have given it more thought.

My thoughts went to Lauren and I had to sit down again. I had made her feel inadequate, like I was with her because she was the only other option I had. In reality, she was the next girl that came along and I wanted to be over and done with Carsen and the hurt. I didn't let myself work through anything before marrying Lauren.

I put my head in my hands and thought of all the damage that had been done. Damage that was on Carsen's head, not mine. The anger was seeping through me. I was thinking how selfish and cruel Carsen was to have done that to me. I deserved to know. And poor Lauren. She had no idea, she had no clue what she had ever even been up against, and now the memory that I had hung on to for over 17 years was nothing but a lie.

That girl didn't exist. The girl I knew was actually cold and calculated, she was vicious and selfish. Time seemed to be passing so slow that I would have sworn I heard the seconds ticking by. I stayed in the chair, my head in my hands. She sat on the floor below me, with her head down. She was waiting for me to speak, to say something. I looked up and saw the clock next to my bed, it was only midnight.

I would have thought a lifetime had passed in the time that she had been here.

She jerked up when she saw my head move. Our eyes met, and I gave her a blank stare and shook my head. "If you don't want to say anything, then may I finish, please?"

"There is more?" I said sarcastically.

"Yes. There is more."

I sat back in the chair and crossed my arms over my chest. I had no words for the emotions I was feeling. Every few seconds I went from wanting to hit the wall, to wanting to kiss her, to wanting to kick her out, to wanting to hold her. I had never felt so much anger and love at one time. I stared hard at her, waiting for her truths to be told.

"I got pregnant on graduation night."

Of course she did. That night had been like magic. I remembered it well and it had gotten me through some tough times over the years, remembering every minute of that night with her.

"I didn't find out until the end of July for sure. I thought about telling you a million times. But instead, I kept looking for a sign that you were in love with me. I was so selfish and so stupid, but I was eighteen. I didn't want to have your baby and you not love me, just for me. I didn't trust that you could love me or be in love with me. I didn't want you to feel trapped or tricked. I wanted you to go to UT and on to law school. I loved you so much that I wanted you to have a great life."

I was still watching her intently. I knew I was making her nervous and a big part of me didn't care.

A baby. She had been pregnant. She had been pregnant with my baby. Something my wife couldn't have ever been. I had never known I really wanted kids until we found out that we couldn't. How bizarre how things work out.

She shifted on the floor below me, and rose up on her knees. Then she sat back on her heels, she put her hands on my knees. I flinched reflexively when she touched me, but she didn't take her hands off of me.

"I decided to come here because my Grandmother Lee was here. I knew I couldn't do it on my own, but I also knew I couldn't do it anywhere near Seabrook either. So, I came here and had our baby. He is wonderful, Joshua. He is such a good boy. And Lilly is amazing, Joshua."

Suddenly I was on my feet. I am such an idiot. I didn't even think about that fact. Tyler was her son!

Tyler was OUR son! Tyler was dating Lilly. Carsen fell back on the floor when I got up. I hadn't meant to push her, but I had moved so quickly. I began pacing back and forth in front of her.

"I. Don't. Understand," I whispered.

She stood up and came to me, she tried to reach for my hand but I pulled it away from her.

"Do. Not. Touch. Me, Carsen."

If I hadn't spoken the words myself, I don't think I would have recognized the harshness in my voice.

"I am going to go out to the patio and I think you should go home."

"I can't, Joshua. This isn't just about you and me. We can deal with that later. But our children what about them? I can't leave here not knowing what you might do. I haven't had a chance to even tell Tyler. Regardless of what you think of me, we have to make this decision together," she said so sweetly.

"Oh so now I have an opinion? So now what I think matters? Interesting. Again, I'm going to go outside, I think you should leave."

"No," she said adamantly.

I turned to her. "No?"

"No. I am NOT leaving. I might have run 18 years ago, but I'm not running now. I'm not leaving this to chance. We will make a decision tonight on what to do about Tyler and Lilly, and we will do that together. Again, Joshua, this isn't about YOU or ME. It is about them."

"Well, aren't you the patron saint? Look how selfless you are? It's not about us, it's about them. It's about them because you never told me. It's about them because you lied. I think I'm going to throw up," I walked into my bathroom and slammed the door.

I found myself locking it, too. I wasn't going to be sick, I was so furious I thought if I didn't get out of there I might do or say something that I would regret. I just needed to think. This was too much information for me to process. It was just a few hours ago I had found Carsen and that alone had its own issues. But, now Tyler was mine?

God, I wished I had been paying more attention. I wondered if I would have known? Does he look like me? Is he like me? How much does he look like Carsen? Of course, the answers to these questions were just sitting beyond the door. All I had to do was open my heart and listen to her.

But, I couldn't! She lied! She left me! She left me and she took my kid!

I started to think that maybe I had never really known her. The Carsen I knew was so caring and nurturing. She had always taken care of me, even when I knew it was hurting her. It wasn't hard to believe that she did all this for me. Yet I couldn't hide how angry I was either. There was no right or wrong reactions here. What are the odds that this would happen? How could I end up in HER town?

How could my daughter end up with her...my son? HOW???

I threw the bathroom door open and found her sitting on the floor again, head resting on her knees. She looked up at me, nothing but fear in her eyes.

"Sarah knew didn't she?" I screamed at her.

She closed her eyes and I could see the tears streaming down her cheeks. For a moment I wanted to wipe them away, but the anger hit me again and I knew that I couldn't touch her.

"How long? The whole time? Recently? What?"

"She figured it out a few weeks before I left. I begged her not to tell you, ever. I convinced her that this was what was best for YOU. I swear to you Joshua, I have never thought of anyone else BUT you. I just wanted you to be happy, and I knew that having a baby at 18 wouldn't make you happy, at least not a baby with me anyway." She hung her head again.

The shame and remorse was oozing out of her.

I felt so bad for her. I felt so bad for me. And our son. I had a son!

"What does he know? What did you tell our son about ME?" I screamed at her.

She stood up to face me. She looked confident and sure of herself now.

"I told him the truth. I told him that I ran away. I told him that I believed what I did was the right thing at the time. I told him that when he was ready, I would help him find you. I think he never asked because he didn't want to hurt me."

I was shaking my head. This was insane! I had thought of her so often over the years and always wondered what it would mean if I ever found her. I guess I was hoping for some romantic second chance.

It's funny that when you are a kid, you think you have all the time in the world, but then one day you wake up and you are choking on the regret of all things you didn't do. I should kick her out. I could take Lilly and leave. I could never know my son. I could never know Carsen again. I could leave just like she did and she did it so easily. But, I had all the pieces of this puzzle that was our life and I wasn't the kind of man to give up and leave. I wondered if she would LET me leave.

"Joshua?" she asked dragging me back to our conversation.

"What?"

"I just want to tell Tyler first, okay? Whatever else you choose to do, will be up to you. All I am asking is that you give me some time to tell Tyler. Can you give me that, please?" she was begging.

Suddenly I was scared. I was scared of losing her again. I was furious with her but I wasn't stupid enough to not also see the possibilities that were in front of us. I was getting more than I ever thought to even dream about. I sat down on the corner of the bed. I was exhausted, furious and even a bit excited. I could feel the anger lessening. I looked up at her. She was still beautiful, I didn't see a woman standing there instead I saw my best friend. The first girl I had trusted.

The first girl that I had done so many things with, the girl that I dreamed about at night sometimes. She must have seen my resolve fading because she came very close to me and stood only inches away.

Without even thinking, I wrapped my arms around her waist. Her arms immediately engulfed my head. She played with my hair, rubbed my back. I began crying.

I could hear her whispering, "I am so sorry. So very sorry. Sorry. Sorry. Sorry."

I didn't say anything to her I just clung to her, afraid of letting go, but more afraid of what was to come.

I remembered the deals I had made with God in the days and weeks following Lauren's death. I realized that while it was a different woman, I was still being given a second chance. A chance to do it right this time. I stood to lose so much more by walking away. I couldn't let my ego get in the way this time. Carsen was not the 'perfect' woman. She has many imperfections. She is only human, too. But, I knew, that regardless of this revelation and the weight it carried, she was the perfect woman for me.

27

Lilly, 2010

"Tyler?" I whispered.

"Yeah?"

"I think I'm okay now. I think I can tell you everything." I wasn't sure that I was going to tell him everything, but I would tell him about what would be happening over the next month or so. I still didn't think he needed to know everything else because I was terrified that he wouldn't look at me the same again, knowing what I had done.

I turned so that he had he had to turn, too. I wanted to face him. I wanted to look him in the eyes and explain myself the best that I could. It wasn't going to be easy, and I knew how much I stood to lose. But, if he loves me, really loves me, he will find a way to forgive me. It might not be today, but maybe someday.

"I was a pretty wild child. I know I've alluded to the fact more than a few times, but I was really really wild. I was lost and confused. My parents' marriage seemed to make no sense to me. They both drank a lot. I could tell they put on a happy face around me, but it just seemed so impossible that they were even together. I guess I blamed my mom for that. She was so uptight and trying to be perfect all the time. Once I turned thirteen I turned into someone I didn't even recognize." I looked away, trying to picture me back then, it was hard even now. I didn't like to even think of how little regard I had for anyone or anything back then.

"I dressed to shock. I talked to shock. I just wanted to make everyone feel as uncomfortable as I did. I started drinking, sneaking out and by the next summer, I was doing drugs, too."

I paused and looked at him. I searched his eyes for judgment or disgust, but didn't find anything but his sweet eyes watching me. I felt comfort in the fact that he was not your normal seventeen year old boy.

I took a deep breath.

"I was sneaking out, hanging out with the wrong kinds of people. I was a mess. And I dared my mom to do anything about it! I was really mean to her, Tyler. I was pretty awful."

"You were a kid, Lilly. Kids do stupid things. It's kind of what makes us kids. I'm sure she knew that was all it was," he said so convincingly.

If I didn't know what I felt in my heart, I might have believed him. I knew how I felt, and that even with her death, it hadn't changed all that much. I had enormous guilt, but it didn't make me love her any more than I had before. I still thought she was weak and stupid.

"I want to believe it had to do with me being adopted. But, in reality, I love my Dad. I mean I have always felt nothing but love for him. It was just different with her. Anyway, the night she died I snuck out and she went looking for me. Normally it would have been my Dad. I realized later that the reason she went instead of him was because he had been drinking – a lot that night. The thing is I was so messed up that night. Some bad things went down where I was hanging out and my friend and I were trying to get out of there, and I don't know what all happened." The tears started to come then, but I fought against them. I had to tell him.

I cleared my throat and continued. "We hit something that night. We were both so messed up. I can't even tell you how much we drank or what all we took. But, we hit an animal. Or at least that is what I remember us hitting."

I looked to him now, but he didn't seem to grasp what I was trying to say. He really was that naïve. One of the many things I loved about him.

"My Aunt called last night and told my Dad that it was my friend's car that hit and killed and my mom. I was in that car, Tyler."

His eyes froze. He didn't move. He was very still and very withdrawn. I gave him a few minutes to comprehend what I had said. I immediately felt a huge relief. Now that he knew, there were no secrets between us. I knew he would forgive me and that everything would be fine, even if that took a little time.

He moved so that he was facing forward again. Both of his hands were in his lap now. He was thinking. God, I wish I could make him talk to me. But, he deserved some time and space. I got up and walked into the house. I needed some water and to pee.

Everything felt different as I walked through his house. I wasn't sure how he was going to react or how he would feel about me now. I didn't even get to tell him the worst part. The worst part was I would have to go back to Austin, and for how long, I wasn't sure. I didn't even know what was going to happen to me. My Dad had been so angry and hung over, I didn't even know what he thought might happen.

While I was in the bathroom, I heard the front door close. I really hoped it wasn't Carsen. I didn't want to be here when Tyler told her what I did. He might forgive me, but his mother was like some perfect mother/woman/person and she would never look at me the same way again. Some mistakes are forgivable, and some mistakes alter the course of your life in a way that you can never imagine. Nothing would be the same after this and that I was sure of.

I came out and started walking to the kitchen. Tyler was sitting at the bar now, playing with his sandwich. I walked past him and went to get my glass and filled it with water. As much as I didn't want to look at him, I knew I would have to eventually. This is when I wished I had my license and could have driven myself home.

I turned to face him.

"Hey!" I said.

He just looked at me. I saw his eyes dart to the clock on the oven, it was past midnight. He stood up and grabbed his keys. "It's late. I need to take you home now." He turned to go towards the door.

"Wait." I said, but he didn't stop.

"Tyler?"

"What?" he said with his back to me and now he was almost at the door.

"We can't leave it like this. You have to say something. You have to let me say something else."

He turned towards me slowly. "I don't have anything to say, Lilly. And unless you can tell me that this is all some sick joke, then you don't have anything to say that I want to hear."

"That isn't fair, Tyler! It took everything I had to tell you that. I KNEW it would change things, but I told you anyway. I trusted that you might listen and hear me out before passing judgment. I guess as wrong as you were about me, I was even more wrong about you."

I knew it made no sense, but the best offense is to turn on the defense. I would act injured and pathetic. I would do anything so that he would give me a few more minutes. I watched as his shoulders seemed to relax a bit. He walked to the couch and sat down. He looked at his watch. He didn't look up at me, he just said, "You have exactly five minutes to say everything and any-thing you want to say. Then I am taking you home."

I rushed over to him and sat down on the coffee table in front of him. His eyes wouldn't meet mine, but that was okay.

"Tyler, I didn't know that we hit her! At least I don't think my subconscious would allow me to believe that. It was an accident. It was a terrible horrible accident. And I will have to go back to Austin soon, and I will have to beg to not be punished. I can deal with whatever comes my way, but I have to know that I have you behind me, with me. I am different now. You KNOW that! I have changed so much and mostly that is due to you! I love you, Tyler. The two have nothing to do with the other. You know how guilty and horrible I feel about my past. All of that was the truth. And as soon as I found out about this, I knew I had to tell you. I was just so scared that you would act this way. That you would shut me out, that you wouldn't love me anymore."

I was staring directly at him, waiting for any kind of response. He was digesting my words.

He was thinking very hard about what I said. I knew that was all I could ask for.

"Can you please say something, Tyler? Something? Anything?" I begged.

"What do you want me to say?" he said bitterly.

"What are you thinking? What are you feeling?"

He was quiet for a moment, thoughtful. I thought I saw a small glimmer in his eyes.

He looked straight at me then and said, "I was just thinking that everything can change in a split second. One minute things are going along fine, almost perfect, too perfect. And then BAM – nothing is as it seems at all."

He looked away from me and shook his head. I knew he loved me, that wouldn't have changed from one moment to the next, but I also knew that he didn't like me right now. He didn't like who I once was. I would just have to be patient with him and give him time. I had plenty of that.

He got up and said, "Let's go."

I picked up my stuff and looked around his living room. The once inviting welcoming room felt almost foreign to me now. I stared at the couch and thought about just last night. How we had been together so completely and totally in love last night. He was right. Everything could change in a split second.

I felt the tears brimming in my eyes. I closed the door behind me and followed Tyler to the car. I wondered if this would be the last time I would be here? Another wave of sadness hit me, and then I was crying.

He turned to get into his jeep and he looked over at me. He must have seen the tears in the moonlight. The next thing I knew he was at my door and his arms around me.

"I am so sorry, Tyler. I am so so sorry," were the only words I could find to say.

"I know," he whispered. "I am too."

28

Carsen, 2010

Joshua was wrapped around me! Joshua knew the truth and he was here. He was letting me be here with him. I was afraid this was all some kind of terrible dream and that I was going to wake up soon and find that none of this was real. Had it really all just happened in this very short night? I was thinking back to this morning, when I woke up and didn't know that he was here. I didn't want to let go of him.

I wanted to make love to him. I wanted our future. I wanted our past. I wanted it all. I wasn't stupid enough to think that everything was okay.

I knew it wasn't. I knew there were a million more questions and a million more tears, but at this second he was letting me in and I wanted to cherish this time with him. He smelled just like I remembered him. He was that boy that I loved. The boy that had turned into this amazing, flawed man. He was the man that I still loved and wanted. He was the father of my child. I thought to myself that my fairy-tale was coming true.

I knew that there were kinks, and I wasn't sure that Tyler would be on board with all of this. It would overwhelm him and he might be angry for a while. But, I knew that if we did all this together, then it would work itself out somehow.

I had no preconceived notions that it would easy, but I also knew that is was possible. I kissed the top of his head very lightly. I wasn't even sure he felt it. He was still holding on to me, like if he let go he might drown. I knew that feeling and I relished being here with him. Of course, I also had to realize that most of his pain was my fault. I had done this to him. And I would have to live with those consequences the rest of my life. I could only hope that he would be with me for the rest of my life.

I hoped that he would give it some thought and find that this was all supposed to happen just as it had. The optimism that I typically reserved only for my thoughts about Tyler now included mine and Joshua's future. Could I be so bold as to assume that we had one? Wasn't I already assuming that?

I felt him start to pull away, but I moved with him, I couldn't let him go. We were both now standing.

He towered over me, and his chin was on the top of my head. We fit together perfectly, still.

I glanced around him, and saw his bed there. It would be so easy to just lightly push him back, and have him fall on to the bed, where I would fall right on top of him. But, I knew that wasn't how this should start. We had tried that once before and it had nearly destroyed both of us in the years that followed.

Instead, I swayed back and forth. He moved with me. I wanted to speak, but knew that I didn't have the right. The ball was in his court and I would have to be patient.

I rested my head on his chest and just swam in his essence. I felt his lips brush my ear. Instinctively I turned my head up and then his lips were on my neck. They weren't really even kissing me as much as they were just brushing against me. I could feel the hunger coming from deep down, and I knew how easy it would be to give into him, to give him everything I had. He took my face in his and kissed me.

It was a slow and gentle kiss. He kissed both of my cheeks. I opened my eyes and found him staring at me. He smiled.

"You are in no way off the hook here. We are nowhere through figuring all this out. And I don't know what will happen either.

But, I need you to do one thing for me, Carsen."

I nodded. "Anything."

"I need you to take me to our son. I want to meet Tyler. It is something we should do together. I don't want you to do it alone."

My first reaction was to tell him no, but then I realized, that I had been calling the shots for too long and my way had been wrong. I made all the wrong choices, the wrong decisions even though they were for all the right reasons. It would be better for Tyler to hear it from Joshua.

I nodded, "Of course, whatever you want."

He kissed me again and there was more force behind this kiss. When he pushed his tongue through to my mouth, I melted into him. His kisses were just as I had always remembered. It was like going home.

We stood there kissing for a long time.

He eventually was the one to pull away, "It's getting late. I want to do this tonight. Let's go."

We walked out to my car. We stood there for a second, looking at each other. I knew I had to say something before everything else that was going to happen, happened. I didn't know how things would go with Tyler. I knew he would embrace Joshua, but that didn't mean it would happen overnight. I knew that nothing about any of this was going to be easy.

"I love you, Joshua. And now that you know that, I can handle anything else that happens." I smiled at him and put my arms around him, one more time.

I wanted to ask him to pinch me, to make sure I wasn't dreaming. He hugged me back, tightly.

He whispered in my ear, "I love you too Carsen. I'm just sorry it took me a lifetime to figure it out."

"Does this mean you will forgive me, in time?" I asked boldly.

"I will try to understand. I will try not to blame the woman you are now for the mistakes of the girl you once were, if you promise to do the same with me."

"I know it's not going to be easy, Joshua. And I know there are a million things we will have to work out and work through. But, I really believe that together we can do all that. I'm so tired of being alone. But, even more than that, I'm tired of living without you."

He kissed me again. I knew that nothing had been resolved. I was prepared to do whatever was necessary to make sure that we all came out of this okay. Tyler, Lilly, Joshua and me. I felt so optimistic about what lay ahead. I had never allowed myself to really believe that I would find this kind of happiness and acceptance. I guess because I couldn't allow myself to want Joshua like that.

I thought that when I walked away from him, I had walked away from any future I would have outside of Tyler. Maybe you have to truly lose something, live without it, to know how important it is to you. Maybe we all do deserve second chances because it takes us some time to get things right. You certainly don't know who you are going to one day become. You can't know your own future even if it is planned out and seems perfect. People make decisions every day that not only alter their lives but also those around them.

"I am sorry for all the hurt and pain I have caused. I know that there is probably more to come. But I promise not to run if you can promise to be honest with me. No matter how much you think it might hurt me, just promise to be honest with me," I begged him.

His hands were on my face. He was smiling down at me.

"You are right, it's not going to be easy, but nothing worth having ever is. I've waited for you for a lifetime, Carsen. I love you. The rest we will figure out together."

I believed him. I saw our future. It was complicated and messy but we were together. I kissed him one more time and opened the door.

He stopped at my door. "Do you want me to drive? You have had a few glasses of wine."

"You are right. Do you mind just driving my car?"

"Not at all. I just got you back and we have a lot of time to make up for." He kissed my forehead and I walked around the back of the car and crawled in.

29

Joshua, 2010

As I got in and started Carsen's car, a life I hadn't thought to dream for began to unfold before my eyes. I saw Sunday barbecues and nights at the river. I saw coming home from work to see her in our home, waiting for me. I saw our children growing up and starting their own lives as we finally got to live ours. I realized that this is all I had ever wanted, I laughed out loud at myself.

"What are you thinking over there?" she asked.

"I was thinking how scared I used to be of you, of us. And then my mind let me catch a glimpse of what might be coming for us, and I wasn't scared at all. Instead, I can't wait for every day, every night and everything in between." I looked over at her and took her hand.

She folded her fingers around mine, and placed her other hand on top. She lifted them up and kissed every single one of my fingers.

"I'm glad you can finally see everything I have ever wanted," she whispered.

"But, you do know it's not really as simple as that, right? We have Tyler and Lilly to factor in. That's not going to be easy." She looked down and I could tell she was very worried about that.

"Yeah, it's not going to be easy, but we'll do it together. And we'll make it through because we've made it through worse." I heard the confidence and the resolve in my voice.

"So can I ask you something, Joshua?"

"Shoot," I smiled over at her, and I could see she was not feeling quite as optimistic as I was.

"Does this mean that you don't hate me? I did keep your son from you and it would only be natural for you to have resentment and anger directed at me."

I thought carefully about the words I was about to say because I knew she was hanging on every one of them. "Look, Car, I'm not happy about all that. And I'm sure there will be good days and bad days. I'm trying really hard not to focus on the past though. I know what it's like to lose someone in an instant, and I am not stupid enough to let a bad decision you made as a child, affect the possibilities of our future. With that said, I'm sure we will discuss the topic too death. I'm sure there will be a lot of words said and tears shed, but at the end of all that, there will be us."

She turned to look at me. "Wow! I never would have expected this from you, Joshua. Never."

"It's amazing what almost twenty years of regret can do to a guy."

We were on the highway now and she was giving me directions to her house as we went. The rest of the conversation was pleasant, almost light. It was until she brought up Tyler's name.

She said, "I still don't know how Tyler is going to react, Joshua."

"What does he know exactly? Tell me what I've got to work with."

"He knows the truth. He knows I never told you about him. He knows I ran away. It's funny the night we discussed it for the first time, I think he was like thirteen. I told him I thought I could find you, if he wanted me too." Her voice faded away. She was thinking something to herself.

"What, Car? What are you thinking about?"

"I was just recalling what he had said. He asked why you didn't come looking for me. I honestly didn't think about that until now. I don't really know what I said back to him, but don't you think that is a strange question for a kid to ask?"

I swallowed hard. The kid had a point. Apparently he was smart like his mom, not slow like me. "I don't think that is strange for your kid. He sounds a lot like you."

"He's so much more like you though, Josh! He looks like you and he has so many of your mannerisms. Or, well, maybe I just wanted to see all those things in him because I was trying not to let go of who I thought you might be. I don't know. Nothing makes a lot of sense to me now. I guess you are right, we have a lot of time ahead to figure all this out. I guess we will need therapy, huh?" She squeezed my hand tight then.

"Whatever it takes," I said.

I could see the smoke ahead, but before I could even think about what exactly to do, I made the car swerve to the left to miss the wreckage on the road. I heard Carsen scream. I swerved head on into a pair of headlights. Everything went black.

30

Carsen, 2010

I can't move my body. I wasn't even sure exactly where I was. It felt like my body and my mind were almost disconnected. I tried hard to remember what had happened. I could hear voices speaking. I concentrated hard to see if I could make the voices out. I knew I heard Tyler's. He sounded so upset. He might have been crying but I wasn't actually sure. I listened again and I heard Joshua's voice, he was talking to someone, a man, a voice I didn't recognize. I struggled to hold on to their voices and to pull myself out from under this huge heavy blanket.

The blanket was stifling me. I tried to breathe, but I couldn't. I didn't feel the air go in and out of my body. I couldn't do it. I concentrated harder on the voices, trying now to hear the words. The male voice I didn't recognize was talking about something to do with a ventilator and the next 48 hours would be critical. I heard sobbing again. I was sure it was Tyler, but when I tried to open my eyes all I could see was black.

I heard Josh say, "Come on son let's get you back to your room. She's not going to wake up in the next hour or so."

Then I felt squeezing on my hand, I tried so hard to squeeze back, I wanted them to know I was here.

I could hear them. Nothing happened as I tried to squeeze my hand. It was as heavy as my eyelids and my attempts to breathe. I then heard something spinning, or did it sound like a chair being moved away on a tile floor. Then I heard what sounded like a door open and then close. There was nothing but silence except for that sucking sound. I concentrated on it, began counting with it until the blanket was so heavy it pushed me under again.

31

Tyler, 2010

One minute Lilly and I were singing to some U2 song, the next thing I was swerving to miss an accident on the two lane highway. It came out of nowhere. I saw the accident first, but there was little time to do anything except swerve to miss it. I felt the impact on my side immediately. I could hear my own voice screaming. The other vehicle slammed into my car and I started to roll. All I could think about was that this was the main reason she didn't want to buy me a jeep. She was afraid of it rolling during an accident.

I don't remember how many times we rolled, but luckily when we landed, we were on my side. Lilly was able to get out of the car quickly. She was banged up a bit. The air bag had gone off on impact and she had a few bruises on her face and there was blood. I couldn't tell where the blood was coming from.

I was trapped inside at first. I couldn't move my leg either. It was crushed below the steering wheel.

I wished we hadn't left then, I wished we had stayed at my house. Eventually I heard the sirens of the police and the ambulance. I knew help was on the way, so I just kept humming to myself. I knew I needed to stay calm and awake. It was hard to do either. Moments passed that felt like hours, when I suddenly heard Lilly crying, loudly.

She wasn't too far away from me. I knew I was hurt, things definitely hurt. But, the pain was somehow manageable. I figured I was in shock. I had watched enough ER and Grey's Anatomy with Mom to know a few things. My Mom. She was not going to be happy with me. She had always said, "If you can just make it to 18 without a wreck, I'll be a proud momma." I had almost done it.

I knew it wasn't my fault though. I had tried to miss the other wreck on the highway. The car on the bottom had looked familiar. I was trying to concentrate now, and remember what I had seen. I couldn't make it out exactly.

I could feel wet all over my arms and coming down my head. My left arm was pinned into the door, but my right one was free so I tried to wipe away the sweat. It wasn't sweat though, it was blood. I decided to just sit still and switched from humming to counting. I think I got to like 25 before everything started to get fuzzy. My head was hurting so badly. I couldn't hear everyone outside the car anymore. I just wanted to sleep. I eventually gave in and closed my eyes. I have no idea how much time passed before I woke up again, but when I did, I was in the hospital.

I could tell by the walls and the smell. I looked down and saw that both my left leg and my left arm were in casts. I was hooked up to some machine and had a few IV's in my arm and right hand. I heard a gasp.

It was Lilly.

"Oh my God, Tyler. Tyler? Can you hear me?"

She was crying, leaning over me. She smelled good, sweet, my favorite smell these days. I tried to smile, but the pain was too much. I felt like someone had punched me right in the mouth.

"Shh. Shhh. Don't try to talk. Just listen, for a second," she whispered. "We were in a car accident. Do you remember that?"

I tried to nod.

"We hit another car it was a head on collision."

I nodded again.

"The other car, Tyler, the car that we slammed in to, it was your Mom's Range Rover. She wasn't driving though," her voice cracked and I could see that now she was crying. She looked like she had been crying a lot. I kept focusing on her eyes, trying to make the picture clear.

"My Dad was driving your Mom's car. They were together. I have no idea how or why, but they were in her car."

I must have looked as confused as she sounded. She answered my questions before I had a chance to even try to ask.

"I don't know why they were together. But, my Dad is okay. He got banged up pretty bad, kind of like me. But, your mom, she wasn't wearing a seat belt." She broke off again, I could hear her sobbing.

"She's here, in the hospital in the ICU. It's really bad, Tyler."

I had been able to push the darkness off of me for a little bit, but now, as it started to cover me again, I welcomed it. I let my hands, my arms, my chest, my eyes become heavy and covered in darkness.

I quit trying to fight it. I embraced the heaviness. I could no longer hear Lilly or her crying. It was dark here, but it was also quiet. I surrendered.

32

Lilly, 2010

I can't remember the actual impact of the collision, one minute we were driving down the highway towards my house, the next thing Tyler is screaming at me to get out of the car. He was asking me how I was, if I was okay. I remembered climbing out. I ran around to Tyler's side of the jeep. He was bleeding and he was trapped. I grabbed my phone out of my pocket and dialed 911. They had already been called.

I went back towards Tyler's jeep. He was in and out of it. One minute he was talking and the next he was counting. I was help-less. I could do nothing. I just sat there by him, crying.

"Stay with me Tyler. Everything is going to be okay."

The words just kept coming out of my mouth and I had no way of knowing if they were true. I wasn't sure he even heard me. I heard a voice that I thought I recognized. I looked about twenty or twenty five feet behind me, and I could see a figure in the grass. There was a lot of moaning and I thought she said, "Help me."

The cops came running up to me then.

"How many people were in the jeep?"

"Just us."

"Okay, please go with Officer Pearce, she is going to take you over to the ambulance."

"No, that's not necessary, please just help Tyler. I think he's trapped in the jeep."

"We've got it young lady, you go with Officer Pearce please."

Once the officer grabbed a hold of my arm, I felt my balance and my resolve faltering. She grabbed me quickly, "That is why we are going to the ambulance."

As we got closer, there were lights everywhere. There were so many people running frantic. I just stared in disbelief. It was late for a Sunday evening. I still couldn't figure out exactly what had happened here. I noticed there were two cars on top of each other. The car on the bottom was barely visible. The Officer saw me look that way, and she quietly said, "Please just keep your eyes straight ahead. This is a mess and I don't need you to pass out."

"Uhm. Okay."

"Lilly?"

I turned towards where my name was being called, and I saw my Daddy. I ran towards him less about being able to and more about needing to. Everything hurt, but seeing him, made it all seem like it was going to be okay. I ran into him, and hugged him tight.

"Oh my sweet girl, are you okay? Are you hurt?" He rubbed my head and held me tight.

"No, I'm fine. Tyler is trapped, Daddy. It's so awful, there is blood and…" I couldn't finish talking all I could do was cry.

"It's terrible, Lilly. It is awful. They will get Tyler out of the car, don't worry."

I looked up. "Why are you here? Did someone call you?"

I followed his eyes and I saw the Range Rover on its side passenger side down. "Carsen?" I whispered.

"She was thrown from the car honey, she isn't in there. She wasn't wearing her seat belt."

"She always wears her seatbelt," I said reflexively. "Wait passenger side? Was she not driving?"

"No, I was driving her car."

I was so confused. Why would they even be together? Nothing was making any sense. I looked up at him and saw that he was covered in blood. It was on his head, his arms, his shirt.

"Daddy," I screamed. "You are covered in blood. Oh my God."

He bent his head down and I thought I saw him heave a little bit, like he might throw up. "It's not my blood, honey."

We heard them then.

"We found her, get a stretcher over here now, she's barely breathing."

"Lilly go over to the ambulance. I have to go to her."

Then he was off. I walked over to the ambulance and was trying to wrap my head around everything that just happened. Tyler and I had collided with his Mom's car, which was being driven by my Dad.

My Dad and I had both walked away from the collision. Tyler was pinned in his jeep, although it sounded like they had flipped it right side up and they were getting him out now. Carsen had been thrown around the car and then thrown out of her car. I hung my head and began to sob. I didn't understand any of this.

One minute life was just happening and the very next second, everything was falling apart. I was shaking and crying when the paramedic finally got to me. They were making me ride in the ambulance, but I knew I was fine. There was nothing broken or much more than bruised. But, my family, Carsen and Tyler were both hurt badly. My Dad reappeared before we drove off he banged on the door until they opened it up. He crawled in, and kissed my forehead.

Finally, he spoke, "Lilly, you are going to have to be really strong now, okay? Tyler is pretty bad, but most of his injuries are repairable. He's already been sent on to the hospital. They are taking him in to surgery when they arrive. They hope to save his leg. It's barely hanging on. But, Lilly, Carsen is not even conscious. She is barely recognizable. I am going to ride with them to care flight her to the hospital. Are you okay to ride by yourself?"

I nodded at him. I didn't want to be alone, but I didn't want Carsen to be alone either.

"I will come see you the minute I know what is going on with Carsen, I promise."

"Daddy?"

"Yes, sweetie?"

"You were driving?"

"Yes, I was."

"Had you been, uhm, drinking?"

He looked at me carefully and very humbly. "No, I haven't had anything to drink at all today, sweetheart."

"Good. But one more thing, why were you driving her car?"

His smile faded.

The tears were brimming in his eyes then. "That is a long story, honey. One I will tell you soon, I promise."

The paramedic interrupted him, "I'm sorry, sir. But we really need to get going. If you aren't riding with us, then I need you to get out of the ambulance."

Then he was gone.

33

Joshua - 2010

I jerked the wheel and the vehicle skid across the highway. Somehow, I saved Carsen's SUV from the pileup on the highway, but not the headlights coming at me in the other lane. It was too late once I saw it. We hit that car head on.

I clutched the steering wheel tightly and closed my eyes. It was over in a split second, and so were we. We landed on the passenger side of the SUV. I was still strapped in and practically swallowed up by the airbag. At first I remained perfectly still in the seat. I felt fine until I looked down to check on Carsen and she wasn't in the car. I closed my eyes again, wondering if this was really happening.

I could smell burning rubber and an overwhelming smell of rusty metal, and I knew that was bad. So I opened my eyes and I looked around and saw there was blood all over the roof. It was splattered on the console, the windows, and me. And that is when I looked at the windshield and saw the gaping hole in the fragmented glass. I realized why Carsen wasn't in the car, she had been thrown out. I tried to remember whether or not she had fastened her seat belt. I realized that she hadn't. We had been holding hands. I had to let go of her hand to grab on to the wheel. I had no choice. Now I had to find her. I tried to get out, but the seat belt clasp was stuck. It wouldn't budge. I began yelling, "Help! Someone help me!"

It felt like an eternity before I felt the fireman's hand reach in and start cutting the seat belt off of me.

"How many people were in this car, sir?"

"Two. Carsen isn't in here! Oh my God, where is she?" I was still yelling.

The big, burly man tried to keep me calm, "Okay sir. Let's get you out of here and checked out. We'll find her, sir. What was her name again?"

"Carsen, Carsen Wylder."

He said something under his breath and then asked, "She owns the Floral Shop right?"

"Yes," I moaned.

I could hear them all shouting at each other, trying to find her. I was lifted out of the car and Carsen's name echoed all around me. A young paramedic briefly examined me. I believe he said I was "lucky" but I felt anything but lucky at that moment. I felt like I lost everything I had just found. I looked towards the flashlights and that is when I saw the jeep. It was Tyler's jeep. And then I saw an officer walking with Lilly. Just seeing her walk helped me breathe easier. She was okay, or so it appeared. When I got close enough, I could see that she was bruised pretty badly, but everything was superficial. I was relieved and grateful for that. I got her into the ambulance and went to search for Carsen again.

As I ran up to the helicopter, I saw the medics lifting the stretcher. She looked horrible. Her hair was matted with blood. Her face was white, splotched with blue and was swollen. I called out to them, "Please let me go with her."

They let me climb in. I found her hand. It was bruised, bleeding and limp. Her eyes were closed. I imagined that this is what she would look like while she slept. She was still beautiful, even with the large, yellow stabilizer enveloping her head. There was so much blood everywhere though.

"Is she going to be okay?" I heard myself say to the paramedics that were working on her.

"We won't know the extent of the damage until we get her to the hospital," the female paramedic said as we rapidly took off. "Her pulse is weak and there is a lot of fluid in her lungs. Sir, I promise we will do everything we can to save your wife."

The words stung. She should have been my wife. She should have been so many things, and now she lay here fighting for her life.

"Do you think she can hear me?"

"I don't know, sir, but it can't hurt to talk to her."

I leaned as close to Carsen's ear as I could get, still holding her lifeless hand. "Hold on, Carsen. Please, hold on. Hold on for me. Hold on for Tyler. Hold on for Lilly. We need you to come back to us, Carsen. We have everything ahead of us, please hold on to that and come back to me," I couldn't say anymore, I just let the tears come.

Everything else seemed to happen in swift succession. They rushed her into the ER as soon as we arrived, and I was left standing there. I was unable to do anything. I just stood frozen watching as they disappeared behind the automatic doors. I looked around for the waiting room. There were a few people in there, and they barely noticed I walked in.

I sat down, put my head in my hands and began to sob. How could this have happened? I found her only hours ago, and now I could lose her. I kept watching the clock. I knew Tyler would be brought in soon, he was coming in the ambulance and Waterbury Hospital was over 20 miles from Beacon Falls. But, it had a much better trauma facility then the Regional Hospital there. Time felt like it was moving in slow motion. The second hand on the clock seemed to move slower than I thought possible. I laid my head back against the wall and began to make a silent deal with God. Please let her live. I will never ask for anything ever again. I'll never drink again. I'll be the man I should have been all along.

I began to hear Carsen's voice. I was listening to our conversation in my head. Her sweet voice, the tears, her explanation only this time, I didn't feel any anger or resentment. I only felt relief. She was talking to me. She was with me.

"Sir? Sir?" I was woken up out of my dream to a pudgy nurse with black rimmed glasses gently shaking me awake.

"Sir? The boy from the other vehicle is about five minutes away. I know you were inquiring about him."

I was awake now. I was immediately aware of where I was

and that I had only been dreaming. I rubbed my face and gently slapped my cheeks. I needed to wake up.

"Is he okay?"

"I don't know sir. He is unconscious. I will know more once he arrives. Why don't you go get some coffee in the cafeteria? When you get back, hopefully they will be here." And she walked away.

I made my way to the cafeteria following the signs. I still was pleading with God as I walked past other people, who were also here for a loved one. I wondered if they were making the same deals with God, I was sure they were. It's amazing what we will agree to do when everything is truly on the line and about to slip away from us.

The coffee was awful. It was bitter and tasted stale. But, the warmth felt good against the back of my throat. The heat reminded me of the crash though, and I began to feel anxious again. As I turned towards the nurses' station, I saw a group of paramedics pushing a gurney. I could see that it was Tyler. I dropped the Styrofoam cup and ran towards the boy.

Instinctively I grabbed his hand, but he lay there unresponsive. I began walking along side of him. We had the same chin.

"Sir, only family members are allowed to come back with us, please move."

"I am his father."

Carsen, 2010

The blanket of darkness ebbed and flowed. I was never able to focus long enough to know exactly where I was. I didn't trust the things I saw. I trusted what I heard even less. I felt trapped and very afraid. I was worried. Where was Tyler? Did he know I was here? Where was here? Where was Joshua?

He had been driving my car. I tried so hard to remember what had happened. I had been at Joshua's.

We had been fighting, but then he wanted to meet Tyler. I had drunk an entire bottle of wine and that must have caused a dull ache in my head. The pain was weird though. I knew the pain was there, but I couldn't really feel it exactly. I struggled to open my eyes. Or maybe they were open. I thought I saw Joshua pacing in front of me. I tried to listen. There was nothing but that terrible gushing sound. It sounded like a gust of wind being sucked in and out.

I was scared. I was petrified. I just didn't know of what exactly. I heard a door open. I heard voices. I heard Tyler, Joshua and Lilly talking. I concentrated so hard on their voices. I needed to hear what they were saying.

"The doctor should be here in a few minutes. He said he wanted us all here to hear it," Joshua said.

"How are you, Daddy?" Lilly asked.

"I'm hanging in there, same as you guys are."

"She's been out how long now?" Tyler asked.

"It's been over three days. But, that is because of her injuries, Tyler. They want her body to heal before they bring her out of the coma."

"Oh," Tyler responded. "I still don't understand why you were with my mom, or why you're still here."

Oh my God! My mind shrieked, Oh Joshua! Please do not tell him now. Do not tell him without me. I struggled to open my eyes, but it was as if they had been sewed shut. I kept rebelling against the darkness. They needed to know I was okay. I didn't want this conversation happening, not now.

"I told you. Your mom had come over to talk to me about you and Lilly. She had a few glasses of wine and I didn't want her driving herself home," I heard the tentativeness in his voice. I hoped they didn't.

"Yeah, you said that before. I just don't buy it," Tyler remarked.

The heavy door slid open. "Hello, Mr. Hattinson." "Hello, Dr. Bertrand. How is she today?"

I heard a soft shuffling and slow steps coming towards me. I couldn't tell who it was. Then I felt Lilly's small hand in mine. I tried to squeeze it. Still nothing happened. I was becoming very irritated with my body and the incessant beeping that kept getting louder. Suddenly, I felt unfamiliar people around me.

"What is going on?" Joshua asked.

"Her blood pressure just spiked. See the machine over there?"

A collective "Yes" was said by all three of them.

"We are doing our best to manage her pain and to keep her sedated, but she is fighting against us. That's a good sign." Dr. Betrand said. What they didn't know was the pain was completely unmanageable. All attempts were futile; in fact, everything they did seemed to intensify the unexplainable stinging I was enduring. Even the smell of my beloved flowers seemed offensive.

I could feel Tyler's hand in my other hand.

"Mom? Mom? Can you hear me?" he was sincerely begging me to answer him.

I wanted to answer him. I couldn't unlock my jaw, I wanted to scream, but nothing happened. It felt like there was tape over it.

"Can she hear us?" Lilly whispered.

"Well, some people say, after they come out of a medically induced coma, that they did hear bits and pieces. So, if you've got some deep dark secrets you might not want to tell her now."

He was trying to be funny. But no one laughed, not even the nurse.

"I love you, Mom. I miss you. Please wake up soon." As much as I wanted to hear his voice, every syllable scarred a part of me that I never before knew existed, a deep chasm yet uncharted by doctors and scientists. I can only say it felt like my soul was being torn to shreds.

I could feel Tyler's head on my hand. I could feel his hair tickling against my arm. I wanted to comfort him. I could hear Lilly crying softly. Where was Joshua? I thought he was here, too. But he was being so quiet.

"So the good news is that the internal injuries were not as severe as we had first thought. We were able to remove her spleen and stop all the internal bleeding. We will start to lower her medication dosage tomorrow, if she has another successful evening…. meaning no fever. She will have to have another surgery to put her left shoulder back into place. It was broken in two places, most likely when she was thrown from the car. I do expect her to make a full recovery, physically."

There was silence. The tension in the room was beginning to make me feel anxious and agitated. I started slowly counting, trying to calm myself down.

Finally, Joshua spoke, "So, she might start waking up on her own tomorrow?"

"Yes, that is the plan. Do you have any other questions for me?" he asked.

"No sir. That is great news. Thank you so much for fixing my Mom."

"Of course, Tyler. That is my job. If you guys need me, just page my service."

I heard the door shut. All was quiet again.

Lilly asked, "Tyler? Do you want to go back to your room now?"

"Actually no, I was wondering if I could speak to your dad first, alone, please?"

"Oh, okay, if that is what you want," she said. I heard the defeat in her voice, but she wasn't going to argue with him. "I'll be in the waiting room. Call my cell when I can come back."

I heard the door shut as she left. The blanket of darkness was closing over me again. As much as I wanted to hear this conversation, I didn't think I could hold on.

"Joshua? I have a few questions," Tyler said very bluntly.

"Do you really want to do that here? Now?" Joshua asked nervously.

For the first time since I had been here, I was grateful for the blanket of darkness that was all around me. I was hiding behind it now. I knew that Joshua was going to tell Tyler everything and I would lay here unable to speak or object. I would lay here without an opinion or the ability to respond. For the first time in almost twenty years, I would know what it must have felt like for Joshua.

34

Tyler, 2010

I knew it was the wrong time. I probably should have waited until my mom woke up. But, she was going to be okay. The last three days and all the wondering and worrying were gone now. I had to know what had happened between them before the wreck.

I don't know why, but I thought that the way she acted on Sunday morning was related to her being with him on Sunday night.

Lilly walked out and shut the door. Joshua got up from the chair and walked over to the narrow window in the small ICU room where my mother lay. I really looked at him now, and I noticed how tired and worried he was.

He had rarely left the hospital in three days. He would take Lilly home at night, after the last visiting hours were over. He was always here before me in the mornings. I was being released soon, and I knew my time with him alone was limited.

"Tyler, how are you holding up?" he asked.

"I'm fine. I'm glad that I will heal before the ice season gets going. Different story for football though."

"Yes, it's unfortunate about football, but at least it's just one season."

"Yeah, but it's my senior year. I hope to play in a few games at the end of the season." I lifted my hand from the chair and flexed it. We both stared at my hand, as if it knew something we didn't.

Then there was silence. I searched for the right words. I stared at my mom, wishing she was awake. I wish she could help me understand. For two days, Lilly's Aunt Sarah has been here, and I have been getting this totally weird vibe from her. I feel their stares, and it's a bit creepy sometimes. I'm just Lilly's boyfriend, so I don't know why they are holed up with my mom.

I had suspected they all knew something about my mom's condition, something no one was telling me. But when the doctor said she might wake up tomorrow, I doubted hey could be hiding anything from me. I was still holding my mom's hand while watching him. The awkwardness was killing me.

"Mr. Hattinson? Why were you and my mom together that night?"

She really did look like she was sleeping except for the tube in her mouth, the IV's and the hospital garb. It was unsettling to see her so vulnerable. I hoped she could hear me.

"She had come to see me earlier in the evening, I don't remember exactly what time. She wanted to talk about you and Lilly."

"So, what did she say about us?"

"She wanted to explain the night before. Look, Tyler. It's no secret that I have a drinking problem. And I've not been parenting as I should have been. I'd been through a really difficult ordeal before we relocated here. I was wallowing in self-pity. Your mother gave me a wake-up call."

I smiled. "I bet she did. You know her father was an alcoholic. She doesn't put up with that much."

"Exactly. She also wanted to talk to me about you and the kind of boy, I mean young man you are. She told me how good you are for Lilly." His words were very sincere.

"Yeah, Lilly and I are good together. She's really wonderful to me. I try to take good care of her, too."

"Is there anything else, Tyler?" Joshua asked.

I waited. There was something more, but it wasn't really a question. It was more a gut feeling. I wasn't really sure how to say it out loud.

Instead I shook my head. "No, I guess that's all."

Joshua walked over to the opposite side of the bed and stood next to my mom. I watched the way he looked at her like a friend, not a total stranger. He looked genuinely concerned about her.

I could read the guilt written all over his face. "She's going to be okay. You know she won't blame you, she isn't like that. She will know it was an accident. It was more my fault than yours any way. You shouldn't beat yourself up about it".

He smiled at her and then looked at me. His face changed from being stressed and guilt-ridden to feigning a half smile. He inhaled deeply, and I could see tears pooling in the corners of his eyes.

I tried to help, "Oh man. I'm sorry, Mr. Hattinson."

I'm so stupid! Why did I bring that up? I just wanted him to not feel bad. I was trying to make him feel better, but he looked worse. He put his head down. I wasn't sure if he was crying or thinking. I wished I could just get up and walk out of the room. But, with my broken arm I couldn't maneuver the wheelchair alone. I tried to find my cell phone to text Lilly. Then I felt his hand on my shoulder. I looked up at him and he turned the wheelchair so that it was facing him. He pulled up a chair and sat down.

For the first time, I looked at him directly in the eyes. He was a decent looking guy. He hadn't slept in days, so he had dark circles under his eyes. I just couldn't see beyond the sadness and pain in his eyes.

"Tyler," he began. "There is more about that night. I didn't want to tell you this alone. And I guess I could wait for your mom, but I think I want to do this by myself right now."

I didn't know whether to be shocked or relieved.

"What are you talking about?"

"I want to tell you a story. Well, I want to tell you my side of the story."

35

Joshua, 2010

I was alone with my son. Well, not really alone if we count his comatose mother, but Carsen could not help me now. He had asked to talk to me, but then his questions weren't like I thought they would be. He really had no idea who I am. That both saddened and infuriated me. I had debated for the past three days whether or not to tell him. Now that Carsen was expected to wake up soon, I could not hold back.

I agonized that he would likely be angry that I let this time pass and didn't tell him. Who was I kidding? I was scared to tell him the truth. I might not have been the one who lied, but I was also to blame. I had made Carsen feel like her only option was leaving.

"Your mother and I know each other, Tyler. Not just from here. But, we figured out on Sunday that we grew up together in Seabrook. My older sister Sarah and your mom were friends, too." I paused.

I watched him intently. His facial expression didn't change. He didn't say a word. He just listened.

I continued. "Carsen and I have quite a history." I didn't want to say the words. I thought maybe if I hinted around it, maybe he'll get it.

"Actually, I took your mother to Homecoming our junior year in high school. God, that was a million years ago." I paused, watching him. I was positive he wasn't piecing any of this together.

"So, you used to know my mom?" he asked quietly.

"I did. So imagine the surprise when she showed up on my doorstep, and we realized who we were and who you guys were. It was kind of crazy there for a while."

I was trying to lighten the mood a little. I could see the confusion in his face. I had no idea what conclusions he was drawing.

"Well, your mother and my sister, Sarah. They kept in contact with each other when your mom moved here. And when I lost my wife and Lilly was having all that trouble in Austin, she thought it might be a good idea for us to come here."

My words were failing me now. I was terrified of saying those four little words. I was scared partly because I knew it was going to throw him for a loop, but I was also scared because Carsen wasn't sitting right next to me, holding my hand. If she were awake she would make it all sound so romantic. She would make it sound like it was fate. Me trying to say 'I am your father' sounded nothing short of lame!

"Your sister thought you should come live in Beacon Falls because my mom was here? Then why didn't she know who you were? How did she not know you were Lilly's dad?"

"My sister didn't tell me Carsen was here."

"Either I am missing something or am on too many painkillers. Either way, this doesn't make any sense," Tyler said. He was absolutely correct.

"I know I'm not doing this right. Maybe I should start at the end, instead of at the beginning of the story?"

I wasn't really asking Tyler, as much as I was trying to explain it to myself.

I stood up and walked to the door. I looked out at the nurses' station. I secretly hoped someone would see me standing there and interrupt us. No one came. Tyler was placid. He didn't say anything. I wished now I had just kept my mouth shut. I couldn't do this without her.

Carsen.

I just got her back and hours later she'd slipped away. I could do this. She is here. She is lying right there. I looked up at Tyler and walked towards him.

"Here's the thing, Tyler. It turns out that I'm your dad. I mean, I am your father. God – that doesn't sound right? But, it is right. I mean, that is what your mom told me. I…" I didn't know what else to say.

The tears that had been building were now creeping down my face.

Everything but our breathing had stopped. Time was standing still. This boy, this young man, my son was sitting in front of me, staring at me, processing the words I had just blurted out. He didn't flinch. He didn't move. He just stared at me.

"Tyler? Did you hear me?" I softly whispered.

"Yes, I heard you." His voice had reduced to a murmur. He was too calm. Okay. The hard part is over. He knows. I know. We all know. I kept watching him for a reaction, but there was nothing. He didn't do anything but glower at his mother.

After an excruciating few minutes, his chin trembled and he asked, "So you think she is going to die then? Is that why you told me?"

I dashed over to his wheelchair and knelt beside him.

"No, Tyler. The doctor said she would make a full recovery, you heard him say that. I just didn't want to NOT tell you. I know the timing is wrong and that your mom wanted us to tell you together. And I guess we kind of are together, but I just couldn't sit in the same room with you and not have you know."

How selfish those words all sounded. Selfish, but true.

"Does Lilly know?"

"No, I haven't reconciled that part of it yet. Hell, I haven't really processed most of it."

"Did you and Mom fight about this? When she told you?" Tyler was still staring intently at Carsen. I think he was trying to will her awake, so that she could explain things better than me.

"At first, it was a bit much for me to digest. But, as we talked through it, I understood her reasoning and we agreed to work through all this together."

"All WHAT stuff? I'm almost 18 and I've done just fine without a father."

Ouch. He was so much like Carsen. Stubborn.

"Well, I know that is true. I know because of how you are with Lilly."

"Oh NO!" He screamed.

I stood up quickly. "What? What is it?"

"Lilly is what to me now? A sister? Oh. My. God. I am dating my sister?" Tyler looked like he was about to explode.

"Don't be ridiculous, Tyler. She was adopted, you know that! There is no "relation" between you two."

This was something that had bothered Carsen, too. She knew how deep Tyler's feelings ran for Lilly and this was beyond peculiar.

"It's just something we have to figure out, Tyler."

I took a deep breath. I searched for the right words to convince him it was going to be okay. I kneeled next to him again and I placed my hand on his shoulder. He didn't shrug it off, which I took as a positive sign.

"I have loved Carsen since I was seventeen years old. I never even let myself dream that I would find her again, much less that we would have a child together. The kicker is she loves me, too, Tyler. I mean she really loves me. And that alone will make whatever else comes next easy to handle. For the last three days, I have done nothing but soul searching and making deals with God. I WANT this life. But, I don't just want it for me. I want it for her. I want her to know what it's like to have someone who will always be there for you, no matter what. I could have walked away, been angry with her for lying, but I would lose so much more by doing that. Tyler, we've been trying to do what is best for each of us, but doing it all wrong. And now it's time to start doing it together and getting it right."

I didn't even try to hide the tears that were coming now. He deserved to hear the truth.

"I was such a stupid kid. I was an even dumber adult. I was so angry with Carsen for leaving like she did, it never really occurred to me why she might have left. Her leaving felt like total abandonment. It really was devastating to me, but I was so self-absorbed. I was so used to her just being there. I took advantage of our entire relationship. So much so, that she couldn't trust me enough to tell me she was pregnant. That kills me! I hate that for all of us. But, I also have to be realistic. I have Lilly. I had a wife. I had a whole life apart from the one I might have had with Carsen. I didn't deserve Carsen then, but the man I am, I mean the man I want to be….now he deserves a chance, Tyler. Please give me the chance to be with her and to be with you. I know you don't need a 'dad', but couldn't you use a friend?"

Tyler continued to stare at Carsen. The only thing I knew he felt was a yearning for his mother to open her eyes. I couldn't tell what else he was feeling.

"Tyler? Can you please say something?"

He tilted his head slightly and looked up at me. He was scrutinizing me. I tried to stay calm and let him look me over.

"Imagine if you would have just given me a glance or two over the last six months? You might have noticed that we looked alike. Or if you had ever thought to ASK Lilly what my last name was and maybe things wouldn't be quite as ridiculous as they are now. Did you ever think that maybe all you do KNOW how to do is make the wrong decisions?" Tyler said flatly.

"Why should I trust you now? Why should my Mom trust you now? What makes now different? Nothing has really changed. We are all who we were 15 minutes ago. Nothing is different."

I couldn't argue with him. Everything he said was absolutely true. He might have the same eyes as me, same mouth – upper lip poutier than the bottom one. His hair looked much like mine did at his age, too. But, it was clear that is where the similarities ended. He is Carsen through and through. He is strong. He is smart. He is protective. He is perceptive. He is more a man at 17 then I have been my whole life.

"Tyler? I'm only asking for a chance. I'm not asking for anything else."

36

Carsen, 2010

It's true what they say about people in comas. You can hear the things going on around you. You can hear the crying. The pleading can feel like thorns within your core. You can hear the bargains being made on your behalf with God by the people who love you. The nurses who talk about you like you aren't in the room.

"It's so sad. The family is in total denial."

Really?

"And her son. He's here too. What a tragedy."

Tyler is here? Tyler is hurt? Well, they don't know me very well. I am stronger than anyone has ever given me credit for. The worst part is not being able to move. I can't really feel my body. I concentrate so hard when Joshua is holding my hand. I can feel the pressure of his fingers. Occasionally I feel the dampness from his tears. I can do nothing. I lay here until the darkness buries me. Right now, I hear the conversation between the two people I love most in the world. I fight the darkness to listen.

I hear Tyler refusing to let Joshua in, to even give him a chance. Tyler is more worried about me than himself. I want to tell them both that the only one to blame here is me. I believed that having these conversations first with Joshua and then with Tyler would be the worst situation ever. I was wrong. THIS is the worst situation. I can hear them. Yet I have been rendered speechless. I wonder if this is my punishment. It is fitting.

I believed I always had the right answer. If I could laugh at the irony, I would. I have no voice. I have no laughter. Maybe I have actually died. If that is the case, then I know exactly where I am. I am in hell. This would be my own personal hell, a place where I cannot speak to anyone, a place where I cannot move and cannot react.

The world is crazy like that, this would be my penance for the damage and hurt I have caused. I begin to make my own deals with God. Just like I did when I found out I was pregnant with Tyler. Please God. I don't want to leave them alone. I need time. I need time to make it right. I need time to make them love each other. I need time to love Joshua. I want my family. Please God. Please let Tyler forgive me for what I have done. Please God. Please God, let me wake up from this. Let me ascend from this hell.

37

Lilly, 2010

I don't know what they are discussing. I guess it doesn't really matter. I know it's not about me.

Tyler is fuming. He wants to know why Dad was with his mom. I know he blames my dad. But, the cops agreed that both Dad and Tyler reacted appropriately, trying to miss the first wreck. There is no way they knew the other was coming. He isn't just mad at Dad. He's mad at the world right now. He's mad at me.

Our conversation last night broke my heart. He loves me, but he doesn't think he can be with me anymore. I thought when you loved someone you were supposed to forgive them. Tyler says that some things are unforgivable. I never believed that. Or maybe I did. Maybe that is why I blocked it all from my head and my heart. I just sit in the waiting room, waiting for one of them to come get me. Aunt Sarah walks in.

"Hey Lilly. Have there been any changes in Carsen's condition?" she asks.

"Hey. Yeah, I think so. Doctor said she might wake up tomorrow. They are going to change her medicine so that she can wake up on her own. She'll be on a ventilator for a few days, but she is doing much better now." I gaze out the window. Everything is such a mess. It is hard to believe it is only Thursday.

"Well, that is good news. I think I have some more to share with you as well."

I look up at her.

"Andrea's family met with the DA's office. They are willing to make a plea bargain with both of you. I just met with your current principal and they are sending over your attendance record and grades. These help show the improvements you are making. Most likely you will be on probation and have community service. You will need to thank your Dad for that. He made a very compelling case."

I knew my mouth was hanging wide open. I couldn't believe

what she was saying.

"Do I still have to go to Austin?"

"Yes, but they are willing to work with us, due to the circumstances here. We don't want to wait too long though because we want it all wrapped up before school starts which is barely a month away." She reaches over and hugs me.

I know I should feel relief and joy. But, it all seems pointless if I won't have Tyler when it is over.

"What is wrong, Lilly? I kind of expected a more positive reaction."

"No, I am glad. It's just that I told Tyler everything on Sunday night, before the accident. I don't think this is something he will get over."

"Oh, Lilly! He just needs some time. If any one of these things had happened on their own, it would be difficult to handle. He's just on information and sensory overload. Not to mention his own injuries. Just give him some time, sweetheart." She wraps her arms around me, hugging me tightly.

I just don't think time is what he needed. I have never seen the disappointment in his eyes before.

It breaks my heart.

Tyler is so good, too good. I always knew he was too good for me.

I think I knew deep down from the beginning that girls like me, like who I used to be, we don't get second chances. Lauren wrapped her whole world around me and my dad. I try to remember things that she did for herself. I can't think of any, not a one. I am certain that isn't the kind of woman I want to grow up to be. I know now if Tyler breaks up with me, I will survive. I stand and face my aunt.

"I am going to walk home."

She looks at me quizzically.

"I will see you later."

As I walk out the doors, I let the sun beat on my face. The warmth feels so good, refreshing almost. I have found a moment of truth in my lifetime of lies. As I walk, I begin to choke on my tears, or is it my regret? It doesn't matter. It feels good to be alone and to be honest for the first time in so long.

I begin to admit to myself all the terrible situations and choices I have made. I had started drinking at 12, just to see if I could get away with it. I did. I started sneaking out at 13, again just to see if I could. I did.

I had sex in my parents' bed when I was 14. That was the most painful of all the memories. It didn't make me feel special or loved. I didn't feel all warm and gooey inside. He broke up with me the next day.

My truth is that I was indirectly involved in my mother's death. I cannot run from that truth. I cannot pretend it isn't as horrible as it sounds. My stomach begins to burn. It hurts so badly I can barely walk. I veer off the sidewalk and into a small empty patch of grass. I lean against the fence for a second. I feel the spit gathering in the back of my throat. I pull my hair back and begin vomiting. I have made myself sick.

38

Tyler, 2010

This is ludicrous. Lilly's father is my sperm donor. I can't wrap my head around it. I think some of it is from the painkillers. I also don't want him to be my father. He's not a good father to Lilly. He didn't love my mother enough to even bother looking for her. Oh, but he loved her! Yeah, right!

I just continue to stare at him. I see the resemblance. I look like him. It's weird to see yourself in someone you don't even know. Even harder when it's someone you know you don't like. He wants a chance. I roll over to the window. I don't know what I want. This whole situation is absolutely freaking crazy! Just a few days ago my life was almost perfect. And now… Now I can't even begin to figure out which part is the worst.

I guess the worst part was thinking I might lose my mom. At least I thought that was the worst part until like 20 minutes ago. I wish she would wake up. I want to know what she thinks about him. I want to know what she thinks I should feel about him. She was letting him drive her car. That sounded weird to me. I turned my wheelchair back around so I could face him again. He is holding her hand and I can see that his own hands are shaking. Withdrawals I bet.

I haven't smelled any liquor on him, not once, since all this happened. Maybe he does have a few redeeming qualities after all. He doesn't seem to notice I'm watching him. I don't know much about love, but I think I know how he is looking at her. He does love her.

"Why were you driving her car?"

He looks over at me, tears are on his cheeks.

"She had been drinking wine and I just didn't want her to drive."

"Yeah, that makes sense, I guess. But, why didn't she have on her seat belt? She never rides anywhere without her seat belt."

He is looking at her hand in his palm, "We were holding hands. I guess she just forgot, Tyler. It was an honest mistake."

Wow!

She was still in love with him. I don't think she ever told me that.

"So then, you are just okay with all this? Okay with finding out that she lied to you? Okay finding out that you have a son that you never knew about? You just forgave her, no problem? I guess that shows how much I matter in all of this."

"This is complicated. It's just not that simple."

"Well, try to explain it to me so that I can understand."

"Carsen and I, we had unfinished business. There was no closure in our relationship. Hell, we weren't even dating. There was no terrible break up, there was no dramatic scene. After an evening, spent like hundreds of others, I was left with a note. Not a letter. Just a note."

He pulls up the chair next to her bed and sits down. He runs his hands through his hair and down his face.

He looks at me and begins, "I had such an ego back then. I was livid that she left like that. I went to her house and her mom didn't even have anything to tell me. I figured that maybe she was in love with someone else." He turns to her for a second, "and ran off with them. But, then the rumors started and no one else was gone. I eventually accepted that she just wanted a different life."

"What kinds of rumors? What did people say about her?"

"Nothing really. Nothing that made a lot of sense. There had been this English teacher that she was a little too close to, and rumor had it they ran off. But, a few months later, he reappeared, and she didn't. Her friends didn't know anything, or at least they said they didn't. And by the reaction a few of them had, I believed them. But, she was always over emotional and a bit theatrical. Back then, I just thought that's how she was. I honestly believed that in a few days, maybe weeks she would call or come back. I figured she went to live with her dad."

"What does it feel like to know now how wrong you were?"

"Tyler, you feel free to blame me all you want. I don't really care. You can hate me, blame me and never let me into your life. I will never stop trying. I am going to be here. I am not going to leave."

"Really? And why not?"

"Unlike you, I know what real true loss is like. I've felt it twice in my life. I will not feel it again. I love her. I always loved her. I just was too scared to tell her when I was a kid. Your mom, she wasn't like other girls. Nothing about her was quite 'normal'. She did what she wanted, when she wanted and with whom she wanted. No one could change who she was or who she was going to be."

He stops and seems to be somewhere else for a moment.

"Well, I guess that was until she got pregnant with you. I never would have pictured Carsen as a mother. And maybe that is why it wasn't something that I ever even considered. But now, it all makes sense. Once there was a you, Carsen as I knew her, ceased to exist. She loved you that much. Which I can only surmise means she hated me almost that much. Of course she says she left because she loved me that much, but I know that 18 year old girl didn't trust me."

Now I am kind of speechless. Maybe he was right. Maybe she loved us both too much. That is so her.

I know she struggled, but I never thought about what her life might have been like if she hadn't gotten pregnant. She never would have let me feel like I was not wanted or loved.

"She is a good Mom."

"I know that, Tyler. I see how you are. I probably would have screwed you up, screwed everything up. I guess maybe she figured as much. But, I'm NOT that person anymore, Tyler."

He walks over to me and kneels in front of me so that our eyes are just inches away.

"You want to know what I have figured out over the last four days Tyler? That life…it's all about the journey, the quest to bettering ourselves and gaining greater understanding of oneself and those in our world. We have to constantly try to break free from the chains of our past. It can be extremely sad and painful, as we have both experienced. But, every experience has tremendous meaning."

I recognize his smile. It is my smile, too. I can't be angry with him. He didn't do anything to me. He didn't really do anything to my mom either. She is really the only one I should be mad at. How convenient that she is lying in a coma, not guiding any of us through this mess she made. We are all navigating on our own and she is just lying here motionless, in a peaceful sleep.

I hope she can hear us. I hope she knows that we are here. I hope she wants him here.

I tell him, "I should go."

"Here, I'll leave, Tyler. You probably wouldn't mind some alone time with your mom. We can talk later, whenever you want."

As he turns to leave, I remind him, "What about Lilly?"

He stiffens and without turning around, he answers, "Let me take care of that, okay? I will tell her as much as I've told you. Then you can talk to her later. Is that okay with you? "

He turns back to me and adds, "Don't think that I have all the answers, I know I don't. None of us do."

Then he was gone. And he walks out the door, leaving me alone with my mom and a whole lot of information that I don't quite know what to do with. I feel numb. A world that I was fairly secure in has been turned completely upside down. I know my mom is going to be okay, but staring at her, like this, is nearly unbearable. I try to think back to a time when she ever sat still, I can't recall even one time.

Interesting. Maybe she kept in constant motion so she wouldn't have to deal with everything else that was going on. l will always be grateful for her, but for the time being, I'm just mad.

I know it is almost time for my next round of painkillers. I need to get back to my room, but I have so many questions. I roll up next to her bed. I take her hand and grip it tightly. Both of our hands are bruised but not broken. I stroke her hand and stare at every line and vein, memorizing them.

"Oh Momma," falls out of my mouth.

I feel like I am five years old and someone just stole my favorite car.

39

Joshua, 2010

I walked into the waiting room and saw Sarah staring out the window.

"Hey," I said as I put my arm around her.

"Don't you think it's ironic how things happen? Obvious that something bigger than all of us is pulling the strings?" she whispered.

"Hmmm? I don't know about that. I feel like you might have been pulling some strings of your own," the bitterness of my words was not missed by my sister. I felt her tense up immediately.

"Yeah, I did do that."

"I don't know how I would really feel if that accident hadn't happened the other night, Sarah. I honestly don't. So, yeah, I guess it obvious that something bigger than all of us is actually at work."

She was quiet.

She leaned her head against my shoulder. I immediately felt the wetness on my shirt. I wanted to comfort her, but at the same time, I felt the need to be on guard. I patted her shoulder gently. She wrapped her arms around my waist.

"The worst part, Joshua, is that I don't feel sorry about what I did. I still believe that letting Carsen go was the right thing, for all of you. I am sorry if that makes you angry. If I had to do it again, I would still let her go and not tell you."

"I'm not going to pretend to actually understand that, Sarah. There was a child involved. I think you let your own experiences and prejudices cloud your better judgment. I should have been given the opportunity to make my own choices."

"See? That is why I would do it again. You still think it was about you. Just about you. It wasn't. I don't think you can stand here and say that Carsen was wrong, not completely, if you are totally honest with yourself."

I closed my eyes. I tried to go back to that time in my life. The time that I relied on to get me through so many difficult moments. The fantasy life I created in my mind, the 'what if' game I played too often. I try to be honest with myself. To let myself feel what it would have been like to have Carsen tell me that at 18 we were going to have a baby. I immediately felt fear. I felt trapped, like I couldn't breathe. I wondered if she got pregnant on purpose? Was she trying to trap me? My palms became sweaty and my face was on fire.

"Joshua? Don't be angry with her or with me. We both loved you enough to want a different life than the one we saw coming if she had told you. I'm not saying that it was right. But, Carsen believed she was being selfless and giving you a bigger gift by leaving."

"That doesn't make it right."

We both back down for a moment and just breathe. Too much had happened in such a short time. It seems impossible to process anything past Carsen being hurt and me being Tyler's father. My heart stopped.

"Where is Lilly?"

40

Carsen, 2010

The blanket didn't feel so heavy anymore. The weight that kept it over me seemed to have lightened. I thought I could feel my fingers and my toes. The sounds were the same. The swooshing and the beeping. I listened. I wondered if anyone else was here. I felt like I was alone, but I didn't trust anything I felt. I heard a door open. I fought hard to open my eyes.

Open.

Open.

OPEN!

The lights were so bright. Or had my eyes been closed for that long?

"Hey there! Sleeping Beauty. Let me page the doctor. He wants to speak with you."

The girl, maybe thirty was pretty and happy. She had red hair and a wonderful smile and that New England accent I have missed. 'Doctuh' has never sounded so sweet! I tried to smile back at her, but my mouth wouldn't move. I tried to bring my hand up to touch it, but my arms wouldn't move. I began to panic. Am I paralyzed? I couldn't move my arms or my legs. The tears began to stream down my face.

"Now now. What is the crying for Mrs Wylder? Everything is going to be okay. I'm sure you are very confused. That is totally natural. You were in a car accident. You have been here in the ICU for almost a week. I will go get you something to calm you down."

The door opened again, and an older man in a white jacket walked in. Joshua was behind him. He was still here! He was okay!

The man in white says, "Mrs Wylder?" only it sounds like 'Wild-uh'.

"Just call her Carsen, please" Joshua said.

Joshua walked over to me quickly, my eyes were fixed on him. I wondered if I looked as terrified as I felt.

"Carsen? You are awake! Oh honey. I am so glad." He bent down and kissed my forehead, again I tried to move my arm, but it felt like it was being held down. I felt trapped. The panic came on again in a rush. The tears were pouring. I couldn't move! The redhead came back and I saw the needle in her hand. She looked at me and smiled, "This will help you relax, so that the doctor can explain everything to you. It's going to be okay, Carsen. You are going to be fine."

I closed my eyes. I must be paralyzed from the neck down. I could feel but I couldn't move. I heard them whispering to each other, but I couldn't make the words out. This was absolutely the most terrifying thing I had ever been through. Everyone else was so calm and reassuring. I couldn't speak so I started counting the swooshing sounds again. The beeping began to slow as well. I opened my eyes again. Joshua, you are here. He had a huge bruise on his left eye and his arm is in a sling, too. I pleaded with him using my eyes.

"Carsen? You have been in a medically induced coma. You are on a ventilator to help you breathe. Your lungs were damaged during the accident, but you are healing. You are doing so well. You are alive."

Alive? Yes, I suppose I am.

But if this is what being alive is going to feel like, then I don't want to be alive. I can't be a mother. I can't be a boss. I won't be Joshua's lover. I won't be me. I tried one last time to move my arm with every ounce of strength I could muster until I felt the bed shake.

"Whoa! She's a fighter, doc. Isn't that what I've been telling you? Can't you take her out of the restraints now? Are they really necessary?"

I was begging Joshua to read what my eyes are saying. And he did.

"Car, you pulled out your breathing tube, more than once, so they had to restrain you. Do you promise not to do that again? If so, maybe they will take off at least one of the restraints?"

Joshua turned away from me and was now looking at the doctor. He nodded at Joshua and then walked around to the other side of my head.

"Hey there! You gave us all quite a scare, Ms. Wylder. But, I was able to repair the damage to your lungs. I would like to keep you on the ventilator a few more days though. Until we are sure that your lungs are strong enough for you to breathe on your own. We can take off the restraints and you can write down any questions you might have. Would you like me to do that?"

I nodded with my eyes and tried to with my head. I wanted this thing out of me! I was so thirsty. I felt like I might die if I didn't get something to drink and soon. Water was all I could think about. The doctor left the room and it was just Joshua and I.

"Carsen, thank God you are awake. Everything is going to be fine. I am here. I am going to take care of you, Tyler and Lilly."

Oh. God.

I recalled a conversation that I had heard between them. Was it real? It must have been. I still feel so groggy and so out of it.

"Tyler knows, Car. He's not thrilled, but he's not angry either. I think he's in shock."

My eyes got really big. Where was Tyler? How was Tyler? The doctor removed the restraints and I was able to move my hands. I wasn't paralyzed after all. I had just been tied down.

"Oh. Yeah. Uhm, I guess I need to explain all that to you. The car we hit, it was Tyler's. He has a broken arm and a broken leg, but he's good. Lilly is fine, too."

Tyler was hurt and I wasn't there for him. The one thing I have tried to do, protect Tyler and I have failed.

"Don't cry, Carsen," he says with tears in his own eyes, "He is strong. He is just like you. "

I could only hope he would love Tyler in time. Joshua explained everything to me, and all I could do was listen. That is such a different position for me. I've always talked and here I can't speak. I wasn't in charge. I wasn't trying to make everyone happy. I couldn't do anything that I had long programmed myself to do. I tried to relax and with the help of the Xanax, I began to.

Joshua tried to reassure me, "We are all going to be fine. We are all going to be together."

My thoughts drift to Tyler and then to Lilly. I could only hope that I would be able to ask for their forgiveness and that in time, all would be forgiven.

The doctor returned with a clipboard. I began writing. Unfortunately, it wasn't legible. I become so frustrated that I just scribble 'T?'

Joshua nodded.

"I have called Tyler's room. He's sleeping. The nurse will bring him down as soon as he wakes up. He's good, Carsen, I promise."

I scribbled again. It clearly says 'SORRY'. Joshua kissed my forehead again.

"There is never a need to apologize. Carsen, I thought I had lost you, again. I know that we have a lot of things to figure out and I know that it won't be easy. But, together, with Tyler and Lilly, we will survive. You tried to do it on your own once, and while I will never completely understand, I know you believed you were doing what was right for me. So now, we are going to do what is right for all of us."

I knew he was right. I had made a mess and I would spend the rest of my life trying to clean it up. We had been given more than a second chance. I scribbled again.

I slowly form the letters 'ILU'.

He smiles.

"I love you always."

I can't remember ever hearing sweeter words. I close my eyes and try to imagine our future. It will be easier for us than for Tyler and Lilly. I am convincing myself not to worry so much when Tyler interrupts me, "Mom."

I open my eyes and no longer see a boy. I see a man shrouded in my mistakes. Joshua smiles at him, but Tyler moves nearer to me and leans in so close I can feel his breath in my ear. His words will resound within me forever, "You got your happy ending, but what about me? Didn't I deserve one too?"

That's the thing about collisions. Sometimes the damage is obvious and can be easily identified. Then sometimes, after the smoke clears you see the impact it really had and you realize the extent of it. Can all the damage ever really be repaired?

-THE END-

51517567R10146

Made in the USA
Charleston, SC
20 January 2016